THE MacDONNELL MADNESS

Alasdar looked down at the woman he had always known —the woman now kneeling naked and glorious before him, her long hair flowing.

"I don't know anything about other women, but I think when a woman is mad with love for a man there is nothing, nothing," and she said it with whispered intensity, "she won't do to show him. Alasdar."

"Yes?"

"I am mad with love for you. Come and let me show you. Don't talk," she said. "Come and let me show you. I can't help it. You'll see tonight what's raging in me. Come to bed, and get to know what I am."

That night Alasdar began to learn what a woman really was . . . what kind of man he was . . . what it was to be a MacDonnell and be heir to—

THE RULING PASSION

a sweeping, tumultuous novel of an age of explosive conflict—and of a family with a legacy of rock strength and dangerous desires

Big Bestsellers from SIGNET

**If you wish to order these titles,
please see coupon on the
last page of this book.**

~THE~

RULING PASSION

By
Shaun Herron

A SIGNET BOOK
NEW AMERICAN LIBRARY
TIMES MIRROR

Published by arrangement with the author

 SIGNET TRADEMARK REG. U.S. PAT. OFF. AND FOREIGN COUNTRIES
REGISTERED TRADEMARK—MARCA REGISTRADA
HECHO EN CHICAGO, U.S.A.

SIGNET, SIGNET CLASSICS, MENTOR, PLUME AND MERIDIAN BOOKS
are published by The New American Library, Inc.,
1301 Avenue of the Americas, New York, New York 10019

FIRST SIGNET PRINTING, MAY, 1978

1 2 3 4 5 6 7 8 9

PRINTED IN THE UNITED STATES OF AMERICA

For

Gordon and Mary Robinson

Contents

Contents

Part One

---◄►◄►◄►---

Tomas Carrach MacDonnell

For
RICHARD SANKEY MALONE

✑ One ✑

I did not marry Elizabeth McCarthy because I needed a wife but because I needed an heir. I am the MacDonnell.

I had a quite satisfactory mistress, a woman I met when she was governess to the Clotworthy children. She was dismissed when her endurance snapped and she thrashed one of that peculiar brood and wrote to me, on the advice of a butler who had once served my father, asking for help. A governess who left one of her eccentric and objectionable charges black and blue was unlikely to find suitable employment no matter how justified she may have been in the assault.

My needs with respect to women had never been anything but modest. There were times when I wondered whether I had pressing needs at all. For what needs I had, in 1857 I established this woman—she was at this time thirty-nine and twelve years my senior—in a small but pleasant house on the Cavehill Road in Belfast. At first I rented the house but when it was clear that we found one another quite satisfactory, I bought it, paid myself in cash a reasonable rent in the woman's name—keeping a careful record—arranged with Pollard my solicitor to make her a small but adequate cash allowance that could in no circumstances be traced to its source and visited her for a few hours each Friday afternoon after the work at my shipping office had been completed. Now and then, but very occasionally, my needs unaccountably increased—there was never any easily determinable reason for the increases—and I stayed till Saturday morning or—sometimes—Saturday afternoon. These extensions appeared to give the woman great pleasure.

So there was no need to marry. As I one day heard one of my estate tenants remark: Why buy a cow when ye can git a ha'p'orth o' milk? (Particularly when milk is not something you want a lot of.)

My mother thought otherwise. She knew perfectly well I had a mistress, though she did not know whom or where. Since I am a man of regular habits and did not explain to her why, suddenly, I no longer arrived back in Carrig and at Barn House at my usual Friday time, she drew conclusions. A mistress was assumed; a man's needs are also assumed—even when, like mine, they are small—and a gentleman's mistress is as inevitable as a gentleman's horse, for young unmarried men, that is, and for youngish married men after the first two or three children, when their wives begin to show signs of distaste for the marriage bed or its consequences.

"Carrach," my mother said persistently, in one form or another, "whatever else you need, you need a wife and you must have an heir."

She always said it with a twinkle. "I think," I told her, "you want to go back to Garden House." Mother's returns to Garden House were the subject of affectionate teasing between us.

Garden House is the dower house. It faces the sea at the eastern end of my estate. Mother loved the house and its gardens and asked when she married my father—family lore said—that instead of doing the usual thing and going to the Continent for the statutory two-month honeymoon, they should spend it all at Garden House. When we were young, parents were of course sexless. Now I am certain of the truth of the stories that my parents were passionately in love and loved passionately. The truth is that apart from the stories, my mother herself, and in circumstances I shall describe, told me so. My parents often went back to stay in the dower house, which stood empty. After my father died, Mother went more often. I suspect now she got at Garden House the quite mistaken idea that I needed women and therefore needed a wife who was always available and who would of necessity provide me with a healthy heir.

When she went to the dower house in 1850—to mourn, I suppose, at the scene of great happiness—I was twenty and my brother Hugh nineteen. She took as her only house servant Cassie Hyndman, the wife of an ordinary seaman on one of our ships. Cassie was thirty then and her husband was at sea for as long as eighteen months at a time. She was therefore able to live at Garden House and to close up her cottage in the village of Boneybefore. I own the village of Boneybefore and Cassie's husband was not only a family employee but a tenant. The room she preferred in the limited servants' quarters at Garden House was a small one at the back—the north side—of the house. My mother's room was at the other end of the house, on the south side overlooking the Lough. At night all she could possibly hear was the incessant sound of the sea.

That was just as well, though I think now my wonderful mother didn't need to hear in order to know. Sometimes, when I went to Garden House to see her—for I loved her as much as I had loved my father—I would tease Cassie Hyndman as I passed her, in a corridor, when she was making beds, or working in the kitchen. Teasing progressed to a little harmless tickling. It was something I had never done before and Cassie neither resisted nor protested. On the contrary, she laughed and appeared to enjoy it and said, "You'd better not let yer mother hear ye." One day I accidentally touched one of her splendid breasts and was so stunned by the sensation that I held on. I think that happened because I did not know what to do or how to retreat. Cassie stood still and did not try to stop me. Ordinary curiosity determined the rest. I thought far into the night about her breast cupped in my hand and wanted to see it. The next day I reached from behind her and put my hand down the front of her uniform bib. She stood still, smiling. She said, "That's a nice feelin."

I said, "What would you say if I came to your room tonight, Cassie?"

"I'd say, 'Don't make any noise.' "

That night I went to her room. It was my first experience. I did not know how to go about the mechanics of the business. It all seemed needlessly awkward. But Cassie knew. She taught me.

"Slow an' gentle, Carrach," she said. "That's the way," she said. "Oh, that's lovely, Carrach," she said and I knew this was something it would be quite pleasant to do from time to time.

My life has been set in patterns. Not until I went to America to rescue my niece Isabella did I break the patterns. I went to bed with Cassie every Friday night. She used to pass me in the house and wink and whisper, "Keep in trainin."

Or: "I'm fizzin-ready to be corked." One night she said to me, "What d'ye think yer mother meant, Carrach? She patted me on the arm this mornin and said, 'I hope yer a good teacher, Cassie. Just be careful.' She was smilin that nice at me I didn't work it out till after. D'ye think she knows?"

It spoiled the night. I spent it listening, creeping out of bed to look down the corridor, cocking my ear to hear Mother's advance along it. "Och, she can't know," Cassie whispered. "Sure if she knew she'd put me outa the house." It was no comfort. I didn't go back for two weeks.

When I did return I was reassured on two points; Mother could not possibly know, and from reports at the shipping office I had learned that Hyndman (who sailed on the *Cathleen MacDonnell,* named after my mother) would be home in just over a week. Cassie used to talk about him during the night: about how much she wanted a child and how hard Hyndman tried to give her one and how hopeless it was.

"D'you think I'm a barren woman, Carrach?" she asked me.

"How could I know a thing like that?"

"Aye, that's right enough. Y'always spill on my belly or we'd surely know by now."

"You didn't expect me to do anything else, did you?"

"Can a man be barren?"

"I've heard so. I don't know."

"Try me, Carrach. He'll be home in eight or nine days. If I catch, he'll never know." She was urgent about it and the thought had been on my mind all that day.

"You'll never let it drop?"

"Ye can trust me, Carrach. Ye know I'd never let on. Try me, will ye?"

Afterward she cried. She was happy and excited. "I want to catch, Carrach," she said, "God, but I want to catch. Keep at me." It was a new experience, more complete than our previous practice, and I must say it added a dimension.

I came to her room every night that week. "Keep at me," she urged. "Make sure, Carrach," she said, and did things that were pleasant and made it difficult to refuse her. She is, I kept telling myself, a very nice woman, and if she wants a child, she should surely be allowed to have one. And she would not talk. I was confident.

I was also astonished at my own endurance. She was, of course, using me. I was quite aware of it. I was also curious about the business of conception, and this, I believed then, was the reason for my ability to meet her considerable demands during that week.

Mother is very cunning in a kind and pleasing way. When Agnes Hyndman was born in 1851, Mother went to the christening in spite of the fact that Cassie was a Protestant. Mother also wrote her a letter which said—Cassie told me—"You were always a good and faithful servant and kind to myself and my sons when we were lonely and in sorrow. I am therefore sending you this small gift and I trust you will use it for the child."

The "small gift" was one hundred pounds. That was the equivalent of fourteen years' pay for Cassie in service. I know that Hyndman used it to leave the sea and set up his small boat-building business at which he has been quite successful.

About eighteen months after the baptism my mother said one day that she was going to spend a few days at Garden House and, "I want you to come over tomorrow for an hour or two. There are things we should talk about."

I thought nothing of it. I had no reason to think she meant more than she said. I was delighted to go. It was always a pleasure to be with her over there. We sat by the drawing-room fire and talked amiably for half an hour before she said, "Carrach, please go to the kitchen and have some tea and sandwiches sent in." I didn't know which servants she had brought with her to Garden House and I did not bother to ask why we didn't pull the bell rope and have the servants do the walking. I found out when I got to the kitchen.

Cassie was there. She looked well. She looked happy. She said, "She gave ye a surprise, didn't she, sir?"

"She did indeed." It was then that Cassie told me about the letter and the hundred pounds.

"We had a nice wee talk yesterday," she said. "Och but yer mother's the nicest woman. Onea the best." She said it with feeling and did not enlarge on it. Mother often had nice wee talks with servants. I chatted briefly with Cassie about nothing in particular and was careful not to mention her daughter Agnes; she was careful not to make any reference to my daughter Agnes. Cassie got what she wanted. She was pleased with what she got. There was nothing to say.

When I got back to the drawing-room Mother had what Cassie called "a nice wee talk" with me.

"Cassie Hyndman is a splendid woman," she said, looking at me as if she could at any moment start to laugh. "Very practical," she said. Mother so often was on the brink of laughter and her eyes declared it.

"She is indeed," I said. It was suitably noncommittal. It covered Cassie in bed and Cassie the servant and Cassie the woman who told nothing.

"Sometimes I'm sorry our sons can't go out and find themselves good, handsome, strong, and honest working women," Mother said, and paused, and her smile was lively with the thoughts to come. Mischievous. "And marry them." She settled herself more comfortably as if there was much more to come. "Don't you think so, Carrach?"

It was not what I had any reason to expect. "No," I said, since that seemed the safest thing to say.

"No, I suppose not. So since that can't be . . ." She didn't finish it. "But I do love the thought of good, healthy, well-dispositioned, broad-beamed, big-breasted women getting pregnant and having babies. Have you seen your daughter?" It fell from her lips softly, so casually, like an almost sleepy question from a happy grandmother to a new father.

"What?" It brought me out of my chair. I felt her soft question like a blow on the head.

"Carrach, you heard and understood me perfectly. Agnes is a beautiful child. Have you seen her?"

I was shocked. I was shaken. We had always been close. Our relationship had always been warm and happy and open. But here Mother passed the limit. This was openness gone wild. At the same time, there was no point in waffling. She knew. The hundred pounds was an acknowledgment. It was not, however, a censure.

Mother was a strong woman. Hugh and I often discussed her with affection and admiration. We talked of the way she managed Father, who was a strong and willful man. He needed management. Mother did it with a combination of humor, amazingly complex circuitousness, patience, shrewd sense, and love. He never doubted that she had thought a great deal about the question at issue. It never crossed his mind that she could possibly want anything but the best for him. His trust in her was complete and on those occasions when she was wrong and he knew she was wrong, their mutual confidence ruled out the possibility that feelings might be bruised. She was quick to know when she was wrong and to acknowledge his superior judgment. She was just as ready to acknowledge his superior judgment on those questions to which she had contributed all the answers. He called her his "means of Grace." Hugh and I often wondered whether or not Father knew how superbly he was managed.

Whether he ever knew it or not, I came to know that if I had paid more attention to her wisdom (and if I had been less observant of her methods with Father), I might have saved myself much misery.

"Have you seen her?" she asked again.

"No, I haven't," I said.

"She's a delightful child. She's in the garden asleep at the moment in a crib her mother put on the lawn. When we've had tea, go down and speak to her."

"I don't think that would be at all wise."

"There's nothing unwise about it. All you need do is ask her how she is. Cassie is a discreet woman. She's managed everything very well—including you. I'm pleased with both of you."

I was almost afraid to speak. "Mother, you knew . . . ?"

"Knew what?"

"All the time . . . ?"

"Yes."

"The little room . . . ?"

"Quite shocking, isn't it?" Now she was laughing. "I've had a long and agreeable talk with Cassie, Carrach. A young man needs to learn to please a woman. Your father went to the same school. A working woman wanted a child and you were a fine strong young man. I understand the whole thing. I would disapprove of it only if either of you, or Hyndman, or Agnes, came to any harm because of it. As it is, you're all happy. Your foreman in the hackling shop at the mill? Johnny Davidson? He's an only child. He doesn't know it but his old mother does. . . . When your father was seventeen . . ." She rattled on while I let my mouth hang open. "And now you, young man, are ready and obviously able to please a woman. I know you think I'm being quite scandalous, my dear, but I'm not. I know what it means to a wife to have a husband who pleases her. I suppose you think mothers are different from all the other women you've ever heard of? But Cassie is a mother, so try to recall her in bed. I don't think you'll find that difficult." Her smile mocked me lovingly and I wanted to run. "Carrach, you oaf, I am trying to talk to you about happiness." She looked a little doubtful then. "You are happy about Cassie, aren't you? It all turned out well— for you and for her and for Hyndman. He has a daughter."

"I'm not quite sure I understand you, Mother."

"You're being tiresome, Carrach. So let me make it easy for you. Your father and I loved one another quite desperately." And now she was close to tears, remembering, I have no doubt. "I want you to know that a happy marriage includes this. Your father and I enjoyed one another—in exactly the way I suppose you and Cassie enjoyed one another in the back room."

I was blushing and sweating with embarrassment and confusion.

"Cassie assures me those were happy nights."

"She *what*?"

"I asked her, Carrach. At first she looked the way you look now. Shocked, silly. But," and she shifted in her chair as if to dispose of something, "she got over it. She even got to the point of enjoying our talk about it. She wanted a child. She got one. She admits she enjoyed the process and she still thinks warmly of you. She wouldn't leave her husband for you and she wouldn't go to bed with you again for she has what she wanted and she wouldn't hurt Hyndman. But it all happened and she's glad it did. So, I may as well tell you, am I. Does that surprise you?"

"Yes." Impatiently.

"So. Now it's time to begin the serious search for a wife."

Cassie saved me. Or so I thought for a moment. She came in with the tray and put it on the table by Mother's chair. She stared into the tray, but there was a small smile about her lips.

"Well, Cassie," Mother said, "we've had our talk and he hasn't yet had time to recover. But I want to say this to you now. If you ever need me while I'm alive and capable, come to me. I'm your girl's grandmother. Think of it that way. After me, if you ever need help, come to my son. He's your girl's father. He will take care of you. You will come to him?"

"Yes, ma'am."

"Carrach?" my mother said.

"Cassie understands," I said stiffly. "She will come."

"Thank you, sir," Cassie said and began her retreat.

"Cassie," my mother called.

"Ma'am?"

"You call him 'sir' now. What did you call him in the back room?"

"Carrach, ma'am." She blurted it out before she had time to think. Then she ran from the room, slamming the door behind her. No doubt laughing in the kitchen. They were both some way out of their heads, it seemed to me.

Mother was laughing again, with, I thought, a lack of control.

"You've been drinking, Mother," I said firmly. It was my turn. "That's what led to this, isn't it?"

She cut her laughter short with surprising control. "Yes," she said, "I've been drinking. Good Scotch whiskey. So has Cassie Hyndman. How else could we have done it?"

She stood up and put her arms around me. "Oh, my darling Carrach," she said, "how I love you, my boy, and oh how I loved your father. Find a lovely girl and love one another the way we loved one another."

She was crying. I always loved her dearly. I felt a great warmth for her now. She wanted for me and some girl as yet unidentified by and perhaps unknown to either of us, what she and Father had known. That was not strange. What was strange was that she was willing to tell me they had actually enjoyed one another's bodies. Wives were not expected to enjoy, but comply. And to breed. But parents, in spite of the fact of their parenthood, were sexless.

I watched Mother as the days and months passed and marveled and loved her more. Naturally, I had no special feeling about Cassie Hyndman. Certainly I liked her and I had unquestionably enjoyed her in the little back room and she had just as surely enjoyed me and got from me what she wanted, a child. Not only that, mind you. There was mutual physical pleasure. Cassie was much more active in this respect than I was; more demonstrative; more emotional and also more physical. But, as I say, my needs are modest and I am a man of singular restraint. The experience was, let's say, for me a pleasure. It was my mother's attitude to Cassie and to me, and to that encounter and to its consequences, that released something in me and allowed me to entertain for Cassie a kindly feeling that persisted far into the future.

It persisted in Cassie also, as I was in time to discover.

But I resisted Mother's importunings about a wife and an heir for close to eight more years. Until, I think, in 1861. I do not easily remember anniversaries, but I try to forget the year of my marriage.

"Surely, Carrach, surely," she would say in her mischievous way—that grew less mischievous as I got older—"you've had enough practice with this woman you visit on Fridays? Get yourself a wife and give yourself an heir."

✑ Two ✑

I did not want a wife. My modest needs were being met by a woman whose talents as a mistress outweighed her value as a governess. But I had to agree at last that I needed an heir.

I was myself heir to a shipping line of six sailing vessels trading to the East and to America, a flax-spinning mill and 1,500 acres. Barn House was the nerve center of a modest estate consisting of tenant farms and the home farm, Court House, in the town of Carrig, Garden House, and the village of Boneybefore.

The 1,500 acres were all that remained of a kingdom. That may sound self-pitying but I do not mean it so. My lineage means more to me—to all the MacDonnells—than any hopeless romantic notion that we could ever again be in Ireland or Scotland what we once had been. The world moves on, and only fools look back with longing. Sometimes though . . .

My MacDonnell ancestors were the Gaelic-Norse rulers of the Hebrides, Argyll, and Cantire—the Lords of the Isles. That, I suspect, is why my father went to Scotland for a wife and married the daughter not of a great but impoverished Scottish line but of a wealthy distiller of Scotch whiskey, Sir Patrick Forsythe. We were always conscious of our Scottish past, near and distant, but time taught us the indispensability of substance. It is a more negotiable asset than lineage.

The MacDonnells came first to Ulster to fight. (And I may say in passing that though the Americans talk today of Ulster-Scots and mean the descendants of the Presbyterian and Anglican settlers of the seventeenth century, the MacDonnells too are Ulster-Scots and Catholic and came here first in 1257.) We came as *galloglas* which in the Gaelic is *gallóglách* and means "foreign soldier." We came because the Normans were attacking Ulster from Connaught and O'Neill called to us for help from across the Irish Sea. So MacDonnell, the Lord of the Isles, brought his armies to Ulster and our captains were given estates in payment. In time Hebrideans formed a substantial part of the population of Ulster and today, as a consequence, almost all Ulstermen, Catholic and Protestant, are Ulster-Scots, not Irish. They are a different people from the Irish. Ulster is a different country. The MacDonnells married Bisets and O'Neills and in time were Viscounts of Dunluce, Earls of Antrim, and Lords of the Glens (of Antrim). And so, with our lands in Scotland and in Ulster, we created once again the fifth-century Ulster-Scots Kingdom of Dal Riada—Antrim in Ulster and Argyll and the Isles in Scotland.

Only 1,500 acres of it remains to us today. Acre by acre it was whittled away in land grants to Scots Protestant planters. We bow our heads.

But my father was shrewd and farsighted. During the famine, it was he who brought the light swing plow to Ulster. With some of his tenants dead or dispersed he regrouped his land, made larger farms from it, let them to his remaining tenants at fair rents, gave them security of tenure before the law required it, gave them seed and foundation stock from which to build small herds, extended or rebuilt farmhouses, and made the tenants better and happier farmers. It paid, naturally. It paid the tenants. It paid the landlord. That is how it was meant to be.

I will say this for us, though: our footwork never equaled that of our cousins the O'Neills. They after all learned the skills of survival in a great school. Did not Great Hugh O'Neill, the Earl of Tyrone, learn the art of survival at the court of Queen Elizabeth herself? The MacDonnells are Catholic still; the O'Neills are Protestant. Could they see the wind?

It was my great-grandfather who decided that if we were never again to be rich in land we could try to be rich from commerce. He bought ships. They were tubby coasters in the beginning. They were deep-sea sailers in my grandfather's time. They are clippers now, trading East and West. Sail is no longer monarch but it holds its own. It was my father who built the flax-spinning mill. The industrial revolution came late to Ulster, but it came as linen, rope, shipbuilding, and for a time cotton, and Belfast grew and still grows like a morning mushroom. Commerce could not restore our lands but it restored some of our fortunes. In the days of our greatness and greatest power we lived in stone towers and slept on straw. Lesser men now, in these days of our decline and exclusion from power in Ulster, we live in some splendor in the house my great-grandfather built.

So I needed an heir and was not enthusiastic about having to marry to get one.

"Male bastards," my mother said in her direct and twinkling way, "complicate wills."

There were few Catholics of our substance or lineage left in Ulster and the choice of a wife was difficult. There were considerations. If we were to protect our commercial interests we must not provoke Protestant commercial suspicion of our political connections. What we once earned by the sword in Ulster, we now earned by trade. After all, our customers for spun flax were the new Protestant middle-class linen manufacturers and there were other flax-spinning mills in Ulster owned by Protestants. The linen manufacturers were not likely to buy spun flax from a Catholic company with family connections hostile to their interests. They could close our mill by simply refusing to buy from us.

But I wanted no such hostile Catholic family alliance. We are Ulstermen and our sympathies were never with the undisciplined and feckless peasantry of the South, or with their intellectual leaders whose inspiration grew out of the ideas of the French Revolution. What was best for a growing industrial and commercial life in Ulster was best for the Catholic MacDonnells. Our interests and those of the Protestant manufacturing class were identical. But in Ulster one always needs to prove it, even in the choice of a wife.

I ought to have followed my father's example and found a wife in Scotland. A Scottish wife, an outsider, could not be an instant symbol in our limited and bigoted Ulster world where code words, code gestures, code actions triggered hostile passions. She could be no more than a woman, a bed-and-board companion: a breeder. With love, if one were fortunate. Father, on a visit to Edinburgh, met and loved Mother and married her. He was fortunate. I had never, even in my youth, fallen in love. Nature did not make my choice, indeed I was in the gravest doubt that I was equipped by nature to experience that irrational convulsion, love of woman. Therefore, I had to select, get the best I could for what I was, avoid the mistake of falling in with some congenital republican family—Irish politics and Ulster politics are congenital—and surrounding the MacDonnells with a thick shroud of suspicion about where our loyalties lay.

It seems to me now that one doesn't begin the search for a wife on some appointed date. If one's situation demands an heir, then a wife is an assumption of one's life and somewhere in the obscurer recesses of the mind, even people like myself are making observations, preparations. When Mother's insistence became to me legitimately insistent, I believe these early and continuing observations and preparations surfaced and served their purpose.

This is how Elizabeth McCarthy came into the business.

You see, my brother Hugh is an exciting fellow, handsome in what people call a "dashing" sort of way. I always called him the Eagle. I was always a dull fellow. Hugh's mind was on adventure and beautiful women. Mine was on the MacDonnells, their heritage, their interests. Sometimes I saw in my brother our great ancestor Sorley Boye MacDonnell, whose grave is in a little churchyard near the town of Bally-castle. I saw myself always as one of the clerks of the family; an elder son prepared for commerce; a useful featureless fellow. Other people saw me as I saw myself. I could have no objection. I was what they saw. Hugh had been to bed with women—not girls, mature women—by the time he was in his sixteenth year; women of quality, married women, even the middle-aged wives of powerful Protestants. That, he said, was "the reconquest of Ulster." He was "seduced" by them if they were young and beautiful, he used to tell me. If they were middle-aged, he "exacted their Protestant tribute." Cassie was my first—a sewing woman in my mother's house. It was commentary enough. Hugh went, a mere youth, as supercargo—business agent—to America, India, China, on my father's ships and was immensely successful at it. His authority on board ship was equal to the captain's in all matters except seamanship. I went staidly to Boston and New York in our ships "to broaden my outlook" and meet our American cousins. I wore a top hat.

In our youth, we went to balls, Hugh as often as they took place and we were invited; myself, infrequently. That is how we met the McCarthys, Catholics, without detectable family politics, the daughters of a decent Catholic family of some substance. There were pitifully few Catholic families of substance. They had gathered their modest wealth in trade. Since Catholics were barred in my father's day from the learned professions, they turned to trade, to such things as the export of salt, beef, butter, cattle and hides, and from these made reasonable fortunes. There were always small landlords in financial difficulties and anxious to hide their condition from their peers. Quietly, a few Catholics with money to spare went into the mortgage business. Quietly, the impoverished little Protestant squires sought out what they contemptuously called "the Popish Jews," to refinance them. McCarthy was one of these.

There were three McCarthy children, Elizabeth, Emily, and John. John was a silent, watchful boy, a hidden child and not easily likable. Elizabeth was sixteen when she was given Hugh's full and self-entertaining attention. She had a kind of prettiness that diminishes with the years, and Hugh did to her what he had power to do—he flirted her into love of him. He was eighteen. How great and enduring a romantic passion she had for him was not known to me till I was called on to pay the price it exacted from me. John was the second child. He was at that time fifteen. Then came Emily, aged nine, with perfect features and a faint cast in her left eye. She was a darling child who spent her waking hours drawing and dabbing paint and she thought of little else. In the years to come, Emily, who later became my dear friend, told me that it was Hugh who made Elizabeth peculiar—not peculiar in any sense our doctors could have put a name to, but peculiar enough to make life miserable for others. He led her to believe, as she believed in God and Hell and Salvation, that when she was eighteen he would marry her.

I think, in extenuation, he was a little mad. We reacted to my father's death in our different ways. Hugh's grief was wild and crucifying. Mine was what you would expect of me: cold, orderly, my agony hidden. I turned increasingly to a companionable intimacy with Mother. Hugh drank more, fornicated more, struck savagely at life and devised ways to punish.But punish what? It was my question; he didn't ask it. Elizabeth was one of his victims. Women stuck to him and he took all they offered. He stuck to Elizabeth. His amusement was another kind of revenge.

Then suddenly he came to Mother and like the Prodigal Son asked for his portion and disappeared into the world and silence. I had a great love for Hugh. I missed him and sought news of him everywhere, and what I got was vague and probably misleading. Our captains brought snatches. There was word of Hugh MacDonnell in Shanghai, in India, in America. He was captain of one of the Astors' Yankee clippers, I heard; he was married to an olive-skinned woman, Spanish, they thought. She sailed with him to far strange places, they believed, and had been seen with him in New York and India.

There was in this last snatch of news, if it could be called news, something that rang true. He loved the Spanish. We had gone together to Spain. I loved the north, he loved the more exotic south. He went often alone. I was now persuaded that he had gone first to Spain, to someone he already knew (didn't we inaccurately call the Andalusians olive-skinned? and he loved them) who could salve his wounds.

Then I had small firm snatches from my uncle and cousin in Boston and Lowell. Hugh had visited them. For one day. He was rich. He said he was married. They did not see his wife. They knew he was loitering in Boston but did not see him again. The company they heard he was keeping caused them concern—the Catholic Irish. The agitating Irish. The English-hating Irish. They heard stories of visits to New York and the same company. They were disturbed. They did not want to be identified with this sort of Irish. There was great loathing for Catholics in Boston, most particularly Irish Catholics.

My American cousin was the son of my father's brother James, who went to America aboard one of our ships as a visitor and stayed on as an American. James was a discreet man. He became a Congregationalist, "a very good club here," he wrote to Father, who laughed at that, but not very sincerely.

Then there was no more news of Hugh. Not even snatches. He had gone to earth somewhere and the years went by now in absolute silence.

Yet I always remembered something he said to me before he went away, and wondered often where it might lead him in life.

"If I stay here among these accursed condescending Protestants, they'll turn me into a Fenian."

I watched Elizabeth McCarthy come of age and Emily grow up into a beautiful girl. Elizabeth had offers and refused them, waiting for Hugh to return. Emily had no offers. In a small provincial society, who wants a wife, however beautiful, with a cast in one eye? Who can endure the laughter of small societies? It was fortunate that she did not want a husband. She wanted beyond all things to be a painter, and she painted and was a figure of fun and indifferent to it. The Blue Lady, they called her in Belfast. She painted blue Irish landscapes. She was the only woman I knew now as a friend. We were good friends, talking friends. Sometimes, as Mother's marriage pressure increased, I thought of Emily. I could enjoy her companionship. But I could also hear the laughter about her eye, and being what I was, I put the thought of Emily from me, supported by the conviction that—being what I was—she would refuse me anyway.

When Mother's insistence became real to me, I looked at Elizabeth. She was familiar. I did not have to search for her or get to know her. She had some good points so far as appearance went, and a mouth too thin, but I needed an heir, not a beautiful woman. And she was almost certain to refuse.

Mother said, "You'll regret it. She'll end up as an old Irish crone with a clay pipe in her mouth. Look at her mother and you'll see."

Emily said, "No, I will not advise you, Carrach. But I know she won't love you. Does that matter?"

"No."

"Do you love her?"

"No."

"I'm not advising you, but I should have thought . . . Never mind what I should have thought. It's none of my business."

Mother said, "No, no, no, Carrach." At a critical moment in my life she lost her skill.

"I'm going to get it done with, Mother," I told her. "You want a grandson. I need an heir." I was thirty-one and she was tired.

To my astonishment, and, I confess, to my dismay, which had to be disciplined, Elizabeth McCarthy said yes. She was, in fact, quite charming. Hugh had been too long away. She was twenty-eight years old.

Emily, when I told her, said only, "Good God."

Mother said, "I'll be nice to her. God help you, darling."

I looked at Elizabeth and supposed the slight sharpness of

her features would soften as she ripened. She had a pleasant smile, her figure was adequate except for her breasts which turned out to be even more inadequate than it was possible to discover in time. She obviously thought well of me and made that clear at every opportunity. I even persuaded myself that perhaps, after all, Hugh had been only her passage to my door.

I married her.

The whole thing seemed quite simple to me. Elizabeth wanted a rich husband—I had no doubt about that; didn't every young woman—and was getting one. I wanted an heir and would get one. Both of us would get a certain amount of pleasure in bed—enough for two people of presumably reasonable but not excessive needs. I came to this conclusion because she was—to me—undemonstrative but also because when I spoke of an heir she said without fuss, "We should begin with a boy, then," and there is only one way to begin. Obviously, she did not expect to find a child under a cabbage. All we could expect after that was agreeable company. I saw no great difficulty. Nor did I see any great happiness in it. It was an arrangement.

"You'll be miserable," Mother said miserably. "But I'll support you both in every way I can."

My mistress was a little upset. Pollard, my solicitor, made the final arrangements for the severing of our relationship. She could remain in the house, rent-free of course, until she made "other arrangements," which meant, in Pollard's language, until she found "another sponsor." A cash settlement was negotiated. She was, Pollard said, a very shrewd negotiator. He had her kept under observation and was amused to report to me eight months after my marriage that she had found a "sponsor" in a man of some seventy years whose demands might be minimal but whose substance was adequate. I sold the little house. That was that. I did not feel it right to keep a mistress when I had a wife who was willing.

Willing?

Our problems began at once. The honeymoon, she was insistent, must be abroad, and that took time away from my business interests. It had to be abroad, she protested, because her bourgeois friends expected her, having married a landowner, to do the standard European tour. But she had plans to go further afield. We must also go to America, she said, to meet our cousins in America. We could well afford it, she said frankly. We could, but to this I could not agree. Nor would I visit Paris, where disloyal Irishmen fled or where they met to plot revolution. Rome, then? The Vatican was there and I was not willing to suggest to those with whom I had to do business that I was part of what they believed to be a continuing and perhaps eternal "papist conspiracy." The thought always amused me that a rich Catholic who went to Rome could very well be going there to be briefed by His Holiness. No Ulster Protestant ever said this to me. It was in the air around them. I took account of their quaint prejudices. Elizabeth accepted Spain. I gave her no choice. Barcelona was on the Mediterranean, and "Mediterranean" was impressive enough for her friends. I knew Barcelona. That, I told her, is where we are going.

We went to Dublin by train. I had a suite engaged at the Gresham. Through some clerical error, they gave us one with two bedrooms and it was an unfortunate mistake that enabled her to play out her unexpected part for a period longer than I would in other circumstances have allowed. Elizabeth to my astonishment announced that she felt quite ill. She did not look ill, but she felt so ill, she said, that it would be best if that night I used the second bedroom. I did not see her undress. She ushered me to my room as if to ensure that I went there and stayed there. I had that night a certain small measure of interest in the marriage bed—nothing unreasonable and nothing urgent, but enough to justify a small pleasant expectation—and while I was bound and willing to be reasonable and considerate, she looked so well that I was a little upset. But perhaps she was nervous? Tired? I had assured Mother that nine months away she would have a grandchild. I suppose it was my orderly way of attending to things that made me a little impatient. I had a timetable, as it were.

We sailed for Holyhead from Kingstown, and that night it was the motion of the ship that postponed the initiation rites. I need not detail the evasions stage by stage to Barcelona and the gloomy splendors of the Plaza Hotel. But there I was determined to bring the matter.to a conclusion. I did, but the occasion was not without retrospective humor—retrospective, because at the time I saw nothing amusing about it and must have looked a bit ridiculous even to somebody as ridiculous as Elizabeth had turned out to be.

This time our suite had one bedroom. The thing had to be done, and it was going to be done. Elizabeth escaped to the bathroom and emerged from it in a voluminous flannel nightgown, a monstrous enveloping thing, I was waiting, naked, on the bed, obviously ready. She stopped and looked. At the time I thought her look was of distaste. It quickly became clear that it was fear.

"But you will wear something?" she said in a voice of astonishment.

"No. Come and join me." I was prepared in every way, and she had not pleaded illness, or tiredness, or any form of reluctance.

She stood in the bathroom doorway and I went to her and took her in my arms. The setting seemed peculiarly inappropriate. My feelings were carnal rather than loving. Not immoderate by any means, but adequate to my intentions. She did not rest easily in my arms, but I had accustomed myself to thoughts of consummation, and time had passed. Enough time. Slowly, with consideration I'm quite confident, I began to lift the skirt of her nightgown. She pushed it down. Hastily.

"I'm cold," she said sharply.

"It will be warm under the covers. Come to bed, Elizabeth."

"I shall keep my gown on," she said.

"Very well. Keep it on. Come to bed."

"Put yours on."

"No." I picked her up and put her under the covers.

She cowered. Yes, quite literally, she cowered. "Please don't hurt me," she said pathetically.

"Of course I'll not hurt you."

"How can you fail to hurt me?"

"How can I hurt you?" The thing was becoming preposterous.

"That," she said, staring at the ceiling. "It's monstrous. You can't get it . . . How can you possibly. It's cruel."

"What are you talking about?" I knew very well what she was talking about. What irritated me was that the thing about which Elizabeth mumbled her complaints was the very thing that drew compliments from Cassie Hyndman.

"Mary Forgrave told me her wedding night was agony. Cruel," she repeated plaintively. Then, with a rush, "She said he forced . . . it was torture . . ." It may be that I ought to have listened and understood. I did not.

"Your wedding night was a week ago," I said, "and I did not share it. How do you expect to have children if we don't make a beginning?"

Then she stunned me. "I don't want to have children."

I sat up in bed. The thing had to be thought about, but all I could think of and wish for was Cassie Hyndman. My God but Cassie would be in a different mood. "You do realize," I asked after a while, "that failure to consummate a marriage is sufficient ground for its dissolution?"

"Yes." She said it crisply, like an unpleasant truth that could not be denied.

"Is that what you want?"

"No."

"You are not ill. You have not been ill since we left home. You have been postponing, because of this Forgrave woman's chatter, what you believe to be the evil day." It was pompous. Even so it was better than what I wanted to say. "Is that not so?"

"Yes, I'm afraid."

"Of what?"

It was almost a whisper. "It," she said.

My God. It. Did she mean my organ or the act itself? She had had an excellent view of my organ, ready to serve. Cassie and my former mistress had both admired it. I was too impatient to ask what she meant by "it." I said, I think with some show of patience, "We can start our journey home tomorrow morning or we can consummate our marriage. Which do you prefer?" I knew it was heartless, but it had its effect.

"Oh, God," she said. "Very well," she said, and closed her eyes and drew her lips tight, preparing to suffer. In this atmosphere the thing was done.

It was a very unsatisfactory occasion. I am a large man and she is right, large in all my parts. Elizabeth is a small woman, small in her parts. The thing was a struggle and she kept her hands by her sides and refused to help. It was awkward. If I had been more interested in sexual pleasure than I was in begetting a son, I would have abandoned the effort that night. She cried out. I soldiered on in fear of injuring my parts, and it was done. But it was of such a nature that thereafter with Elizabeth I was always in fear of doing damage to my parts.

And the thing having once been done, I kept Cassie's formula for sure conception in mind and once each night for the following week "kept at her."

"My God," she said on the third night, "are you going to put me through this every night?"

I assured her that I was, for the time being. "Conception, not carnal greed, is the purpose," I said.

By the time we came home to Barn House, Elizabeth was reconciled to one of the facts of married life and submitted to the necessity. I say submitted. Each of our three children was conceived—indeed every Friday night rang—to a familiar chorus: "Will you soon be finished? Will you be much longer? Will you please be quick? Stop. Stop now."

All the births were difficult. I cannot deny that. They were difficult for me also. I had heard of the commotion some women make in labor and at the delivery, but I had never in any circumstances in life heard anything like this. Mother, on the other hand, told me Cassie had laughed about her delivery.

"Aggie just slid out like a wee darlin as if she couldn't wait to get here," Cassie said, and Mother roared her delight at that. Elizabeth was not like that.

When our first, Alasdar Carrach MacDonnell, was born, I was certain she must be dying. It was very difficult for her, and I think I had more sympathy for her than at any time in our married life, even though there were grave and perhaps ruinous concerns on my mind. The American Civil War was in its third year and I had committed four of our six ships to running cotton through the Union blockade from the Confederate states to the starved cotton mills of the North of England. It was a worrying time. I had made a serious and inexcusable mistake in committing so many of my ships. Elizabeth's cries and my other anxieties divided my mind and shattered my nerves. It was a very difficult time for us both.

When Morag came, I was sure Elizabeth could not survive.

When Cathleen came, I had to leave the house to escape from cries that sounded as the damned in hell are said to howl in their eternal anguish. I know nothing about what the damned in hell suffer or how they sound—I have some doubts also about the place and its location—but those great and continuous deep-throated yowlings and howlings came close to stopping my heart. They froze Mother to the chair she sat in.

"Merciful Christ," she whispered, "let it be over."

Later, weak from the misery of it all, she said to me, "You would have been better off with a woman like Cassie Hyndman."

The servants stood still in their places whether it was

kitchen or corridor, and the groom at the stables ran into the walled garden to escape the sound.

And it was over.

Two months after Cathleen (we call her Kitty) was safely delivered, Elizabeth and I were at breakfast. Breakfast was a silent meal. By now our life together was almost entirely silent. There can be no doubt she hated me with a dark hatred. Day by day, her hatred for me increased. Hatred was too strong an emotion for me. I can only say that year by year my distaste for Elizabeth grew. She hoped, I soon discovered, to dabble in my business. Presumably it was some sort of compensation for things lost; for life's disappointments; for love's disappointments. What she had reached for in our marriage was place and power, and since it could not be with Hugh, then with me. "You must turn from sail to steam," she said. "No," I said. "Sail is holding its own. It is not yet time." She insisted, "It is time." I was forced to say at last, "Tend your business, I'll tend mine. Do not interfere in matters you do not understand."

And at breakfast this morning she said suddenly, in her voice of censure, "I have provided you with an heir and two daughters."

I said agreeably and without suspicion, "Yes, you have," for I could hardly deny it.

"No more. There will be no more."

It was almost a shout. There was something hysterical in it, but it went deeper than that. I am not expert in states of mind, for it seems to me people who want to be stable and are determined to be stable can be so. There was a wildness in that voice and something of the deep-throatedness of her labor howlings that alarmed me.

"That is reasonable," I said, and because I was sorry for her and anxious that she should be reassured by my sincerity and concern, I added, "I have been reading the pamphlet by Bradlaugh and Mrs. Besant about anticonception methods. They are of course forbidden by the church but . . ."

"No more," she screamed at me, and crashed her plate to the floor. *"There will be no more."*

I still supposed she meant children. She did not.

"Do not come to my room again," she said, almost growling, or so it sounded to me.

"I see," I said not very helpfully.

"You have violated me to satisfy your lust for the last time," she said. *"No more."*

It was the reference to lust that offended me. I am far from being a lustful man. Furthermore, men do not lust after their own wives, but it was hardly a time to argue about that.

I said, rather stiffly, I think, "Very well." Since she said nothing, I added, "As you please." I wanted to say, "In bed you are scarcely a source of undiluted joy," but that would have been out of time. I left the table thinking how in bed with her I had always feared injury to my parts. There was a certain measure of relief for me in her unilateral decision.

She called after me, "When you come back today I shall have moved from our apartments to the little apartment in the west wing."

"That is much too close to the maids' quarters," I said.

"Then you'll not find your way to their quarters, will you?" And she rose and swept past me, a small, birdlike, and now very sharp-faced figure with a tongue like a kestrel's beak. And as she passed me, her arms swinging violently, she did something for which I find it hard to forgive her. She swung her left arm, her little fist clenched, across toward the right side of her body and brought it back in one uninterrupted movement and struck me savagely in my parts. It was treacherous; utterly unexpected. I was blinded by the agony.

Then, while I was bent in torment, tenderly grasping my parts and doing them no good, oohing and aahing and mygodding in near despair, she stood in the doorway and laughed as if she had just heard a very funny story. I was too harassed by fearful pain to notice when she left.

Later in the day I went to see Dr. Houston, who had delivered all the children. I could not allow her the satisfaction of seeing the doctor arriving at Barn House. There was, he assured me, no damage done, but I could expect my parts to be tender for the rest of the day and perhaps a little longer.

"Why in God's name would she do it?" I asked him.

He was very solemn. "In the texts," he said, "they call it geographical reciprocity." Then he roared and his big belly quivered.

Even Mother found some humor in it. "I didn't think she had the intelligence to relate one part to another," she said.

Both of them are no doubt very humorous, and that is easy for them. Mine were the aching parts.

✐ Three ✐

Barn House did not darken because of Elizabeth's defection to the west wing. If anything, it lightened; a certain daily strain diminished; there were times when I forgot about her entirely, and the children, who rarely saw her, rarely spoke of her.

But she was busy. She spent more time at Court House on the sea front in Carrig with the castle in the corner of its eye. And she wrote letters. She wrote to my cousins in Boston. I am certain of this because their letters ceased to mention her, even to inquire about her. Mother had made her disapproval of our marriage plain to them and said, as she told me, "but since he is determined on it, I shall not make matters difficult for them." I interpreted their silence about Elizabeth as a sign that she had written to them of our difficulties and they were not anxious to involve themselves to their or our embarrassment. These are the difficulties that frighten relatives away, and since none of them really knew Elizabeth—though I had visited them in America and Cousin James had been present at my marriage—what could they do but shrink from the retailer of bad family news and fall silent?

She wrote also, I was certain, to Emily, who was now living and painting in Dublin, sustained by an allowance from her father. My friendship with Emily was deep and, I suppose one would say, sexless. She had been a frequent visitor to Barn House in the first two years of my marriage. One day she said simply that she would not be back.

"Elizabeth would prefer me not to come," she said.

"Did she say so?"

"In her way. And please remember that I know her way. I have lived with it longer than you have."

Soon she went to Dublin, but our correspondence was full and frequent, not to or from Barn House but to and from the shipping office. Emily would not write to the house. "I want no quarrel with Elizabeth," she wrote.

Now she wrote that she wanted to visit me "for a short break." She was "tired." She would, she said, be happy to stay alone at Court House. She would be happier to stay at Garden House with Mother to avoid any possible strain at Barn House.

What strain? I said nothing in my letters about our domestic separation, which was now more than nine months old. I pondered a lot on Elizabeth and her letters and her motives, and ordered a room made ready at Barn House for Emily. I chose the room. The one next to mine. The one the wife who leaves her husband's bed usually moves to.

There are no secrets in houses like mine. I knew this all too well and knew my orders would filter through to the hermit of the west wing, almost certainly through the housekeeper, the guardian of the linen—who must still discuss with Elizabeth all housekeeping arrangements. Yet not a word came from the west-wing nunnery. Nor did I send any. This is my house. I shall have in it whomsoever I please. Elizabeth was not in the dark. Her separation was her choice. She repudiated her marriage obligations but clung to the place they had given her. If she wanted to live in the light, let her come to me for immediate information. I would not acknowledge her existence or her place in the house by volunteering information.

I met Emily at Carrig station.

Perhaps she was emboldened by my decision that she must stay at Barn House. I did not think at all about her motives. Why should I? She was a trusted friend. When we met, she kissed me.

I had never kissed nor had I ever been kissed by anyone in public. There were in the station people who knew me. Everyone in Carrig and for miles around knew me. And Emily kissed me.

I was not shocked but I was taken aback, and she saw it and was amused. (She did not look tired or ill or under any strain. She looked happy to me.) So she kissed me again, this time holding me so that I could not withdraw.

"Carrach," she said, laughing, "give these gaping locals something to wonder about."

"Don't you think they have enough already? They know where Elizabeth lives in the house and what time I go to bed."

"Now they'll wonder who goes with you."

That did disturb me. The servants of a large house are often related. A girl who is well regarded by butler or housekeeper will recommend her sisters, or cousins, or second cousins on the strength of her own good reputation. So Elizabeth's move to the west wing was known and discussed and interpreted in Carrig and the country around. The second time Emily kissed me, I felt a faintly rebellious tremor against the pressure of opinion and against the insolence of inside observation and outside speculation. The trouble with this public knowledge of our domestic affairs was that while it was usual for women to leave the marriage bed after a few years of childbearing, Elizabeth had chosen not to occupy the room next to mine but to remove herself to the small apartment once occupied by a butler and his wife who acted as housekeeper. And this was of great interest to the household staff, who conveyed their interest to anyone who would listen. Everybody wanted to listen. For a moment, on the station platform, my resentment of this public invasion of my private life made me want to give them, as Emily said, something to wonder about. Only for a moment; no such impulse touched me again for several years.

Emily read my mind. "Don't worry,"she whispered. "The maids always know how many people slept in one bed."

The coachman loaded her baggage and prevented further talk.

"Let's take the longest way home," she said, "I want to talk before we get there."

So we drove up North Road and around Lovers' Lane, a tree-sheltered little road that earned its name every evening when the sun set. I did not on that ride think I would have been wiser and happier to have pursued this pleasant girl who was now twenty-five rather then be reeled in by her sister. The thought did come to me later. It came with unhappier thoughts of the sort that I think now and then haunt the waking hours of cautious men. I have never been free of the frightening notion that my survival thus far in life has been mere chance; that anyone's survival is mere chance. It is not true that men believe mortality belongs to others. For cautious men their mortality, the prospect of tragedy or capricious disaster, is always present. This thought leads to states of anxiety about oneself and one's children that have to be ruthlessly controlled. What chance happening would destroy me or mine? Once when I was young I sailed to Boston aboard the *Cathleen MacDonnell* in company with the *Eóin Mor MacDonnell*. The *Eóin Mor* went down with all hands in a fearful Atlantic storm. Separated by the storm, we never knew her position when she foundered. It might just as well have been the *Cathleen*. Chance. So with good things: good events to me are chance that might as easily and by some small margin have brought tragedy. One's life is always a hair's breadth away from triumph or tragedy, and the determining factor is a random thing. But at this time, with Emily, the thought was not in my mind that I might have had her and not her sister.

"Now, Carrach," she said, "what's this about Elizabeth?"

"What about Elizabeth?" If she knew something, she would have to tell me what it was and how she knew. I have tried all my life not to walk blindly.

She took my hand under the rug that covered our knees on a cool spring day. "Carrach, do you need to pretend with me? Elizabeth writes letters. She has written me several scorchers about her removal to another part of the house and about your"—and she leaned close to whisper what the coachman must not hear—"fearful lust and insatiable appetites." And she laughed, a ridiculous little laugh that made what she said immeasurably more ridiculous. "That makes you very interesting," she said.

Emily is what is called "a free woman," sometimes "a modern woman," and I had always supposed that with most people when these words were used about a woman, they had scandalous meanings. She didn't look scandalous as I turned to face her. She was laughing, true enough, but at Elizabeth, not at me. "It's preposterous, of course," she said. Then she added, with mischief in her eyes, "Do you really have these awful virtues?"

We were riding in an open carriage, and in spite of the noise of its wheels and the clatter of its horses, this was no matter to be talked about behind a coachman. Words drift through all but the most thunderous noise, and one word heard or misheard can lead to the most outrageous invention. Emily had already thought of this. "Let's stop and walk a little," she said.

Precisely at the halfway mark along Lovers' Lane a narrow path leads northward along the edge of a field. It is sheltered on one side for the length of that field by a high hedge. In the next field the path is sheltered on both sides by thick hedges and under the hedges are manmade bowers where country girls and their lovers conduct their rites. I thought nothing of this when I walked on the path with my sister-in-law. The occasion was serious, the intent innocent. The coach waited, for all to see, on Lovers' Lane. There was neither attempt nor intent to conceal.

"Well," she said along the path, "are you a lustful man with insatiable appetites?"

"How can I talk to you about such things?" I talked with Emily about almost everything, but never about matters such as this.

"You can surely say yes or no?"

"Emily," I said, "how can I talk about something as intimate as this? Your sister is also involved, you know. It's her intimacy also." I was fumbling. The truth is, I saw no reason why I shouldn't talk about it. My problem was that I didn't know how to talk about it.

"Tosh," she said.

"Tosh, is it?" I stopped in the path. "You want me to stand here in the open air and discuss the intimacies of the bedroom with you?" Of course it was a ridiculous thing to say, but I wanted to peer into the green bowers under the hedges to make sure there were no couples listening. The cool air moved, suggesting exposure. This sort of thing was discussed behind closed doors with every assurance of privacy.

"Yes," she said emphatically. "Oh, God, Carrach, would it be more in keeping with your sense of fitness if we brought the rug from the carriage and draped it over our heads?" She crouched and threw an invisible blanket over her head.

"It would not." But I confess the thought and her action amused me.

"Then have some sense. She's discussed all these 'intimacies' with me. In great detail. In writing. Some of the details . . ." And she was laughing again, but as if the matter had suddenly shed its humor for her, her laughter stopped abruptly. "If these things had been about Hugh, she would have written to me about her ecstasies. Carrach," she said sharply, "I'm trying to find out what she's really talking about."

"Why?"

"Because I want to know. Because I know her. How well I know her." There were many years of feeling in it. "Because I love you," she said. "Don't misread that," holding up one palm to block misunderstanding. "I love my father also, and my friends."

I had not misunderstood her. I loved Emily in the sense that I valued her, would have wept at her funeral and missed her presence all my life. It was the only kind of love I had ever felt—for my father and mother, for Hugh, for the children, for Emily. It was then that I thought of it. God, if Emily had been the marrying kind, she would have been the one, with enough carnal knowledge to meet my meager needs, companionship, friendship, and without draining passion. Emily would have been comfortable—to live with, to be with. But that was that.

"Don't ask me to defend myself," I said.

"I'm not asking you to defend yourself, you dunderhead," she said, waggling her hands at me.

Another thing occurred to me then. We could also have disagreed without pain, in the certainty that there was no malice, no intent to hurt or diminish one another. Elizabeth needed to diminish me.

There was something going on in Emily's head that made it hard for her to keep outrageous laughter away. She was shaking with crushed-down laughter. "Nature betrayed you."

"What does that mean?"

"It would be impossible for you to defend yourself against one of her charges," she said, and she said it sputtering like a dying engine. "She says your member was transplanted on to you from a horse . . ." And her laughter broke. "Monstrous," she shrieked. "I can see it!"

I looked down hastily, looked up foolishly, and felt foolish.

I was sure the coachman heard her. How could he know what caused her laughter? But what you think determines what you fear, and I feared a servant's dirty mind.

"For God's sake, Emily."

"Don't be a prig. I'll not talk with you, Carrach, as if I were the Virgin herself."

It broke my own reserve. I could talk about anything with Emily.

She took my arm and drew me along the path, walking slowly. We were out of sight of Lovers' Lane, between the hedges. "Look, Carrach. I'm not a wicked woman. You think the way I live and the work I do are the ways of the loose woman . . ."

"I do not." But I had always wondered.

"But you assume that I'm . . . experienced."

"I do not." Speculation is not necessarily assumption.

"I am not. With that understood . . . It is understood, isn't it?"

"Of course it is. Perfectly."

"With that understood, Elizabeth is trying to hurt you. She's written to John and Father and Mother . . . no, no, no, not about what she tells me are your fearful lusts and your insatiable appetites . . . It's your cruel, heartless, brutal lack of thought, consideration. All that."

"She is a cold woman," I said in my own defense.

"She is not."

"I should know."

"Should you indeed? I suppose when you and she were girls together she talked to you about Hugh? Did she describe to you all her sex fantasies with Hugh? How she couldn't wait for the marriage bed?"

"I don't believe it. It's impossible."

"It's true. I'll put it to you plainly. There was never anybody of my acquaintance as horny as Elizabeth. It was her constant conversation at night—but always about Hugh. She lusted after Hugh."

"So did a lot of women. Quite successfully."

"But he never attempted to seduce Elizabeth. He merely teased her. He was laughing at her. She waited a long time for Hugh before she realized what he did to her. She married you when the poison had worked its way into her brain. She settled for position, money, and stuffy old sexless old Carrach. She's still keeping herself for Hugh, because she knows what he did and can't let herself believe it . . . somewhere in her head I'm sure that's how it works."

"You're saying she's crazy."

"Crazy? What is crazy? I'm saying she hates you."

"I know that."

"I'm telling you why she hates you. Someday, maybe sooner, maybe later, she's going to gather up all the threads in her malignant mind and hurt you and Hugh."

"If she can find Hugh."

"She can find you."

"What am I supposed to do?"

"Get a legal separation. Get her out of your house. Give her a big settlement, but get her outside your life, where she can know nothing that matters or can be used."

"If you're right about her, she wouldn't agree."

"Or you don't want to face it in public."

"I don't."

"Well, I've told you. Let's go back to the carriage."

"You're blaming me."

"Let's go back to the carriage."

We had nothing to say. We came out from between the hedges into the field that bordered Lovers' Lane. And stopped.

There were two carriages waiting in the lane. My coachman was standing by Elizabeth's, pointing toward the path. Pointing now toward us. She looked. She stared for a long time. She gestured toward the groom who drove her carriage, and went slowly on her way. She turned in her seat, looking back at us, and then was lost against the trees that lined the lane.

Emily looked grim. No, she looked frightened. She did not speak again till we reached Barn House.

The servants took her baggage to the room next to mine.

"Not here," she said briskly, nervously. "Put me in another room."

That too would be reported. I felt bruised, and waited for the storm to break.

❧ *Four* ❧

Emily stayed for a month. For most of the time Elizabeth behaved reasonably well, emerging from her redoubt beyond the maids' quarters to help entertain her younger sister. They went riding together, looked at the countryside from the open landau, visited Mother at Garden House, and held a tea party or two at Court House for some of the women of the district. Yet all the time, Emily seemed puzzled. "I expected a row," she said. "Elizabeth can conduct very nasty rows. She used them at home as emotional blackmail. They were always hanging over us like a threat."

"What has she got to row about?"

"We were walking on that path," she said. "You spend your day thinking about business. I spend mine thinking about Elizabeth. Because she . . ." She did not go on and I did not press her to.

It was the end of the month before I heard what she . . .

In that time, brother-in-law John came frequently to Barn House. He had changed the English John to Seán and was being very Irish. He made me nervous, talking a great deal and with favor in the hearing of the servants about the Fenians. My servants were almost all Protestants. Some of them are the sisters, daughters, and nieces of ardent Orangemen. It would have been very unwise of me to fill my house with Catholic servants, giving the impression of a center of papist clannishness or something much worse. I could have no doubt that John's conversation—or if I must, since that's what he calls himself, Seán's conversation—was reported out-

37

side the house and it could do me no good. Therefore, I countered it, assuming an even greater impatience than I felt at his eulogies of men like John Devoy in jail now but who had in the past and would again from New York at a safe distance urge the Fenians to acts of violence and revolution in Ireland and raise money to finance Fenian actions. Devoy was, I said in the hearing of the servants, "heroic on the pennies of Irish servant girls" and I hoped he would come to a bad end, hoping also that I would be quoted as widely as my chattering brother-in-law who from his days of silent watchfulness had traveled a long and articulate way. Emily helped as though she saw the danger of it. "Home Rule," she said, for Seán talked incessantly about it, "would not be good for Ulster. Ulster is different." I did not know whether she believed it. What worried me most about Seán was that he never attacked me for my views when there were servants within earshot; he ignored my views and talked always as though we were in complete agreement, and I was forced again and again to enter into long repudiations of his opinions when I did not want to talk about them at all. When I launched these repudiations, he sat smiling and would say repeatedly, "Very discreet, brother Carrach. Very discreet," as if all that I said was intended to mislead the servants.

Even so, Emily brought some happiness to Barn House. The children loved her and she spent a great deal of time with them. Mother enjoyed her company. For that matter, she spent a great deal of time with me, riding, driving, talking, visiting Mother at Garden House and cheering her failing days, for she was now quite ill. Elizabeth emerged from her redoubt to dine. Otherwise she never joined us as a family but confined herself to dinner and occasional expeditions and tea parties with Emily. But she smiled, always shrouded in an atmosphere of watchfulness, and welcomed her brother to dinner with an excess of enthusiasm that was manifestly artificial and, I began to suspect, was meant to be seen to be so; like a threat that was being carefully nurtured, an act of slow and careful intimidation.

It came first from Seán. It came when Patton, the butler, an ardent Orangeman, was in the dining room supervising two serving girls who were the daughters of Orangemen. The Orangemen were still alert and angry about the last Fenian "uprising" in 1864. The very word Fenian filled them with militant rage. Into this explosive context, Seán fired his shot.

"Carrach," he said, when all three servants were together

about the table, the girls removing dishes, "I have pledged you for a hundred pounds for Fenian funds."

Elizabeth smiled and looked at me. Her smile said, "Talk that away."

"You have what?" I shouted, and decided that since he had said something so deadly before the servants, I had to deal with it in the harshest terms in the same company. "Then unpledge me," I said. "I will never contribute one penny to that murdering rabble, and I have this to say to you. Since you choose to identify yourself with them, do not any longer identify yourself with me or my house. You are no longer welcome here. Do not return." I do not know whether I sounded impressive or foolish, but since the Orange moved about the room slowly, drinking in the talk, I added, "This is a Unionist house. It stands for the ancient connection with the United Kingdom, and that is to be understood now and in the future." It was like a formal declaration of policy. Even to me it sounded pompous if not downright silly.

He grinned his derisive Irish grin and stood up. "Am I to tell the archbishop," he said, "that you have separated your house from Catholic Ireland?" I doubt whether the impertinent young whelp was in a position to tell the archbishop the time of day.

"You can tell . . ." I was shouting but I didn't know what I intended to say and stopped before I could find out.

Elizabeth left with him, still smiling as though a nail had been well driven. Whether it had been planned between them I could not know. What I did know was that a version of it would spread through Carrig the next day, and whether it would be a version that carried the truth was an open question. The incident left me shaken. What followed left me in a state of deep gloom.

Elizabeth came to the library late that evening.

Emily and I were talking by the fire. We rambled on about many things, the children, her paintings, life for a young single woman in Dublin. It was pleasant talk, comfortable talk, friends' talk. It relaxed me and made me happy at the end of a trying day. She was curled up in what I call the captain's chair because it is the chair in which I sit my captains down when they come home from the sea. It was in my mind again that this woman would have met all my needs and made me content. I was ashamed that I had once weighed the faint cast in her left eye in the balance and passed by what I now most needed, domestic tranquillity. It was in my mind,

too, that the relationship we enjoyed made me unaware of
the cast.

"Will you ever marry, Emily?" I said.

She shook her head. "No," she said to the flames. "Do you
have a mistress, Carrach?"

The conjunction of the questions was surprising.

"No," I said.

"Will you take one now?" It was so casual.

"No."

She grinned. It was more robust than a smile. "Not even to
assuage your lust and fearful appetites?"

"They're too occasional and too feeble to need one.
Unless," I said, "I found the right one and it wouldn't be lust
or fearful appetites that made me ask her."

"You sound as if you already know her."

"I do."

"Do I?"

"Better than anybody except myself."

She looked into the fire for a long time, and I had nothing
else to say. Only the fire made a sound.

"Thank you, Carrach," she said at last, and did not look
my way.

"And the answer?"

"No." She wiggled about in the captain's chair, sinking
deeper, like a cat half asleep. "I would want to come here,
live here, sleep with you, eat with you—every night, every
day. There are many reasons why I can't do that and you
wouldn't. But my main reason is that I am going to make
them change their minds about my paintings and stop them
laughing at what they call my Blue Landscapes. I am going
to be a famous and a respected painter. Nothing will get in
my way. Do you understand how I feel?"

"Yes."

"So what is *your* main reason for not taking me as your
mistress?"

"Because I wish you were my wife."

"Do you love me that way?"

"I love you as my friend. You make me content and
happy."

"Have you ever loved anybody with a great passion?"

"No."

"Could you love anyone with a great passion?"

"I've seen no sign of it in myself."

"You think married love is mutual kindness and respect?"

"Yes."

It was soft almost languid talk. Talk between trusting friends. Our voices barely carried across the fireplace. Neither of us had any more to say, or if Emily had, she was not in a hurry to say it.

"It would probably have been very nice, very comfortable," she said, but I had no chance to ask her to explain.

Elizabeth, literally, with violence, threw open the door and marched in, leaving the door wide open. Since her retreat to her nunnery, she had dressed entirely in black, perhaps in mourning for her lost maidenhead, brutally murdered by the wrong man. Now she marched across the room toward Emily, her arms swinging as they had swung the morning she struck me in my parts. I thought her clear intention was to strike Emily, and rose to be prepared to stop her. But she stood over her sister, her face red with accumulated anger and immediate exertion.

Emily looked up at her placidly, no longer with any sign of fear.

"I have come to have it out with you," Elizabeth said.

Emily sat up defensively and said quietly, "You have come to what, Elizabeth?" Its quietness made Elizabeth's storm look oddly extravagant.

"Why did you come here?"

"Because your letters alarmed me," Emily said, and moved slowly from the chair to stand before the fireplace. It seemed to give herself the advantage of reach and height. "They were very alarming letters."

"Why wasn't I informed of your coming?"

"I informed your husband."

My wife turned on me. "And you chose not to inform your wife?"

I was tired of all her antics. I was weary of her. She was an alien in the house. I could not imagine myself trying to still her frenzy. I said, "I do not have a wife. You may recall that she abdicated and went to her cell." I picked up a newspaper.

She tore it from my hands, pushed Emily aside, and threw the paper on the fire. It was open, part in the grate, part trailing outside it and going up in flames. I threw her aside, grabbed the tongs, and lifted the burning pages into the fire.

"I think you'd better go back to your apartment," I said to her. "Better still, go to Court House for a few days. At least until you collect yourself."

"Oh, no. Oh, no." Her little frame was bursting with fury. "I came to have it out with her and I'll do it. Here *I am home*. Here in this room *I am home*. Everywhere in this house *I am home*. You will not consign me to the servants' quarters."

It was very perverse, very Irish. Create a situation, then accuse others of having placed you in it. I said so, but she had done with that theme. She was standing in front of Emily, fists clenched, face blotched, eyes burning with hostility out of control.

"What were you doing in Lovers' Lane with my husband?"

"Talking." Emily was admirably cool. She had made up her mind how to deal with her sister.

"*About what?*" It was a shriek.

"*About you.*" Her coolness was like fuel poured on Elizabeth's rage.

"*What about me?*"

Emily struck. She struck with a smile and a soft voice. "About your letters to me. About your husband's animal lust and his huge organ, which you said must have been transplanted from a horse."

Elizabeth's little fists were raised before Emily's face. "*And I suppose you found out for yourself?*" she screamed.

Emily took my wife's wrists firmly in her stronger hands and softly struck again.

"Not yet," she said, smiling.

There was malice in the smile and the voice, and the malice I did not understand.

"I think this has gone quite far enough," I said reasonably, though I wasn't displeased with Emily. The whole thing was distressing, but my distress was in seeing Elizabeth as the fish-wife I had never seen so convincingly before. There was nothing distressing about Emily and her way with her sister.

Elizabeth tore her hands free and struck me on the cheek. "Keep out of this," she yelled, and turned again to Emily. "Not yet," she said with menace, "not yet, is it? That's what you're after, my girl, isn't it? You came here like a whore, didn't you? I told you he was a lusting animal, and you couldn't wait to get into his bed, could you?"

A maid was standing by the door with a tray of the hot milk Emily and I drank every night before we retired. Elizabeth could see her. My wife was insanely destructive, a woman burning her boats; she had crossed over to the other side with no wish to return. Suddenly she smiled.

"Well, you can't have him, can you? We're all good Catholics together, aren't we? So you can't have him, can you?"

Emily was not smiling. Her face was frozen. "That," she said, and struck again, "is entirely up to him." I do not think she intended to say it.

Elizabeth screamed in Emily's face and turned about in wild frustration in small despairing circles, her hands locked together, and ran to the door. She knocked against the maid; the tray and the milk and the Jacob's Cream Crackers crashed to the floor, and she was gone.

"Leave it," I said to the girl.

Emily stood very still, staring at my bookshelves, not seeing them, I am certain.

I took her in my arms. "Emily, Emily, Emily," I said uselessly. I could think of nothing else to say.

"I shall take the early train in the morning," she said gently.

The maid backed slowly to the library door.

ᏬᎧ *Five* ᏬᎧ

And the children grew in our shadows.

And other shadows. These were prosperous times, for the Civil War in America and the devastation of the Confederate states, while denying the cotton mills of the North of England all the cotton they needed, had created a great opportunity for the Ulster linen industry. Linen mills expanded, their need for spun flax increased, and I expanded the spinning mill and seeded increased flax acreage on the home farm and on the tenants' farms. It was not enough. We bought flax in Belgium, so much flax that we had to maintain an agent abroad to ensure the quantity and quality of the crops committed to us.

But this of itself raised questions. Were the prospering MacDonnells "solid"? Were they, that is, solidly loyal to the Crown and the Union of Great Britain and Ireland, governed from Westminster as one nation? We were. But it soon became necessary to prove it, due in large measure to the activities of Elizabeth's brother, Seán McCarthy, now an active Fenian propagandist. I confess I was angered by the necessity to prove it. Why should it be necessary for me to prove my interest in my own interest? Because I was a Catholic, and for no other reason. It was humiliating. It was, I suppose, like a Confederate who had accepted the American Union and come to live in the North as an ordinary American and found that he lived with constant suspicion and doubt about his good intentions.

My forebears served Ulster and ourselves in it before there

44

was a Protestant in Europe, long before there was a Protestant in Ireland. We had always, with the O'Neills, put Ulster first and resisted any domination from the South. Yet, with longer lines than any substantial family in the land, I had to prove my loyalty to men who were latecomers to it. Because I was a Catholic.

Now that the O'Neills were Protestant, there was no truly Irish Catholic aristocracy in the North, for we, as I have said, are Ulster-Scot and a different breed. Yet, being Catholic, we had to be circumspect. The small Catholic middle class lived lives quite indistinguishable from their Protestant neighbors. The Ulster Evangelical Revival had left its mark on the Protestant and there was a new moral censoriousness in the land so that even Catholics with pianos in their parlors would not permit them to be played on a Sunday, unless they were used to play hymns. Catholics, Hugh once said, are always ducking their heads to avoid Protestant beams.

The United Irishmen failed because Catholics and Protestants could not trust one another, and distrust was as rife as ever. Anger and ugliness were rampant in the land. Mr. Gladstone was ready to take power for the Liberal party in England, talking of reform in Ireland and talking far beyond reform. The Fenians O'Donovan Rossa and James Stephens, Devoy, O'Leary, Luby, and others were in jail and their Fenian paper, the *Irish People,* closed down, but the *Nation* published a damaging story about me in which I saw the fine and venomous hand of Seán McCarthy, my less than loving brother-in-law. This story said that in their councils Fenian men like Kelly, Halpin, and the American "General" Millen dined sparely on dry bread and tea. A rich and sympathetic benefactor in the North had sent them a feast of wild duck and snipe, walnuts and oranges, the finest Irish whiskey and adequate supplies of Guinness's porter. The donor? Tomas Carrach MacDonnell. I had also, it seemed, contributed a hundred pounds to the Fenians' treasury.

I had not. I would not. It was unthinkable for me. I was sick with anger and dismay. I could see and hear the Fenians laughing at the impact of this announcement. I could see Seán McCarthy's sleeked mind and his derisive grin. There was nothing to do but deny it in the daily press in Dublin and Belfast and to see Robert Garrett, a powerful Orangeman but also my largest customer for spun flax and a man who shipped linen to Boston in my ships. Cousin James's company imported it. It was a cooperative and profitable alliance. Cousin James's business was some assurance to me of Garrett's self-serving interest in listening to me.

We were friends insofar as an Orangeman and a Catholic could be friends. This is to say, we had a relationship of trust in all our business dealings: we were honest men and knew one another to be honest. But I am a Catholic and therefore by nature part of a universal conspiracy to make the Pope of Rome the ruler of the world and of men's minds and spirits in it. In the English House of Commons the Irish Catholic members were even known as the Pope's Brass Band. I never give a second thought to the Pope of Rome. I have no knowledge of any such conspiracy. If I knew of it, I should oppose it. Nor am I acquainted with a Catholic who knows of its existence. Garrett is confident of its existence and that it exists especially in Ireland, even though the Catholic clergy are almost to a man in favor of the United Kingdom of Great Britain and Ireland and actively hostile to the Fenians. The *Irish People* had attacked the Catholic clergy almost without respite. For issues on end it seemed that its only policy was to attack our clergy for their loyalty to the government. They had scandalously, even scurrilously denounced Archbishop Cullen of Dublin for his condemnation of Fenianism.

I went to see Robert Garrett. Cap in hand? Not visibly, but that is the humiliating truth. My method was nothing more, at its heart, than an aristocratic plucking of the forelock. It left and has always stirred in me a hardening core of bitterness that makes me think at times and with sympathy of my brother Hugh and his need to get away from Ulster before its Protestants and their condescensions turned him into a Fenian.

These powerful industrial and political linen men were not always powerful. The linen industry in Ulster had been a cottage industry. The spinning and weaving and bleaching were done in cottages and farmhouses, and the product of the people's industry was brought into the town markets and into the commercial stream.

Not so long ago the weavers and spinners from the farms brought their cloth to the towns and sold it in the marketplace. So important were these day-long markets—where as many as a thousand weavers would sell their wares—that the Linen Halls were built to display "the white cloth." It was the

Famine that reduced their numbers—a weaver would in that dark time sell sixty yards of cloth for three shillings and sixpence—and changed their lives and ours.

The linen magnates built mills, installed power looms, and drew into the city the country men and women who live now in poor cramped houses in mean streets and war on one another according to their faith. I never believed faith had much to do with it, but the city grows at a great rate and the factional warfare grows with it.

The new magnates, with good sense, acquired fine estates in the country, away from the conflicts.

Robert Garrett grew with the new linen industry. He is a stocky, heavy man with a growing belly and in most circumstances an open, genial disposition. That alters when his political prejudices are touched or challenged; or when he talks politics with a Catholic. Then he is a wary, cold, and a hard man. He belongs to the second level of Ulster Protestant society.

The first level is what it amuses me—in a bitter sort of way—to hear called "the landed gentry." These "gentry" are the Brookes, the Coles, the Conynghams, the Chichesters, the Stewarts, and others, all seventeenth-century English planters but all belonging to the Episcopal Church of Ireland, which is the Church of England in Ireland. (One Brooke, the head of a family that received its first land grant in Ulster in 1645—the lands of the Donegal O'Donnells—said, "I take unkindly to being called an Irishman.") Nobody loves them. The Catholics hate them, the Presbyterians hate them, all for the same reason—their power, their arrogance, and their assumptions of superiority. They belong to the gentlemanly top story of the Orange Order. Their word—that is, their social authority—is their only link with the rest of that order.

Robert Garrett is a leader of the second level of Ulster Protestant society, the rich bourgeois who manufacture linen, build ships, or make rope. Subservient to the episcopal gentry, they also envy them and dislike them. The Protestant bourgeois are for the most part Presbyterian, and are as bitterly resentful of the establishment of the Episcopal Church of Ireland as the state church as they are of their social subservience. They burn with anger at the inequity of the tithes they have to pay to a church to which they owe no allegiance. But they are closer to the Orange mass, which ranges in social standing from solicitors, schoolteachers, craftsmen, and farmers down to the warring illiterates of the workers' ghettos; and all of them are separated, level by level, by class walls of impenetrable stone.

Garrett received me cordially and invited me to be seated, in an office that reflected the austerity of his Ulster Protestant character more than it did his wealth.

"How's Elizabeth?" he said, and his smiling eyes told me he knew and found humor in my domestic situation.

"Well, Robert. Quite well, thank you."

"And her sister, Emily?" he said, with the direct indelicacy that marks his breed. His smile was now a knowing grin.

"It's some time since I've seen her. She was well while she was here on a brief visit." I watched him sit there behind his desk, full of strength and confidence, and I marveled at the strange contradictions in these people. Rough as he was and indelicate as he was, he was charming. There was nothing malicious in his amusement at my domestic predicament. He half-expected me to share it. That is their strength. They expect you to share their convictions, to share their tastes, their prejudices. Those who do not are peculiar people. Or enemies. They speak with an assumption of your agreement. They are bewildered when you do not agree. How could you disagree?

"It's a bad thing, Carrach," he said companionably, "when a woman leaves your bed. My wife is always ready when I am. Better than that, as often as not she's ready before I am. But why should you care if yours falls short? That sister of hers should be able to take care of you. From all I hear, she's a lively one."

What could I say to the man? I ought to have spat on him and walked out. He was talking about my wife, my sister-in-law, my morals, and assuming that all I needed was ready to hand. A cold wife was no loss. There was a ready substitute in an agreeable sister-in-law. Gossip grows. They harvest it; there was, was there not, something entertaining about a Catholic who could not get rid of a wife? I felt enclosed by eyes and ears that surrounded and penetrated my household. I felt naked.

"I'm afraid all that's a bit far from my style of life, Robert," I said, hanging on to my control, protecting my privacy, and trying not to sound like a prig. And not succeeding, I think. But a man does not discuss his wife in this way. Garrett does. So do Arabs. That is as much as I need say. "I came to discuss something with you, Robert—something we had better think about." Cap in hand against companionable and insufferable intrusion. But I had suffered it, to my shame.

"And what's that?" He was no longer looking at me but at the wall to his left; at once he was wary.

"Mr. Disraeli's failing ministry," I said.

"And what about it?" Still looking at the wall. I was on ground that was riddled with potholes. Dangerous ground.

"Mr. Gladstone and his Liberals will win the election that is coming."

He looked at me then, with speculation. "How can he? Disraeli brought in his second Reform Bill and passed it. He extended the suffrage in boroughs to all householders paying the poor rates and to all lodgers of one year or more paying ten pounds a year. Those are all new votes for the Tories. He can't lose."

Surprisingly, it does not always occur to the men behind the members in parliament that one man's favor is another man's inflammation. "First," I said, "not all the newly enfranchised will cast a vote. For most of them, much as they wanted the vote, casting it is a new idea. It's an action. But in addition, Disraeli by this act has angered as many as he has enfranchised. They'll vote for Mr. Gladstone."

He thought about that, rubbing his nose, pulling at his ear, lighting a pipe and putting it down at once. "You could be right," he said at last. "So?"

"Mr. Gladstone," I said, "has declared that if he is sent to power, he will regard it as his first responsibility to pacify Ireland."

"Ireland" and "pacify" touched him like code words. They set moving in his head a whole range of questions. They were in his eyes as he looked at me. Why was a Catholic raising this? What does it mean to this papist? He stared straight into my eyes, and his eyes were hard. All companionableness had disappeared from them. Carrach MacDonnell was an honest businessman but he was a Catholic and that posed the question: Can he be trusted where this is concerned? But he did not speak. Let him talk, his face said.

I said, "Mr. Gladstone will offer the Fenians concessions—rent rights, security of tenure for tenants, things of that order."

"So he should, if it keeps them quiet," Garrett said brusquely. He had no use for Southern landlords.

"But it won't keep them quiet." I thought of explaining but said no more. I wanted to make him talk, to discuss the thing with me. He merely watched me as though I had to be watched carefully.

"They want independence," I was forced to say. "He will make more concessions. In time—quite soon in fact, he will offer them something short of complete independence. He will offer the Irish members what before long they will all ask for—Home Rule. That will not be enough. The militant Fenians want nothing less than Ireland's complete independence, a separate nation."

He looked puzzled now, but he did not speak. He was puzzled by me, not by what I was saying. What's he up to? he must have been thinking. His look said so. And by silence he forced me to talk. I wanted to get up then and walk out of his office. Surely men can talk together? Surely I could be trusted to serve my own interest, which was also his interest? What had my being a Catholic to do with it? I think I almost hated him then, but I tried instead to ease his mind.

"Count von Bismarck offered Queen Victoria a solution to the Irish question. He said the Dutch should be sent to Ireland and they would make it a land flowing with milk and honey and the Irish should be sent to the Low Countries and they would neglect the dikes and all be drowned."

He almost smiled. "Yes, indeed," he said, and left his chair. He stood by his window, turned to his desk, and took up his pipe. He lit his pipe and puffed on it for a while. I was determined to say no more till he unbent.

"Carrach," he said, "why do you want to dabble in this sort of thing?"

"What sort of thing?"

"Politics."

"Because I have an interest to protect. The same interest you have to protect. Robert Garrett, linen maker, and Carrach MacDonnell, flax spinner, have the same interest to protect. Am I wrong?"

"No."

"Robert," I said, "did you know that my coreligionists who want to break up the Union and elect an Irish parliament are holding lotteries on the Protestant farms they will win, the Protestant mills and factories they will win as prizes when Home Rule comes to Ireland? Did you know that?"

"No."

"My mill is the prize in a Ballycastle lottery, and I am a Catholic, Robert. But I am also for the Union."

"It's a lot of damned nonsense."

"Yes. But it is also a state of mind. Mr. Gladstone in time will offer us both to an illiterate peasantry."

"Why," he said, "did you contribute to the treasury of the Fenians?" He did not turn to face me.

"I didn't. And you know it, Robert. I've issued a denial today in Belfast and Dublin. I think Elizabeth's brother told that tale to the *Nation*. He's an enthusiastic Fenian."

He turned to me at last. "Is it true that you've barred him from your house?"

"Yes."

"Is that the trouble between you and Elizabeth?"

"In part."

"Are you now coming to the point of this political dissertation of yours?"

"Quite close. Though I must say, Robert, it's hard to talk when you know you're not trusted merely because you're a Catholic." I said it too crisply, more so than I intended, and for a second I thought I saw honest regret in his eyes. I think sometimes they would like to see an end to the incessant tension and pressure. I think sometimes they would like to trust somebody, to end the state of siege that is always in their minds.

"Come to the point, Carrach," he said.

"Count von Bismarck also said democracy is government from the nursery."

"What does Carrach MacDonnell say?" A small, sly smile, as if to say, That's a natural belief for a faithful adherent of an authoritarian church.

"I say that an independent and enfranchised Ireland will in time be governed by an illiterate peasantry and that my deepest interest, historically, economically, and in every way, will be threatened by people who know nothing about business, or economic necessity, or how a nation pays its bills. I say that your interests and mine are identical and that it's time to show Mr. Gladstone and his Liberals that Ulster Catholics and Protestants have a common interest in the Union."

"You've made that point already, and I never doubted they had a common interest," he said, as if I had brought him old news. "But the way they're behaving, they seem to."

"That is why I want to stand as the member of parliament for the borough of Carrig. As a Unionist." It was what I came to say. It was how I had chosen to defend myself and my interests against all attack, in a bigoted situation.

"You *what*?" He was dumbfounded. I might have suggested that I should replace Jesus Christ as the Second Person of the Trinity.

"I think you heard me clearly, Robert," I said.

"I did, by God, I did. But I don't believe what I heard."

"You can believe it. It's time Catholics who agree with you were seen by the English to do so." I hated to say that: Agree with you. It was a blanket declaration and I was far from agreeing with them about many things.

I didn't agree with them about the Catholic conspiracy, either Irish or universal. I didn't agree with them that there was something congenitally inferior about the Irish as a race and that a name like McCarthy or Muldoon was a label advertising a kind of Untouchability.

I would have agreed with them that the Celt is emotionally unstable. It was this "wild" inheritance that I fought against in myself to the point where I had turned myself into a man of almost iron and certainly boring propriety. Irish ignorance, Irish dirt, Irish laziness didn't frighten me. Irish volatility did. As much as Protestant self-righteousness frightens me.

I could see Robert Garrett looking at me with an earthy brutality in his eye, and the word "infiltrator" was written on his forehead. The Catholics have a sickness in their heads and hearts about informers. They believe their own brothers, their own mothers, are capable of being agents of Dublin Castle. And indeed they are, for the Celts are a treacherous race. We know that about ourselves and fear it in ourselves. But the Protestants are sick in their heads about traitors, to the point where even the suggestion that Queen Victoria's retreat from public life since Prince Albert's death hinted at a degree of melancholia was regarded by them as the equivalent of Guy Fawkes's attempt to blow up parliament. An alliance between Catholics and Protestants in Ulster meant unresting watchfulness on the part of the Catholics, that no word might ever be spoken by them that could trigger Protestant fears, suspicions, certainty about the long and hidden purposes every Catholic harbored in his poor head. If we were capable of entertaining all the long thoughts with which they credit us, we would indeed be fearful foes. And Garrett was silent again. Staring at me as though I were a species of poisonous snake and if he took his eyes off me I would strike.

"Why hurt yourself?" he said.

"Hurt myself? How?"

"By proposing a thing like this. By drawing political attention to yourself."

"Explain that to me, Robert."

His right hand flickered in an impatient little gesture. "I don't need to," he said. "You know very well."

"Yes. I'm a Catholic. I should sit in my corner and be quiet."

"That kind of talk does you no good. You know that too."

"What will do me good, Robert? Do I have to sit in my Catholic corner until Mr. Gladstone is convinced he can hand me over to an ignorant peasantry just because I'm not allowed to raise my Catholic voice to prove I want the Union to continue? Before I let that happen, I'll fight. And I mean fight."

He stared and made no effort to reply.

"I would fight before I'd let it happen." I hadn't intended to say that or anything like it. I'm not the fighting sort. His silence and his stare were making me angry. It was his kind I wanted to fight. I suppose that somewhere deep inside us, deflecting us from our worst errors, there's a cunning we're not properly aware of. I knew as soon as I said it that it was the right thing to say. His right hand was resting, palm down, on his desk. It closed into a huge tight fist. The cold expression on his face remained. It was the fist that mattered. That was Ulster bourgeois eloquence. I must have touched his own secret thoughts, perhaps the yet undeclared intention of his Orange friends to fight the breakup of the Union.

"That would be treason," he said without expression.

"How can it be treason to fight to preserve the United Kingdom of Great Britain and Ireland?"

He said, "How would you vote on a bill to disestablish the Anglican Church in Ireland?" It was one of his passions to see it done, "to end this Anglican affront," he always said.

Any question was a distant point of light, though this one didn't mean much to my chief concern. I said, "Why should a Presbyterian farmer ever have paid tithes to support the Earl of Enniskillen's church?" I knew he hated Enniskillen, who summoned high and low in the Orange Order as he mustered his servants.

"I'll take advice," he said, and stood up. "Good morning, Carrach."

I was dismissed. His big red face had on it the wariness of a bull instinctively alerted by some invisible danger to the herd.

There was no way in which I could possibly know what went on in their councils. If Garrett bothered to take it any further it would first be with his bourgeois Orangemen. They would meet and talk and speculate and calculate, first about me and my motives, then, if they saw some small merit in me, in spite of my Catholicism, about what advantages they might squeeze from allowing a papist to run as a Unionist (a Tory), and if they saw none, I would hear no more from Robert Garrett. They would simply ignore me. If they saw some, or enough, they would have to consult the Coles, the Brookes, the rest: the Episcopal "gentry." And that was hopeless.

I walked back to the shipping office regretting I had ventured out of my commercial shell. All I had accomplished was to put myself in the way of another humiliation. They would talk about me, almost certainly in terms that didn't flatter me, laugh about my Catholic cunning, then drown me in their arrogant and condescending silence. I would never hear what they said or thought, but I would know. I assured myself that at least I had been cunning. They could not easily believe that I would propose myself for Carrig and contribute to the Fenian treasury. But the comfort of that thought did not last long. That is exactly what they would believe. I am a Catholic.

Already I felt the humiliation and tried to hide from it in intensive work. I suppose a visit to my little governess would have done something to salve my wounds—so far, self-inflicted, for what did I know?—but she was no longer available and hadn't been for years. It was a measure of my gloom that I thought of her at all. I had no real heart for a mistress.

I took my usual train home, wallowing in self-pity. There were glimpses of the sea as we passed Whiteabbey and Whitehouse, then the Lough was shut away and we were enclosed in patterns of hedges and small green fields. Knockagh Hill cast its flat-topped shadow on the left. The land was green and good and tranquil and I wished that I might build a high wall around it and enclose myself, my house, and my children in a safe and private place. I resented this railway that

carried me home. It was built in my lifetime and heightened
the pace and tension of our lives. True, it brought greater
prosperity with it, but it also diminished Carrig as our chief
port in northeast Ulster and compelled us to move our shipping offices to the now dominant port of Belfast. The old arrangements were so relaxed and restful. Once we were a
self-sufficient world at Carrig, now we are on the fringes of
an expanding, even exploding world. My thoughts were the
fruit of my self-pity. I was running away, in my mind. There
are days when I want to conquer that world. There are days
when I want to hide from it, and this was one of them. I felt
weak from anticipated rejection.

But I was resentfully angry. I knew I could win Carrig for
the Tories. Enfranchised Catholic and Protestant would vote
for me—the result would be a declaration to Mr. Gladstone's
Liberals. I had reduced the hours of my workers from 60 to
54 a week and paid them not the Belfast average of 11s. 6d.
a week but 13s. My carpenters at the mill got 32s. 6d. for a
54-hour week—a shilling more for less time than in Belfast.
Clerical workers in Belfast got £60 a year or less. I paid my
shipping clerks £70 in Belfast and my mill clerks £65 a year
in Carrig. I was a good employer and a good landlord. It was
well known.

Hawthorne, my coachman, met me at the station with bad
news that drove all this from my head. Mother's health has
been poor. She is failing far too quickly. The acceleration became clearly visible when Elizabeth retreated to her west-
wing nunnery. It galloped when she told Mother to reduce
the number of her visits to Barn House. That directive followed Emily's visit and led to a fearful storm in which I
shouted at my wife and she remained coldly and derisively
calm, having, I imagine, learned something from her sister's
method of dealing with a raging antagonist. I "counter-
manded the directive to Mother," as Elizabeth put it sneeringly, but without effect. Mother said only, "Come to see me
often, darling," and did not come again to Barn House. The
meaning and purpose of her life had gone; she appeared to
have decided to die quickly. Now, three years after my wife
had left my bed, Emily refused to come again to my house
"while Elizabeth is in it," Seán was barred from it, and
Mother was not only the legitimate occupant of the dower
house—and had been now for six years—but an exile from
her own old home.

I took the children to see her often, but it soon became obvious that all her strength could bear was a brief visit from them; a kiss and an embrace and they were sent back to Barn House with the governess. She loved them deeply but I was slow to see that what I thought of as mere tiredness was deepening exhaustion. I stayed when the children had gone, holding her hand. She sat, sometimes she lay, with a frightening stillness and silence, looking at nothing. Waiting, I thought. When I squeezed her hand, not talking because listening tired her almost as much as talking, she smiled and said in a small voice, "I know you're there, my love." I was often uncertain whether she spoke to me or to my father.

Now, Hawthorne told me, she had been left alone for a moment in her chair at the top of the steps leading down from the center lawn at Garden House to the shore and had tried to reach the shore without her maid. She fell down the steps and the maid returned to find her unconscious on the sand. Dr. Houston was at Garden House. We must hurry, Hawthorne said. Dr. Houston wanted me there at once. When we cleared the streets of Carrig, Hawthorne put the whip to the horses.

Houston met me at the door. He was not one to show deference.

"Hurry up, man," he said, "you can do no harm." He was one of Mother's great friends. She made friends with servants, doctors, family solicitors, tradesmen. If she liked them, she made friends of them, and no amount of social disapproval inhibited her. She seemed not to notice, from some servants, familiar speech I could not have tolerated from any. Perhaps that was because she regarded them as friends?

I scarcely glanced at Houston, but he sniffled and I looked at him quickly. He was crying. "Go on up, for God's sake," he said, and turned his back to me.

I do not know whether she knew me. She was conscious. In a way she was conscious. I took her hand, and what might have been a little smile lingered around her mouth. I kissed her, and like a child—I felt like a child—said close to her ear, "Mama."

She did not try to speak. I think now she was not there.

I sat for an hour, sometimes kissing her hand, sometimes stroking her hair, sometimes saying only, "Mama." No, she was not there.

Then suddenly her limp hand tightened a little on mine

and she said, very clearly in a happy voice, "Yes, yes, my love. Of course, my love."

That was all. In less than a quarter of an hour the faint thin breathing stopped. I saw the living eyes die. I shouted, "Mama! Mama!" I know, quite certainly I know, that the last words she spoke in life were to my father.

Behind me, Houston said, "You needn't bother." His eyes were scalded by his tears.

Now I was alone.

The only people in the world to whom I could talk freely, with confidence and trust, were gone. Emily was not here. Hugh was not here. I had no wife in any sense, only a waspish enemy in my own household. Emily did not come, though she wrote with affection. "It would add to your pain," she said. The children were too young for real companionship. My brother-in-law, Seán McCarthy, was a lurking enemy. His parents were distant, siding with their elder daughter and their malignant son.

I had always thought it strange that the Irish should take such a pride in their family funerals, pride if they attracted a great crowd of followers, shame or hurt if they did not. Yet I was myself proud of Mother's funeral. She was held in great esteem. She was held fondly in the hearts of all who ever had dealings with her—with the single exception of my wife. Mother's funeral was much larger than Father's. She had been more visible to the people of Carrig and the district around. She knew the tradesmen and treated them without condescension, never calling one of them by his surname but always, as in the case of the butcher, Mr. Robinson. She never called a servant girl by her surname (thereby fixing her inferior status) but by her Christian name, as in the case of Cassie Hyndman. She never spoke in the presence of a servant as though the servant did not exist. That, she taught us, is arrogant and inhuman. But it was the practice among her peers. So everyone who could came to her funeral, Catholic and Protestant. I closed the mill. The women in their black shawls came to the funeral. Robert Garrett and his bourgeois Orangemen came to her funeral and were astonished at the crowds gathered outside our Catholic chapel.

But only Catholics, or as many as could crowd inside, went into the little chapel. A great mass of the people gathered outside were Protestant. If the chapel had been as large as a field, they would not have entered. They might have caught some corrupting papist infection, borne to them, perhaps, on clouds of incense.

Nor would Catholics have entered a Protestant church where so many dangers to their eternal souls might lurk in the very air.

But for Mother, they were there to say good-bye.

Robert Garrett said to me later at Barn House, and with what I took to be surprise, "Your family is greatly loved in this borough, Carrach. I can see that. By Protestants and Catholics."

Was he counting votes? Foolishly I said, "My mother was greatly loved, Robert."

"Where is Elizabeth?"

"In her apartment, I suppose."

"She didn't come to the chapel?"

"No." I had no wish to discuss the matter.

"Pity," he said. "Great pity." And did not enlarge on that. He did not enlarge on anything. He had not, I concluded, taken my proposition beyond his office. He had much more interest in my cousin—mother's nephew—Sir Patrick Forsythe, the whiskey distiller from Edinburgh. Patrick had his grandfather's title. Garrett longed for one of his own.

I turned more and more to the children. Morag and Kitty were delightful little girls. Morag was four now, Cathleen three. They rode their small Scottish ponies with confidence, and we rode together a great deal. But five-year-old Alasdar warmed my heart in a very special way. He was a loving child. He reminded me constantly of Mother. At five he talked beyond his years and was a joy to me and a comforting companion. Each day seemed to draw us closer. I paid small attention to anything except business and the children but thought a lot about Alasdar's education. I had never been to school, but tutors were no longer adequate for the education of boys who must one day shoulder responsibilities in an increasingly complicated—and democratic—world. School and university must now take their share of the burden of preparation, and the more time I spent with Alasdar, the more I thought with distaste of the decision I would have to make to send him away. Perhaps that intensified my attachment to my son. It could not have intensified his to me, for the question of school was never mentioned to him. Simply, a strong love grew stronger.

Sadly, I was not able by my nature to express or display my love as freely as he expressed his. That has always been a problem. In bed with my mistress, I was never able to take the reins off what pleasure I enjoyed. With her it was not required, of course. It might have been different with Cassie Hyndman, for that relationship was of a different nature, but, in fact, I was restrained in pleasure, unable to cast aside limiting inhibitions. Cassie used to say to me, "You're always a gentleman, Carrach," and it was some time before I came to believe that she meant it and was not mocking my self-control. Cassie had none in bed, and I marveled at that.

So Alasdar grew with me, and all I could do to tell him of my deepening love was occasionally to touch him, take his hand, lay my hand on his shoulder. He seemed to understand. When I touched him he would look up at me and smile and say, "Papa." Words were not really important.

It was three months after Mother's death that I was summoned to Florence Court by the great Enniskillen himself. He was the czar of all the Orangemen, though he rarely met most of them and spoke to few of them. He governed them through the socially inferior and self-consciously subservient second-level bourgeois, like Garrett. I had not and did not hear at all from Garrett. Presumably he had now been pushed aside, but he had done something, else why should the Earl of Enniskillen send for me, a papist?

It was quite certain that he did not wish to see me for my lineage, though beside it his own was paper-thin and comparatively recent. The first Cole at Enniskillen was a captain who served in the armies of James I in Ireland—that same James who loaned an army to my own ancestor, Alasdar Carrach MacDonnell, to secure the MacDonnell hold on the Glens of Antrim and to lay our hands on the lands of the McQuillans of the Route—some four hundred years after we first came to Ireland. For his services to James, Captain William Cole was granted extensive estates around Lough Erne. Later, this mere captain was knighted. In the hierarchy of rank, it was the humblest, a long way below the Earls of Antrim, Viscounts of Dunluce, Lords of the Glens, Lords of the Isles. If I speak with what appears to be bitterness, appearances do not deceive. The humble captain was given the

Maguire castle and lands at Enniskillen, not after he fought for them but after English and Irish forces (the O'Donnells) had, in alliance, at last subdued and dispossessed Maguire, whose lands and castle were granted to Cole. That is part of the story of Ireland, is it not? The Irish betrayed one another for gain—and in 1645 the first Sir Basil Brooke in Ireland received the lands of the dispossessed O'Donnells who had been willing tools in the dispossession of Maguire. It is the history of the Irish.

The Coles rose in the world. They built Florence Court in 1764 to fit the dignity of the Cole who had now become Lord Mount Florence, a title that caused great merriment in the North. "Lord, *mount Florence*," small boys cried out when the great man passed by in his carriage. Florence Court is a large, square, naked center block standing three stories high and from which extend to left and right two colonnaded arcades with offices at the end of each. The place has austerity without dignity. It was built for someone peculiarly devoid of taste and bears some resemblance in its stone and its style to a penitentiary. In 1748, "Lord, mount Florence" was created Earl of Enniskillen, which deprived the children of their catcall.

His grandson received me now, as a king might receive the least of his squires. I had traveled more than 120 miles to be received by him and like the least of his squires was not a guest at Florence Court. I put up at an hotel in Enniskillen. How could he ask me to be his guest at Florence Court? As a Catholic, might I have the table manners of King Henry VIII? Well-slept, clean, and patient I next morning sent a messenger to his lordship that I was all present and correct and available, ready, willing, and able to wait upon him if he would send a carriage. He would send a carriage or I would go home.

I was cold on my walk to his library. I was cold through my rib cage to my spine. Coldness of the heart and spirit. I no longer knew why I ever raised with Garrett the question of standing as a Unionist. I no longer knew why I answered his Lordship's summons. I do not know now why I did not turn on my heel in his corridors and go home to my children. They were in my mind. My treatment was their treatment. My dignity was their dignity.

He was comfortable by the library fire and did not rise to greet me. He said,

"Ah, MacDonnell," and did not offer me his hand or a chair.

I said, "Enniskillen," and sat down across the fire from him. He was twice surprised. I spoke to him as an equal (no "my lord") and I sat down. Did the man expect me to travel from the east coast almost to the west coast of Ireland and stand in his presence? I watched his eyes move uncertainly, avoid mine, and settle their look on the mantelshelf. A papist equal was an intolerable thought.

"You have created a difficulty for me," he said, not looking at me.

"How have I done that?"

"This matter you raised with Robert Garrett. It has been brought to me." The decision was in the tone. I had already accepted it so there was nothing much to say now. It was curiosity that kept me where I was, to observe this omnipotent Orangeman who looked like a farmer and talked like a monarch.

"What matter?" It ought to have been: How have I done that, my lord? and: What matter? my lord. The omission clearly irked him and made him uncomfortable and that pleased me. It was an insolent challenge to his dubious supremacy.

"That you should be the Unionist member for Carrig." He said it with peculiar clarity as if to say: You know damned well what matter.

"Why would it be brought to you? I should have thought it concerned the electorate of the borough of Carrig much more closely." It was cheeky and I was suddenly enjoying the occasion. He brought me all this way to say no; to see me come expectantly, like a plowboy; to see me go empty for my papist presumption.

"You don't know how things work, do you?" he said as to a plowboy who could not be expected to know how things work.

"I do. But the facts leave my question quite untouched."

"You think so? Then let me clear your mind on this."

My mind was very clear on it. I thought of smiling and decided against it. There was no need to be too deliberately insulting in the man's own house. "Please do," I said, which was impertinent enough.

"There are things you could not possibly do, things a Unionist member would be required to do."

"What things?"

"You would, naturally, be required to join the Orange Order."

"I'll join it."

"You can't, you see. You're a . . ." and he paused. To kill the word papist? ". . . Roman Catholic. You wouldn't be acceptable to the order."

"Would I therefore be unacceptable to the people of the borough and to the Imperial parliament?"

"That is not the point." His patience was already filtering away. He didn't need much patience. He was dealing with a papist.

"What is the point? Is it that only Orangemen may loyally represent loyal Ulstermen?"

But he hadn't summoned me to debate with me. Only to inform me.

"You could not join in Orange marches, you would be conspicuously absent from important gatherings where a member's presence is necessary. You would not . . ."

". . . fit," I said.

"What did you say?"

"I finished your sentence. I said I would not *fit*."

"I see." I wasn't sure what that meant. Perhaps: So that's your attitude?

"Enniskillen," I said, enjoying his annoyance at my assumption of equality. "O'Donovan Rossa is in prison."

"Where else should that blackguard be?"

"One of his jailers treated him with constant and deliberate contempt. Do you know what Rossa did?"

"Why should I need to know?"

"Because things understood in time bring wisdom—even common-sense self-interest, if there is not enough intelligence to acquire wisdom."

"Am I now supposed to ask you what this Fenian did?"

"I could scarcely hope for that, but I shall tell you. He shit in his prison bucket and pissed in it, then he threw the mixture in his jailer's face."

He sat back in his chair, his nostrils twitching as though he could smell the pudding.

"What wisdom am I to find in that, MacDonnell?"

"You? No wisdom. Not even common-sense self-interest. It is, however, a little morality about self-interest. You do not appear to know how to serve your own. And that makes me sad. And afraid." I got up.

Then I made a mistake. I had revealed to him something of my scorn and bitterness. Now I exposed something of the reasons for them. I said, "Enniskillen, I know this province. In my blood I have known it longer than you or Brooke or Conyngham or Chichester or Stewart—longer than any of you. I love it. I wanted to do it some service. Help to protect it, it might be. My forebears loved it and fought to protect it when they were the Earls of Antrim, Lords of the Glens, Lords of the Isles . . ."

"Once upon a time," he said, sadly smiling.

"Blind men on the shore," I said, "walk into the ocean."

"You could begin your probation," he said with a calculated insult, "by proving your good faith with money." He was still smiling, but now with satisfaction. I had come. I was going empty away. It was a splendid triumph. A lesson to a presumptuous papist.

I walked out of the room.

He called after me, "Talk to Garrett about money."

I refused his carriage and walked the four miles to my hotel. It was raining now. Rage propelled me. I sometimes marveled that I am capable of such unbridled anger and incapable of unbridled passion with a woman. It seemed a contradiction in my nature, but I am not analytical enough to find an explanation. What I knew was that this arrogant upstart had summoned me across Ireland to his dreary house and his mindless presence to set me firmly in my papist place and in my rage I even thought of sending the Fenian treasury the sum of £100. It seemed that Catholic Ulstermen could not be trusted to be loyal Ulstermen—not even self-interested Ulstermen. And the thought would not leave my mind that, one day perhaps before long, the Orangemen and their detached and condescending leaders—condescending even to the led—would pay a heavy price for their refusal to receive men as men. The rejected make poor allies and worse friends.

In Belfast I read in a newspaper that James Stephens, the Fenian leader, had escaped from jail. My own laughter startled me. Later, it shocked me.

At home again, I sat by Alsadar's bed and watched him sleep. Bad times were coming and would go on far into his lifetime, and he must be prepared to play his part in them, to protect his inheritance . . . and I realized that in the half hour I sat beside my son, loving him, thinking of him and for him, my thought had narrowed. I was not brooding on the kind of education that would best equip him to protect Ulster's interest; what would he need to help him protect the interests of the MacDonnells? Nothing else. That might mean a broad concern. It might mean a narrow concern. It must be thought about and thought about. I went to sleep thinking about it and woke with nothing else on my mind. Yes, there was one other thing lurking in a corner of my mind, teasing me, provoking me.

It was O'Donovan Rossa's bucket.

❦ Six ❦

At noon the next day, which was Saturday, Patton, the butler, came to me in the library. A child, he said, had come to the house in a carriage hired from McMurtry's in Carrig. She spoke, he said, with a strange accent and wished to be taken to Mr. Carrach MacDonnell. She would give no information about her identity. She had simply refused to go away and when the groom was brought from the stables to remove her, she quite successfully scratched his face and forced him to retreat.

Things like this do not happen, and I was curious. Children like this do not come to my house. "Bring her and wait," I said.

The child was dark and tall, not beautiful but striking and wonderfully made. She stood before me and said nothing but her smile was as brilliant as a small sun. She stared at me; no, she glowed at me. Once her lips moved as she said something to herself. The butler stood by the door, waiting, as I had told him to do. I do not think he waited merely to be told to remove her.

"Well, child?" I said. "You wished to see me."

"All the way from West Cork," she said triumphantly.

"And what did you come for?"

"I am Isabella," she said, and the name and the accent met in my mind. She was Spanish. Yes, her accent was Spanish.

"Isabella? Isabella what?"

"Isabella MacDonnell," she said, "and you are my Uncle Carrach."

"Your uncle? Well, I think you've . . . I haven't got a niece whose name is Isabella. The fact is, I haven't got a niece."

"But my father, sir. Hugh MacDonnell. I am his daughter, Isabella."

My life was about to change. The child flung herself into my arms and kissed me, and I was not alone.

Hugh, the thought of being in touch with Hugh again, filled me with peculiar joy.

But caution always commanded me. I was willing enough to be kissed by this delightful, shining child who was more than a child and not yet a young woman, but who she really was had to be established.

She had photographs, taken in America and in Spain by some American photographer. She had pictures of Hugh in America with cousin James and his family; of Hugh and his wife in Spain. In the pictures the woman looked dark-skinned. There were pictures of a house which she said was home, "in West Cork, on the road a few miles east of Goleen," a finely proportioned house with ample grounds; pictures of Hugh and herself sitting horses in the parkland around the house. I did not know Hugh was in Ireland or in West Cork—or anywhere. If his house and his horses were to be believed, he was not living on his portion. If I believed what I saw, Isabella wore tight trousers when she rode. It would not do here. It might do in America.

"Papa lived in America," Isabella chattered. She chattered with excitement, answering my questions. I forgot about Patton standing obediently by the door, waiting. In my excitement at this visitation and revelation, I did not even see him or think about him. There was much for him to tell, I suppose. So, since he had not been dismissed, he waited.

"Tell me about your father," I said.

"And Mama?"

"Both."

The child rattled on, excited. I was perhaps less excited, but not much less. I showed it less.

Yet I learned nothing much in manageable chronology about my brother. Long, long ago he married "a woman of Andalusia," the child said proudly. There were four children. "Myself, and three boys stillborn. I am a few days away from being sixteen."

I heard of his travels with and without the woman of Andalusia, but not in their order. Their home for many years was in Spain. It sounded more like a base than a home. And then they came to West Cork to live. How long ago? "Oh, many years ago." She didn't seem to care. "Papa often goes to America, but we do not go with him." What does he go for? "Oh, business." So he was still in business of some sort.

Her dark hair and eyes and high cheekbones and wide full mouth were the Spanish things about her. Hugh, it seemed, "many, many years ago," entered into partnership with a Spaniard who raised horses and fighting bulls and married his daughter and could not endure the tightness of Andalusian family ties. But the horses explained what we discovered about Isabella. She was a superb and daring horsewoman.

"But why will he not write? Why has he not brought you to see us?" I was amazed and delighted even by this torrent of vague news, consumed by curiosity and determined to understand my brother's silence and his refusal to communicate with me.

"He says he will not come," Isabella said. "He told me you would laugh at Mama and at the way we speak English. He says that here your neighbors would be suspicious of a foreign Catholic woman, especially if we spoke a strange language together. He says they would think we were plotting."

It wasn't unfair to our neighbors. "But why did he let you come, if that's what he says?"

"He didn't. I came. I wanted to know you. Papa talks of you. He loves you so much. He doesn't know where I am. I ran. He will be very, very angry." She was immensely amused by that. It was some sort of victory over Hugh, a sort that entertained her. It made me even more curious. What sort of relationship could she have with her father?

But it worried me. "You ran? Ran away?"

"No. No. Just for a visit. To know you."

"He'll be very worried, and when he knows, he'll be very angry that you came here against his wishes." He'll be angrier with me for harboring his runaway. That was in my mind.

"Yes!" She leaped up and went through the motions of a bullfighter playing the cape to a charging bull, and laughed at her pantomime. "Toro, Toro," she muttered dramatically. "He'll be like that."

I had never seen a child like this, never heard one like this. Her face had not one beautiful feature, yet it was to me beyond beauty—and its magic grew the longer I observed her.

Now, when she moved to demonstrate her father's bull-like rage, I saw Patton, still waiting, still absorbing details to repeat later.

"Thank you, Patton," I said. "That will be all." He went slowly, making a display of his reluctance.

The children adored her. She was their contemporary. She was, in a very strange way, my contemporary. I adored her. She adored us.

Elizabeth was for a time the mystery. She emerged from her nunnery the day after Isabella arrived, having learned of her presence only from the conversation of the housekeeper. She was not dressed in black, a fact that impressed itself on my staff as it did on me. On that second day the change in her appearance did not reflect any significant change in her behavior. She was still distant and not cordial to Isabella.

Elizabeth led her across the drawing room away from where the five of us had been huddled together, chattering, laughing. Her reappearance was surprise enough; her dress probably meant nothing to the children, but I was sure it had some meaning for me, and probably an unpleasant one. So I listened as she set Isabella gently in a chair as if the child needed help.

"Now." She sat down in front of her, knee to knee.

"This is your Aunt Elizabeth," I said, and felt a little guilty, as if I had concealed her existence like an embarrassing secret, though I had not done so in that sense. I did say to Isabella, "Your aunt lives elsewhere in the house and emerges when it pleases her."

"Is she all right?"

"All right?"

"Yes. I mean, in the head?"

I had to suppress laughter at that, for I was far from certain Elizabeth was quite right in the head; but it was this child's directness that I thought funny; perhaps also the notion that anyone who separated herself from us might not be all right.

"Oh yes," I said. Then, smiling and unkindly, "At least, I think so."

Now, sitting knee to knee opposite Elizabeth, Isabella studied her face. She might have been reading a book. Her eyes examined her aunt feature by feature, line by line. "Yes," she said. "I see," and nodded. It was, for a girl of her age, an extraordinarily mature and self-possessed scrutiny. Moments before, she had been laughing like a child.

I expected Elizabeth to complain that Isabella had not come to see her. She said only, "You are Isabella MacDonnell."

"Yes."

"Hugh's child."

"Yes."

"Tell me about your father."

"What do you wish to know?"

"Why do you speak with a foreign accent?"

"I have lived most of my life in Andalusia, speaking Spanish."

"I see. How is your father?"

"Well."

"Tell me about him."

"What do you wish to know?"

Elizabeth glanced at me, then at the children. She was going to have to ask her questions. "Leave us, please," she said to me.

I sent the children to the nursery and did not leave the room.

"You also, Carrach."

"I'm interested in Hugh," I said, and sat down again. I had no idea what the woman had in mind. I was not going to leave the child to her mercy till I knew what she was up to, how she was going to behave.

Then began a long and intensive questioning about Hugh. She made no effort to conceal her detailed interest, and there was no aspect of Hugh's life that went unexamined—except his marriage. One might have supposed that Isabella was received direct from heaven rather than from the loins of the dark-skinned woman in the photographs.

"You have photographs of your father," Elizabeth said.

They were on the mantelshelf, and I acted as bearer and took them to her. She looked with care at the pictures of Hugh and Isabella but set aside the pictures of the dark-skinned woman. Then she took them up, glanced carelessly at them, and put them down again.

"Is that a white woman?" she asked.

Perhaps she took no warning from Isabella's reply, but it was there in the sharp light in her eyes.

"Nobody is white, Aunt Elizabeth," she said. "White people would look peculiar. Like dolls with linen faces."

Either Elizabeth misunderstood or chose to ignore it. "How long will you stay with us?" she asked.

Isabella glanced at me. "Till the end of the month," I said, "then she must go back to her parents."

"I shall take her home," Elizabeth said, and stood up.

"That can be discussed later," I said.

But Elizabeth had changed only her clothes. She said to Isabella, "I shall take you home. I shall inform your father. Your uncle will see to the travel arrangements. I shall see you tomorrow."

She withdrew to her nunnery.

She was better than her word. She came forth with a certain cheerfulness and had breakfast with us each morning. Her cheerfulness blossomed, and the catechism continued. With whom did Hugh visit? Ah, the Whites of Bantry, the Earl of Bantry.

"Yes," Isabella said, "King Pilchard," with a small smile that was Hugh's ironic smile.

"I beg your pardon?" There was a little sharpness in it. Elizabeth knew very little about family histories, but she read the smile. Perhaps she saw Hugh in it and knew?

"King Pilchard. The noble earl's family made their money out of pilchards and herrings." There was more to Isabella than her sixteen years could justify. Her body, her humor, and her understanding were mature beyond her years.

"Indeed?" Elizabeth got away from it quickly. "He has a fine library?"

"Very fine. In French, Spanish, and English."

"You have callers, of course?"

"Very few. We have no roads, only tracks too narrow for carriages. The carriage road ends at Schull—eleven miles from Goleen and seven miles from the house. We shall have to ride horseback from Schull."

"Why did he choose such an isolated place?"

"He prefers it." She was concealing something. Her tone, her smile, announced it. She was tired of Elizabeth's probing. As the days passed, she discovered that the way to put an end to the probing was to mention her mother. Her shrewd young eyes twinkled as she timed her strokes. "Mother loves the land there. It is beautiful and wild and violent like Andalusia. Mother is like Andalusia."

"Indeed," and Elizabeth tried to change the subject. "What do you do for recreation?"

"Fish, ride horses. Mother is a splendid horsewoman."

Every morning after breakfast they rode together for an hour and a half, then Elizabeth returned to her west-wing refuge and Isabella was ours for the rest of the day. I stayed at home. Messengers from Belfast and the mill brought office work to me at Barn House, and I attended to matters of business each morning, made decisions, and left the day-to-day things to my clerks. Then each day was holiday.

And the house was happy. The servants were Isabella's happy serfs. She bubbled with good life. When a maid did her some small service, she embraced the girl. Everything about her was giving. I wanted to explain to her that this embracing of servants was unwise, but whatever magic she possessed made my stuffy cautions unnecessary. I say my stuffy cautions because I knew, in spite of myself, that my concern was stuffy. The servants never presumed. Like the four of us, they adored. Adored? It is a feminine word for a man to use, yet it is the right word.

She had come quite unprepared for a visit, and Elizabeth's seamstress wanted to make some clothes for her. Elizabeth encouraged the woman to do so. She even entertained Isabella to tea in her apartment.

"What do you talk about in there?" I asked her.

"Papa. That is why she is nice to me, isn't it? She wants me to tell Papa?"

What could I say? "Why do you say that? I can't read her mind."

"I don't need to. Papa told me things."

"Then you don't need to talk to me about them."

Every day was a celebration. Isabella saw the mill, the shipping office, and two MacDonnell ships in port, and wanted all of us to leave for China. She rode to call on all my tenant farmers and made their wives and children her friends. She rode with us through Boneybefore, and Cassie Hyndman was at her door, her daughter with her.

"This is my niece, Isabella," I said, and Isabella charmed her.

"This is my girl, Aggie. That means Agnes," Cassie said, and smiled and looked up at me and said, "I miss yer good mother that bad, sir. She was the great one."

We rode to Garden House. "Oh, it is beautiful," Isabella

said. "I want to live here." Often, in the weeks she spent with us, she rode alone to Garden House. Always when she came back to Barn House she said, "Oh, how I love that house. I want to live there."

I wrote to Hugh on that first day, of course. Now that I had found him, he must be told of Mother's death. I wrote again four days later to enlarge on my original letter, to tell him how happy I was to find him again, how we loved his child, what happiness her coming brought us all, and that I would bring her home in a few weeks unless he chose to make us all happier by bringing his wife and coming north for Isabella. I did not mention Elizabeth.

His reply was brief. It said only, "Dear Carrach, I look forward with great happiness to seeing my daughter again. I have things to say to her. It will make me happy to see you also. I cannot trust myself to write of Mother. Hugh."

He loves you so much, Isabella said. He did once, I know. Now, if he did, he expressed it with great economy. But I was going to see him, welcome or unwelcome.

For a while that made shadows, at least in my mind. I did not tell Isabella what her father said. She wrote to him several times. He did not reply. "He is angry," she said, "but not worried now. I shall kiss him and he will call me terrible names, but there will be no more anger." I believed it. When the child kissed me or smiled, I could not be angry.

To the servants I must have seemed strange and much changed in my ways. I am not a singing man, but we sang in the library, we sang in the drawing room, we sang in the nursery, we sang when we rode; little songs the children knew, songs Isabelle taught us. We taught her to sing an Ulster children's song in the accents of my tenants. It went:

> My Aunt Jane she called me in,
> She give me tea outa hur wee tin;
> Half a bap and shugar on the tap
> An' three black lumps outa hur wee shap.*

Then, repeat the last two lines, with gusto:

> Half a bap and shugar on the tap
> An' three black lumps outa hur wee shap.

How we shouted those last lines.

* Bap: loaf; shugar: sugar; black lumps: a kind of sweet; shap: shop.

Once I heard Kitty saying to Morag, "Isabella makes Papa so happy and jolly."

She did. She had dark qualities also. Once, when she walked through Boneybefore with the children, some village lout tripped Alasdar, and Isabella was on the bully, Cassie Hyndman told me, "like a savage." The boy was bigger and heavier than Isabella, "but she near clawed the face off him and sent him skitterin down the street wi' the blood running outa his cheeks." After that, in Boneybefore, they called her the Spaniard. The incident reminded me of the groom's attempt to send her away. Alasdar was her knight and faithful servant.

"Papa," he said to me as leader and spokesman for all the children, "why can't Isabella stay here forever when she makes you so happy?"

Still, she had to go home and Barn House was heavy with dark spirits. The children wept inconsolably, the maids wept discreetly, and if I had not been going with her I might well have gone to my room to weep for the departure of this magic child.

I had other cause to lament. A maid brought to me the message that "The mistress wishes to see you in her apartment." This sort of thing had been going on for some time. Even the form of words was prescribed. If I did not respond at once, she sent her maid again. And again. It was what I thought of as "the little tyranny of the west wing," and at first I responded to her first summons if it were possible to do so. Young girls found it difficult to suppress their smiles on the second and third command, and it was intolerable that I should allow her to use the servants as accessories to blackmail. When it was credible for me to send my regrets, I did so. ("Please explain to your mistress that I am rushing to complete some work for the office," or some such fiction. The forms of words themselves became a language. This meant "Go to hell," and she did not persist. The servants, I was told, used the formulae for their entertainment.) I was forced to the silly device of always having some work on my desk so that the servants could see I was occupied with important matters. It was all so petty and malicious and so calculated to make me in the servants' eyes a figure of fun or a puppet on her string. I was tempted to send her one final uncoded answer, "Tell your mistress to go to hell," but that would have advertised what was already all too plain to them and it would have pleased her to think she had harried me into a major indiscretion. If she felt entitled to revenge, she was having it.

Since I was in the drawing room with Isabella when Elizabeth's most recent summons came, I could hardly claim work as an excuse for refusing, so I went.

"Ah, there you are," she said like a great lady from some English ducal house, and I couldn't help thinking that her Belfast bourgeois preparation for the royal role was comically inadequate. There was a touch of lunacy or hysteria in her high manner, in her tone, in the brightness of her eyes.

Without preamble she announced, "I am absolutely determined to accompany Hugh's daughter on her return journey to Goleen. I shall take charge of her till she is safely in her father's hands."

I was having none of it. My hopes were set for a rambling journey to Goleen, with all the hotel arrangements completed without provision for Elizabeth. I had worked them out with Isabella, and Elizabeth had not again made reference to her intention to travel with us.

"You are not coming, so you will not take the child in charge," I said.

She didn't intend to argue in the privacy of her apartment. She said, "I shall come to dinner tonight. I take it you will be willing to debate the matter in Patton's hearing in the dining room?"

"That's contemptible. It's blackmail."

"I have been watching you. You are contemptible. After my sister, Emily, you now want to practice your clumsy arts on your brother's daughter."

"That is false and even more contemptible. Your only motive in wanting to come is to see Hugh again. He's married and out of your reach."

"You are married and out of Emily's reach but it didn't prevent your fornications with her on the grassy bowers of Lovers' Lane. In Garden House too, maybe, in Court House certainly, probably even here in my house." She smiled at me as though she felt happy, as if my alleged fornications with Emily carried the key to something she had in mind for herself.

"I'm not at all certain you're in your right mind."

"I understand you've been trying to create that impression abroad."

"That is utterly untrue."

In her absurd ducal part-playing she dismissed me with a small movement of her hand. "There's nothing more to say. I am going with you to Goleen."

"You are not." I left her.

Within five minutes her maid was back in the drawing room. "The mistress," she said, "asks me to tell you that she'll be goin w'ye to Goleen, sir."

A household like ours is a community. We live, in a measure, in the public eye, our staff being "the public" from whose scrutiny we are never entirely free. Elizabeth had staked a "public" claim, and if I wished to challenge it, I would have to do so at dinner, in Patton's hearing and for the subsequent entertainment of his Orange Lodge. Her message was like an announcement in the *Northern Whig*. I could hear the Orange discussing it over glasses of Guinness's stout.

"Och, the reason he didn't want the wife to go was he wanted a good go at the sister in Dublin. They're right thick thegither, thon two, aren't they, Patton?"

"Maybe he wanted a wee go at the Spaniard?"

But how could I know they would think and talk in these terms? Why should such things come into my head? I put them out of it and told the maid to tell her mistress I would have all the arrangements made. What else could I do? Announce to the servants and the entire district that I wanted the child alone on a journey to the Southwest? I say the child; but I no longer thought of her as a child. I did not see her as a child.

Two days before we left I took Isabella and the children on a carriage tour of Carrig. She passed through the town on many of our drives, but she was always rattling on, fussing over the children like a young mother, looking at the people who were looking at us, and paying small attention to the physical presence of the place. I often thought of this small town—for Carrig is a small town—in a very special way in the years still to come and while we look back on the past and on our motives for past actions, do we not often read the present into them? Yet I think I understand my motives for that last drive. I am satisfied that I wanted Isabella to keep in her mind the physical setting in which I lived my dull and commonplace life. Would it not add a little color to the

memory of a drab personality? The truth is that I was afraid
I might fade entirely from her memory.

We drove along the sea front up the street—a sort of utili-
tarian promenade—that began at the Fishermen's Pier, a
massive stone structure where people gathered to buy their
fish when the fishing boats came in, and ended at Carrig
Castle, an eleventh-century structure, still in use as a gar-
rison. The castle had played a part in my family history. One
of my ancestors and a namesake of mine, Carrach MacDonnell, had ambushed and beheaded the English governor of the
castle. This stretch of seafront road is known as the Scotch
Quarter.

"This is the part of the ancient town where the Scotch
lived," I explained to her.

"Why?"

"To keep them separate from the Irish."

It wasn't quite true, but it created a picture of racial separation that I for some reason wanted to emphasize. We
passed Court House in the lea of the castle, passed through
the square with its great Celtic Cross which laid stress on our
Gaelic past and which some Orangemen wanted to remove—and in time succeeded in having removed and replaced by an ugly lamp that became known as the Big
Lamp—and drove down a narrow street of mean houses.

"This is the Irish Quarter," I explained.

"This is where the Irish lived?" Isabella asked.

"It was outside the town's old walls." Why I wanted to
make the point was not in my mind. What I felt, though, was
a little spasm of resentment that brought Lord Enniskillen to
mind. "Beyond the pale" were the words that came into my
head, and I put them away from me. There were enough sad-
dening things to think about: Isabella was going, Elizabeth
was coming. I showed her the bleach green where the gray
spun flax was whitened; the North Gate, an archway from
the ancient town wall; the old law courts, next to Court
House; then we took the children home and rode together to
Boneybefore. There were two houses I wanted her to see, one
in the village and one beyond the village, at Kilroot. These
things were part of the color of my place and my life. I was
framing my poor person for her so that I might sit in her
mind as someone never quite forgotten. Why? I did not want
to tell that, even to myself.

"That cottage over there," I told her in Boneybefore, "was

built from the stones of the cottage lived in by a couple named Andrew and Elizabeth Jackson. They sailed to America in 1765. Their son Andrew was conceived in this village and born just after they reached America. He became president of the United States. And over here," we rode a little way, "was where the cottage originally stood. It was moved from here and rebuilt over there to make way for the railway. The Jacksons were poor Protestants. If they had stayed here they would still be poor Protestants and still be my tenants. This is a rigid society, an excluding society."

I was not thinking of the Jacksons, but of myself. The Jacksons were poor Protestants—poor is the key word—who sailed for America to escape exclusion, and their son became president. I was the descendant of rulers of Antrim and Ulster and my uncle and this girl's father were Catholics—and Catholic is the key word—of two generations, multitudes of whom had gone away to escape exclusion. But I remained and, being Catholic, was excluded. It struck me suddenly and bitterly as I sat there on my horse that the proper alliance against the likes of the Earl of Enniskillen was of poor Catholics and poor Protestants and their employers. I thought of mentioning that to Robert Garrett, but O'Donovan Rossa's bucket chased it from my mind.

"The kind of society we need here to protect Ulster," I said to Isabella like an unskilled schoolteacher, "is the kind Cousin James and his family live in, in America. Andrew Jackson, James Knox Polk, James Buchanan, were all of poor Ulster stock and all became presidents of the United States. Andrew Johnson, the present American president, comes from a family that lived ten miles down the road, tenants on what was once MacDonnell land."

She said nothing, showed no interest. I was a gray bore. We rode on to Kilroot, talking of trivial things. But we were subdued.

"Uncle Carrach," she said, "I want to see Papa and Mama, but I do not want to leave."

"I don't want you to leave. You must, but think of all the years ahead."

"I do. They make me sadder."

I did not ask her why.

The house I wanted her to see was the Kilroot Rectory, called by us the Kilroot Roundhouse because it was stone, whitewashed, and completely circular, with a thatched roof.

One of the men I most revered when I was young had lived in it. I knew his book, *Gulliver's Travels*, as I knew the soil I sprang from.

"This was Dean Swift's first parish," I told her, "and this was his rectory." I couldn't be sure that with her foreign background and upbringing she would know anything about Dean Swift, but she surprised me. Surprised me? She almost knocked me off my horse.

"I know a verse he wrote," she said, as though there might be a prize for knowing.

"Tell me."

She was herself again, full of sudden laughter, and I could not anticipate the verse.

"Sometimes when Papa is cross with me he shouts it at me." She recited:

> Disgusted Strephone slunk away
> Repeating in his amorous fits
> Oh, Celia, Celia, Ceila shits!

I had never heard a woman use such a word. I had never heard a child use the word. I must have looked as I felt—shaken. She was laughing as she recited, and her laughter died. She looked dismayed.

"Uncle Carrach," she said like a small lament, "did I give you offense?"

The two of us were saved by an incongrouus thought that leaped into my head: Why hadn't I known the verse so that I could recite it to his Lordship of Enniskillen? My laughter was at this thought, not at Isabella's recitation, but it swept my shock away and let me escape from my obligation to express an opinion about it. It did more, and what it did came to me as we rode back along the shore to Garden House: Isabella is magical, it said, and, Why am I not a different sort of man? it asked. Why am I not capable of consuming passion? Why do I live under such interior restraint, like an arid puritan who, stunted in spirit, feared and rejected joy and closed theaters? My head and heart were jammed with and confused by questions. Was it all about Isabella? The name in my head was Cassie Hyndman. The thought in my head was: God, if at this moment I had her in bed, I would ravish her like a satyr. The mind and the heart are cunning. They cheat the accusing conscience. The name in my head was Cassie Hyndman. The figure in my fantasy was not, and fear struck me and caution overwhelmed me and all my restraints were triggered like a snare that snapped its teeth shut on my desperate longing thoughts. You are lonely, the snare said. That is all—a poor dull lonely man, and your lonely illusions are obscene. She is sixteen. She is Hugh's only child. She is your niece. She is *sixteen*.

One question was persistent, through the self-flagellation, like a needle thrust into my flesh by an enemy intent on destroying me, and withdrawn to be thrust again: Why am I what I am? Can I feel as Cassie can feel . . . ? My head was like a dam of water, and the water was pounding at the walls, trying to break them down.

We wandered through cold, empty Garden House and did not talk. As she mounted, she said, "Oh, how I love this house. This would be home, Uncle Carrach."

I thought of many things I wanted to say, and said none of them. She was sixteen. She was my brother's daughter. I was twenty-one years her senior. I have a wife and three children and things to protect. I am a fool. I am what I am. I said it all again and again and again.

But all the way to Barn House the water pounded and I watched Isabella and felt as I had never felt before, and for the first time in my life had within my spirit movements that frightened me by their force.

I needed to be alone. I did not want to be away from Isabella, but I had to be alone. The disturbance in me would not consent to be put away. Yet all the fears of the cautious man shouted at me of folly, stupidity, tragedy, mockery. You are infantile, they said, retarded, presumptuous—silly. The weakness of that word made me sweat. It was cruelly fitting. I was silly. At twilight I rode back to Garden House. It stood empty and seemed as desolate as I was. Gardeners from Barn House came over to keep the grounds tidy; two servants came occasionally to air the place, light fires, stand mattresses before the fires.

I came to the house from the north side, down the bridle path through its woods. I did not know it then, but it was the way I was to come in the future, as regularly as I rose in the morning, and, I suppose foolishly (though I have no regrets, only joy and great thankfulness) the time came when I called it the Magic Forest. Foolish? I wondered often in the years ahead, whether for us poor, lonely humans there can be full life without folly.

For some reason that was not then and is not now clear to me—I didn't think about it at all—I stabled my horse. It was hidden, but that was not in my mind. In the house I lit lamps, lit fires in the drawing room and in the main bedrooms, and decided something more must be done to keep the place dry. The servants would have to come oftener, do more. For a while I sat by the drawing-room fire, thinking about happy days spent here with Mother, thinking about the love my parents bore one another, thinking, as I tried hard not to think, of what Mother would say about the turmoil the daughter of her younger son was stirring in my spirit. With Isabella, I told her in the flames, I could know all that you and Father knew of warmth and ardor and love. I had never been a truly happy man, merely a cautious and an orderly one. It was too late now to be anything else. Conscience and caution and cowardice would not let me go.

It was dark outside, and I could not sit for long. Restlessly I went out and walked in the woods behind the house. I wanted to hide in the dark, I think, not see or be seen: to think my terrible thoughts only in the dark. The gloom of the woods fitted the miserable gloom of my spirit. The figure standing in the fringe of the trees just off the bridle path startled me. I was ready to protect myself.

"It's Cassie, sir. Cassie Hyndman."

"Cassie?" My relief was like a cool drink. "What in God's name are you doing?"

"I was pickin up dead sticks, sir. Kinlin. You rode past me before it was proper dark. Is it all right for me to pick up the dry sticks?"

"Of course, it's all right." I was close enough to see her face clearly now. "Where are your sticks?"

"At m'feet. I have a rope on them."

A scarf covered her head. She looked cold.

"Are you cold?"

"A wee bit. I was just standing here watchin the lights on in the house. It looked that nice and warm."

"It is now. I have fires going. Come into the house and get warmed. There'll be tea in the kitchen. We can have a cup."

I groped for her bundle of sticks and carried them by the rope to the back door. She went to the kitchen to light the range and boil water for the tea, and while we waited she crouched close to the drawing-room fire. We didn't talk.

Then she said, to herself I thought, "It's awful nice here." Her lined and weathered face was tranquil.

"Yes, it's nice here."

I was thinking about the house and its care, honestly, I think. "Cassie," I said, "they're not doing enough to keep this house aired and dry. If I left it to you, could you find the time to give it two days a week?"

She was watching the fire. "I could," she said. "I would like that fine," and went to make the tea. She would like that fine. Was she thinking of other days in the house? It is possible that women think with affection of a place where a child was conceived. But perhaps not. Perhaps people do not think the thoughts that wandered in my head. Other people are happier, I think, more capable of happiness.

My thoughts had moved a long way when she came back with the tray. I drew the curtains. "Come and look at what needs to be done, Cassie," I said.

"Don't ye want yer tea, sir?"

"Later. Let it sit on the range till we come down."

"Yes, sir," she said. "It'll be time enough when we come down."

She followed me upstairs. The master bedroom was warm. I drew the curtains there also and came to her. She did not speak and did not move, but she looked in my face. I took the scarf from her head and laid it on a chair. In the back room she had always looked frankly into my face with her warm docile eyes as if whatever I did was an undeserved favor and a service.

"D'ye want everythin off, sir?" she said. Had I a right, established by bonds wrought long ago? She didn't question it. Perhaps she believed it, and I knew then that she knew as she sat before the fire that this would be done.

"Everything, Cassie," I said.

"I'll be ready by the time ye lock the doors. Jist in case, y'know?"

Going downstairs, locking the doors, and then climbing the stairs again, I thought passion. I commanded passion. I ordered up lust fit for the satyr I thought of earlier. I am going to ravish Cassie, I told myself, let passion run riot, and habit and caution and cowardice and order in the spirit are going to be crushed or transformed. Whatever I was in my hidden places, I was going to show it freely. I was capable of it. I felt capable of it. I rushed to her.

She was naked on the bare mattress, ready, waiting, smiling. She always smiled when we did it. "I'm always wonderin would ye ever do it to me again," she said. "I couldn't very well ast ye to."

I took my clothes off and she reached for my parts with greedy fingers and greed in her eyes and was already a woman of passion. "Come on, Carrach love," she said. "Enjoy yerself on me, love, afore I'm past it." It showed in her face, but not in her white strong body and not in her passion. Cassie was forty-seven then.

When it was done she said, "Yer just the same, Carrach, after all them years. Y'always did it like a gentleman. Och, it's awful nice that way."

"Like being ridden by a stone statue, you mean."

"No. Yer always that nice to me. A real gentleman."

"I'm tired of being a gentleman."

"But that's what y'are, Carrach. Y'couldn't be anythin else."

Whatever I was, I was going to show it freely? Not keeping myself hidden? Well, there was nothing there to hide, merely what Cassie called "a gentleman"; what I knew now to be merely a careful man, a self-protective man; a dead man or a coward. That was all there was to me.

"What days will I be comin?" she asked.

"Wednesdays and Fridays."

"Will ye come at all yerself?"

"Fridays." Great God Almighty! Fridays! I wanted to scream. It was always Fridays. Even if I wanted desperately to let my spirit loose—my puny self-exposure of nothing at all had to be on a Friday. It always had been. I was pitiful.

Cassie had a flawless sense of place and station. In bed I was "Carrach, love." With our clothes on I was "sir."

"There's somebody out there on the gravel, sir," she said.

Fear ran through me. It was Elizabeth, following, snooping, sneaking, malignant. The thought of discovery made me shake. Exposure, humiliation, and worse than all, trapped in Elizabeth's bludgeoning knowledge. She would own me utterly and command me like a serf if she could catch me here with a middle-aged serving woman.

"Go to the kitchen," I said. "I'll call you from the back

door. Whatever I say, use your wits and give me the right answers."

She ran, coat on, scarf on her head. I went downstairs slowly, self-accusation lashing me. To be caught in my own house like a fornicating stableboy, to be afraid of discovery in my own house, head weak, fumbling in fear for something plausible to say when I opened the back door; overwhelmed by the thought that for all I got out of fornication, it wasn't worth this. It wasn't worth anything.

I opened the back door and stepped outside. Whoever was lurking was coming slowly around the house. I could hear but not see. I stood in the doorway and called, "Cassie? Where are you?"

She came running from the kitchen and stood on the doorstep, an oil lamp in her hand. We were in the light. I might have known Cassie would do the right, the bold thing. Whoever was along the wall of the house was still and quiet now.

"I was clearin up a few wee things in the kitchen, sir," Cassie said. Probably putting away the tea tray that would have told its cozy tale.

"Are we clear about the arrangements now?" I said. "You'll give two days a week to the house? Air it, light all the fires, dry the mattresses, do whatever's needed? It's not being properly done now."

"Och, I can do it easy, sir. It'll be no bother at all." She sounded comfortingly relaxed and confident.

"Very well, then, and thank you, Cassie. Take the house key from the kitchen and keep it at your house. I have keys at Barn House. Good night."

"Good night, sir." She turned quickly away and closed the door.

I walked toward the hidden lurker—or toward where I supposed she must now be.

Cassie hadn't finished. I heard the door open again. "Sir," she called, the lamp held high.

"Yes?"

"Y'didn't mention pay, sir. How much would that be? It's not that I'm anxious, sir, but there's things I . . ."

"Twelve pounds a year. Is that agreeable?"

"Aye, that'd be very good, sir. Thank ye very much, sir. That's very good."

It was the figure that came to mind without thought, and I

said it, too wary to think of anything but the solider figure now darkly visible against the wall. It could not be Elizabeth. I walked on, stopped to confront the lurker.

"And what the devil are you doing here?" I asked it.

"It's Hyndman, sir. Cassie's husband."

It was then that I realized the annual wages of a servant working six days, often seven days, a week in the great English ducal houses were twelve pounds a year. Here in provincial Ulster, they were seven. Well, extra service merited extra pay. Juices raced up from somewhere into my head. I was floating.

"Good," I said, controlling with the discipline and practice of all the years a compulsion to hysterical laughter. "You'll find your wife in the house, Hyndman. You'll be able to see her safely home. Good night."

"Good night, sir."

Two days later we departed for West Cork on the journey that began with my visible life as it had always been, ordered, staid, inhibited, and dull, and ended with my inner life so transformed that I could not that day have credited the change.

Seven

We traveled by train. It had been possible to do so for ten years now. The mail coach made the journey from Belfast to Dublin in twelve hours. It was a hard and wearying journey. The train takes five hours. First-, and second-, and third-class carriages are now a feature of the rail service, and I engaged all six seats in a first-class compartment at a cost of 18s. 6d. a seat. I wanted to ensure our privacy in case Elizabeth should decide to behave eccentrically on the journey. But she had, as it were, her cards to play with Isabella, and she played them with care, even with a measure of artificial charm. Her charm might persuade a stranger. It nauseates me.

Originally, I planned a dawdling journey, to keep Isabella in my company for as long as I decently could. Now, with Elizabeth in tow, I curtailed my plans and made all possible haste to West Cork. Our first night, in Dublin, we had a three-bedroom suite at the Gresham Hotel on Sackville Street. Elizabeth was too tired after the train journey to come with us to look at Trinity College, but in any case, having insisted on opening the compartment window to stick her head out, she got a cinder from the engine in one eye and had to stay in her room waiting for a doctor.

I have, I'm afraid, an obsession about Trinity College, perhaps because Catholics are barred not from attendance but from taking its degrees. When I'm in Dublin I always go to College Green and walk in the college yard; on this occasion

85

Emily joined us for an hour and we took Isabella. She had only one question, and it was not about the granting of degrees to Catholics at Ireland's Oxford-and-Cambridge-in-one. It was: "Do you think women will ever study here?" What could be more unlikely? But I asked her, "What would they study?" Without the slightest suggestion that she saw anything incongruous in her statement, she said, "Why, whatever there is to study." It struck me as a very odd thought. She had been to Mass each Sunday morning and was careful of her religious duty, yet it did appear that she supposed the granting of degrees to Catholics as such at Trinity to be a matter of less consequence than the admission of women as such. Indeed, in support of Isabella, Emily said exactly this, and the two of them laughed at my disbelief.

I have to assume that the times we live in, with change and development so explosively rapid, are creating in the young and especially in women the illusion that radical thoughts are normal and not at all dangerous to the stability of society. But they probably are not dangerous. Most of them will pass harmlessly away.

Then by train to Cork, where we spent the night in preparation for the dreary coach ride to Schull and a third night's rest there before we rode to Hugh's house, seven miles to the west over narrow cart tracks.

But in Cork that night there was news that set the place talking and almost sent me scuttling back to the North, though it made Isabella silent, her face tight with excitement held firmly in check. I mistook it then for fear.

Behind us, on tracks down which we had traveled that day, a large body of Fenians had torn up the rails, cut telegraph wires, and derailed the Dublin express. It was said that nobody had been hurt. And at Knockadoon, Fenians had raided and captured the coast-guard station and then withdrawn with all the arms they found there. Before the night was old we knew, too, that the police barracks at Ballyknockane had been raided and captured. They were not great actions, one man in the hotel said; the coast-guard station was lightly held, and the police barracks were taken by two thousand men against the resistance of a handful of policemen. How could one know the truth? Rumor spread.

In the morning there was more news. A Fenian force at Ballyhurst had attacked and been routed by one return of fire from an army flying column let loose, in response to Fenian actions, all over Ireland. The telegraph wires sent rumor, gossip, and fact, without discrimination.

"We are going back north," I told Isabella.

"How are we to get there with the tracks up?" she asked me sensibly, and I settled for the remote security of Hugh's house. All we "knew," and we knew it only because it was inevitable and an often-repeated story, was that Fenians were scattering, running for hoped-for safety with police and military flying columns in pursuit. And that day it snowed. It was late for snow. We do not see much snow. Men were walking in it, running in it, trying to hide in it. The coach to Schull was stopped four times before we reached there. We were cold, our feet frozen. We were nervous. We were silent. Isabella was grim-faced.

"What are you thinking of?" I asked her.

"Papa," she said.

What danger could Hugh be in? None that I could imagine. "Don't worry about him," I said. "Worry about us."

There had been no snow in Schull or near it. There had also, it appeared, been very little news. No news at all, Mr. O'Keeffe said.

Isabella had assured me the place to stay in Schull was O'Keeffe's inn. It was the only place to stay. Schull was a clutter of miserable cabins, a short street of stone houses, and a good rock-slab quay, half breakwater, half harbor. Schull had been burned to the ground by that same poor humbly born Captain, William Cole, from whose loins and in mounting consequence had descended the present Earl of Enniskillen. Burning a clutter of miserable mud and thatch cabins was the zenith of Captain Cole's military talent. From this great achievement had come after centuries of progress what now was Schull—a clutter of miserable mud and thatch cabins, a short stone street, and a breakwater. Why Hugh would choose this desolate and isolated landscape for his home I could not understand. This part of the country, west to Mizen Head and east to and beyond Skibbereen, had been decimated in and after the years of famine. The landscape was like the face of the moon as I understand it to be: rock and gashes of golden gorse, and red, purple, blue, and yellow lichen, patches of green between the rocks—an awesome spectacle of satanic beauty. And roofless cabins whose former inhabitants had died of typhoid, or cholera, or mere starvation, or had been evicted. In the intervening years since the famines, the land had been reclaimed—by the marauding bushes. What could such a landscape hold for Hugh, who grew up with our own rich pastoral landscape in his eyes and heart? Perhaps he would tell me?

O'Keeffe's inn was reached through an archway that had on one side, on the street, a provision shop and on the other a haberdashery that served the countryside halfway to Bantry and, though the sign said Haberdasher, this place sold everything from candles and bill hooks to heavy boots, rope, fishing gear, and, if you knew what to ask for and were not an obvious excise man, as much as you could afford of the products of the stills that worked hard on the moors. Both shops belonged to O'Keeffe. Through the archway you came to the courtyard around which the inn gathered like a sheltering arm. In the middle of the courtyard grew a great tree whose branches reached almost to the windows of the bedrooms on the second floor.

Seamus O'Keeffe was a young man to own an establishment of such dimensions and so well-equipped, for it was comfortable and spotlessly clean. We ate that night with confidence, and young Mr. O'Keeffe, who was well known to Isabella and clearly intent on being better known, came often to our table—we were his only guests—not out of concern for the comfort and satisfaction of Elizabeth or myself, but to keep himself in Isabella's eye. I found his cheerful reappearances annoying, and to divert his attention from Isabella, questioned him about his business. But first I questioned him about the Fenian raids.

There are Irishmen whose faces, under questioning, are so improbably innocent that they cry out their duplicity. Mr. O'Keeffe's was of this sort only when I asked him for news of the Fenians.

"Ah, you'll find none in these parts," he said in a voice that dismissed the possibility as equal, say, to a man from the moon.

"But they took the coast-guard station at Knockadoon."

"They did *not?*" It was dumbfounded question and assertion in one.

"I'm afraid they did."

"There's no word of it here. Maybe there'll be word tomorrow?"

"Maybe." There was no point in pursuing the matter. He had no intention of elaborating. I passed to the less-dangerous question of his years and his well-equipped businesses.

"How did you come to acquire this place, sir?" I asked him. "It represents a considerable investment."

O'Keeffe was Irish-handsome, that is, he had a good-looking face of a racy and insolent cast, and he spoke with an assurance that to strangers might sound easy but, to those of us who knew the breed, covered a deep uncertainty. He was the kind who scaled church steeples when he was drunk to answer questions nobody asked about his manhood, nor even thought about it. The questions are theirs alone, and this is what compels them: They answer their own questions out of the nagging fear that nobody else will ever ask them. Or so I judged this young man on our first acquaintance.

"The investment was heavy," he answered me, but I saw his wink to Isabella, who looked away from him stone-faced and not amused. "Very heavy," and he measured an imaginary weight in his hand, a weight that slowly forced his hand to the table. It was a performance. "Take a look at the window frame in your room," he said. "I bought this place for very little. It was not in a good state of repair. But the windows were in a good state, and I could not understand why they were so hard to open. They weren't stuck. They weren't warped. They hadn't been sealed by a careless painter. Then why wouldn't they open? Hasn't Miss Isabella told you?"

"Told me what?"

"The way I took them apart, opened them up, and examined the leads on the window ropes. She didn't tell you?"

"She did not." Isabella ate. She was listening. Waiting, I thought.

"Do you know what I found?"

"Perhaps you will get to it before we leave in the morning?"

"I'll tell you now." With a careless hand wave that brushed away sarcasm: "There were no lead weights at all on the window ropes."

An Irishman does not rush to the end of a story. Needing an audience, he holds it. I decided not to encourage him, and ordered more wine. It was a very fine wine. Not surprising that it should be served here: amazing that it should be served. I remarked on it. He ignored my digression.

"Gold," he said.

I thought it was a tribute to the wine. "Gold?"

"There were no lead window weights. They were gold. Solid gold bars. Bullion." He was as earnest as a priest.

"Those weights on the ropes were solid gold bars. Now, there's a mystery for you."

"Brandy," Isabella said. "Wait till you taste his brandy."

"Ah, now, there's something else," Mr. O'Keeffe said.

"No, not something else, Seamus," Isabella said. "There's the gold."

It was not clear to me, but at least it was beginning to be entertaining. A good meal, good wine, a little entertainment, and early to bed. "I want to hear more," I said to Isabella.

"Seamus O'Keeffe," she said, "has a great passion for boats . . ."

"Ach, it's not only boats," he protested, and what he meant was obvious enough to me, and irritating enough. I was possessive and helpless.

"He is a superb seaman. Skillful, cunning, and daring."

"Now you're getting too close to the bone, Bella," he said. And to me, "She's saying more than there is, sir. Not much more, mind you. Not much."

Why did he call her Bella? I found it displeasing.

"Fine wines," Isabella said, "fine brandies. He finds them, he buys them, he loads them, he transports them, he unloads them, and if he does not leave us now, I shall tell you where he finds them and where he unloads them."

"France?" I said.

"France. And since you know where he loads them, you may as well know where he unloads them. At high tide in Toormore Bay. And do you know where Toormore Bay is?"

"I do not," I said. I could not decide whether there was humor or anger in her.

"It laps the seaward boundary of my father's land," she said. "The wines and the brandies are run from the shore on slide cars up to our stables, and there they are, or they are somewhere around, I don't know exactly where. Except for what Seamus brings here to serve to his customers, of course." She looked at Elizabeth, who was holding her knife and fork in the air. "What do you think of that, Aunt Elizabeth?"

"I should have preferred not to hear it," Elizabeth said severely, and put down her knife and fork.

Very seriously O'Keeffe said, "I should have preferred you not to hear it. Why, Bella?"

There it was again. Bella. I did not like the name.

The thing was no longer amusing. It was shocking. It was not the time to ask questions. There was too much confusion in my head for me to find the right questions to ask. But my reaction was more than my Ulster predisposition to obey the law. The Catholic Irish have no great regard for the law, most particularly in the South. It has not always—not often—been on their side (I think of Trinity College) and they have come in a way to regard lawlessness of a certain sort as an assertion of their liberty, even their common humanity. I understand this very well. What I could not begin to imagine was my brother's need to be involved in this sort of plebeian lawlessness. It certainly could not be for any need of money. I knew enough from Isabella—apart from the snatches of news that formerly came my way—to know he was wealthy. Was it that living in this desolate isolation, his life lacked the excitement he had known? He was an adventurer. Yet it seemed such tame adventure in a place where in the past even those who were charged with the prevention of smuggling and piracy had what I can only describe as working contracts with the smugglers and pirates, affecting the division of the spoils. I was frightened for my brother, bewildered by him, and at a complete loss to see any sense in what I had heard.

Elizabeth was upset. "If you will please excuse me," she said, and went to her room.

O'Keeffe was upset and angry. His Irish tall tale had turned on him, biting. "Why, Bella?" he said again.

Isabella was serious in a way new to me. "Seamus," she said, "call it blackmail if you care to. That is what it is."

"About what, for God's sake, girl?"

"About me. I want you to know that I mean what I say. *Leave—me—alone.*"

No, there was no humor in what she was doing to O'Keeffe. There was deep anger, about something personal between them, and I was jealous again. They were young. O'Keeffe was no more than ten years her senior, and that was about the usual degree of separation that marked wives from their husbands.

"What in the name of God happened to you in the North?" he said.

She rose from the table. "And what in the name of God could that have to do with you?" The Irish form of the words and the faintly foreign accent did not go together. Or perhaps they did, in a darkling fashion. Together they gave what she said the impact of a hammer on an anvil. The expression on

O'Keeffe's face made me wonder if he had a sudden and severe headache. As if his head were the anvil.

She was gone, and he started after her. I caught his arm. "Sit down again, Mr. O'Keeffe. I think you'd better talk to me first." I pulled him back to his chair. "Talk to me about brandy and seamanship and my brother," I said.

"I'm damned if I will. I'll talk to you about her," he said. "Whom did she meet up there?"

"Very few."

"Men? What men?"

"Well, my son."

"What age?"

"Five now."

"You're not the big laugh you think you are. Who else?"

"I can't think of anybody. Why?"

"You? She spent a lot of time with you, did she now?" He asked it in the tones of sneering Irish derision.

"Most of it."

His face was clouded by what I could only read as disgust. "Merciful Jesus Christ," he said. "It's you. An old married man. Her old uncle." He leaned forward over the table. "An old man that doesn't even sleep in the same room with his own wife. Now, how does that look for dirt to any decent man? She's sixteen. By God, when Hugh hears this . . ."

I was alone. He went like a charger, and I felt the cool stream of the air he displaced.

I could not sleep. What O'Keeffe might in his anger say to Hugh worried me, more now than the Fenians. Leave them to the army. But O'Keeffe could so misinterpret what he thought he had understood that a reunion of love would be turned into venomous enmity. There is no enmity like that between brothers. The business of the brandy and the wine was irrelevant trivia now. I spent a large part of the night composing denials and defenses against false charges. But uneasily, in my heart, I knew that had I been as bold as Hugh and less cautious and less cowardly, they would all be true.

It must have been three in the morning when I heard the gravel rattling a window in the yard, but when I got up to look, there was nobody to be seen. I heard it again as I walked back to bed. And again before I could reach the window. But there was nobody in the yard. Where did the gravel come from, and whose window did it rattle?

That was answered. Isabella's window opened, and she looked out.

O'Keeffe's voice hissed to her, "Bella, will you for God's sake come down and talk to me?"

"I will not."

Then I saw him. In the tree.

"I told you to leave me alone, Seamus," she said. "Get down from there or I'll start to scream and waken the house."

"Bella, will you listen?"

"No. I will not listen. Go away, you fool."

"It's your old uncle, by God. Isn't that the truth? Isn't that the dirty truth?"

"Don't you try to talk to me like that. Don't you dare talk to me like that. Don't you dare talk about him like that."

"Merciful God," he said, "you've got a child's infatuation for an old man. He doesn't even sleep with his wife. Has the dirty old man tried to get you yet?"

I ought to have spoken then, or closed my window noisily. Perhaps it was just as well that I did not. But I was choking with rage.

"That does it," Isabella said. "Come near me again, speak to me again, and I'll take a gun to you." Her window closed.

Then I spoke. I spoke before I knew what I would say. Indeed, I spoke before I knew I had made a decision to say anything.

"Is that gravel you're throwing also gold, O'Keeffe?"

He had supposed me, I have no doubt, to be deep in weary sleep. The shock made him turn quickly on his perch. He lost his footing, lost his balance, and crashed among the branches. He grabbed and hung suspended from a limb.

"Are those cobbles below you also gold, O'Keeffe?" I asked him.

"No," he said, short of breath, "but they're just as hard."

I closed my window and went back to bed. I do not know how Mr. O'Keeffe got down from the tree. He was not there in the morning. He did not appear at all in the morning. A stableboy saddled the horses we hired from the inn and came behind us with our baggage on a small flat cart that was almost too wide for the track.

So we came to my brother's house.

"Why," I asked Isabella on the way, "did your father not ride into Schull to meet us?"

I was afraid that O'Keeffe might have ridden ahead of us.

"He is angry," she said. "He will be angry till I kiss him."
But she added, "Or so it has always been."

Only Elizabeth rode up the avenue to his front door with
an easy mind, confident of her welcome.

Eight

He was waiting on the steps. His woman of Andalusia stood on the top step, perhaps the regulation distance behind him. She was a tall beautiful woman—as we say inaccurately, olive-skinned. She was smiling. He was not. He was watching his daughter as she rode between us toward the steps.

I reined my horse. Let them meet. Let that at least be done with. Elizabeth stopped with me. Isabella went on, at a slow walk, watching her father. Not smiling.

Hugh is tall, as tall as I am but harder, stronger, looser in his frame. My face is square and without interest. I am not noticed. Hugh's face is dark, distinctive, aquiline. It reveals his restless nature. Our Norse-Gaelic ancestors speak in that face. People see Hugh and overlook me. My face speaks of the lowland Scot, the farmer turned whiskey distiller giving life to the flax spinner. Hugh is loved, admired, yet he makes men wary. I am trusted. I think it is always assumed that I am too commonplace to be feared. I have found that useful.

Isabella stepped down from her horse. She was smiling now. She walked toward him slowly, mounted the steps slowly. Her smile was for him. It enveloped him. It was full of love and a conqueror's will. His hawk face thawed slowly with her slow approach. She is melting him with that smile, I thought, and glanced at Elizabeth with distaste and pronounced an anathema on my age and my marriage and my close kinship with Isabella. Yet my anathema did not diminish my desire for my brother's daughter. Now I had no sense of shame, only of need. Devouring need. I wanted that smile to be for me.

At times I have thoughts that contradict my mood. I expect that is the safe cautious man in me. I have an inconvenient sense of the ridiculous. As I watched Isabella, Elizabeth watched Hugh. Her eyes were hungry, and as I glanced at her, I crushed down laughter. I did not find myself ridiculous. I had brought Isabella to her home, to leave her here. This poor woman, though, had come here like a girl fixed in her adolescence, to take Hugh from the Andalusian.

Then Isabella sprang on her father. Her arms were around his neck. She showered kisses on his face, crying, "Papa, Papa, Papa," and Hugh was laughing, lifting her off the steps. He said distinctly, "Bella, you're a self-willed little bitch." He dropped her on the steps—dangerously, I thought nervously—and demanded, "Where did all that finery you have on come from?" He was still my Hugh, the one I remembered.

He ran down the steps to me, and I leaped from my horse. I did not expect him to embrace me. He did so so suddenly that my arms were pinned to my sides and I had to struggle to release them and return his welcome. He welcomed me with love. Every fear was driven from my mind.

He turned to Elizabeth, who was now standing beside us. "How do you do, Elizabeth?" he asked her civilly. And, "My wife will take you to your room."

Elizabeth smiled on with determination and went up the steps to meet the Andalusian. It was not what she had hoped for, that was plain.

Isabella had my arm. "I'll take Carrach to his room," she said. "You have a hot whiskey ready for him, Papa."

"You don't know which room," Hugh said.

"The best room."

"The east-end room, in front, where he can see the sea."

It was an excited, disorderly reception. I had not yet met his wife, who had taken Elizabeth into the house. For all I knew, it was organized disorder. I followed Isabella into the house and up to my room.

"Do you want hot whiskey, or is that young savage just giving orders?" he called after me.

"I want it." It would keep him downstairs.

Isabella closed my bedroom door. "Carrach," she said urgently. "Seamus O'Keeffe."

Carrach; not Uncle Carrach. It rang in my head. "What about him?"

"In the tree. I saw you at your window. Carrach, that was before I went to Barn House."

She was standing very close to me. She was not a child. She did not look and now did not act like a child. I could not say what I wanted to say. "I once knew a man who used a drain pipe."

"He tried that. Here at the house."

"Without encouragement?"

"Carrach. That was before I came to Barn House. It was only entertainment."

Carrach. She could not think of me as her uncle. But I could not say what I wanted to say or do what I wanted to do. I wanted to take her by the arm and rush her from the house and disappear with her into the wild and lonely landscape outside. I think Irishmen have been affected in their own wildness and irresponsibility by that landscape, as if they lived at the end of the world where nothing could reach them or hold them to account. But even these thoughts were disciplined by fear of consequences. My own world was too much with me. I did nothing. I said nothing.

She looked disconsolate. "I will tell you anyway," she said.

"Tell me what?"

"You'll laugh."

"I shall not laugh."

"I'm not a child. I'm a woman. I told Emily in Dublin, and she didn't laugh at me."

"What did you tell her?"

"How desperately I love you."

I could not speak. I was afraid to speak. The room closed in around my mind, on all my senses. I ought to have been jubilant. I was numb.

"What did Emily say to that?" I was trembling. With fear. What if Hugh or his wife walked in on such talk?

"She said, 'I can see you do, my poor darling.' "

"Isabella," I said, and my voice shook. "I am on my way to forty. I'm married. I have three children . . ."

"You don't love her."

"I never did. But I married her."

"Yes," she said. "Yes," nodding. "Papa said it was a blunder."

"In a month, six months, you'll scarcely remember this," I said.

She spoke very firmly. "When you know me as well as I know you," she said, "you will know how silly that is." She opened the door. "Come and have your whiskey. Six months from now, I shall tell you again. Two years from now I shall come to you and say, 'To hell with Elizabeth.' Will you remember that I said this?"

"I'm not likely to forget."

In the doorway she said, "You love me. I know it. There's no point in your denying it merely because you think I'm out of my head for a little while and will get better when I don't see you every day. I know you love me, and in case you think so—I am not a little girl sick from reading the works of the Brontes. Now, come and have your whiskey." She said it impatiently, like a mother to a naughty boy, and ran downstairs.

It was too adult. It sounded rehearsed, and for the first time I thought sympathetically of Mr. O'Keeffe and wondered if she took after her father, charmed people into love for her—then made them victims. I know now how resolutely we throw out our doubts and fears about the people we love deeply. Nothing despicable can be true of them—till we catch them in the act. Isabella spoke and acted like a practiced tormentor. But I would not believe it.

How was I to face my brother? Or his wife, who was now with Elizabeth in the drawing room? Whatever their daughter might for her amusement be doing to me—what was there to love in me?—I was not playing games with myself. I loved this woman-child and was guilty in my thoughts. But Isabella was composed and Hugh happy and relaxed. His wife came eagerly to greet me, and when Hugh made short work of the formalities, she said, "Always he talks about you. All the years, he talks about you. I know you very well from his talk, and you are welcome in my house."

There it was again. "I know you well." Did everybody know me well? I knew myself too well, but can I be read like a book set in large type?

Elizabeth stood alone by the window, looking over Toormore Bay; a separate presence, and listening, no doubt. I thought resentfully: Why does this outsider have to be here at this moment?

"Mama," Isabella said, "when Carrach has gone from here, I shall talk about him too."

Her mother laughed at that. "You talk enough, Bella. I think." She said to me, "You will call her Bella also? I am Isabella. She is Isabella. We call her Bella."

"I shall call her Bella," I said obediently. I shall if I must, but it is not to my taste. Inside I was still shaking from the hopeless encounter upstairs. I wanted more than anything else to sit down and drink my hot whiskey to calm my nerves.

It was one of those fragmented moments when something new is happening and nobody has found comfort in any other. It would pass. So I prayed.

Bella was smiling at me, a small sweet smile with mischief in it; a mischief that raised questions and heightened my sense of being an old man who harbored self-destructive passions.

"And I shall call you Carrach el Cojo," she said.

Her mother protested vehemently. "You will not do such a cruel thing," she said. "How could she say?" she asked Hugh.

I knew what it meant, and it was not unjust. Carrach the Cripple, she would call me. I felt like a cripple.

"But to me it means 'Carrach the Wounded One,' Mama," Bella explained innocently.

Hugh was happy enough to be amused. "I think she's been watching you too carefully, Carrach," he said, "and she sees under the skin."

Elizabeth turned from the window. "Wounded?" she said. "How has he been wounded? Who has wounded him?"

Who indeed had wounded me? There are times when I examine myself without mercy and think I was born middle-aged. At such times I know the motive force of my life can be stated in one word: Survival. I am a Survivor. When we were boys sailing in the Lough, it was Hugh who piled on more sail to get more speed. I wanted more speed, but my cry always was: The important thing is to get there alive, Hugh. Hugh rode to hounds, in the Irish way, as if the horse and not the hounds should get to the fox; I merely rode. The important thing was not to break your neck. When there was fighting to be done with boys who thought drawing the blood of their betters was a fine sport, Hugh did it wildly in a whooping, joyous rage. I could see him in the midst of battle, his sword like a flail. I went to an old professional bare-fister and learned to do it with cold scientific precision. Do not risk needless damage: inflict it coldly, surely. My demon was Survival. Yet there was another one there, always lurking, always peeking out, always longing for release. I read Mr. Melville's *Moby-Dick* and longed to have sailed on the *Pequod*. I read Mr. Dickens's *A Tale of Two Cities* and imagined myself as Sidney Carton, willing to die . . . but if I died, how could I preserve what place the MacDonnells had in the remnants of their old kingdom? For survivors there are always higher considerations than the reckless indulgence of one's irrational impulses. My grandfather was a builder, a commercial adventurer, a MacDonnell. My father was a consolidator, I was merely a Survivor, preserving what I had, yearning at times for what I might have been if I had been born young and not in middle life. Perhaps that is what I yearned for: my never-existent reckless youth? Was that what drew me to this joyously living Isabella? Was she my compensation?

But in some measure are we not all Survivors? I may be the Wounded One, Carrach el Cojo indeed. But what was wild and exuberantly dominant Hugh? I was to find out.

Why did Hugh run off to Andalusia, to this woman he must have known and, maybe, always intended to marry? The next day he told me it was so. Was it that there is in him a streak of cruelty that was matched in his Andalusian? They were gay, generous, and—secret; as hidden in their open way as I am in my enclosure. They too, in their fashion, were Survivors. Elizabeth was taken over by his wife and kept away from Hugh. I saw them smile about it and heard them whisper about it in Spanish, though I could not follow quickly enough what I thought I heard. And Elizabeth diminished and fell back into silence, aware of what was being done to her. She knew, I am quite certain, that they had read her foolish hope, laughed at it, and arranged for the woman and not Hugh to crush it. I do not like Elizabeth, but as I watched her shrink away, my heart bled for the poor creature who was as much sinned against as sinning.

"I want to go home," she said to me.

"I know. But there are things I want to know. Give me three more days and I'll take you home."

They were eventful days. At night I watched Toormore Bay from my window and of course saw nothing. I could scarcely expect to. They were not likely to put on a show for me, and in any event, Mr. O'Keeffe was at home. I saw him twice about the place. Since there was no change in Hugh's happy attitude, I assumed O'Keeffe had thought better of his threat. He came, Hugh said, to take his horses home. I heard nothing of the Fenians. There was no strain here. It was as if they knew nothing of it, and I decided not to speak of it. Not yet.

I saw more than Mr. O'Keeffe about the place. Why, with

so many stableboys at Hugh's, did Mr. O'Keeffe have to come for his horses? One of the stableboys could have taken them back. Why were there so many stableboys, and why did they appear to change? I was certain, over the first two days we stayed, that some of them changed. Yet I did not see them come or go. The answer was obvious: they came at night and left at night. Horses had always been for Hugh the noblest and most useful of beasts. He was breeding them here. On his land there was not more than a hundred acres flat enough to run them on, and these were in separated parcels of from six to twenty acres. Why did he need so many young men about the place?

We rode each day, Hugh and myself and Isabella, who was now Bella. She made no effort to conceal her affections, and that entertained Hugh.

"Carrach," he said, "you made a conquest in Bella."

"The church will protect me. Forbidden relations," I said sourly, and he misread it, supposing me to be displeased by Bella.

"It protects Elizabeth also," he said.

"How?"

"You can't divorce her."

"Do I want to?"

Bella was running her horse in a long narrow field. We were dismounted, watching her. It was safe to talk.

"Bella told me how things are at Barn House."

"She couldn't tell you all of it."

"It was my doing, wasn't it?"

"How could it be your doing?" I ought to have said: Yes, it was your doing.

"I don't need to explain it to you. I told Bella about Elizabeth. She knew enough to understand what happened. I owe you a great deal for what I did."

"You talk about deep things to a child, Hugh."

He looked at me soberly. "Bella is no child, Carrach. Sometimes I think she was born middle-aged."

"Does that alarm you?"

"No, but it should alarm you."

"Why do you live here, Hugh?" I had no intention of getting into any talk of that sort about Bella. But what did he mean or think he knew?

"You want to change the subject?"

"Why did you stay away? Never write? Come home to Ireland and not tell me?" I was determined to change the subject.

"We would quarrel about that, Carrach."

"We'll never quarrel about anything."

"I'm too happy to see you to want to risk that. Just say I could never have been a flax spinner, and I'd have had to run the mill if I'd stayed at home. And add also that when I heard you married Elizabeth McCarthy, I felt too guilty to face you. When you wrote that you were coming, I wanted to run away."

"Did you ever run away from anything? Apart from what you did to Elizabeth McCarthy?"

"No. No, I don't think so."

"Then why are you here? Why did you run to here?"

"I didn't run to here. I chose to come here."

"Why have you so many stableboys, and why do they change? I see new faces, Hugh."

He mounted his horse. "Spin flax, Carrach. Send out your ships. We were never the same. We are not the same now. Leave it there."

"What are they, Hugh?" I took hold of his stirrup.

"Friends, Carrach. Friends in need. Tomorrow I'll show you something. If you are not angered by what I show you, you are not a MacDonnell."

I got into my saddle. Bella was working her horse close to us now, her hands on her hips. There was no point in more talk of this sort with Hugh. I watched her instead. Our saddles were deep Spanish armchairs with pommels. She was working her horse with her knees and heels, wearing close-fitting Spanish trousers. I had never seen a woman in trousers. They made her look naked from the waist, and my eyes were burning. I kept my back to Hugh.

I did not see the movement of her legs that set her horse at the gallop. It leaped into stride and thundered down the field. She rose in one stirrup, hanging on to the pommel, and stretched herself along the horse's side, one arm reaching almost to the ground. The movement that put her back in the saddle was single and smooth. She reined to a rearing stop beside us again, laughing.

"Showing off," Hugh said.

"Of course, Papa," she said. "You taught me to."

They were friends. Were they as alike as they seemed? In many ways they were, I was sure; but there was something in Bella that was not Hugh and not the Andalusian woman, something softer and gentler and more in need. Something like me, maybe? She looked at me then with an expression on her face that startled and hurt me, for in her eyes was the look that sometimes I saw in Alasdar's eyes when I touched him to tell him of my love—and could not declare it to him. It was Alasdar's look that always said to me: Tell me, Papa. Was it a father and not a comrade Bella needed, and was I the Chosen? That was what it was? That was all it was?

The night was wild. The wind disturbed my sleep and made its banshee wailings in the chimneys. I stood by my window and watched the sea below the house. The clouds raced like grotesque chariots across the sky, and the moon came and went behind them. Fastnet Lighthouse on its lonely rock seven miles out in the Atlantic may have been flashing its powerful light—Hugh told me—every six seconds, but the storm hid it from me.

I wanted to stand on the shore, close to it, to feel the salt in my face. I remembered thinking once, watching with Hugh as a storm raged on the Lough below Barn House, that the tumult around us was like Hugh's interior life, while mine was like a cool autumn day. I amended that a little now. I was a man on my way to forty, and for the first time in a cold and careful life I was in love, with passion—with a girl of sixteen. That was improbable enough. Now I wanted to go out in a storm, to feel the storm. I wanted to know a storm within me. I wanted some kinship with the tumult. I dressed, happed up warmly, and went out.

The wind tore at me, and I liked it. It pushed me and I had to fight it, and that made me laugh. A week ago I would have turned back to the house unwilling to be disturbed by the wind. Now I wrestled it all the way to the shore and made my stand behind a defending rock. The sea thundered into the bay and lashed the shore like a malignant monster.

Somewhere out there I had ships and seamen. When I was a child and heard the sea in rage, I cried for the safety of my father's ships and his men. I thought of that now and thought at the same time that passion in the spirit was as threatening as rage in the sea, and turned my back and crouched behind my rock with my back against it. The respite from the wind made my small pocket of comfort seem warm. Hugh's house was a dark shape up the slope from the shore. There was a light in Bella's window at the west end of the house. It had not been there when I came down the hill. She too was sleepless, and I willed her to come.

She came. I saw her first when the front door opened. I watched her in the light of the lamp she placed on a small table in the hall. Then the door closed and she was out of sight in the darkness. The moon was hidden. My first impulse was to run up the hill, the wind on my back, and find her; but she would come this way. I was sure of it.

Then she was above me, on a shelf of flat rocks less than twenty feet from me. There was something long in her hand; a stick? Too long for a stick. It was a gun, and I did not move. Did she bring it for protection? What would harm her here?

I moved for my own comfort and the wind lulled, and in the brief silence the stones under my feet rattled together and she spun. The gun pointed in my direction, moved slowly left and right and back to my rock. The moon came out and the gun settled firmly on me.

"Seamus?" she called, and the wind whipped in again. She walked slowly toward me. She could see the darkness of my frame, but not me. She dropped from the rock down to the shore, but the gun did not waver. "Seamus?" she shouted against the wind.

"Carrach," she said with the gun three feet from me. "What in God's name are you doing there?"

"Come into my shelter," I said, and she came and put down the gun and nestled against my side, sharing my shelter. I put my arm around her. "What's the gun for?" I asked her.

"Go back to the house," she said, "and go to bed and don't look out again tonight. Please."

"There'll be no brandy coming in here in this weather," I said. "So tell me what you're doing. You expected O'Keeffe."

"I still do."

"But that was before you came to Barn House." I was in a storm of jealousy as tumultuous as the sea.

"No, no, no. Don't think foolish things."

"I've already thought foolish things. About you. About what you told me in my room. Stupid thoughts." I was shouting.

"What stupid thoughts?"

"Why should I tell you now? You were mocking me the way your father mocked Elizabeth when they were young. I was sport—that kind of sport."

"That's a damned lie." She leaped from my arm and pinned me against my rock. Her arms were about my neck, not like the arms of a woman, but like bolsters, so well wrapped up she was. "Don't you think that, you fool."

"Then explain it."

"I'm waiting for Seamus, yes. And two men."

"What two men?"

"From the Knockadoon coast-guard station . . . two of the ones that took it."

"And what in God's name have you to do with them?"

"They'll be hiding here. In an old cabin up Knockna-madree."

"What have you to do with them?"

"Will you shut up and not roar at me? We're hiding them. Isn't that plain enough?"

"Hugh?"

"And me. And Mama. Now, will you get down behind your rock and stay down? But before you do . . ." and she kissed me on the mouth and I lost my senses and held her and kissed her and never knew the like either of my passion or the wild turmoil in my head. "Someday," she said, "you'll do that every day. Now, get down out of sight before you get shot." She pulled herself free and picked up the rifle.

"Isabella," I said.

"Shut up and get down and don't show yourself. I'll come to your room when I get down from the mountain. I knew damned well you loved me."

She climbed back to the rocks and stood facing east, watching the shoreline. Soon she dropped to the shore again and came back to my rock.

"Move around it," she said, "and stay down behind me. They're here."

She laid the long rifle across the top of my shelter and leaned against its sloping face. The gun was aimed eastward, at what, I couldn't see. Presently she laid her cheek on it and was very still.

Then she fired.

"Seamus," she yelled.

"What the hell are you trying to do?" It was O'Keeffe, all right.

"Don't come any nearer," she called. "Send them on and go on back home."

"I'll see them right there," he said.

"Will you?" Her cheek was still on the gun. She fired

again. That told me a great deal. It was said that the American repeating rifles made for and rejected by the Union Army in the Civil War were finding their way to the Fenians from America. That had to be one of them. "Go on home, Seamus," she yelled. "And send them on."

There was no more talk from O'Keeffe. I took it that he was doing what he had been told to do. I could not see the two men who came forward now.

"Which one of you is Harrington?" she said, and the man may have raised an arm. I did not hear his voice.

"You'll be Donovan?" This time I heard a voice, but what it said, I did not hear.

"You see the house up the hill? Walk around the west end of it and go on up the mountain. I'll come behind you. There's a cabin halfway up. You'll see it when you're near enough. Go into it. What do you know about horses?"

This time I heard a young voice. "I know all about horses."

"There's a horse in the middle room. Go into the end room to the right. The end room to the left is boarded up. The front and back windows are boarded up. There are no lamps. There's straw, blankets, food, and water. There'll be somebody up to see you early in the morning. Go on, now."

I saw them climb from the shore and walk slowly up the hill. They dragged themselves up the hill. How far they had walked or where they had hidden, I had no way of knowing, but they were weary young men and wet and cold, without overcoats or caps. Wet, cold, exhausted young men, and happed up as I was, now I was cold and felt their chilled, wet weariness. I was not even surprised that I thought not at all about what they had done. They were hunted. Where were the hunters?

Bella still stood beside me where I crouched behind the rock. "I'll have to go now. Go back to bed. I'll come to see you," she said. "Wait a good while before you move."

She was gone.

When she passed the house and was out of sight, I went after her. Protectively? I had to smile at the thought. She needed no protection. But I had time to be surprised at myself. No censure. No caution, except the necessary caution of staying well behind her. A little excitement at the thought of what I was observing. At what I was doing, for I was aiding and abetting. But here on this wild night in this desolate place, it all seemed unreal. No, real enough, but removed from reality. The reality I felt was in my legs as I scrambled up the mountain, and in my chest as my breath shortened. But Isabella was up the mountain, and I would not leave her. I felt young. Well, quite young. My desk at the shipping office, my desk at the spinning mill—my wife, God save my soul, alseep in the house—were far away. The whole world I knew was far away and less than tangible. I wasn't sure I would recognize myself when we met again in daylight, but daylight was many hours away, and the darkness was like a blanket over conscience and caution and cowardice. I was a stranger to myself. The Earl of Enniskillen came into my head, and I wanted to laugh at the thought of the fool.

Isabella—I cannot call her Bella in my own mind—rose beside me from among some bushes and paralyzed me. Soldiers, my God! Police?

"I told you to go back to bed," she said.

"I'll stay."

God forgive me and understand me. I carried the rifle up the mountain to the cabin door. It was closed. She opened it and called to the men inside.

"Are you all right in there?"

"There's no bar on the door, missus," one of them shouted.

"There will be in a minute."

I could hear the horse moving inside on the earth floor. Isabella groped against the base of the cabin wall and found three bars. Their slots were on the outside, and she dropped them into place.

"Now they can't run if they need to," I said. "That door opened outward."

"Last night it didn't, and they won't need to run. We'll come back tomorrow when the soldiers come."

"They'll come?" It was my first twinge of alarm.

"They're in Schull tonight. Come home."

"What will happen when they come?"

"Nothing. They won't find them. Papa will deal with them."

In the dark, I felt her confidence and shared it. I didn't understand myself, but as we came down the mountain I didn't care. I cared less as we came close to the house. She was clinging to my hand, and in my stomach was an excitement that shattered me.

"You love me," she said happily.

"I love you," I said. At that moment I would have said it if Hugh and Elizabeth were beside us.

We were walking along the west gable of the house. One step, and we would turn the corner.

"Kiss me," she said.

I took her in my arms and kissed her. I was drunk with love for her. I cared about nothing but that.

"We must go inside," she said. She was bold and passionate and sensible.

We turned toward the steps.

O'Keeffe was sitting on the top step.

"Holy Jesus Christ," he yelled at me. "A filthy old cradle robber."

He leaped down the steps and ran toward the shore, into the storm.

The night fell in fragments about my feet.

Nine

It was raining now. The rain lashed my window, the branches of a bare tree whipped and cracked outside it like evil spirits struggling to get in, and the wind wailed in the chimney. The room and my bed were cold; the earthenware hot-water bottle a servant girl had placed in my bed was cold. The world was a hostile place without comfort or consolation, and sleep denied me. For all I knew O'Keeffe was prowling malignantly outside. I am no warrior.

In the early hours of the morning I must have slept from exhaustion. Hugh shook me awake.

"We have guests," he said.

I was thick with weariness and incomprehension. My body was stiff, my neck sore. It must have been the way I was lying, we say. I knew it was because I lay rigid with tension. What did his guests have to do with me? Sleep had come. I wanted it to stay.

"I'm tired, Hugh. Leave me for a while."

"The army would like to see you," he said.

I cannot claim that I sat up in bed. I wrestled myself up on one elbow. "The army? What do they . . . ?" and it all poured back and I sat up.

"I understand you helped," he said. "Bella told me. But you slept through the storm, didn't you?" He was grinning, in a way I knew well from the far past. He kept that grin for the edge of danger, as if whatever threatened made him even more fully alive—planning and executing a fornication with Lady Carbery under her jealous and ineffectual husband's nose during his own ball and returning her to public view with a contented expression on her plain face and that grin on his. The grin was for me and for himself. "Come and enjoy the play," he said.

"What did Bella say?"

"The bare facts," he said, "but not what goes on in her head and heart. I just happen to know that part because I know her. If it was anybody but you, Carrach, I'd lock her up, or him. She'll come to no harm with you, though that's not what O'Keeffe thinks."

"What does O'Keeffe think, if it matters?"

"It doesn't matter. He thinks you're a lecherous old bastard. He doesn't read character too well. Sometimes I find his impertinences a bit trying. He seems to think he's set his seal on Bella. Get up and dress."

Dressed but limp, I went downstairs.

A young lieutenant was engaged in agreeable and harmless conversation with Elizabeth, Hugh's wife, and Isabella. I cannot bear to think of her as Bella. It is a working-class diminutive for Isabella, like Cassie's Aggie for Agnes, and I cannot understand why Hugh would tolerate it, but he has a perverse streak in him. No doubt he's asserting something against the pressures of his youth. I don't know. The lieutenant greeted me cordially, as an equal. My God, the presumption of these English puppies. His easy assumptions pumped my adrenaline and made me think of Brooke's down-the-nose declaration, "I take unkindly to being called an Irishman." This youth was the hunter, and weary myself, I thought of the weariness of the two young men up Knocknamaddree. It was irrational, but I had discovered in myself a new—or was it a latent—capacity for the irrational, and the storm had died, the wind was not battering my window, and daylight was all about me. Isabella glowed on me and said, "Good morning, Carrach," as if the day had suddenly brightened.

"You'll forgive this intrusion, I hope?" the lieutenant said.

"I should have preferred to sleep," I said, "but I forgive you." I was at my most dignified, my very proper self. "I did not sleep well."

"Ah. Your brother said . . ."

"My brother does not share my room and he does not have a young pliable tree outside his window. Don't think me ungracious, but what did you want of me?"

"I must ask my questions, sir." He was a little less equal.

"Please do ask them." Isabella's grin was Hugh's grin. And she winked at me.

"This is not your home?"

"I take it you know the answers?"

"I am required to ask."

"This is not my home. It is, as you must know by now, my brother's home. His daughter has been on a visit to my home in the North, and I have brought her back so that I might enjoy a few days with my brother and his family. I am, in the North, a Unionist, a flax spinner, and a shipper . . . You have questioned my wife, I take it?" I felt spiteful about his youth, I suppose, and his presumption and his presence.

"Yes, sir," the lieutenant said in retreat. "I think I shall dispense with any further questions."

Hugh said, "Have your men finished in the servants' quarters and the outbuildings, lieutenant? In Ireland, one cannot always speak for one's servants."

Hugh, I thought, was becoming very Irish. His impertinence bore a close resemblance to O'Keeffe's—and his solemn mockery.

"Quite," the lieutenant said primly. "We must comb the mountain." It sounded as the Lord God might have sounded when He announced His intention to begin the Creation.

Hugh said, "Anyone who might have been lying on that mountain last night will be cold and wet and likely to be dying from exposure."

"There's a cabin . . ."

"It's mine. Do you want to see it?"

"I have to see it."

"Come, Carrach. We'll show the lieutenant."

It was not what I wanted, before breakfast. I couldn't understand Hugh. The hunted were up there. "I'd rather have breakfast," I said.

"You came to visit me. Spend time with me." The grin was the same old grin—the circus performer with his head in the lion's mouth, I once told him.

"I'm coming," Isabella said.

"I think your mother has business with you," Hugh said, and her mother nodded vigorously. I did not always understand what passed between them, but Isabella did not argue. The lieutenant seemed disappointed. She was wearing her close-fitting trousers.

We rode up Knocknamaddree, Hugh and the lieutenant talking idly while his men combed every spot that might give cover to the hunted, and found nothing. They had been doing this across endless open country for days, hunting men, finding some, missing many, the lieutenant said. People shelter them, he said, even people who do not agree with their activities. It is a strange thing, he said.

"There are several reasons for it," Hugh said. "First, they are Irishmen, like the hunted. But you are an Englishman."

"Two-thirds of the men in the army are Irish," the lieutenant protested.

"Officered by Englishmen." Hugh said it very pleasantly. It was merely a thing to talk about. "Another reason is that many who say they disagree with the Fenians, do not. Another is that many of them are afraid of the Fenians. Fenians do not believe killing informers to be a mortal sin."

"Ah." The lieutenant nodded in strong agreement. "Murderers."

"Another is that they are human."

"Who?"

"The sheltered and the shelterers. Compassion can make politics look very unimportant, lieutenant."

He was talking about himself now. But how could I be sure of that? He could be talking about poor farmers in the hills, O'Keeffe in Schull—or me. I was bound into this compassionate conspiracy.

Then the thunder reached us, still more than two hundred feet from the cabin. It was the horse, rearing, kicking, smashing wood, screaming with rage.

The lieutenant reined up. "That's a horse," he said, looking at Hugh, then at me, with a stupefied expression. "In the cabin."

"He's a rogue. He went crazy."

I thought of the two men in the cabin and was utterly bewildered. The horse was moving last night, but it did not act like a rogue. It was not my place to speak, but why put those young men in there with a crazy brute? We pushed our horses up to the cabin. The door shuddered. I noticed now what I could not see last night in the dark—the boarding over the window of the small end room where the men were lodged had a knot hole in it. They could have watched us coming.

"The bars are on the outside," the lieutenant said.

"You're an acute observer," Hugh said, and the door cracked. "Do not mention this to my daughter, lieutenant. I'm using this old cabin as a loose box. We're going to shoot this beast up here, but I have to get my daughter away for the day before it's done. It's her horse, and I'm going to have trouble with her." So that was why she couldn't come.

"Well, there'll be nobody in there," the lieutenant said confidently. "Or they're kicked to death."

"In any case, as you said, the bars are on the outside."

"Of course. Well, gentlemen, we'll move on to Goleen and Crookhaven."

"Good luck, lieutenant." Hugh was his most charming self. His grin was his most lunatic. I knew he was roaring inside.

"Why have you so many horses, Mr. MacDonnell?" the lieutenant asked suddenly.

"I breed horses and sell them."

"In this country?"

"When they're trained here, lieutenant, they never get winded." He looked at that moment like a tinker horse thief.

"Who buys them?"

"The army."

The young officer was like a man who swam constantly too far out of his depth. He gestured hopelessly with one hand and swung his horse away. With relief, I thought.

We turned back down the mountain and were silent most of the way.

"Is that horse crazy, Hugh?" I asked at last.

"No."

"Then how is it done?"

"I was up here before dawn with a long probe with a small harpoon lashed to it."

"And they tormented the beast?"

"Yes."

"I thought you loved horses."

"Which do you prefer, Carrach? Two men hanged or one horse shot?"

"You'll shoot it?"

"If that English boy comes back, he'll ask that, won't he?"

No doubt. I said no more.

Breakfast was a silent meal. We were all tired. It was plain that several of us had had little sleep the night before. Hugh reminded me that he had promised to show me something today. It would take time. We would leave after breakfast. "Bella will come." That, I supposed, was to remove her from here while the stableboys slaughtered the horse.

While I changed for a long—and unwelcome—ride, Elizabeth sought me out in my room. She had faded again and was as colorless and fragile-looking as she had been before her hopes were roused. Her face was even sharper than before, her thin mouth tighter.

"Take me home," she said again. It was a plea, not a demand.

"The day after tomorrow," I said. "There are arrangements to be made."

"This place is hostile. That woman is hostile. Hugh is hostile. That mountain is hostile."

"You ought not to have come."

"Don't you think I know that?" She was snarling again. She may look fragile. She is like barbed wire. Her talent for killing sympathy is limitless.

I was alone for a moment with the Andalusian woman before we left; she said to me gently, half watching me, "Your Elizabeth is a silent woman."

"Yes." It covered all my thoughts, all my feelings. I could have said: You destroyed her into silence. But it was in my mind that I had made my own contribution to that. Committed however uselessly and hopelessly I was to Isabella, pity for Elizabeth stirred a little. I wanted nothing to do with her. I would gladly have paid her to go away, live at Court House, live anywhere but at Barn House, and failing that, stay in her nunnery out of my sight. But now too I pitied her. Is it not a form of contempt?

We rode the cart tracks west to Goleen, a collection of habitations without even a church of their own. The people walked two miles to Rock Island, crossed the bay by boat, and walked another mile to Crookhaven, where there was a tiny church and a priest with a horse. This, Hugh said, was where young Harrington came from. He might never see it again. He might hang. He might somehow get to America. He might find a hiding place and work, in the North—if he could find a compassionate patron and a new name. I did not respond. Hugh said, "They're planter stock, turned Catholic and Irish."

Through Goleen. The entire population of the place was gathered in the muddy street, and two policemen and a man Hugh identified as "Townsend's land agent," and another man he did not speak of. I knew the signs. I did not ask questions.

Still going west, and no sign of the soldiers. Then left on the track toward Rock Island. It was not an island but an immense rock formation on which a small lighthouse and the coast-guard station had been built. Halfway to the Rock, on high ground, Hugh stopped us. We were above a green hollow that ran down into a small bay. At the head of the hollow, a cabin of mud and thatch. The thatch was rotten, overgrown with weeds. There was no sign of life about the place. It had no windows. The half-door was closed.

"We shall watch from here," Hugh said.

"Hugh, I do not want to watch."

He paced his horse, back and forward, back and forward before me. Isabella sat hers, beside me. Hugh reminded me of a general pacing before his gallopers while he decided with what orders he would send them galloping. His face was dark, and darker still with gathering anger.

"There is an old man in that cabin," he said. "Do you see smoke from his chimney? No. Do you see sons in his field? Two acres, Carrach. That is a farm? That place is fit to live in?"

I knew the story. A farm was one and a half acres, two, three, four acres. A "rich" farmer had twenty acres, and here half of them might be unfit for plow or cow, pig or potato.

"That old man had three sons, Carrach," he said as he passed again. "One drowned out there," and he pointed to the sea, "two months ago. One died of consumption," he shouted back, turned and came again, "six months ago and one," as he turned again, "you helped to shelter from the storm last night. The old man in there, his name is Harrington. He just sits there." He pulled up beside me, knee to knee. "They walk from Goleen to feed him, Carrach. He never speaks. He is sitting, waiting to die, to get out of this midden of a world. But his youngest son fights."

I watched the cabin. I could see the old man, sitting by his cold fire. Perhaps by now lying in his own mess on his own bed?

"We never did it to anyone, Hugh," I said lamely.

"Townsend does it still," he roared at me. "He owns most of this peninsula east far beyond Schull almost to Ballydehob, and how much does he take out of it in rents? Three landlords here in the west take fifty thousand pounds a year. Does the Queen of England have that much in rents from her English tenants? Look," he said, and pointed.

Beyond Harrington's cabin, on the track that turned into the Rock, they were coming: two policemen, the land agent, the bailiff, and three laborers with a flat cart drawn by a don-

key, and on the cart, two ladders, picks, forks, and sledge-
hammers. The policemen carried rifles.

"To protect the wreckers," Hugh said. "They're probably
scum from as far away as Waterford."

They came to the cabin. The policemen and the bailiff
opened the door and went inside. They came out carrying the
old man and laid him on the grass. They pulled up fistfuls of
grass and wiped their hands with it. It was not enough. They
walked down the hollow to the sea and washed their hands.

"He was lying in his own shit," Hugh said.

Isabella pulled her horse away from me. She was fixed on
the scene below, as if it mesmerized her.

The wreckers put their ladders to the thatch and went to
work with picks and forks.

Six women came up the tracks, carrying an improvised
stretcher. They lifted the old man onto it and carried him
away.

There were holes in the thatch now, and odd pieces of
homemade furniture piled away from the cabin. But no bed.
It was, very likely, too filthy to save. Maybe it was no more
than a straw mattress on the floor. The bailiff handed to the
men on the ladders two cans. They half-emptied the fluid in
them over the sections of thatch still intact, poured the rest
through the empty spaces, and threw the cans down inside.
Then they came down from the roof, loaded their ladders
and tools, and led the donkey and cart up onto the track.

The bailiff went inside and came out running. The flames
leaped. He threw a forkful of burning straw up onto the
thatch, and the flames roared. The men drew back and stood
in a cluster, facing the fire. The black smoke billowed.

Across the track to Goleen, high above it on a ridge, the
people of Goleen watched.

And Isabella put her knees to her horse's shoulders. This
time I saw the movement, and the horse leaped like the
flames.

"Bella!" Hugh screamed, and lunged for her reins, but she
was gone, rolling in her saddle, one foot in the left stirrup,
the other hooked into the right stirrup, the stirrup strap
caught around the back of the saddle, her foot on the animal's rump. She was screaming, one hand gripping her
horse's mane, the other the pommel, her body along the
beast's side and bumping against it helplessly.

The horse thundered down the hill toward the cluster of
men facing the fire. They can have heard only its roaring till

she was almost on them; then they turned and leaped. It was the bailiff who in panic leaped the wrong way and hit the horse's shoulder and flew like a crippled bird trying to rise and struck the ground tumbling and rolling and lay grotesquely splayed in the field. His companions ran to him.

But Isabella went on, clinging to her galloping runaway.

I had seen her do it more elegantly, but this was not meant to be elegant.

"We'll go after her now," Hugh said, "no faster than a canter."

"Where will she go?" I shouted.

"I don't know, but she'll have to keep that beast running for a long time if she's going to convince anybody. Sometimes she's a self-willed bitch."

We did not catch her. We saw the Goleen people turn to watch her round the low end of their high ground, and we followed their line of sight. When we saw her again in empty country she was comfortably in the saddle, at a canter and far, far away.

We reined, and Hugh fumed. "Now we'll have to go back and see if she killed that man. God blast the bitch, I could do without that sort of attention." His rage was murderous.

They had the bailiff on the flat cart. The police said both legs were broken and one of his arms and his skull was maybe cracked and maybe his ribs were broken. The man was crying in great pain. It would be a long journey to a doctor at Ballydehob.

"There'll be charges," one of the policemen said.

"It was a runaway," Hugh said.

"There'll still have to be charges, sir."

"He jumped into the horse," I protested. "I saw it, you saw it." I was once again a co-conspirator with them, a pliant confederate for Isabella.

"I saw nothin but a flyin horse," the policeman said.

Hugh at once sent a rider to the magistrate with a long letter of explanation and a request for immediate charges and a quick hearing. You must stay, he argued with me, and "bear witness." I could scarcely deny him. The thing must be "handled," he said. He was cold and strong and ruthless about how it would be done. But his rage as he prowled the house waiting for Isabella to return, arranging for the shooting and burying of the horse up the hill, was not exhausted by this massive expenditure of energy.

He was not cold when Isabella returned to the house, later in the afternoon, leading a lame horse to the stables. It was out of the question, she said to Hugh's order that she come at once with us and her mother to the drawing room, till she had hoof-picked the stone that lamed her horse. She met his rage with a cold eye.

"And do not order me," she said with frosty quiet.

"I wish to God I'd thrashed you," he shouted.

She dug at the horse's hoof. "And there'll be no talk at all while you talk that way."

Yet there was nothing of the shrew in it. I wanted to ask Hugh: Is she really sixteen? She was going to be a formidable woman. I had had three women in my lifetime, one unwilling but legally bound, one bought with a place to live and an income, and one—what was Cassie? Submissive, lusty, socially inferior, maybe flattered, but hungry for soft affection and a child: none of them like this woman. I lusted at the sight of her strong thighs as I had never lusted for a woman, as I never believed I would be able to lust, as I had tried to lust with Cassie and failed. I lusted after her strength, the force in her, her certainties. With that sometimes annoying split in the mind that makes me think of the ridiculous in the midst of the gravest or most disturbing circumstances, one line slipped quickly across my mind: A mighty furnace is my girl. It was more acceptably ridiculous because Protestant Luther wrote the original line, "A mighty fortress is our God." With Isabella there would be no question of what I could be. It was said in Catholic mission books that once there were Indian tribes who ate the hearts of men who fought them bravely and died, that the Indians might take to themselves the courage of their victims. That, I am sure, was how I lusted after Isabella. To take into myself her strength and courage and passion. To plunge myself into hers. I could feel, I could see how it would happen, what I would become. I am quite aware that what I was saying was: If I conquered her (ate her heart) I would have her power. My rational world was as far from me as the planets.

The stone lodged in the horse's hoof was pried to the ground. She called a stableboy from the yard to rub down her horse and water it.

"Now," she said to Hugh. First, my horse, she was saying, then I have time for you. She walked away. Strode away without a look at him. God, I was thinking, I want to consume that arrogance.

We followed her into the house, upstairs to the drawing room. We were like courtiers giving the queen her space and precedence.

Her mother was already there, sitting by the window waiting to ride out the storm, her hands locked in her lap like the hands of a woman who had ridden out many domestic storms that were not her own. "Ah, yes," she said to me the other day, "we fight. Then we rush to bed and make ourselves tired. But our poor Bella—who could make her tired?" I didn't say it was my great desire to try; to make her cry "enough" long after other women would cry "too much."

Hugh slammed the door. He had climbed the stairs muttering "arrogant bitch," and now he shouted, "What the hell did you think you were doing?"

"Riding them down," Isabella said without emphasis or repentance.

"What were you trying to do to me?" His big hands made enormous fists.

"It had nothing to do with you. It was my anger."

"You drew attention to me. You're putting me in danger, damn you. Police, charges, magistrates . . . I don't want them . . . I can't afford them . . ."

It is impossible to recall all they said to one another. Hugh storming, thumping tables, and making things jump, and Isabella standing, very erect, very still, answering in an almost inaudible voice that rustled at Hugh like leaves in a movement of air. What I remember, for it thrust from my mind most of what they were saying, was that she stood there like a cold flame. And I understood one thing as I watched them. These two loved one another with a tumultuous love, and if they had not been father and daughter, they would have fought this fight and then "made themselves tired." Hugh's hands hovered near her. He wanted to strike her, embrace her; his love for her was spilling through his fury. She, standing still and, I'm certain, unaware of it, was receiving his anger and his love as her right and her possession. It excited me wildly, and the woman of Andalusia watched me and, I swear, understood them and me.

I saw Isabella's lips move and did not hear what she said.

Hugh did. His mobile face was frozen in shock.

"What?" It was a change of tone so complete that it was itself shocking.

"I said: What is that mound on the edge of the two-acre hayfield?" She asked it gently.

"We'll stick to your stupidities," he said feebly.

"The mound in the hayfield," she said softly but relentlessly. "What is it?"

"Will you listen to me?"

"Where is my horse? Still up the mountain?" She had not moved since the row began; she stood like a statue of flesh.

"It's in the hayfield," he shouted. "What do you prefer? Two boys hanged for armed insurrection, or one horse dead?"

He had used it on me. It was reasonable, but it was also desperate. He had stormed, raged, fumed, stamped, and strutted, come close to seizing her, and she had, without speaking much above a whisper, forced him to talk instead on her chosen ground about her slaughtered horse.

"Because of this goddamned bailiff, they'll come back," he said, trying again. "They have to find a dead rogue horse."

She was not drawn back. "You got rid of me so that you could slaughter my horse," she said, "and you talk to me? You were afraid to tell me." She moved for the first time. Her body softened, relaxed. "Papa," she said, "I expected something better from you."

She walked past him to the door. His hands opened and closed as she passed him. I thought, this time he will seize her. But his arms fell to his sides. He was defeated. I wanted to laugh.

Isabella opened the door and turned to her mother, sitting by the window watching the sort of scene she must have watched many times before.

Isabella said, "Mama. You made a dreadful mistake by marrying this man." She was grinning. Her mother was grinning.

"God preserve me," Hugh said.

Isabella closed the door very gently, like a gesture with a velvet hand in a velvet glove.

"The right man will tame her," her mother said. She was not unhappy.

I thought they must live in a state of tension, with a taste for it like the taste for drink. Liking it, maybe now needing it?

We sat in the drawing room, fidgeting for the want of something to say. Isabella did not come back. Her mother watched the sea. Hugh stared into the fire. Sometimes his lips moved as if he were belatedly rehearsing what he might have said to his daughter.

"Hugh," I said through his thoughts. "What are you afraid of?"

"What do you mean?"

"It's not just the bailiff or those two young men up the mountain. What is it?"

"I have to think about young Harrington," he said. "I have to get them traveling tonight. If Harrington hears about his father, he'll be out looking for somebody to kill. He'll very likely decide he wants to kill the landlord, and that's Townsend."

That too was plausible, probably true, but more than likely already arranged for. "Twice now, you've involved me in whatever you're involved in here. You don't want to tell me, but I want to know. I'm your brother. I have a great deal at stake, and you know it. What are you hiding?"

He took a long time to answer. I could see the doubt in his face. Every now and then he glanced my way like a man debating my reliability.

"I've done things, condoned things I would never have tolerated in the North, Hugh," I said. "I'm involved now in things I don't approve of. If you don't tell me yourself, I'll ask Isabella."

The Andalusian woman still looked at the sea. "And she will tell him, Hugh," she said.

"I'm sure of it," he said, and to me, "You're sure of it too, aren't you?"

"Quite sure of it."

"Guns, Carrach. Guns and ammunition. The boarded-up end room in the cabin up the mountain is stacked to the roof with them. And it isn't boarded up. It's walled up."

"Where do they come from?"

"From America. Where else? They're old Civil War loaders and a few repeaters. We would hardly expect to get them from England."

"We? Who are we?"

"Oh, why should I lie to you? I'm a Fenian, Carrach. A Fenian quartermaster. You may as well know. Does it frighten you?"

"Strangely enough, it doesn't, and that surprises me as much as it must surprise you. The way these young men were brought here, the changing faces of your stableboys. I

thought of the Fenians when I saw you and O'Keeffe at
work. I ought to have cleared off home as soon as I thought
of Fenianism. I think I'm losing some of my senses down
here."

Hugh's wife looked around at me, sharply, I thought. "And
found some new ones?"

I didn't care what she took from it. "And found some new
ones," I said. If this shrewd woman saw through me, let her.

She said, "Then you can help us."

"I was coming to that, Carrach," Hugh said quickly, taking
control.

"To what?"

"When we get this bailiff business out of the way . . ." It
wasn't easy for him to say whatever he wanted to say. He
blurted it out, "Take her north with you, Carrach."

✌ Ten ✌

It was preposterous, of course. I was being asked to do what I would never have dared to propose. It was my turn to be silent, to stare into the flames. I could feel them watching me. In the corner of my eye I could see Hugh watching me.

"Carrach?" he said.

"Give me time," I said, and waved him to silence. "Give me time."

I could see all the problems. I could see them, and my mind was brushing them aside; not my mind; my eager and self-regarding emotions. How could I treat her as a young woman in my charge, my brother's daughter, for whom I had accepted some sort of parental responsibility? How could I be honorable about it when what I wanted . . . ? What I wanted, my mind told my emotions, was simply to have her near me. My emotions told my mind: What you want is to have her near like a fond habit, a right arm, till propinquity leads where it leads—to bed. How could I conceal from Elizabeth, the servants, the neighbors, that my passion for this girl was overwhelming? Well, I had concealed it from her parents. I think. Why would they entrust her to me if they knew what was in my mind and heart?

I found a new kind of cunning in myself. I was not myself.

"Why?" I said. "It's a heavy responsibility. She's at a very difficult age. I'm not the sort of person. And there are problems with Elizabeth . . ."

"You mean her sister, Emily?" the Andalusian said.

"Emily?" What had this to do with Emily?

123

"Carrach," Hugh said hesitantly, "that is none of our business. I wouldn't have mentioned it," and he glanced impatiently at his wife. "But Elizabeth told Isabella—this Isabella—that you're carrying on a liaison with her sister."

"I would have mentioned it," this Isabella said stubbornly. "At home I would have said: Do you lie in the perfumed garden with this Emily? If I was like your Elizabeth, I would know Hugh was lying in it with somebody. Why would he not?"

"My wife is part Moor," Hugh said, shaking his head.

So Elizabeth was back where we started. It would have enraged me if it had not also been so useful. If Hugh thought this about Emily, he couldn't think it about Isabella. "Elizabeth is not a happy woman," I said. "What I meant was that she's just—well, she's difficult. Not pleasant. Hostile." I assumed a deeply thoughtful posture, licking my domestic wounds for them.

"Ask her if she'll agree," Hugh said.

"Tell her," his wife said. "She has no rights now." She understood very well, in her Andalusian way, that a woman who denies to her husband access to her loins no longer has rights. That was, among her people, a law of nature. We acknowledged a different law, and I did not bother to explain to her that when a wife has at some time permitted her husband access—and has children to prove it—the marriage is confirmed in heaven. The question then, in Andalusia or in Ireland, remained one of mere power. Andalusian women bent it; our women, accustomed to other ways, did not. Andalusian men had a right to relief, and their wives accepted it. Our women did not. So our men did in secret that with which Andalusian men taunted their unwilling wives. Sometimes, of course, both murdered their husbands, from the same question, for the same reasons. Elizabeth would rather keep me alive and, if she knew my sins, punish me for them into all eternity. I changed the subject.

"You're not being open with me, Hugh. I want to know why you want me to do this. I want to know it all."

"I can't, Carrach."

"Then neither can I." If he couldn't tell me why he wanted his own daughter far away from her own ground, it had to be something serious, something dangerous. This Harrington boy and his companion up the mountain and Isabella's horse charge at old sick Harrington's evictors could be read as standard reactions to situations that repeated themselves often in Irish life. Hiding the hunted was in part a question of compassion, in part the Irish love for a little lawlessness, and Isabella's charge was understandable anger at the inhumanity of homelessness, desperate poverty, despair, the death wish of the utterly defeated—and the callous, even vicious heartlessness of a landlord. It made me angry. But it wasn't Hugh's idea of danger. He had always felt himself to be invulnerable until he stood in the jaws of death. The repeating rifle and the guns stored up in the cabin were closer to the meaning of Hugh's concern—and his activities. He was sitting gloomily, looking at his wife as if to ask: How much do I tell him? I decided to force the issue. To force the issue? I decided to force him to talk because he wanted Isabella away from here and I wanted her at Barn House and neither of us would get what we wanted unless he was open with me. I had made that certain.

"Don't ask a brother to involve himself in your life unless you're willing to show him what your life is, Hugh," I said. "You're a Fenian. What else is there?"

"Why should there be anything else?"

"I'm your brother, man. I know you. That O'Keeffe fellow comes here to report to you. Faces change among your too numerous stableboys. They come at night and go at night. You're not one compassionate soul, you're a part of something, and in the absence of other means, in this end-of-the-world place, you're the hub in some sort of communications wheel."

"Is it that obvious?"

"It isn't obvious at all. I'm your brother, living in your house. I know you. You are storing American repeating rifles. Not anybody else. You. You're more than a quartermaster. Now, will you stop these Irish evasions and tell me what you're trying to involve me in?"

"So I'm Irish?" He was smiling. There was a little Irish derision in it.

"You always were. Just tell me." Even if he told me something, he would hold back a great deal. I had to have something.

"All right, Carrach. I'm the Fenians' armaments organizer. Does that shake your Unionist heart?"

I ought to have been shocked, horrified, outraged. I was not. In this place, with Knocknamaddree shutting the world away from us to the north and Mount Gabriel to the east, with the Atlantic ocean before us, the rest of the world seemed neither serious nor real.

"Does that frighten you?" he asked me again.

"At this moment," I said, "your Fenians are like characters out of Mr. Carleton's Irish tales."

"Go on thinking that," he said.

"You think otherwise?"

"No. I agree. I'm going to change it. At the moment, we're plagued by an excess of American Civil War soldiers who think they can repeat their Civil War on Irish ground. I don't know what they were in their Civil War, but by the time they get here, they're generals. They want fine heroic set battles. The Irish aren't made for that sort of warfare unless they are British- or French-trained and -officered. They simply run away. They ran away at Ballyhurst the other day—after the first volley from the soldiers. The Irish are devious. Their proper kind of warfare is sneaky. I hope to persuade them, then they'll not look like characters from Mr. Carleton's Irish tales. You don't believe me? You're laughing."

"I don't believe you. All you've given me so far is a theory. What are you afraid of?"

"I've said enough." He waved his hands in a gesture of finality.

"I'm afraid not." Quite apart from any question of Isabella leaving with me, I was curious. I was in a world I didn't know, touching things I had never touched before. It was to me an Irish underworld, but my strange brother was in it, part of it, from what he said, a very important part of it. I was in a sense visiting a slum, but in the abstract. I could touch it here in my brother's comfortable house without risking the infections or contaminations of the slum. And in any case, nothing could come of it; nothing ever had. Mr. Gladstone was a far greater danger than were armed Fenians. They were always crushed. They always ran away. They dreamed great battles and talked defeats into famous victories. Here, where I sat, they were a sorry lot. Even Mr. Gladstone, dangerous as he was, seemed less dangerous here between Knocknamaddree and the sea. Mr. Carleton, talking of his Irish tales, said the Irish Earth was to him a character like Neal Malone, like O'Connell and the schoolmaster composing an oath against drink, like Phelim O'Toole, and now the Irish landscape diminished Mr. Gladstone and enlarged my curiosity. There are many worlds, and in our minds, according to circumstances, they are not always related to one another.

"The repeating rifles, Hugh," I said. "Isabella goes with me if I know exactly what I'm involved in."

"All right," he said. "I have no right. But I want to trust you."

"You know damn well you can."

"The cabin up the mountain," he said, "as I told you, one of the end rooms is walled up, and the room is stacked with guns and ammunition, up to the roof. There will be more—much, much more. I go often to America to arrange for shipments from the Irish there. They're landed wherever they can be around this coast. So far, all's well. But now we're going to start training officers on this ground. Not set-battle officers. What the Spanish call guerrilla captains—it comes from the word *guerra*, war, *guerilla*, a small war. Sneaky war. Hidden war. Hit-and-run war. It will be very dangerous. I want Bella away from here, Carrach." It was a plea.

I kept him waiting a long time, thinking not of him or the plans he had for his undisciplined Irish. Improbable plans. Plans like Carleton's two drunks drawing up oaths against drink. None of that mattered to me, here at the foot of Knocknamaddree; only Isabella mattered. He hated to tell me what I had insisted on knowing. He was caught between his daughter and his Fenians, and Isabella came first. Unlike the English, the Irish are deficient in institutional loyalty. They are loyal to persons. I was surprisingly unmoved by his traitorous intelligence, having been made whole, single-minded, by my own obsession. I wanted only to take Isabella home with me, and wait decently . . . and with difficulty . . . till she was . . . till I honorably could . . . till the image of O'Keeffe's dirty old cradle robber was a distant ghost. The Fenians with their passwords, their secret signs—rubbing the nose while pulling the ear, and things of that order (there were hilarious tales of signs and phrases confused while they were drunk)—were mere entertainment compared with my single purpose.

"I would like her away from it too, Hugh. It's lunatic nonsense."

The woman crossed the room and kissed me.

"I'll speak to her," Hugh said.

"Carrach will ask her," his wife said. "We tell her nothing. She will go for Carrach."

I could not tell what the woman had in her head. I think

she is much subtler than my brother and sees more of what goes on in other people. But my mind was already scheming ways to hide my passion and my intentions before and after they came together in their appointed time. I was already eating her heart. I closed my eyes to hide them from her mother, and felt no shame, no guilt; only the will to do, and the joy of expectation.

In a while I went to find Isabella and asked her to come back north "for a long visit to Barn House."

"Have you asked Papa and Mama?" she said.

"No." I hadn't asked them.

"Good." There was a twinkle in her eyes. The corners of her mouth were turned up, but only a little—a trace of a small smile, no more.

"Well, are you coming?"

"Of course I'm coming." The twinkle was gone from her eyes. What took its place? It is hard to describe. The eyes were even darker than usual, and very warm, and the warmth seemed to come from tiny points of light deep inside or behind them. They made me think of a cat's eyes. A cat? Not a small domestic cat. Something much larger, much stronger, much more elemental. Something much more worth the struggle to overwhelm, but never to subdue. There was nothing unknown between us, though everything was unspoken. "We'll have to think hard about how it's to be done," she said.

I was immobilized by the eyes, imprisoned in them. "I can't marry you, Isabella," I heard my distant voice say.

"Of course not," she said, and sounded as distant in my ears. "Perhaps not," she said. "Maybe not for a long time." She kissed me. First, a touch, no more, on my cheek. Then a touch, no more, on my lips. My numbness was sweet numbness. "We don't care," she said. "I'll tell them I'm going."

They were still in the drawing room, waiting to hear from me.

"Carrach wants me to go back to Barn House with him," she announced with what I did not see then as conscious ambiguity, "and I'm going."

Hugh's performance was quite convincing. "You are, are you? And what are we supposed to do about that? Don't you think we might want to have you near us?"

"I'm sure you do. I know you do. So now you'll have to come north often to see us, won't you, Papa?" There she went again, ambiguously, like a bride leaving on her honeymoon, or a niece leaving with her uncle. "To see us."

"We'll come often," her mother said. "I shall see to it."

It was all so easily accomplished in that enclosed and distant place in which there were no points of reference to my commonplace world.

I went riding with Isabella in the afternoon. Elizabeth was more and more reluctant to leave her room, and while it was a little awkward, it was only a little. It meant, to me, that Isabella was slipping naturally into the role of companion—almost constant companion—without interference and by virtue of Elizabeth's own default. I was able to say to Hugh, when he asked me about Elizabeth's virtual disappearance, that this was how she behaved at home. "Her behavior when we arrived here was not usual. She hoped to interest you in her again. Now she probably wants to punish you as much as she tries to punish me." I didn't know how true that would prove to be or how costly it was going to be for Hugh and Isabella and for me.

So I said to Isabella as I would to a beloved wife of long standing, "Let's ride over to Crookhaven," and we did. We wrapped up well, saddled side by side, said very little, were filled with a glowing contentment because we were "we" and not separate (whoever else might suspect this—the Andalusian woman cunningly looking in this strange country for a safe hand, even an uncle's hand on her daughter's life?—or might not be able to imagine it, we knew it) and we rode out knee to knee to the west.

Crookhaven is the last port in Ireland. It is a very small place, a cluster of cottages at the throat of a long deep harbor created by Streek Head, the thick finger of land that turns its back on the harsh Atlantic gales and runs east for over a mile. The result is the harbor, deep and safe, a quarter of a mile wide, and once, before the famine, a busy place. Now there are safe moorings, a quay of great stone blocks from the quarry on the north shore and a few stone cottages and a tiny church. Yet there is no road to it—only the track that runs from Schull. In the last century fishing fleets worked from this harbor after pilchard and mackerel, shipping from the West Indies waited here for favorable winds, and the ships that carried American mail left it here to be forwarded in other ships to other ports, or carried by riders to Skibbereen. They still left the mail from America here. There was an American ship in the harbor. But fish or quarried stone, they left here by sea.

We sat on the ridge above Rock Island and looked over the coast-guard station to Streek Head at the mouth of the long natural harbor.

"There's a hole in Streek Head," Isabella said.

"There's a what?"

"A great long hole like a tunnel. You see the teeth of the rocks running out from the Head? They're called the Black Horsemen. Straight in from them, there is this natural tunnel of rock and water, right through the Head. Tonight the two young men up Knocknamaddree will leave Toormore Bay in a small fishing boat. It will wait in that hole till that American ship is leaving Crookhaven, then it will go out under cover of the Head. The Americans will throw ropes across the fishing boat, the two men will hold them and jump into the sea and be fished out of the water, very cold but quite safe. Come away from here, Carrach."

"Fishers of men," I said.

"What?"

"Fishers of men."

"Yes." But she was not amused. "Everything goes out from here," she said, "but nothing comes in. We send a lot of young men out. A few farming fishermen are willing to take them out to meet American sailing ships—but not many. It's too dangerous. The young men never come back. Do you think some day everybody will leave Ireland?"

"Down here? All but the old."

"The copper mine over on the Head ia almost worked out. The quarry on the north shore is dying. I love this place, but I want to leave it. Even the seaweed smells like death."

"Is that why you want to come with me?"

"I love you."

"You're too young. I'm too old."

"If you believed that, you wouldn't take me."

Twice that afternoon we saw searching soldiers on the hills, and once we saw policemen at a cottage on the north side of the peninsula. It was dark when we got back to the house. Hugh was on Knocknamaddree. He brought the two young men down the mountain, fed them a hot meal in the kitchen, gave each of them a bottle of whiskey and money, and led them to the shore. He was in a surly mood and would not talk. We were not allowed to go.

"There are soldiers and police everywhere," Isabella told him when he came back.

"Tell me something I don't already know," he said, and after dinner went to his room.

I heard him and saw him again that night. His mood now was ugly, as if something over which he had no control was out of order.

"What is it?" I asked Isabella.

"When he's like this," she said, "we keep out of the way and don't ask. Asking makes him worse. If he needs me, he'll tell me and I'll tell you."

He did not come from his room to confide in her.

That was the night I started keeping the Book. There is a shop at 51 Grafton Street, Sibley and Company, Booksellers and Depot for Fountain and Stylographic Pens. I find it difficult to pass these shops, and while we were in Dublin, Isabella, Emily, and I browsed in Sibley's. I bought one of those heavily bound notebooks with the clasp and lock on them, intending to give it to Isabella. I hadn't done so. Now I began to write in it. I had no idea then that in the years to come I would fill many of these books and keep them in an old iron safe in the library at Barn House.

I knew when I began to write that I would go on writing in books like this one. My son, Alasdar, was much in my mind that night. Elizabeth ignored him almost entirely. She ignored all the children. I suppose she associated them with suffering in labor and my unwelcome attentions in bed. There was in my head when I began to write a vague assumption about Isabella and my motherless children. I was scheming half-consciously, I think. We'll have to think hard about how it's to be done, Isabella said, and at the back of my mind the solution lay ready to emerge. Isabella loved the children, they loved her. She was eleven years older than Alasdar—old enough to be sister and nurse and substitute mother. She would grow by habit and propinquity into her mother role and into the proper place for the mother of my children: into my bed.

But one day Alasdar would have to know about such things. There must be explanations. That is how I began writing the Book.

"Alasdar, Alasdar, Alasdar," I began. I found it so much easier to open my heart as the words crossed the page and not my lips. I knew then I would fill these books for the rest

of my life and leave them to my son. "I want you to understand about your cousin, Isabella," I wrote, "and to know the
extent and meaning of my love for you and my love for her.
You know, even now, how hard it is for me to speak what
lies deepest in my heart. In this book and if I live many other
books like it, I shall talk to you and to Isabella about each of
you and both of you. This, if you like, is my Confession: To
you and Isabella and, though I did not think of Him first, to
God.

"Isabella was sixteen when she came first to visit us. You
loved her then. I am sure you love her now as you read my
words . . ."

So it went on, and I wrote far into the night.

When I was done with writing I was still wide-awake with
no need for or taste for sleep. I put out my lamp and sat by
the window, watching the clear night sky, the moon on the
water of Toormore Bay, and thinking of the two young men
cheating the hangmen somewhere out to sea. They might now
be safe in the tunnel under Streek Head, but it was a dangerously clear night. They could not sail straight up the shore on
a night like this. They must go far out to sea in a great arc
and come in toward the Head, covered from the eye of the
lighthouse on Rock Island and difficult to see from the watch-
towers on the northern heights of Crookhaven. On a night
like this, that meant coming in without sail, rowing the heavy
fishing boat from several miles out. Was it any wonder so few
fishermen or fishing farmers would take the risk?

I had asked Isabella earlier in the day, "Why do they risk
it?"

"For a pound each for each man they take," she said.
"Tonight there'll be two men to take, and two men to take
them. Two pounds each for the fishermen. If they're caught,
a year at least in jail, and no money for their wives and children. Sometimes in some places, they inform for extra
money, but not here, and certainly not tonight. Every man
here has old Harrington on his mind, his cabin burned and
himself dying in the poorhouse. Townsend probably ate a fine
warm dinner tonight and washed it down with good port.
That stiffens their spines."

I saw the riders coming from the shore—coming from the
track above the shore, riding hard up the hill to the house.
Two horsemen.

Something was going wrong or had gone wrong, and I was
afraid for my brother and without thought ready to help or

defend him. I ran along the corridor toward his room. But I had to pass the stairwell, and the lamps were lit in the hall. Somebody was up. There was no light under Hugh's bedroom door. I hurried to Isabella's room and opened the door. She was sound asleep.

Go down? Would he want me down? The horses were in the yard, the kitchen door slammed, and booted feet clattered. Hugh's voice was raised, angry and accusing. I stood back from the top of the stairs in the darkness of the unlit landing, and Hugh came from the kitchen across the hall toward the sitting room, followed by two men. One was O'Keeffe, grim-faced. The other man I had never seen before.

Hugh was yelling again, "You're a stupid bastard, Millen, and I want you out of here in five minutes and your ship out to sea as soon as you get back on board. You're taking that ship back to Sligo Bay."

The man who must be Millen said only, "Shit to that." He had an American voice. "I unload here or I go to Waterford."

I could not follow the storm, but I could feel the rage.

"Neither, neither, neither," Hugh yelled close to the sitting-room door. "The place is hiving with soldiers and police, and you bring the stuff in here . . ." But he was moving about, pacing with rage I couldn't doubt, and only snatches came to me.

". . . O'Sullivan Burke was the only Fenian above ground in Sligo . . ."

". . . hunted, you goddamned fool . . . soldiers . . . Fenians crawling in ditches for the love of God . . ."

"I'll deliver only to an active command . . ."

"There isn't one." It was an enraged bellow. "They've been trying it your way and it doesn't work here . . . We're back to scratch, you stupid fool . . ."

"Standing off Schull . . ."

"This isn't America and it isn't your Civil War . . ."

"Training, the right training . . ."

"Get the stuff to hell away from here . . ."

And once, O'Keeffe, "You godforsaken know-all bastard, you'll have the rest of us in jail or on the gallows . . ."

And after much more that must have come from the far end of the room and was incomprehensible, three men charging back across the hall to the kitchen. Millen in the lead this time yelling, "I'm taking it to Waterford, and if you don't like that, stuff it up your . . ." The kitchen door slammed behind Hugh.

Something touched my arm, and I spun. It was Isabella in a nightgown as wide and full and heavy as the one Elizabeth wore on the night of her tormented deflowering.

"That was Millen," she said.

"Who is he?"

"He's an American Civil War soldier. Papa hates him. He hates Papa. They disagree about everything. Millen thinks he has nothing to learn about Ireland."

"They were fighting about a ship. I heard Sligo Bay. What's it all about?"

"An arms shipment. The American *Jacknell Packet* was expected in Sligo Bay. What's Millen doing here?"

"I think Hugh wants to know that too. Go and put your clothes on."

The storm was still raging in the kitchen but there was nothing to be learned from it. I was trembling. This was a place of rage, a land of rage, men enraged, allies and coconspirators enraged. Isabella had to be gone from it. Tomorrow the magistrate had to be seen, the business about the bailiff settled, and the next day our journey home begun. She must and I must leave this place of rage. And, it came to me unwillingly, Elizabeth also. There was no help for that.

They were still yelling in the kitchen when we went down to the sitting room to wait for Hugh. Then the back door slammed. The kitchen door slammed, Hugh was in the hall, in the sitting room.

"I could do without both of you," he said, and the horses pounded around the house.

"But you've got us," I said. "What's the danger to the house?"

"Demolition for the house and jail for the lot of us, including you. Ten years, twenty years, life. Five thousand breechloading and repeating rifles, one and a half million rounds of ammunition and three cannon, standing off Schull in the *Jacknell Packet* renamed at sea *Erin's Hope*, with a fine American flourish and a lunatic disregard for everybody's safety."

He poured whiskey into a glass and poured the harsh Irish fluid down his throat, filled the glass again and poured again. "I should have killed him," he screamed, and poured and drank again.

His body couldn't take his rage and the whiskey he was

pouring into himself. "That's enough, Hugh," I said, and took the bottle.

"Enough what? What do you know about it, you Protestant bookkeeper?" he said, and snatched the bottle from my hand. "They'll not even get back to Schull. It's that sort of night." He was slipping quickly into drunkenness. That was what he wanted, and he poured again unsurely.

"Maybe that's what you need. More cautious bookkeepers and fewer blustering heroes," I said.

Hugh sat heavily down, shaking his head. "Maybe you're right," he said. "Maybe Mr. Isaac Butt is right. Maybe. Maybe we can only win in parliament. Maybe, maybe, maybe. Ireland is the land of maybe. Maybe this, maybe that, maybe today, maybe tomorrow. Maybe if we had one sane leader big enough, strong enough, honest enough . . . what does the bookkeeper say to that?"

I said nothing.

"Nothing?" he said. "You know, Carrach," and he brandished the bottle at me, "you know enough now to hang me. Don't you? What is your Unionist soul telling you to do?"

"What I did to you once when you were fourteen—hit you in the face."

He wagged his head and looked thoughtfully at the floor. "Yes, you did that, didn't you? But I got the best of it, Carrach. I bequeathed you Lizzy McCarthy, than which revenge nothing could be harsher, and for that I will be ashamed till the day I die." He was close to tears, maudlin. He drained his glass again and filled it again.

"No more, Hugh. You'll kill yourself," I protested.

"You will not believe me, Carrach," he said sadly, "but sometimes I want to. Do you believe that?"

"Yes, I believe it."

"Isn't it a very sad thing, brother, that people like me who were too good to stay at home, too clever to stay at home and went out and strutted about in the world, always have times when they long to be at home and wish they'd never left home?"

"I believe that too."

"Careful, careful Carrach," he said.

"Papa," Isabella said, and went to him and held his hand to her breast. "Papa, don't do this. I love you. Don't be like this."

He put his arm around her. "I know you do, I know you do. And that's a miracle." His speech was not clear.

"Go to bed, Papa," Isabella said, and then I thought I knew why she loved me. Under all the flaming *machismo* of her father's life, she could see the waste, the empty desolation of it. The sham. Was that why she came to Barn House against his wishes? To see if, in her family inheritance, there was more than the pseudo-cavalier? Something solid? Survival?

Hugh didn't speak. He rose uncertainly to his feet and wove his way to the door, carrying the bottle. We came close behind him as he hung with one hand to the balustrade and started to climb. Twice we had to catch and hold him. I took the bottle from his hand, and he did not protest. He began to sing, a muttering kind of sound. The tune, more or less, was "God Save the Queen."

> God save me, great John Bull
> Long keep my pocket full.
> God save me, great John Bull.
>
> Ever victorious,
> Haughty, vainglorious,
> Snobbish, censorious,
> God save me, great John Bull . . .

It trailed away at his bedroom door. The lamp was lit. His wife was waiting. She took him in her arms and laid him on the bed. "I will take care of him," she said. "Go to bed."

Isabella was close to tears. The great man, her father, the Soldier of Fortune, the captain of his fate, needed a woman to look after him. She followed me to my room. "Let me stay with you," she said.

"No. That would be unwise." But I stirred up the warm ashes of my bedroom fire and put more turf on it. I lay down on my bed, fully dressed. "Go to bed, Isabella," I said, my eyes closed. "You need sleep."

"Yes," she said, and lay beside me. "Keep me, Carrach," she said. "Keep me near you. How I need you."

"Yes, yes." Her head was in the crook of my arm. All my energies were drained, and I was drowning in a deep sorrow. We must have slept in seconds.

In the morning when I woke she was not there, but there was fresh turf on the fire. She had taken care of me.

❧ *Eleven* ❧

Sometimes, when there is a winter storm on the Lough at Carrig, the sea breaks over the battery wall and hammers the houses on the other side of the Scotch Quarter. Often, walking down that street, I have been drenched by the spent fury of the breakers.

The commonplace world struck me like that icy water when we reached Cork: there were crowds of people in the muddy streets, people were going about their business, walking, talking, looking in shop windows, riding in horse-drawn trams, dodging across streets in the traffic; going home. Everything was ordinary, known, familiar. In Dublin, things were not different.

"Come and visit us, Emily, please," I pleaded with her. "I have difficult things to work out at home. Come and help me."

"No." But she waved from the platform till we were out of sight.

Belfast was dirtier than Cork and Dublin, but not different. By the time we reached Barn House, the world I had been to was hard to recall in detail; it was foreign, distant, scarcely to be believed. Isabella was the only tangible evidence that it existed, and she was subdued till she saw the children. After that she was herself. That was the iciest shower of all. She was one of them: not the hard-riding independent young woman of her own alien ground, but of the children. Had I brought home a child for my bed? Illusions or dreams were harshly stripped away.

137

One thing I remembered with peculiar clarity: our visit to the magistrate to expedite the case of the bailiff and Isabella's horse. We went, my brother Hugh, Isabella, and myself, to his house at Ballydehob. It was a fine house above the sea. The Protestant landlords have all the best sites.

He is a small man and a small landlord. He sat in his chair, not unlike a child with an old bespectacled face, and set about first to determine that we were not intimates of the landlord Townsend who evicted old Harrington. That wasn't reassuring. The question, surely, was not who one's intimates were but whether the bailiff jumped into Isabella's horse or was ridden down with malice. There was no doubt about the latter, but the man did jump the wrong way. We were, Hugh said, groping for good references, intimates of the White family, the Earls of Bantry. The magistrate laughed at this with a heartiness that shook not only his little body but the big chair in which it was half-concealed. "Ah," he said when he had breath to say it, "old Pilchard White? Decent fool. He's not fond of evictions. He evicts only proven Fenians," and Hugh laughed heartily at that. I think the magistrate took this for Hugh's approval and called for drinks and drank heavily and heartily for the rest of our visit with him. (It is said that he often appears on the bench in a state of great jollity and universal affection and is therefore much beloved by the unfortunate.)

"This bailiff was acting for Townsend, was he?" he asked at last, and slyly.

"Yes."

"And you, young woman, ran your horse at him?"

"Oh, no, no, indeed not, sir," Isabella said humbly. "He jumped at my horse."

"Townsend is a scoundrel," he said waspishly. "Did you know that in the famine one of his relatives, a Church of Ireland clergyman, died of typhoid from caring for the sick and dying?"

"I did not, sir," Hugh said respectfully.

"Ah, but he also took eight thousand pounds a year in rents from his poverty-stricken tenants—think of it, a man of God!—and did not reduce their rents. That is the moral philosophy of the Townsends. A life is only a life, but a rent is always an obligation."

"A great pity," Hugh said, meaning nothing.

"Young woman."

"Sir."

"Next time, ride a little harder. Have a solicitor represent you at the Petty Sessions. The case will be dismissed. Accident. No question. Nooo question. Now, there's more port. Let's talk of pleasant things." He did not love justice, but he hated Townsend. One way or another, righteousness is served.

We left the next day and came at last to Barn House. That other place was another world, the sort you leave behind on waking.

Elizabeth said when we were alone at home, "So your lady Emily would not come? She sampled your bed and came to my conclusion, did she?" I chose now not to deny it. If her eyes were on Emily, her mind would not be on Isabella. She summoned the children dutifully to kiss her cheek and went at once to her retreat. The world was normal.

There was work waiting to be done. Some of it I could have done without. Coming out of Hugh's enclosed world was like the shock of moving suddenly from a secret culture to an open one. One's emergence led to a reawakening. The contents of the sealed envelopes on my library desk were the larger, fiercer, icier breakers that threatened to knock me off my feet.

My senior clerk at the mill, William Buchanan, reported:

Pat Haggan and Boysie Aherne [presumably two of my workers, for I did not know their names individually], assisted by a Belfast man by the name of Patrick McGladdery, are trying to organize a Workers' Combination Society or Trade Union at the mill. Most of the workers are cautious. They are waiting to see what you will do about Haggan and Aherne. I am informed that about one-third of our total number is openly willing to join the Society. Almost all of those willing are Catholics.

I found this news distressing. The scutch mill was everywhere else in Ulster a dangerous place: I had made ours safe. Pouce (an accumulation of pus in the chest and throat), bronchitis, and other chest complaints were common in the textile industry. They were caused by dust, heat, and the moisture necessary for the successful operation of the mills, and by poor ventilation. I had devised and installed a ventilation system of pumped fresh air and suction fans that greatly improved conditions and reduced sickness.

My father built Barn School for the children of our workers, and had financed it until it was taken over by the new National School system. I allowed no half-time children to work in the mill for more than two days a week, and none under twelve years of age. The school system kept them till they were fourteen, but not on a compulsory basis. Other employers used half-timers (half-time in school, half-time in the mill) from their eighth year. I would not. I had done all I could in this regard. I employed at the mill a woman part-skilled at nursing, and I laid aside in what we called the Sick Fund a sum each year to help men or women who were prevented from doing a day's work by illness for which the mill might be to blame.

I am a good employer. I paid wages higher than the Belfast level and kept a week's working hours to an economic minimum. In Lisburn, hacklers, scutchers, and spinners worked sixty hours a week; in my mill, fifty-four. I was already in trouble with my manufacturing customers—and ahead of my time—because of their fear that I would pass all my additional costs to them. I did not.

What I read in Buchanan's report made me unhappy, especially since this outsider from Belfast was taking a hand in upsetting my workers. The thing had to be attended to quickly. But not at once. I took the reports to my room to read while I rested a little. Before I could do anything else, and while I was reading a report that William Johnston of Ballykilbeg House—the founder of the Orange Society—was out of jail and planning a great meeting of Orangemen in Belfast, another annoyance came to me.

The housekeeper put Isabella in a well-situated, large, and comfortable guest room. Now the unhappy woman came to me with an air of lamentation.

"Miss Isabella," she said, "has refused the room."

"She wants another room? Well, put her somewhere else."

"She wants in there." She nudged her head at the door from my room into the bedroom next door. I thought her eyebrows would be lost in her hair.

That was a different and not a reassuring matter. I said, as casually as I could, "I'll see her. Don't worry about it. She's very tired."

I went to see her. She was lying facedown on the bed. All she wore, and that was evident, was a thin silk gown. It lay on her body like a skin. I sat down on the bed.

"You're tired."

"Very." She turned on her back. That made her look even

more naked and my condition even more disturbed. "I've been so anxious to get here, I was pushing the trains all day." She was happy. "We're home now," she said contentedly and took my hand. "I love you so much, Carrach."

"I love you very dearly."

But tonight she looked sixteen. With the children swarming over her, rolling with her on the floor, she had looked and sounded even younger.

"We'll have to be very careful," I said, preparing the way.

"Of course."

"I'm going to be very busy and preoccupied with business for a while now."

"I know." She held my hand to her cheek. "But not at night?"

"We'll have every evening together."

"And every night?"

"Not yet. That's what we'll have to be careful about. You understand?"

"I don't want to. But I do understand."

"At first, we'll be very ordinary about everything. I'll attend to business, you mother the children. Settle in. Be at home, yes? We're together, Isabella. Take over the children. Be skillful about it. Establish your authority over them so thoroughly that nurse, governess, and the servants know better than to challenge it. We'll slip into everything slowly and easily. In a natural way . . ."

"I will not be your mistress, Carrach." That startled me. I had never thought of her as a mistress; only as my consuming love. "I'll be your wife. To all intents and purposes, that is," she added, grinning at me. "I feel I'm your wife."

"That's how I think of it. But gradually, carefully, not to cause . . ." I was about to say "scandal," but I think she would have laughed at that. I said, "Pain. We mustn't cause ourselves or others pain."

"Oh, no. Of course not."

"We'll talk more about it. A lot more. You like your room?"

"I want to sleep near you. In the room next to you."

"It wouldn't be gradual or careful, would it?"

"You want me to stay here?"

"For a while."

"Whatever you want I shall do. Whatever you want, when you want."

It was less difficult than I had expected. I kissed her and

went back to my room. I could think only of how young she seemed, how uncertain her emotion might be, how terrible it would be for me, but much more terrible for her if after six months in my bed—a night, a week, a month in my bed—she wearied of me and was, before she was seventeen, what men called "damaged goods." The thought frightened me. Soon she would have to face that, think about it, take it into account. She could change her mind. Then what?

I was wrong. But that is miserable hindsight with much grief to salt it. Wisdom, or what sometimes passes for wisdom, and looks exactly like it, is often folly. Statesmen know it, mere politicians know it, practiced lovers know it. I did not know it. So I attacked my work, thinking myself wise, honorable, and protective. I was honorable and protective, but I misread Isabella, and that was folly. And my folly became more deeply rooted as the weeks went by, for Isabella was apparently happy and patient and at home. Very much at home. So much at home that I did not see her waiting to erupt. I was aware of the dangers of her youth, and stupidly unaware of its impatience and intolerance. She mothered the children and loved me and loved them, and I grew complacent, waiting for her to grow into my bed.

A month went by during which there was no sign of any Workers' Combination Society activity, and I supposed it to have been a move made in my absence and suspended on my return.

Elizabeth was now spending two or three days a week at Court House, a development I welcomed but in which I took no interest; nor had I any curiosity about the reason or reasons for it. During that month she did approach me for sums of money beyond, but not much beyond, my obligations under the marriage contract, and since she was out of my way and this was probably part of the price of keeping her out of it, I made the money available to her.

It was with Isabella and the children that my happiness lay, and it was intense. Unquestionably, we were a family, a very young mother, three children too old for her to have borne, and a middle-aged husband. We rode together—under Isabella's instruction, Alasdar was becoming a horseman of extraordinary skill and courage—and spent weekends without servants at Garden House, which was an error of judgment on my part. Isabella was patient but persistent on each of those weekends. "Why not here, Carrach?" she said, and I wanted to and would not. "I'm a woman, not a child, Carrach," she said, and I was not warned.

One morning while Isabella and I breakfasted together, a clerk came from the mill with a note from Buchanan. It said only, "During the night the mill was entered and the belts cut on three spinning machines. The watchman saw and heard nothing. My conclusion is that the damage was done by someone familiar with the mill."

The thing enraged me. Isabella got a hasty peck and I left for the mill. But rage is a poor counselor. I decided to walk. It gave me time to think and to regain my composure. I went through the courtyard into the gardens, through the gate in the garden wall into the yard of the home farm. Our potting sheds were built against the wall on the farm side, and I stopped there to have a word with Hodges, the head gardener, who was at work with his son in the sheds. It had been my intention to tell him to cut some flowers from the conservatory for Isabella.

The first thing he said put that out of my head. "Mornin, sir. I hear tell there's wreckers up there," and he nudged his head toward the mill.

"So I hear." It was enough. I walked across the farmyard and the field beyond and came to the mill by the back gate. My anger was cold by the time I reached my office; it was anger now, not rage. I knew how I intended to deal with the business. During the walk, I had thought about Haggan and Aherne and Workers' Combinations, as they were sometimes called; or Societies, or Unions. I was certain they were the source of the trouble now. They were making belated progress in Ulster. Their progress in England was much greater. Around the turn of the century they were at first illegal. Their members met in taverns, and for a time their meetings were largely fraternal. As they made a little progress they became much more purposeful and in spite of arrests, fines, imprisonments, and dismissals, there were men strong enough to face all these risks and persevere. Where Unions or Societies were successfully formed and in time made legal, their members were levied one and a half pence a week for the support of sick members. It was this that persuaded me to establish the Sick Fund for employees who needed it. I was not unsympathetic to trade unions. I must confess that much of my sympathy derived from my resentment of the Enniskillens and the Garretts and was the real source of my belief that if Catholic and Protestant working men combined to improve their condition, they might at the same time contrive with sound judgment and self-interest to save Ulster from the angry and illiterate peasantry of the South. And the facts of life are facts: I thought much during that walk about the names of the three men with whom I would no doubt have to deal in this matter of the Union: McGladdery, Aherne, and Haggan. They were all Catholic names. That is Ulster. Some Orangemen said—and believed—they could tell us papists by the color of our eyes; but we all know one another's religion from our names. My senior clerk Buchanan is a Protestant. His name declared it. I sent for Haggan and Aherne.

They came unwillingly. They came, I am quite certain, to "get their time," as they called dismissal. They had families. Haggan had a son who was a half-timer in the mill. I had already been informed that Haggan did not like the fact that his son was a half-timer. He wanted the boy to get a better education and "be something." But what? What could a working man's son become? A clerk with a clean collar, more standing and less pay than his collarless father? A clerk in Belfast earned £60 a year. Haggan earned £80. They came in, anxious and, in Aherne's case, surly. I was civil.

"Buchanan," I said, "have one of your clerks bring another chair. Sit down, gentlemen."

Their faces lightened a little. The cashier in an outer office gave men their time. Men who came to get it did not find themselves invited to sit down in their employer's room.

Haggan was a small plump man, normally of a genial disposition, Buchanan told me. He was known as a nondrinker who spent his Sunday afternoons walking with his family. Aherne was tall, thin-lipped, and intense. He was not a disagreeable man but, Buchanan said, was known to be short-tempered and apt to defend himself before he was attacked. Both of them had families to feed and shelter. I was not unsympathetic to their concerns.

Haggan sat on the edge of his chair twisting his cloth cap in nervous hands. Aherne sat back, stiffly upright. His cap was stuffed into his jacket pocket, perhaps to keep it away from his hands. Even so, his hands spoke. With the nails of one hand he picked at the nails of the other as they lay in his lap, simulating composure he did not feel. I felt sorry for Haggan. His mind, I had no doubt, was on his family. I had no sympathy for Aherne. His mind, his eyes told me, was on me.

"So you are trying to organize a Workers' Combination?" I said.

Haggan nodded and swallowed, looking condemned.

Aherne said, "It's legal."

"Yes, it's legal," I said, and gave them a long time to think. "But wrecking machinery is not."

"Mr. MacDonnell," Haggan said pathetically, "I had nothin to do w'that. I'm not for that sorta thing, honest to God, sir."

Aherne glanced at him resentfully. "It wasn't us," he said.

"Who did it?"

"We don't know," Aherne said aggressively.

"That is all I wanted to ask you," I said to them. "I shall be speaking to all the workers in the yard in half an hour. Be there. If after you hear what I have to say, you should find you know more than you've admitted, come and see me afterward. Very soon afterward. That is all."

Haggan stood, leaning over my desk. "Afore God, sir. Ah don't know. If Ah knowed anythin Ah'd tell ye now."

"I believe you, Mr. Haggan," I said. "Aherne."

"Aye?"

"There are four women on each of those three machines. That means twelve women who make no money today, maybe also tomorrow, till new belts are installed. Somebody did them a poor service."

"Ye don't need to tell me that. Ah know it. Ah work here."

They were at the door. "There's one more thing," I said, and they waited. "You're Catholics."

"Aye."

"Think about that. Two-thirds of your fellow workers are not. My information is that almost all those willing to join your Union are also Catholic. Think hard about that. I'm sure both of you want to feel safe as you go about your work. If you have any sense at all, you can see forward from there."

Perhaps they could. Haggan could. I had doubts about the other one. In other circumstances I would have dismissed him for his insolence. In these circumstances he was more useful to me where he was and as he was.

In the half hour that followed, I did no work. Most of the time I thought about Haggan. We had a lot in common. We were Catholic. I wanted my son to take a degree at Trinity. He could not take his degree there because he was Catholic.

Haggan wanted schooling for his child, schooling that would lift him out of his class and his condition. There was no escape for either of them. They were excluded by their class; beyond the school the boy went to, there was nothing Haggan could pay for on his wages. A woman spinner earned 7*s.* 6*d.* a week. Haggan, a skilled workman, earned thirty shillings. But even if he could have saved enough to send his son to a good private school that took him beyond what the little Barn School offered him, his class, his accent, his dress, would have excluded him: the sons of those who could speak well, dress well, and had an acceptable social presence would have made his life unendurable. His kind would never be presidents of anything except, perhaps, Workers' Combinations: they had to go to America to become Andrew Jacksons, James Knox Polks, James Buchanans, or Andrew Johnsons—and even then only if they were Protestants. My beloved Ulster was a ghetto with a hundred subghettos. I, a rich man, a landlord and employer of labor, would vote Unionist, give money to the Unionist cause—but I could not stand for parliament as a Unionist in the coming election. I too had my ghetto, like any Jew in Europe or any workman in my own society.

But this was not the issue now. Someone entered my mill and damaged machinery. That was the issue. I would find the person or persons who did it. My workers would help me. I knew how to make them help me.

I stood on a box in the mill yard. Their faces meant nothing to me. A few were half-familiar but had no names. Most were strange. It was cold. The women had their heavy black shawls about their shoulders and covering their heads. The men were at the front, the women behind them.

Without preamble, I said what I had to say. It was simple and brief. "Last night someone entered the mill and cut the belts on three machines. Because of that, twelve of you have no work. I am informed that it could only have been done by someone familiar with the mill. There is no sign that anyone broke in, so someone who works here had access. Therefore, some of you may have information that will be useful to me in bringing this person or persons to justice. If any among you do know anything, I shall wait until ten o'clock tomorrow morning. If no information is volunteered by that time, I shall take other steps. Thank you, that is all."

I descended from my box and walked away. I did not expect any information to be volunteered in time. I was right about that.

At ten minutes past ten next morning, notices were posted in every part of the mill and folded into the little tins in which the workers received their pay. The notices said: "The mill will close at six o'clock today for an indefinite period. Hands will be recalled when work resumes."

It was a prosperous time. Work was plentiful. But there was only one mill in Carrig. Only the stupidest would misread the closing. I did not expect to be kept waiting.

But Haggan was the only one to come.

"Mr. MacDonnell," he said with more pride and dignity than he had shown the day before, "thons an awfa cruel thing t'do."

"What is?"

"Closin the mill. Aye." He was not twisting his cap. "Ah don't know who done this wreckin, sir. If Ah knowed Ah'd tell ye. But maybe nobody knows and yer taken the bread outa their mouths fer not knowin."

"Somebody knows, Haggan."

"Oh, aye. The one that done it knows. Yer not expectin him to come an tell ye, are ye?"

"Hardly. But somebody will."

"An if nobody does, how long d'we go w'out wages?"

"I should think somebody else will think of that too, Haggan—and come forward with the information."

He had something else to say and was in two minds about saying it. He turned to leave, turned back and said, "Sir, there's them that's fer goin off t'America, seein there's nothin much for them in their own country. I'm thinkin there'll be a lot more. This is an awful place to get a dacent chance for yer wains." He hesitated a moment and said, "Yer a good man, Mr. MacDonnell, I'm not saying anythin different. But Ah'll tell ye this, sir. Ma wee boy needs a new suit a cloes. Ah had the money saved up for it. Ah'll have t'use it now to keep the house goin, and that's a right cruel thing."

It was. I agree. Haggan didn't wait to hear my agreement or my justification.

"Have the gates locked, Buchanan," I said to my senior clerk. "Only the maintenance men are to get in." I went home, walking, through the home farm yard and the garden. Isabella and Alasdar were sauntering among the vegetables, hand in hand, and they ran to meet me. Alasdar climbed on my back and Isabella took my hand. After the sort of day I'd

had, it was homecoming, comfortable, a season of contentment. We walked into the courtyard, and without being
aware that she was on my mind, I looked up at the windows
of Elizabeth's west-wing apartment. She was there, watching.
How much time did she spend watching by her windows?

"Papa," Alasdar announced happily, his head forward
beside mine, "I'm going to marry Isabella."

"Immediately?"

"No. Isabella says I must first go to school."

"That's very sensible." It was something to smile about, not
think about; little boys, I understand, are always anxious
to marry their aunts, cousins, teachers, even their mothers. Isabella at this moment looked like a young mother, not a
young girl, and I longed to take her to my room. Elizabeth
was still there in a corner of my mind, but like a shadow, not
real, not related in any way that was tangible to the content
of our lives. I could not think of her as my wife; there was
no reality in that. She was there, lurking, an intruder in a
way, but one with some vague claim to her intrusion. I would
at that moment have happily locked her in her retreat.

Isabella squeezed my hand hard. "When, Carrach?" she
said.

"Not long," I said, believing it at the time.

"What's not long, Papa?" Alasdar said, and reminded me
at once that should he some morning wander from the children's quarters to mine (as he often did) and find Isabella in
my bed, he would think it perfectly natural—and with perfect
naturalness would mention it to someone else. Most likely to
the governess. She was a discreet spinster and loyal, but I
have not found that discretion or loyalty can outweigh the
triumph of being privy to the best "secret" of the year: "The
young niece comes to his bed." Very soon—that evening—every Orange Lodge in the countryside would clang with the
new revelation. "Stuffy MacDonnell stuffs young girls." Every
young girl employed in the house would be asked by her fellow servants and her friends: "Has Old Stuffy tried to stuff
you yet?"

"Dinner," I said to Alasdar's question, and he was satisfied
with that. It wasn't interesting.

Dinner was a happy meal. I explained to Isabella all that
was going on and what steps I was taking to kill at the outset
any possible trouble with workers who might suppose trouble
could benefit them. I felt almost sodden with domesticity. I
could never risk talking like this to Elizabeth. She always

tried to make my decisions and was always stupid about them.

"Do you think it's fair to put them all out of work like that, Carrach?" Isabella said.

It leaped to my mind at once that when in an earlier time Elizabeth had made comments of that order, my resentment roared. Isabella's question was to me no more than a caring question. But no less. I was even prepared to consider it, discuss it, when Patton returned to the dining room.

"Sir," he said, "Cassie Hyndman and her girl, Aggie, are here to see you. Cassie says it's very important. They're waiting in the hall."

"Put them in the drawing room."

"The drawing room, sir?" His voice said he had not heard me properly. They were not drawing-room people.

"The drawing room."

Every conceivable cause of alarm raced through me. Cassie had Agnes with her? Why? But Cassie was stable. Trustworthy. I reassured myself and at once destroyed my assurance. What day was it? Friday. I was to be at Garden House on Fridays, when Cassie would say, "Everythin off, sir?" No, no, no, no. It could have nothing to do with that. That was a stupid fear.

"What is it, Carrach?"

"Oh." I fumbled for something to cover whatever concern I might already have revealed. "Cassie was Mother's favorite servant. Her name made me think of Mother." And, to sweeten my own thought, I made a foolish mistake. "If she were alive now, she would look at us, sitting here together, and she'd say, 'Come live with me at Garden House and do what will make you happy.'"

"Why don't we?"

I knew at once it was a mistake to say that. "Come and meet Cassie Hyndman and her daughter. I want you with me." Nothing dangerous could even be approached before a witness like Isabella.

I rang for Patton and told him to take them to the library. I always felt safer in the library.

Meeting in your own house your own daughter, born of a devoted servant, is an unsettling experience.

Agnes Hyndman was a handsome girl; handsome in an alarming way. She looked very like Mother now. Nobody would think of it? Hyndman wouldn't think of it? Or was that the occasion of this visit? They were dressed in their best. We were barely into the library when Cassie spoke, justifying her presumptions.

"Aggie has somethin t'tell you, sir," she said quickly.

Agnes did not look pleased. Whatever she had to tell me, she was not here willingly.

Whatever it was, it could wait for a moment. "This is my niece, Isabella," I said. "You met my brother's daughter one day when we were riding through the village?" What else could I have said? This, Isabella, is my daughter Agnes, who is your own age?

Cassie said, "I'm very pleased to meet you again, Miss Isabella," in her best voice.

How short a time it was since I was naked on her naked belly. Tonight she looked old. She said, "Tell Mr. MacDonnell, Aggie."

"But first, sit down, Cassie. Agnes." It was a strange occasion; the mother of my daughter, sitting uncomfortably in my house; my daughter as uncomfortable as her mother on the edge of her chair and even more unwilling to be here. And of an age with the Isabella I wanted in my bed and who wanted to be there.

"What have you got to tell me, Agnes?"

"I don't want to," she said, head down.

"Then I will," Cassie snapped.

"You didn't see him," Agnes said sharply.

"Who didn't your mother see, Agnes?"

"The one that cut the belts." She looked guilty, as if this was an act of betrayal.

"You saw him?"

"I saw him going in." She spoke more carefully than her mother. I could hear Cassie, "Don't forget yer g's when yer speakin, Aggie." Preparing her for something better than she had had herself. For what?

"Who?"

"Wee Mick—Mickey Cafferty."

Cafferty. Another papist. Great God Almighty. What were they trying to do? "Tell me about it, Agnes."

"Well, we were over on the home farm, just about dawn, gatherin, gathering mushrooms. I was wandering a bit away from her when I saw him. He was speelin up over the top of the back gate, and I went and watched him. He . . ." She had doubts about telling me something.

"He what?"

"He had a key to the door into the spinning floors. Either he stole it or somebody give . . . gave it to him."

"I see. You didn't want to tell me, did you?"

"No."

"Will you tell me why?"

"You closed the mill." She looked straight into my face. "Do you care?"

She was indignant. "Certainly, I care. I make seven and six a week as a spinner, and I'm savin up t'git married. I'm losin wages." She forgot her careful speech and glared at me with hostility, and I could not forget she was my angry child.

"You work at the mill?"

"Aye. What's wrong w'that?"

"Isabella," I said, "will you take Agnes to the drawing room for a little while? I want to talk to your mother, Agnes."

"About what?"

"About you. Off you go."

Isabella, acting the mistress of the house, took Agnes away. I stood for a while, my hands on the mantelshelf, my back to Cassie. She did not speak, waiting for something. I knew no more of what was coming than she did.

"She," I said at last, "is a spinner in my mill. In God's name why?" I turned to face her. She would be herself, I thought, now that we were alone. But she was in my house and could not be herself. Barn House was not Garden House; not the little back room, not the master bedroom with the bare mattress and the fire going. Here in the Big House, Cassie was consciously my servant and would not allow herself to forget it.

"She can't work at anythin' else, sir," she said. "There's only the mill."

There was domestic service, goddammit, and suddenly I was angry. The alternatives open to my own child whom I had ignored for sixteen years were the spinning mill or slaveying, as those who are not servants call it. I was angry with myself. I took it out on Cassie.

"Oh, for God's sake, stop calling me sir. I'm her father. I have rights too." What that meant in the circumstances, I tried to imagine and couldn't.

"What rights?" Cassie asked me quietly without the "sir." And before I could think of anything to say, "I ast you to give me a child. It was me got you into bed. Hyndman was on the sea and I wanted a man, and when it worked out good for the two of us, I wanted a child. You fathered her, but Hyndman's her father. He has the rights, Carrach."

It was a slap in the face. My instant assumption of rights was arrogant, and it certainly stopped short of recognizing Agnes. There is more to fatherhood than flesh and blood. For sixteen years I had pretended not to see Agnes and was always aware of her. Now I wanted to help her. My pride demanded it. My own daughter working as a spinner in my own mill was too much for me. Any other man's daughter could work there. Not mine. I remembered that when I looked out over them in the mill yard, none of them had faces. They had faces now, and in future I would see their faces.

"I'll talk to her," I said.

"What about, Carrach?"

"About work. About this marriage she's planning. Surely to God I can do something?"

"She's doin it herself. She's that kind. She's part MacDonnell."

"She's the spitting image of my mother."

"Aye."

"Has anybody ever said so?" It was a frightening thought.

"Aye."

"Who?" That was even more frightening.

"Hyndman."

That reached me like a small explosion. "What did he say?"

"Nothing much. 'She looks a lot like oul Mrs. MacDonnell,' he said. That's all."

"When? When did he say that?"

"The night he came up to Garden House when I was puttin on my cloes."

The floor under my feet seemed to give way. The movement was in my head. I was so certain I had handled him well that night that I had not since then given him another thought. "What did you say to that?" I had to know exactly, clutching at calamity or reassurance.

"I said he could see more'n I could. That's all."

"What did he say to that?"

"I don't want t'tell ye, Carrach."

"*Tell me.*" I would rather face armed Fenians than dangers like this.

"He beat me. He hasn't spoke t'me since."

I was red-faced and perspiring. I was cruelly humiliated.

Maybe Cassie was mocking me? But she looked miserable. I saw her lying naked on the mattress in the master bedroom at Garden House, asking me to hurry on to her, and I could not believe she would mock me with such a terrifying story.

"What will he do, Cassie?"

"Nothin. He's not gonta tell people you could do what he couldn't—make me pregnant."

I stood silent, shaking, sweating, for a long time.

"What can I wisely do for Agnes?" I asked her weakly. Wisely do? Safely do, did I mean? Self-knowledge is a fearful scourge. What I was really feeling rather than thinking was: Why did I ever touch this woman?

"Nothing. But ast her herself."

"Does Agnes know?"

"Not now. Someday I'll tell her. She hates Hyndman."

"Do you need to tell her ever?"

"Maybe someday she'll need to know. You know yer own father, Carrach."

I could not deny it. I hauled on the bell rope and sent a girl to bring Agnes back.

"Carrach," Cassie said, "don't think wrong things. Y'give her t'me. I'll always love ye for givin me Agnes. Hyndman couldn't. I didn't just want a man, Carrach. It was you I wanted. Y'know? Don't be afeared of him, love. He'll do nothin to harm ye or shame ye. He'd have to shame himself to do it, an he won't do that." She read my fear in every inch of me, and I shamed myself. "I'm not cheeky, Carrach, but I'm going to say it. I loved ye then and I'll love ye all my life."

Isabella opened the door. "Carrach," she said gaily, "Agnes is going to America when she gets married. When we go there, I want to visit her."

I didn't know we were going, though everybody in Ireland wants to go there. But it eased the strain a little and created a diversion, though it didn't ease my frightened mind.

"When are you getting married, Agnes?" I asked her. I had a sudden and desperate need to know my daughter and to help her. Perhaps it was no more than an instinctive need to protect myself from her poor opinion when Cassie told her who I was. Even then, another protective instinct told me not to be dangerously insistent.

Isabella had fish to fry. "In three months," she said, before Agnes could speak. "She's not too young, is she, Cassie?"

"She's full grown," Cassie said, and left no doubt of her meaning.

"She's marrying a Belfast carpenter who's finishing his apprenticeship a month from now." Isabella was full of Agnes's information, all of it directed at me and my failure to deflower her promptly enough.

"If I have a ship sailing when you go, Agnes, you and your husband will sail as my guests," I said. "Will you accept that?"

"For clypin on Wee Mick?" she asked.

Isabella saved me. "I'm almost three months older than Agnes," she said, grinning at me like a challenge. At that moment she looked a great deal older.

"Agnes," I said, hoping for some small sign of approval, "the mill will open in the morning. Nobody will lose a day's pay over this."

"Except Wee Mick?" She might have found a congenial spirit in Isabella during their time in the drawing room. She had no intention of getting on well with me.

Cassie covered her discomfort and perhaps a little pain. "Well, sir. We'll be gettin away on home."

"May I come to see you, Agnes?" Isabella asked.

"Why?" With my mother's frank eyes and her direct look.

"Because I want to."

"I work from eight in the morning to six at night, and my fi-ancy walks down from Belfast on Saturday and walks back on Sunday after we have our tea." It was not a rejection. It was not an invitation. Nor was it an explanation. It was an Ulster version of an English device that infuriated Ulstermen and turned Ulster women into spitting felines: "You must come to tea," they say, and do not say when.

"It's awfa nice of ye, Miss Isabella," Cassie said, smoothing things and I suspect warding off dangerous relationships. "She has no time t'herself at all. Y'know?"

"Indeed," Isabella said with icy regality and looked like the mistress of the house.

Cassie knew what it meant. Head down, she said softly, "I'm sorry, missus," and unawares accepted the appearance Isabella intended to create.

Isabella pulled the bell rope. "Patton will show you the way," she said.

"That's all right, missus. I know the road out." Cassie raised her head. "I was a skivvy in this house when I was Aggie's age."

I felt it like a blow in the face.

"Why does her carpenter walk the twenty miles from Belfast and back, Carrach?" Isabella asked me. "Why doesn't he take the train?"

"Because he's an apprentice and he's earning two shillings and sixpence a week after nearly five years."

I could almost see his face. Or it was Haggan's? How could I know? I had looked at so few workers' faces. Only at Agnes's, and only because I saw Mother in it.

✑ Twelve ✑

West Cork was an alien and a secret place where men hid, whispered, moved at night, and made sudden, foolish, and incompetent gestures and then claimed sanctuary in the houses of those who, for the most part, deplored their methods. Hugh was right about the Catholic Irish. It was not their talent or their character to fight by day. At the first smell of their enemy's powder they ran at Ballyhurst, and their compensation was a song of glory.

> Thus handicapped on every side, what wonder that we failed,
> And none but knaves and cowards say our spirit ever quailed,
> And Ballyhurst did more that day to raise all England's fears,
> Than all the blatherskite I've heard these five and twenty years ...
>
> It makes me sick to talk to you and those who agitate*
> Oh, give us but ten thousand men with rifles up to date
> Then Saxon laws and Saxon rule may do their very worst
> To men behind the rifles like the men of Ballyhurst.

There is a pathos about Irish self-deception that has driven many Irishmen to tears and many more to drink: We failed,

* Those who seek change through argument or parliament.

but it was the fault of others; we ran away, but those who say so are cowards and knaves.

The Irish snatch themselves up out of the real world of grim and sad defeat and weave heroic fantasies for their comfort, and fantasy becomes their reality.

Ulstermen run special trains and challenge that which threatens them and grind their teeth, and if they run, it is toward their enemies.

William Johnston of Ballykilbeg House led a march of some thirty thousand men from Newtownards to Bangor for no other reason than that such marches were forbidden by the Party Processions Act, a measure designed to keep masses of demonstrators off the streets. He was sent to jail for one month, and now he was out, and special trains were running to Belfast taking men to the great meeting Johnston had called.

Mr. Gladstone, not yet even in power, was talking publicly of the disestablishment of the (Episcopal) Church of Ireland and talking privately but not secretly of concessions to the Irish. Mr. Disraeli had already given money for the papist seminary at Maynooth, and Mr. Gladstone, panting after power in the coming election, might have even more sinister plans. Do not snipe by night at those who would betray us, the Orangemen declared: Show them what they face. Do not fear them—engage them, that they might understand the papist determination to "subjugate all nations beneath the sway and tyranny of the Roman Pontiff." As I say, I was not myself and do not know of any Catholic who was privy to this universal conspiracy, but these Orangemen had no doubt of its existence and there were priests and politicians in the Catholic community whose wild talk of a "Catholic Ireland for the Catholic Irish" gave a measure of substance to Orange arguments.

In the morning I did not go to the mill. It seemed best to absent myself and let the workers wonder what had happened about the cut belts. Instead, I took Isabella and Alasdar to Belfast; Isabella that she might see how formidable were the enemies her father wanted to defeat, but Alasdar because these were the people among whom he must grow to manhood and with whom he must do business and in spite of whom he must manage to survive. Not merely to survive, but to survive with his family's interests intact. True, he was of tender years, not close to years of understanding. But I wanted on his mind, in these years, an impression of the brutal strength and the political ferocity of the men whose kind would always dominate his life.

A year ago, in 1867, five hundred people died of cholera in Belfast. It was the dirtiest and unhealthiest city in Ireland. It had more mills and more people and more sectarian violence and more industrial violence. Now, some concern was manifest over drainage, a sound water supply, the health of the people. Belfast was also Ireland's most vigorous and most prosperous city. As commerce and industry and population expanded, the need for solicitors, accountants, lawyers, doctors expanded. There were three times as many doctors in Belfast now as there had been ten years before. Six of them were women. That in itself lent to the place the atmosphere of positive revolution; women were being taken into industry not as spinners and weavers—they were already there—but into offices. They were paid less, of course. They were glad to be paid at all.

The business center of the city was brand new. It had been a mess of ugly and unhealthy wooden warehouses. These were torn away and in their place were fine new buildings, shops, a hotel, and paved streets that met at a point now called Castle Junction and reached south, east, and west. Orange Johnston's meeting was held here at the Junction. The hotel was only the width of one building from the open corner where Johnston and his friends would speak. I was known to the operators of the place and booked a room looking out on the Junction and took the key and went back to the street.

Isabella held hard to my hand, Alasdar sat on my shoulders. He was getting bigger, stronger, heavier by the month. We stood on the edge of the granite-slab pavement (the Americans more sensibly call it the "sidewalk," which is what it is; they call the street the pavement, which even here in this part of this muddy city it is: paved now with square cobbles or "paving stones.")

The special trains were emptying their masses, the bands and drummers and Orangemen were forming ranks to march from the two railway stations, Victoria and York. The Orange were ready to show and to tell Mr. Disraeli and Mr. Gladstone how far Orange strength reached and where the limits of its tolerance lay.

And they came. An Orange parade is an awesome sight, except to a young boy perched on his father's shoulders. What are these men to him but marchers, dressed up in their

Sunday best, wearing colored sashes around their necks, some wearing short aprons and sashes, all walking behind bands and painted banners, singing Orange songs to the tunes the bands played. The banners had on them portraits of Orange heroes, notably Protestant King William (William of Orange) on a white horse he is reputed to have ridden at the Battle of the Boyne on the Twelfth of July when he defeated Catholic King James and maintained his hold on the English crown. It was not a battle about Ireland or for Ireland but about the succession to the British throne. It was not about Catholics or Protestants but about parliaments and kings. Had I been alive in those days and a Catholic and of my present mind, I would have been for Protestant William and parliament over any return of the romantic and despotic Catholic Stuarts.

Now they came past us marching and singing,

> D'ye think that I would let
> A dirty Fenian get
> Destroy my loyal Orange lily, O . . .

"What does that mean?" Isabella shouted above the din.

"Later," I yelled. Who were these people crowding the sidewalk? Packed elbow to elbow. How could I know? It would not have been expedient to yell to her now: "It means a dirty Fenian bastard . . ." Later, in our room, it would be time enough to tell her how they sang of her Fenian father, my Fenian brother.

These men were survivors from the seventeenth century, in dark blue suits. Pikemen walked like outriders on the edge of the marching masses, their pikes always ready to rap or prod any who strayed from the sidewalk or presumed too far. The thunderous drums went past, blood streaming from the wrists of the shirt-sleeved drummers who laid their wrists against the rims of the huge drums and beat out their barbaric rhythms with bound and baked bulrushes. The new stone buildings along the street threw back the battering sound and made the eardrums ring.

Erratic movement on my shoulders and against my head made me look up at Alasdar. He was leaning forward, gesturing and making ugly faces at a red and neckless pikeman who had paused to survey the crowd on the sidewalk. The boy had his fingers spread and was moving his hands sideways from his neck as if to indicate that where the pikeman's neck should be it was not. His face was drawn in an ugly contortion and his tongue stuck out. The pikeman glowered at him like a bull about to charge, and the boy yelled, "*Bull! Bull!*"

I turned quickly around and dragged Isabella behind me through the crowd. We pushed our way into the hotel and went up to our room.

"You must never do things like that, Alasdar," I admonished him.

He was unrepentant. "He was a very ugly brute," he said. It was not my way. But he was a child. He would learn discretion.

It was almost time for the speeches. The two east-west streets were packed as far as I could see from the window of our room. The third, running south, would not be less so.

The great mob sang with fiercely militant fervor till the speakers were ready:

> We'll fight for no surrender
> We'll make the Fenians run . . .

The crowd was too great for unison. The lines rolled from front to back down the three canyons at the city's heart, line behind line rolling and rising like an ocean rumbling on a rising shore.

Then, the Queen. It was a ritual. Always, the Queen. A sea of white hands broke like spray, snatching off caps and hats, and the silence roared in the streets. Every man was at attention. No matter who or what he was, his head covering was in his hand and he stood to attention. Catholic spectator, Protestant spectator, Orangeman or lurking, fuming Fenian, he was at attention and his head was bare. Not to be so was a deadly blunder. The Crown and God were interchangeable. This was a martial race. An Irish-Hebridean-Norse-Scots martial race. My race. And I was not allowed to belong to it, though my forebears came here and first created it. I watched them with a sense of loss.

The drums of all the bands gathered around the platform rolled their ritual call.

The bands struck. Fifes, flutes, brass instruments, pipes, melodions. They struck and the great cry of the heart burst forth and rolled in uneven numbers down the streets.

God Save our Gracious Queen
Long live our noble Queen . . .
God save our Gracious Queen
Long live . . .
God save our Queen . . .

They were singing below us, stiffly to attention while the anthem rolled back from far down the streets, two lines behind. It thrust into the Junction from south and east and west, lines rolling over lines till it seemed that in a great echo chamber the whole world was crying slowly Queen, Queen, Queen, Goddd, Goddd, Goddd . . .

And then a dread-full stillness, of men and voices.

And then twenty thousand Orangemen in one long serpentine howl of assurance, strength, invincibility.

The speakers came after it. There was William Johnston of Ballykibeg House himself, and he was cheered till it seemed the buildings trembled. There was the Reverend Thomas Ellis of Newbliss, who had come from County Monaghan, and the Reverend Ferrers of Rathmines in Dublin, who came to represent the solidarity of all Protestants in the land, South and North. There were lesser figures, there to speak for God, who at this moment was impersonating the Crown.

They spoke to this multitude through an instrument of a sort that made their voices carry. It was a metal funnel with a mouthpiece at one end. The other end flared out to enlarge the sound. A megaphone. They spoke slowly, and their very slowness of speech gave to their words, in the presence of these sashed and bannered Orangemen, a special fearfulness.

The Reverend Mr. Ellis, a Bible in one hand and the great horn—like something from the Book of Revelation—in the other, commanded them in God's name to fight.

"We will fight as men alone can fight who have the Bible in one hand," he waved it high, "and the sword in the other; we will fight, nay, if needs be, we will die as our fathers died before us . . ."

I suppose they might have heard the thunder of the cheers he drew as far away as Carrig.

Now came William Johnston, full of fire and the recollection of a month in prison "for loyalty to Her Majesty."

I saw Robert Garrett on the platform. My lord of Enniskillen I did not see. He had not called the meeting.

"Governments," Johnston said slowly, "may trample on

our hearts if they dare, but they should not try to trample on the Orangemen of Ulster. . ."

Orange anger spewed from the streets below, up to high heaven.

There was a word for my lord of Enniskillen and his kind, "who hold our access to the Imperial Parliament in their hands." (And I felt a tremor of sympathy for them all. How much we had in common, if we could only agree together.) "They like our votes," Johnston cried, "but they dislike us. They have used us for thirty years, and now it is time to put their kept members of parliament through their catechism. The government should beware lest they make Fenians of us all. If England, in a moment of infatuation, determined to establish Home Rule for Ireland, we shall take up arms and ask the reason why . . ."

The whole world seemed full of menace and the sound of anger in twenty thousand throats. And I thought: In Ireland, rage is the only constant.

"What do you think of it all, Isabella?" I asked, my arm about her.

She stared into the street. In a while she said, "They are frightening. Like Papa's people, but stronger. These people would never run away." She read them well.

Alasdar, sitting on the windowsill, said, "Papa, when I marry Isabella, I shall take her to America."

Isabella kissed him. "But I want to live in Garden House," she said.

"That is not far enough away."

We dined rather poorly at the hotel and went home.

Before she went to bed, Isabella, still nervous from the impact of what she had seen and heard, said to me, "Carrach, let me come to you. I need to be near you."

"Why do you love me, Isabella?" Like a dull-witted schoolmaster.

"Carrach," she said, "everything explodes. Everywhere there is anger and terror, and there is no safe place. You are my rock. Nothing can shake you. Let me come to you."

"Soon. When I know you are certain." Was I only a safe refuge in a frightening world?

"I am certain. I cannot be more certain. If Agnes at my age can be certain enough to marry and go off to America, how can you doubt that I can be?"

"Soon," I said. I have made many mistakes in my life. This was the worst.

She went to bed alone, crying; like a young girl who was merely afraid, I thought stupidly.

At breakfast she said only, "You think I am a child. I am not a child." She said it with emphasis, but not in anger. Then she rose from the table and said with sudden fury, *"You will treat me as a woman. I am a woman."* And was gone.

I did not see her till we met again at dinner. It was her first outburst.

✒ Thirteen ✒

She did not come to breakfast next morning. I went to her room. She had not slept there. I questioned the housekeeper.

"Oh, she went with the mistress, sir," that stupid woman said.

"And where did your mistress go?"

"She went to Court House to stay there for a few days, sir. That is what she told me. She told me she thought Miss Isabella was unhappy and that maybe she could cheer her up, sir. That is what she told me."

That is what she told me, that is what she told me. What would she talk about next with the housekeeper, who would talk about it to the butler, who would talk about it at his lodge?

I walked to the mill to cool my temples for the things I had to do.

"Buchanan," I told the senior clerk, "I want Haggan and a man named Michael Cafferty in my room in ten minutes. Get Haggan to bring this Cafferty. Do not let anybody from the office go near him." I had enough to worry about without having Elizabeth surround me with questions about what she was up to. Damn the woman.

It was hard to keep my mind on what I was doing. Elizabeth darted into it, and I felt for her something akin to hatred. What did she want with Isabella? What made the woman think she was the one to try to cheer her up? Isabella never left my mind, and I wanted to rush to Court House and bring her home.

But Haggan and Cafferty were here, and I must keep my mind on them.

Cafferty was even shorter than Haggan, but thin, like wire. I thought he had a crafty face, but allowed that I might think so because I knew what he had done to my machines. He sat in his chair like a man waiting to hear the verdict of a jury and expecting the worst. I ignored him.

"Mr. Haggan," I said, "you said an interesting thing to me last Friday. I want to talk about it. It was about people going to America."

"Ah meant no offense, sir," Haggan said, half out of his chair.

"I know you didn't. I took no offense. I want to understand what you were talking about, and I want you to be frank. Why do people go to America?"

"There's nothin for them here."

"What does that mean? There's nothing for them here? There's work in plenty now, isn't there?"

"Ach there's plenty ah work now, sir. But what's work? D'ye honest to God want me to say the God's honest truth?"

"That's why I asked you here."

Cafferty sat like a fox at its run, ready to bolt underground at the wrong scent.

"Well, luk at me, sir. I'm never outa work. But it's not me Ah want anythin for. It's for ma wee boy and ma wee girl. I mean, they kin go to the Barn School, and then where kin they go after that? Nowhere. Ah can maybe git ma lad apprenticed t'the blacksmith at the mill here, or the carpenter's here. But what's that better nor me? Ah want him to be better nor me. Like a solicitor or a doctor, and he'll niver git near aither a them nor anythin else much."

"That's why you talk about America?"

"Well, y'see, sir, ma brother's in America. He's a cabinet-maker and he's got his own shop now, sellin what he makes an takin the profit wi three men workin for im, and he's tellin me when his lad's oul enough he's gonta a university. *To be a doctor.* My wain stays here an he'll make thirty shillins a week, maybe for the rest of his life, an ma wee girl can skivey or maybe get to the spinnin in the mill—if there's work when she's the age."

My own daughter's in the mill, spinning, I wanted to say.

"You would really go to America, would you?" I said.

"If Ah iver got the fare scraped thegither."

Has Isabella come home this morning? Elizabeth is a cunning and malignant bitch. Why in the name of God did I marry that woman? For Alasdar. Well, I've got Alasdar. Why do I have to keep her? Get your mind back to the business on hand.

I went to the window to get a grip on my thoughts, to turn them back to these men. The mill yard was empty. Everybody who worked for me was working, heads down, making the money that kept their homes together and nothing more. All of them had faces. Agnes was in there, breathing flock and wet air, making 7s. 6d. a week. She had a face. Cafferty had a face.

I looked at it. "Mr. Cafferty." He stared past me, full of dread. "I want to understand what the people who work for me want. You know, ambitions? What are your ambitions?" I sat down again, not quite free of malice toward the mean-looking little man.

"Nothin," he said, I think because his mind was frozen.

"Nothing? There's nothing you want? Are you married?"

"No." Looking to my left.

"So you've no children?"

He was thinking. "Ah don't think so." Looking to my right.

"You've never thought of going to America?"

"Och, aye." Looking at the edge of my desk. This was the closest he had come to looking at me.

"Would you like to?"

"How'd Ah git there?" A quick, shifty glance at me that had in it the wish to spit.

"Now, supposing you could get there, would you go? Do you know anybody there?"

"Ah've two cousins there." *Everybody has cousins in America.*

"Would you go if you could?" I said it impatiently. *Isabella was in my mind again and would not leave it.*

"Aye, Ah wud."

"What's your job in the mill?"

"Ahm a hackler."

"You break up the flax fibers?"

"Aye."

"Like it?"

"It's a wage." *Yes, it's a wage. What else is it? My own bastard child who held me in some kind of contempt worked*

in my mill for 7*s*. 6*d*. a week. It was a wage. Save it to get
married and escape this place, this country. Something was
happening to me. A disturbance in my spirit about people
with faces, but the only face I saw in my mind's eye was the
face of Agnes saying, "Only Wee Mick?"

"And you have no family?"

"No. Ony ma mother."

"If I could get you to America, would you go?"

"Ah . . ." His head dipped and came up again. Still he
didn't look at me. "Ah . . . Why?" he said to the wall behind
me, and licked his dry lips.

"Because you want to go."

Haggan's head turned from face to face, puzzled and curious.

"Would you go?"

"Aye. Ah wud. But there's ma mother. She's got nothin."

"Why did you cut the belts, Cafferty?"

His head went down again and stayed down. Haggan's
went up.

"Ah don't know," Cafferty said hopelessly. If there was
spirit in him, it was night spirit.

"But you did."

"Aye." He had been cheated into a sense of security. He
spoke with deadly resignation, without spirit, and I pitied the
man and his kind. He was close to serfdom, and he knew it.
He could get up and go if he could afford to go. I could afford to go. He could not. That was freedom? Agnes could afford to go. She had Cassie and Hyndman to help, and she
kept her weekly wage and saved it. This man had a mother
to feed.

"Should I give you in charge, Cafferty?"

He didn't speak. His hands were on his thighs, gripping
them like vices. "Are ye gonta?"

"Why did you do it?"

"Ah don't know."

"Resentment?"

"What?" He could barely hear me now for the frightened
din in his head.

"Anger?"

"Aye."

"At me?"

"Everythin. I'm a papish workin man." It was the first real
sign of life in his voice.

"I know. So am I. So is Haggan. Do you want to go to America, Cafferty?"

"Aye. If Ah cud take the oul woman, Ah'd be there the day." It was a tiny shout. Anywhere away from here and this. But he had an old woman to keep, and he wouldn't abandon her to the poorhouse.

"You heard him, Mr. Haggan?"

"Aye."

"Then I'll get you there, Cafferty. Go back to your work." He stumbled as he rose.

"Cafferty," I said.

"Aye?"

"I have a witness. I also have a ship leaving for Boston in a month. Your mother will be a passenger on it. You'll work her passage for her. You'll also be paid for your work on board. If you don't go, I'll lay charges. Then who will feed your mother? Have you understood?"

"Aye.' Aye." He staggered as he left, rushing to get out of my sight.

I wanted to stop talking, to think of Isabella, to go and get her. I said, "Mr. Haggan, give your family what you want to give them. I'll get you to America."

"Ah done nothin wrong, sir," he protested. Getting to America was now a penalty for sin.

"Yes, you did. You were born a working man in Ulster. You made it even worse by being born a papist. Do you want to go? Not, in your case, before the mast."

"Ahm not one for takin charity." He got to his feet, ready to leave.

"No charity, Mr. Haggan. How long have you worked here?"

"Twenty years, sir."

"Then I owe you something. Will you go?"

"Aye. If yi put it that way Ah will, by God. Can Ah tell the missus?"

"You can. We'll talk again. And, Mr. Haggan? Cafferty is my business. Nobody else's."

"Aye."

But my daughter Agnes, I was not entitled to help. That, I suppose, is life's or time's revenge. Still, the blind are fortunate if some sight comes to them, slowly and late.

I walked through every part of the mill that day, looking at faces. They were for the most part yellow faces. I looked in Agnes's face. She knew I was there; she knew I was staring at her. I have no doubt about that. She did not look up from her machine. Her head was too stiffly held. And as I turned away, a girl called across the noise.

"Oul Stuffy tuk a right look at ye, Aggie. D'ye think he's after y'to git down on yer back fer 'im?"

How could she know what she had said? It struck me in my inmost parts, but vulgar and gross as it was, there was a kind of truth in it. Agnes was there because her mother "got down on her back" for me at Garden House, and what was the difference between a house servant and a mill servant? Oh, I know that since the Middle Ages there had been an assumption of seigneurial rights for the landlord in the bodies of tenants' wives and daughters. It was no longer assumed as a right, but the habit of generations survived among the sons of landlords—and sometimes their fathers—and the basis of it was a deep assumption of the worthlessness of the servant and a view that attributed to servants as a class a diminished humanity. If you took a servant girl to bed or put her down in a field or a wood, what harm could you do to her? She was still good enough for whomever she might marry—he would be of no more consequence than she was herself. Mind you, that was not my view of Cassie Hyndman, then or now. But she was a servant and I did her a "favor" by making her pregnant at her request—and it was my daughter this vulgar bitch in the mill was talking to and about. I hurried from the place. The lot of these girls might still be a kind of serfdom, but they were a crude and vulgar breed and my actions had set down Agnes in their midst, and there was nothing I could or would be allowed to do to help her. Well, nothing that touched Isabella must ever be allowed to reach their dirty minds. I would run no risks with my darling Isabella, and she must be made to understand that.

But my darling Isabella had not come home, and now I was angry with her.

Pity, disgust, dismay, all in one morning. And now anger. There was too much emotional turmoil.

At home there was a letter from Hugh.

ᘒᘒ *Fourteen* ᘒᘒ

The letter brought news that eased the mind a little. Hugh was not cutting completely his connections with his "friends." They had been too close and intimate for that. But he had decided his and their activities were futile and the talents of the men involved not adequate to the tasks they had set themselves or the larger goals they were meant to reach. He had, however, had several long talks in Dublin with Mr. Isaac Butt, who was looking for new men to run for parliament. It was agreed between them that the victories they fought for would be won in London, in the House of Commons. Hugh had agreed to stand for election in November. This didn't mean, he said like a saving clause, abandoning all other forms of pressure on the British government. It meant combining them so that as the moment dictated, or long-term tactics advised, all forms of pressure could be brought to bear in the right proportions, at the right times, and in the right places. His "friends" were not so sure, but they agreed that some good might come.

At first that puzzled me. It seemed that Hugh might be going to the House of Commons as an undercover Fenian. But if he considered their methods futile, perhaps this was the discreet and the safest way to move away from men to whom human life was cheap? That, I decided, was the truth. He was moving away from them. It was a tremendous relief. My concern was not for his political goals but for his safety. And, I have to acknowledge, my own. If he were caught in

170

his Fenian activities, I could not escape the consequences and they could be disastrous for the mill.

He wrote at considerable length about his conversations with Isaac Butt, who was a brilliant and distinguished Protestant lawyer in Dublin. It may be that Hugh was reading me a lesson, trying to insinuate another point of view into my mind in the hope that I would change my attitude to Home Rule. He rambled on about these things, and it did not occur to me that he might be making this part of his letter unduly long to postpone his arrival at the next part. If this had occurred to me I would have skipped the section on the Parnells and come quickly to the part about my brother-in-law, Seán McCarthy.

Hugh was amusing about the Parnells and about Butt's hopes of getting one of the two Parnell sons to run for parliament in County Wicklow. The elder brother I knew, John Howard Parnell. His estate is in Ulster, in Armagh. Hugh wrote:

> The Parnells have a long history of lunacy in the family. John is sane, but I do not think the young one, Charles, is quite right in the head, and his sister Fanny is given to hysteria. The mother is so given over to hatred that she must have an unbalancing effect on the family. She hates the English with a quite violent hatred and copies them in everything. Young Charles has no use for the Irish and looks on them as useless, worthless, and not to be given thought to. Mr. Butt hopes one day to see him in politics, but I fear if he succeeds, he will be sorry for it. The young man is, in my view, vain, cold, self-seeking, and immoral.

That amused me, coming from Hugh. We never like our own faults when we see them in others. The record of Hugh's fornications would have filled a library. But, being Hugh, he next took up that point. It was all too obvious that he did not care for young Charles Parnell, and I must say, he has always been a good judge of character. Young Parnell, he said, picked on servant girls and farm girls. He, on the other hand, had fornicated only with married women of quality.

It was an odd justification, but there was point to it. All Hugh's women, young and middle-aged, had indeed sought him out and found him eager to oblige, and none of them were of the lower, defenseless classes.

There are times when I think myself a silly man and feel interior embarrassment at my own silliness. Who was I to speak of the defenseless classes after what I had done to Cafferty? Even if what I did to him was for his own good? Wasn't I angry when Garrett advised me "for my own good"?

"I do not think Mr. Butt is wise to hope C. S. Parnell will one day be in parliament," Hugh said, "for I do not think he is always of sound mind."

He had delayed me as long as he could. What he said next destroyed any comfort the first part of his letter brought me:

> Have you seen or heard anything of Elizabeth's brother, Seán McCarthy? My friends are anxious to find him. He was the custodian of some of their funds, and he and the funds have disappeared. I want you to know this because his family connection could be a serious embarrassment to you. Should he attempt to reach his sister, for your own sake please let me know at once. It is better that we should deal quietly and in our own way with the matter. Then, only those who deserve to be can be hurt.

It was ominous. It implied his still-strong connection with his "friends"; and a long reach and quiet justice. Fenian justice is often quiet and final; as often as they can put it into effect. I locked Hugh's letter in my safe.

He sent his love to Isabella. They would come to see us soon—as soon as their current preoccupations permitted.

Long before they came, we had other visitors.

✐ *Fifteen* ✐

The avenue of Barn House is long—some have begun in the American way to call the avenue "the drive" or "driveway," but I prefer the old way—and for most of its sweeping length it is lined with chestnut trees. It emerges from the trees into about two hundred yards of treeless parkland, to the front steps.

I had not heard a post horn for many years. The coming of the railways destroyed the enormous coaching business, except in remote areas where trains still did not run, and in such places the open car or sidecar or jaunting car is the means of public transport.

Now I heard a post horn. It was blowing the code signals that had once been important for the safety of the coach, its passengers, and other travelers on the roads. The sound was coming from my avenue.

I was on my way downstairs and looked out from a landing window. A four-in-hand was charging up the avenue. The horn blew the codes, one after the other: *Passing on the near side; passing on the off side; turning left; turning right; clear the road*, and, as they came into the last stretch before the front steps, *Pulling up*.

What in God's name? I believe in the Resurrection but not of the coaching business. I could not recognize the happed-up driver or his companions stepping down from the coach, or any of the "outsiders" climbing down from the top. Four "insiders" climbed down, two men and two women. They climbed down circumspectly. The other three persons—two

173

from the driver's seat and one from the guard's perch behind—were agile and therefore presumably young.

I hurried to the library to wait for Patton to announce this
peculiar and unwelcome intrusion. I prefer to observe elaborate pranks rather than to be involved in them.

"Sir," Patton said, as though he did not expect to be believed, "Sir Patrick and Lady Forsythe, with their three sons
and two friends. They arrived in a four-in-hand, sir, driving it
themselves."

"It sounds quite improbable," I said. "Ask them for their
proper names or I shall not receive them."

"Sir Patrick was here for your mother's funeral," Patton
said, and irritably, "that's who it is, if you'll excuse me, sir."

It was bizarre but I couldn't argue with him.

Sir Patrick Forsythe is my Scottish cousin, son of my
mother's brother and heir to his title. He was the third to
bear it. My Scottish grandfather was the first—for services to
the Tory party. I do not know how long the Forsythes have
been distilling whiskey, but they claimed to have been doing
it since the days when it was called, in the Gaelic, *uisge
beatha*, the water of life. Patrick had recently been involved
in a bitter controversy concerning the true nature of Scotch
whiskey. He had for some years been marketing blended
whiskey, which, some of his competitors said, was not Scotch
whiskey. A Royal Commission had lately decided in his favor. Blended whiskey could indeed be legally described as
Scotch whiskey, the Commission reported.

Patrick had written quite a long time ago that if the Royal
Commission found in his favor, the field was open, the world
was ready for his blended whiskey, Irish whiskey would be
left standing at the post and when all his investigations and
probes about markets were complete, he was coming over
from Scotland to discuss the matter with me, for "it could be
of mutual interest and immense profit." That was the end of
it. He didn't write again and didn't come to Carrig, and I had
no thought of investing in his distillery.

But I had warm affection for Patrick and his family,
though for some years now we had communicated very little.
"Patton," I said, "have somebody find Miss Isabella. Tell her
we have guests. Send her to me." I ran to meet the Forsythes.

Patrick was ten years my senior and married early, so his
sons were young men and youths; three of them. His wife,
Mary, was a handsome woman who had always been handsome and never pretty; but they were happy and their home

was a happy place. Their Edinburgh house was a four-story building on Morey Crescent. It had fewer books than mine, and more statues. As a child, visiting there with Hugh and Mother in her father's time, the place frightened me, for when we went exploring at night and in the dark, we kept running into people who turned out to be of marble of one sort or another. There was a fountain on a landing on the second floor. A naked white female figure spat water into the big white bowl, and one night while I stood in my nightshirt at the edge of the bowl (examining in the poor light the interesting parts of the white figure), someone picked me up and dropped me into the water. I never saw him—or her?—but Mother was certain it was her father, who till he died "liked practical jokes." Cousin Patrick's family was happy and rowdy. That is, their humor was robust. I enjoyed it so long as it was directed elsewhere. Even so, their coming was a great pleasure, though I prefer my pleasures to be better planned.

This reunion was also robust and happier than any of us could have been expected to be at Mother's funeral. (Patrick took his sons with him like a bodyguard.) By robust I mean that there was much embracing and thumping of backs and Mary kissed me warmly and held me hard enough to make me think their bed must once have been an athletic place. That for some reason rushed Isabella back into my mind, and there was no sign of her.

The Forsythe sons were Rob (Robert) "after The Bruce" (as Mary, who had been Mary Bruce, always remembered to say, and from whom she claimed descent), Iain, and Duncan (after Lady Macbeth's royal victim, no doubt, though Mary never made the claim!). Rob was the one I was soon glad to have out of the house. Big, red, handsome, and quiet, he was also very determined. He appeared to believe there were rights inherent in his self-will. I did not agree.

The other two people were Mr. and Mrs. Ronald Gregor. The Gregors were friends of the Forsythes, and Gregor was an intimate business associate of Patrick's. I never did find out quite what the nature of the business relationship was, but whatever it was, Patrick explained the reason for his long silence about the Scotch-blended-whiskey business by saying he and Gregor had lately returned from a trip to New York to see a Mr. Leonard Jerome, who cavorted in New York with beautiful opera singers while his wife and three daughters, Jennie, Clara, and another one whose name he could not recall, cavorted in Paris with what Patrick called "all those perfumed princes."

All that could wait. Why were they here, and why were they traveling in this outlandish fashion, with a four-in-hand?

It was the boys', Mary said. They had joined a Four-in-Hand Club (there was one in London also, "with the Duke of Bedford presiding") and bought the coach: "They insisted we join them in Larne—we all crossed in the steamer from Stranraer—and ride here without telling you we were coming. We wanted to make an arrival, post horn and all . . ." It was Forsythe fun, not mine.

"When shall we see Elizabeth?" Mary asked.

Patrick had not told her what the situation at Barn House was, after his visit for Mother's funeral. Much less understandable, he had forgotten to warn her not to raise questions.

"You may or may not," I said.

"Poor dear, she's ill?"

"Poor dear is not ill," I said without sympathy. "Suppose we leave it to her to appear or not? She'll know you're here—if she's here. I don't know that she is."

"Oh. Like that?"

"Leave it, Mary," Patrick said.

"Like that," I said.

"Ah well." I half expected her to say something comforting like, "You're well rid of her. I never liked her." Patrick's presence was probably the restraining factor. Mary liked to say what she thought.

The boys would be moving on, "on a little tour." But might we (the Forsythe seniors and the Gregors) stay for a week? For a month if it pleases you. Their coming was a diversion. Their sense of fun was a relief. I found myself laughing very readily, feeling happy, glad of them. But why is Isabella not here? There is business that will take time, Patrick said. That is what we have come about. I did not want business. I wanted family friendship and pleasure.

I rang again and instructed Patton, "Find Miss Isabella."

"We have just found her, sir, and your message is delivered. She is with the mistress at Court House. Miss Isabella will be home for dinner."

"And your mistress?" Goddammit, she was *always* with the mistress at Court House.

"No, sir," Patton said. "The mistress will not be here for dinner."

What was Isabella doing over there with Elizabeth? Why was Elizabeth so much out of her kennel these days? How angry was Isabella? But why was she angry?

"And who," asked Mary, who was barred from talking of Elizabeth, "is Miss Isabella?"

"Hugh's daughter."

"Hugh's daughter!" The excitement surprised me. Isabella was mine. She was home. This was home. Some things I took now for granted. I had to tell the story of Hugh and his wife, Isabella, and of his daughter, Isabella, but not of his politics. The story was now woven into the texture of my life. I did not want to tell it. They wanted to hear it. Hugh was a family legend, as much for the fact that, as the years passed, Mother spoke less and less of him as he was for his mystery; and her relatives did not press her. They knew the thought of her absent, silent son was pain to her.

"Why in God's name does he live down there?" Patrick asked.

"He likes it."

"He was always a queer bird."

"Sir," the silent Rob said, "what is Isabella like? I mean, the Spanish mother and all that."

What is Isabella like? How long was Rob staying? I did not ask him. "Very nice," I said shortly. What business was it of his?

"What's she doing here?" Mary wanted to know.

"Visiting." What more were they entitled to know?

"For how long?"

A lot more, it seemed. "As long as it pleases her to stay."

"With, ah . . . with, ah . . ." But Mary remembered not to speak of Elizabeth. "You'll want her company for as long as you can have it." And then, "How is Elizabeth's nice sister, Emily?"

"Very well. I think." Mary was exploring. I was a man with a wife who was, to say the least, unfriendly.

Patrick is a perceptive man. He reads atmospheres as well as Mother ever did. I must have been sending out nervous signals when the subjects got too near some danger point. "Carrach," he said, "can we send this lot away and talk about a few things?"

"If they wish." I wanted rid of Mary and her questions. I did not want to talk Patrick's business with him. I had no choice.

I learned a lot about the Scotch-whiskey business in the

next hour and about the blended whiskey he had been sending us since before Mother died. She had been drinking it the day she told me I had a daughter by Cassie Hyndman. The best blends, I learned, are of a Highland and Lowland mix, and some of them come from as many as forty different distilleries. I listened with a fair amount of interest. I like the stuff—the blended stuff—but I do not drink it in large quantities. Hugh prefers the harsh Irish brew, I cannot help but believe for political reasons. A man should put his stomach before his politics. Peter the Great, the Russian czar, once said, "Of all wine, Irish wine is the best," which surely raises grave questions about him. The blending of Scotch whiskey, Patrick said, is not a science, but an art, or a mystery. They had worked for many years to perfect their blends, yet there was no precise measurement for their content. It was a matter of touch, taste, and tools, he said. He told me the story of one of his stills which was old and worn. The new one did not for some reason produce the same rich product. Why not? It was a mystery; all the ingredients and their proportions were the same. So he had another new still made, an exact model of the old displaced one, including its patches. The result was the old perfection.

Did I understand?

"Who can understand a mystery?" I asked him.

Then he came to the business he had in mind. It concerned two things: production and distribution. The market for blended Scotch was enormous. They had made their investigations. They were first in the field. The world was at their feet. Another distillery was what they needed. Immensely increased production. New capital.

Ah.

"Preferably family capital."

Ah. I made no response to that.

He returned to Mr. Leonard Jerome of New York. A wealthy speculator. A king on Wall Street. A sampler of beautiful women with beautiful voices. A gambler on futures, though blended Scotch whiskey was not a gamble. It was gilt-edged. Mr. Jerome wanted it in enormous quantities. The excise on a gallon was 10s. It would go up. It would go on going up. Governments always needed more money. They would tax luxuries before necessities, and blended whiskey was a luxury for which countless millions could be given a taste before taxes reached a point where men thought twice about it. Then it would be, for these countless millions, a social necessity, if the campaign to sell it was of the right sort and of the right duration. The future of Scotch whiskey was endless, and Forsythe's Scotch would be out in front.

He talked with great enthusiasm and threw in odd bits of information that were interesting enough: that over two million imperial gallons of Scotch evaporate from their casks every year. The thought crossed my mind: Tour Scotland and breathe deeply. That Scotch aged best in casks of American oak. That struck me. It has to be shipped. So, of course, does Scotch? Ships.

He was back now to the new and much larger distillery and new capital. In my head I was saying no. But I listened. "Give me time to think, Patrick."

"Certainly. Most certainly. Of course. How long?"

"I would want to send my accountants . . ."

"Of course. Most certainly. Time is of the essence, Carrach."

"Of course. We'll talk again at dinner. None of this is secret, I take it?"

"Not from the family. From everyone else, most certainly."

"Good. Well, an open discussion at dinner. Let the family convince me. Or fail to." He must not be encouraged to think he or they would wear me down.

As if they could. My knowledge is of flax spinning and shipping.

Even so, alone till dinner, I thought about whiskey and Isabella. Why had she gone from me?

She came to dinner a figure of splendor and beauty, looking—how old? God save my soul from carnal excitements: a young woman. Radiant. Patrick watched me. Mary watched me. The Gregors and the boys watched Isabella. Rob, the eldest, said nothing, nothing at all. Not even when he was introduced to his newfound cousin. He nodded, stared, and kept on staring like an ornamental dog.

She came straight to me and kissed me on the mouth. It was deliberate, and not coldly deliberate. It was the open greeting of a loving wife, the mistress of the house. My God, I thought: I wish it were true. But I thought also: Patrick and Mary are coming to conclusions. Isabella took Elizabeth's place at the other end of the table as though it were her own. She dealt with Patton and the serving girls as Elizabeth never could. She reigned, and if ever I saw a girl play the role she intended to assume—had already assumed, for

God's sake—it was Isabella. And Rob sat, scarcely eating, his eyes fixed as though they were stuck, and he was spoiling it all for me. I think that when I was young I did not seek to compete for the attention of pretty girls because I was afraid of rejection or, if some attention should come my way, because some other youth might take it from me. In this area I did not believe in competition because I could not face it. Yet here in my own house, this slip of a boy . . . Till I became fully aware of the fixity of Rob's gaze, I had been enjoying the play as much as Isabella obviously was. I must have been showing my annoyance.

"Treat the wine tenderly," Patrick said, and I thought it was a diversion for Rob's mind. "I have an after-dinner experiment I want you all to join me in." It did not divert Rob.

"Rob," Mary said. "Rob." He did not hear her. "*Rob!*" she said.

"Oh? Yes, Mother?"

"Yes, Rob."

He knew. He was back at it again within a minute. There was nothing to do about it.

"My dear," Mary said with the privilege of seniority and family relationship, "how old are you now?"

Isabella's smile was wicked. No, it was not a smile, it was a wicked grin. There was a laughing glitter in her eyes, as if Mary's question delighted her, served her purpose, amused her, and had to be punished.

"How old enough now for what?" she said. "Cousin Patrick," she said quickly, "may I take a handful of your coach and four?"

"Take a handful" meant take the reins, and I had no idea she could know the terminology of a dead trade. But why not?

"It isn't mine," Patrick said, "my sons own it. Ask them. But it's a dangerous sport."

"Good. Rob, may I drive your coach?"

"It's . . . it's . . . it's . . ."

"Dangerous?"

"Yes."

"Do you ride?"

"Yes."

"Then why don't we ride in the morning, then you can decide whether the coach is too dangerous for me?" She was smiling. They did not know the meanings in her voice. I heard them very clearly. I had heard the same meanings in her voice recently. She was smiling now. But she was angry. They were questioning her ability to handle horses, as I had questioned her ability to handle life. She turned to Mary. "You don't mind if I take your sons riding in the morning? It could be quite dangerous."

"I think," Mary said, "I'm sorry for them already."

"I shall look after them," Isabella said with sparkling malice.

In my house we do not observe many of the fixed and useless customs of what is called polite society. For example, we do not, at the end of dinner, segregate the men and the women while the men drink and smoke at table and the women withdraw and gossip. This sort of thing is done by people like the Garretts, who ape the Enniskillens, who ape London society. London is a long way from here, a world farther away from us than it is from Dublin. We are not obliged to them.

"Patton," Isabella said, "bring the cigars, and that will be all."

In Mother's time dinner was a forum. We had talked often and at length about all kinds of things. Isabella, in her element and in the mood to reign and rule, cleared the decks. "Why did you come in that monstrous machine, Cousin Patrick?" she said, opening the forum.

But Isabella was not in complete control. "Before you go, Patton," Patrick said, "you will remember my experiment?"

"Certainly, sir." He opened the sideboard and took out a tray with six bottles on it, all labeled only with manila paper, the paper marked only with letters from A to F. This he put on the cleared table, with glasses.

We watched with curiosity. Even Mary appeared to be without knowledge of Patrick's intentions.

"Now," he said, "whiskey and talk go together. Good whiskey should be drunk only in good company. We have both. One of these whiskeys, Forsythes have blended and casked for twelve recent years. It has no name and as yet no market. We need both for it, and it will be named tonight— by the family. But which one is it? A, B, C, D, E, or F? I know. Gregor knows. You do not know. Find it, then we shall name it."

"Six bottles?" I am not an excessive drinker. "Do you expect us to drink all six bottles, Patrick?" I asked.

"Sip, Carrach. Taste only. Savor a little, one by one." He

sounded Scottish-religious, which is a way they have when whiskey is involved. Sipping seemed safe enough.

"I do not drink whiskey," Isabella said.

"Then when we drink, you shall do the christening," Rob said suddenly.

"I know even less about christenings." Isabella aimed her glittering grin at Mary.

"You have lots of time, my dear, and I think you'll have lots of opportunity."

Isabella laughed. Patrick poured. Isabella said, "I shall call the first one Carrach. That would be fitting, don't you think, Cousin Mary?"

The fun had started before the whiskey was sipped. "Not," Mary said, "if it's a girl."

"It will be a boy."

"Taste," Patrick said, and led the way, casting his eyes to heaven like a Scottish Presbyterian advertising his unction.

I tasted. I was indescribably happy. She was there, like a queen; regal, gracious, confident, clever. Mine. Did they know it? I suspect that Mary did. Women in such circumstances are more perceptive than men. Or more suspicious. Or more prone to envy or censure. We all sipped and tasted like communicants at a conventicle. And Patrick determined the direction of the talk.

It was time to talk business, he said. Family business, he said, as if his affairs were any affair of mine. Whiskey A was good.

This time he was concise and to the point, with a lecture on the almost religious mysteries of whiskey blending. I had heard it. Isabella listened intently, examining Patrick's face line by line, as she did with people. Mary watched her with equal attention, and, I think, deepening bewilderment. She turned to me with open astonishment when Patrick was done with his exposition and Isabella spoke.

"But, Cousin Patrick," to fix his attention.

"Isabella?" He said it politely, perhaps with tolerance, expecting nothing of consequence. What of consequence could this young woman say?

"If this is to be a family matter, why this man Jerome?"

"I don't understand, Isabella."

"We have family of our own in America. This man Jerome is a speculator. Cousin James MacDonnell is a wealthy and a solid industrialist and importer. Wouldn't he be a better agent? Safer?"

"Well . . . but . . . we have . . . we don't know . . ."
Patrick didn't know what to say. I think he didn't want to say
anything to her.

Sip. Taste. Patrick passed out pencils and paper. We must
mark each bottle on a scale of one to six.

I sat back. It was entertaining. It was also useful, for I had
no intention of becoming involved in Patrick's whiskey
business, and Isabella's play, whatever it was, would probably
fog the thing. So would the whiskey. It was fun and not serious. I couldn't escape an honest discussion with my cousin,
but I could do with a timely diversion. If Patrick didn't know
how to deal with a girl who asked intelligent questions, I was
not any smarter; I couldn't have imagined what Isabella had
going on in her mind.

"Well, you see, Isabella," he said, as to a child, "we have
already discussed it with Mr. Jerome." As to a child who had
to be humored but who was dabbling and making him impatient.

"Then why not discuss it with Cousin James? Do you think
he would object to making money from Scotch whiskey?"

Well, would he object? "I suppose he wouldn't," Patrick
said. "But he might not be equipped." He turned to me to begin the serious talk.

Whiskey B. Taste and sip. Scribble, scribble.

"Speculators don't have warehouses," Isabella said. "Impor-
ters and cotton manufacturers do. They also take things to
market and know how to sell. That's their business, isn't it?"

Patrick said nothing. I think he was holding his breath. I
was holding down laughter. Mary was holding her glass, not
in her fingers, but in her fist.

"Why do we not go to the drawing room and talk, my
dear?" she said to Isabella. "Leave talk and tasting to the
men."

"But this is so interesting and so important," Isabella said
with her most brilliant smile. "I think there must be a great
deal of money to be made from selling Scotch whiskey in
America, and all I'm saying is that the Forsythes and the
MacDonnells ought to be the people to make it. Don't you
agree, Carrach?" So she was going to throw a net over me.
That was not so amusing.

Patrick, it seemed, was no longer holding his breath. He
thought he saw an ally. He was looking at Isabella with
speculation. But all he said was, "Why not, Carrach?"

A little more B. please? It's very fine. Scribble, scribble. What were you saying, Isabella?

"I love to think of us making all that money, Carrach," Isabella said. She was wearing the smile she used to turn my head. Her elbows were on the table, her chin cupped on her hands, and I swear she didn't care who read that smile. And before God, suddenly I knew what she was doing. Bitch, Hugh called her, and bitch she was, but to me the most dazzling bitch in creation. *Us,* making all that money! "Why don't we," *we* she said, "write to James? Why don't we outline the whole thing to him exactly in the terms Mr. Jerome was agreeable to, and try James? Better still, why doesn't Mr. Gregor go over and talk to him? Even better, why doesn't Cousin Patrick take Mr. Gregor back to America and see James?" She was laughing into my eyes, and Mary was gaping.

Bottle C. Sip. Taste. Not so smooth. There was loving warmth in my heart and behind my eyes.

Mary said, "My dear girl, there's a lot of Hugh MacDonnell in you."

"Oh, no. There's a lot of Grandmama Forsythe in me. Isn't there, Carrach?"

"You mean Grandmama MacDonnell, don't you?" I said. It was better than trying to make a comment on her dealing, and it was the truth. "She means your aunt, my mother, Patrick," I explained unnecessarily.

"That is exactly what I mean. What do you think, Mr. Gregor?"

"I never knew Grandma MacDonnell," he said, like a Scot stepping his way among puddles.

"You must certainly go, Mr. Gregor. You wouldn't put a foot wrong with James." She made Mr. Gregor smile.

Bottle D. Sip. Taste. The world is a shade of amber. Amber is a loving color.

"Patrick," Mr. Gregor said, "we should look at it. It's a point."

"Are we being perfectly open with one another?" Isabella said. "Cousin Patrick, you have no firm commitment to this Mr. Jerome?"

"No, no."

Patrick pours with such panache. Bottle E. Sip. Taste. Scribble. Isabella would make a splendid advocate, or judge—or wife. Suddenly I wanted to cry out, but Old Stuffy was sitting on the fringes of my mind.

"Are you ready to open the matter with Cousin James in Boston, try to keep the thing in the family? I mean, is there any purpose in discussing a family enterprise unless we make it a family enterprise?" She looked around the table, from face to face. She came to me. How will you treat me now? her grin said to me; shouted at me. Oh, where, oh, where, has your little girl gone? it laughed at me.

"Carrach?" Patrick said. "I'm willing to try to get James MacDonnell in. What do you say?"

"Nothing. Isabella seems to have all the ideas." I was very happy, very proud. A little too easily inclined to laugh, but even Patrick seemed able to laugh now. Cousin Patrick. Splendid Patrick. E is splendid too. Scribble, scribble.

"Well, to that I would say: if James will come in, we should go in, Carrach, right from distillery to shipping to delivery to James." Isabella, still dealing. "And if we don't invest for ourselves—why don't we think of investing for Alasdar and the girls?"

Holy God Almighty! It was brutal, shameless, and cunning, and wonderful. If *we* didn't invest for *ourselves* . . . Alasdar and the girls . . . there she was, sitting at the end of the table in Elizabeth's place. She was taking Elizabeth's place, filling Elizabeth's place; she was my partner, she was the mistress of this house; she was declaring it in the bosom of my family. Not my family: my family and her family. Why am I laughing like this? Who has made jokes? Why is Mary's mouth wide open? Like the mouth of Moby Dick, the white whale? Is Mary Moby? Stop laughing, Carrach.

"It's impossible to lose money making and selling Scotch whiskey," Isabella said, nailing everything down.

Silence. It was as if the entire company was waiting for her permission to speak. Perhaps the truth is that nobody knew what to say. Very likely Mary was thinking: The girl's his mistress, for God's sake. Very likely Patrick was saying: She's the one to work on. What the rest of them were thinking, I didn't wonder. Patrick and Mary were my concern.

Bottle F. Not so good. Back to Bottle E please, Patrick. Sip. Taste. Scribble, giggle.

Concern? I wasn't too concerned. The truth is, I liked what was happening. Delicious. Liberating. I liked the idea of Isabella as the mistress of my house. Patrick and Mary were too happy together to begrudge happiness to anyone else. Of course they were. Now the two of them knew Elizabeth lived another life, remote from mine. Mary was smiling now, nodding at her thoughts. They must have been pleasant thoughts.

Old Stuffy, perched on the edge of my mind, said: Don't
say more than you intend, Carrach.

"Give us a few days to talk it over, Patrick," I said. Us, I
said.

"We've really not had time for anything." Isabella picked
up every thread. "Between Orangemen and Fenians, mill
wreckers and unions, and, of course, the children—well,
there's been no time." She looked directly at me, daringly,
grinning. "And this is the first time I've seen Carrach today,
apart from a very hasty breakfast. We'll talk about it tonight.
I promise you. I love the idea of us all making an immense
fortune from Scotch whiskey. And do you know? I've never
even tasted the stuff." And she collapsed under the pressure
of her own amusement. Or amazement?

We agreed on E. It was beautiful whiskey. And the name,
Isabella? Patrick asked her.

"The Auld Alliance," she said, "not for the Auld Alliance
between France and Scotland, but this family alliance—Ireland, Scotland, and America, MacDonnell, Forsythe, and
MacDonnell."

And that is how it came about that Auld Alliance Scotch
whiskey poured in its torrents around the world. Sip. Taste.

The rest of the evening was pleasant and relaxed. The talk
was good and easy and shared by everyone but Rob, who sat
like the dog, careful of its mistress; a tiresome young man.
Mary was particularly gay, and I got the impression that she
was, or believed herself to be, privy to some knowledge that
either delighted her or at the very least entertained her. From
time to time she glanced at me and at Isabella, who had now
compounded all her other ploys by sitting at my feet, her
head resting on my thigh. And the amber world was clarify-
ing in my head.

"Well," Isabella said suddenly, sweeping to her feet as if
she was in a great hurry, "we always retire early. Please do
not be influenced by our ways," and she pulled me from my
chair. I almost resisted, but I was too deeply ensnared. Humbly I followed her. Did I want to resist?

Outside my bedroom door she stopped, and I was afraid
she had made up her mind to push her way in. But she kissed
me. "My darling Carrach, how I love you," she said, and,
"Do you think they're thinking what I think they're thinking?" Then she ran to her room.

I was in bed, reading myself to sleep, when she came in, closed the door quickly behind her, and hurried to sit down on the edge of my bed. She was wearing the silk robe she wore the day we got back from West Cork, and I was quite certain that underneath it she was in the same condition— naked.

"Now, Mr. MacDonnell," she said, "we shall take matters up where we left them the other day."

"You," I said, "are leaving here and going to your room."

"This is my room because it is your room."

"But not yet, Isabella."

"I got into my bed. I rumpled it thoroughly. It has now the appearance of having been slept in. I am sleeping in yours till the early hours. I may leave it as chaste as a nun, but I am sleeping in it." She moved up the bed, sat on it beside me with her back against the headboard. "I love you," she said intensely, "and I shall not wait any longer for you. Carrach, damn you, I am a woman, and you will treat me like one or I shall know the reason why." Her arms were folded, her mouth tight, her head high. She was angry; after all that loving and compromising maturity and gaiety, she was angry.

I wanted her. Everything in me said: Take her. Everything but my conscience.

"Are you prepared to listen to me?" I asked her.

"For the last time," she said.

"What do you mean, 'for the last time'?"

"I mean this. I love you. I know I love you. I shall always love you. You say you love me. Look at me, damn you, Carrach!" It was almost a shout, and it was full of angry passion, not carnal passion. "I am a woman. I can be all that you need me to be, in bed and out of bed. In your dining room—and by God I showed you—or anywhere else, I am a woman, not a child. Are you listening?"

"You are supposed to be listening to me."

"For the last time."

"Then for God's sake listen." I lay back against the headboard and closed my eyes. That was a blunder. She moved with surprising speed—off the bed and into it, under my covers. Sitting up beside me, against the headboard.

"I'm listening," she said, but quite unsmiling. "Say your piece."

"Isabella." I was pleading. "Get out."

"I'm listening."

I admit I did not try hard. It took all my years of self-sup-

pression, marshaled for her protection, to keep my hands off
her. "All right." And everything I wanted to say sounded
pompous in my mind before I said it. But it was all true and
I said it.

"In London," I said, "people of our class are in and out of
bed with one another's wives, quite shamelessly. Most of
them don't even try to hide it. The Prince of Wales, that
idiot, leads the field. Nobody cares. There is no decency.
Here, on this side of the water, our lives are different. These
things happen. But they are not approved, and the guilty,
when they are caught, are pariahs." Was Hugh once caught?
I wondered. Did the husband of some prominent woman give
him the chance to run for the sake of the man's own public
face, or because he loved his wife or wanted to shield his
children? I didn't know. The thought had never occurred to
me before. "Isabella, I will not have one breath of scandal
touch you. You would be crucified in this society. This is a
puritan land. It is harsh in its judgments. And suppose you
change your mind about me? There was young O'Keeffe at
Schull . . ."

"He was only amusement."

"He is young. You are young. If you changed your mind,
what would become of you?"

"We've been over all this."

I suppose I went on till I was unendurable. She got out of
my bed quickly and stood by it. "I came here to live with
you," she said, "not board with you. I love you. The question
now is: Do you love me? The shoe is no longer on your foot.
In spite of all you know about me, what I am, what I can do,
you want to wait till I become what I already am. Very well,
I'll wait. Not to find out whether I shall continue to love you,
but whether you love me at all. I shall wait, Carrach, but not
too long. So make up your mind, and then make it clear. I
am waiting now for you."

She didn't sound or look like any child. When she was
halfway to the door I said, "Now that you've got that off
your chest, perhaps you'll tell me why you tried to get me
into the Scotch-whiskey business?"

She folded her arms again. "Certainly," she said like a governess, "the continuity of life in this damned and bigoted
province, whether it's business or biological, is questionable. I
should have supposed an astute man would think it prudent
to lay off some of his resources on a sure thing, away from
this bonfire of a place. And if he had some objection to doing

it for himself, he might have the foresight to do it for his children."

She slammed the door. It was that little speech that got me into the Scotch-whiskey business, or, more correctly, got my money into it for Alasdar and the girls. It also, indirectly, got Cousin James into it, for he decided that if a cautious creature like myself wanted to risk money where there was no risk, he might as well take a share of the profits. So he became our sole agent in America and put American money into the new distillery, and we were MacDonnell, MacDonnell, and Forsythe, makers of fine Scotch. The Forsythes made the whiskey, the MacDonnells shipped and sold it, and Auld Alliance blended Scotch poured around the world like the river of life itself.

I tried to persuade Isabella to let me include her in the alliance, but she would have none of it.

"How do I know," she asked me, "that you won't change your mind and regret it?"

When Isabella reached a decision, she had already walked around it and examined all its ramifications. I'm a stupid man or I would have seen that in time. Patrick's boys did not go on their little tour in their four-in-hand. They stayed while Patrick and Mary stayed, and each morning went riding with Isabella, who gave most of her attention to the gawking Rob.

"Rob is a darling boy," she told me.

Each afternoon she disappeared. To Court House, I was informed, to spend the time with Elizabeth. I weighed everything. She avoided me. She gave her attention to Rob. She spent time with Elizabeth. She might very well be waiting for me to prove myself, but what was I to think? Would every young man get her attention till one day she said, "Carrach, you were right"?

I was wrong.

♆ *Sixteen* ♆

I did not know it, but as the months passed into the following year, my life itself was running forward toward its beginning.

Agnes married her William Morgan, carpenter, in the Congregational church. I gave Cassie two hundred pounds for Agnes. It was to be given to her in an envelope at the last moment before she left for America, and it was to be accompanied by a note that said these were her mother's savings. I wrote the note in a disguised hand and felt foolish. Agnes had never seen my hand.

Her departure had a strange effect on me. It was like the end of something that had never begun; a vague sadness at the loss of someone in whom I had no rights. Cassie could not read. Bring her letters to me, Cassie, I said, I'll read them to you. I'll take them to Dr. Lyons, the Congregational minister, she said. I was like the coach passenger who couldn't afford an inside seat. I was an outsider, even to the mother of my daughter; even to my daughter.

It was a sad time, and my relations with Isabella were uneasy and unhappy. She was waiting. She corresponded with Rob Forsythe and gave me his letters to read, but did not show me her replies. He asked to come to see her. I do not know what she said to him. He asked me for permission to come. I had to say yes. He did not come, I do not know why. He wrote to me asking to be allowed to come and talk marriage with Isabella. I showed her his letter and referred him to Hugh. Hugh did not mention him in his now frequent letters (always his letters said, "If you have word of McCarthy,

190

don't fail to tell me, please"), and Rob did not come to Barn House. Isabella explained nothing. Life was unpleasant, uncertain.

But these were unpleasant times. When had times been pleasant? Not in my lifetime. There had been wars and rumors of wars for a generaion, revolutions and unrest. The Prussians were breathing fire against France, looking for an excuse to make war, and the French in response were their usual arrogant and sneeringly superior selves; Hugh won West Cork and Mr. Gladstone went to power in the Commons; Spain was in crisis again; President Johnson of the United States fought off impeachment and Ulysses Grant (both men were of Ulster-Scots stock) succeeded him in the White House; Italy was in crisis; there was no peace in the world. Perhaps there never has been.

And as if the state of the world was not enough, Elizabeth was active. What this meant I could not guess, but whatever she was up to was directed toward Isabella. Warm friendship. That was improbable enough—and unsettling enough—and I tried to imagine the reason or reasons for it and could not. It made me feel threatened, as her earlier alliance with her brother, Seán, made me feel threatened. But there was nothing on which I could fasten. I supposed she must have brooded in her retreat until some notion grew in her mind, and now, I was sure, it was in operation. I was tender and loving toward Isabella, and there were times when she was happy. There were times when she was wary, silent, elusive; sometimes for days at a time she went with Elizabeth to Court House, and I could not understand it.

There was no alteration in Elizabeth's attitude to me or to the children. She ignored them; she came to me to ask for funds in excess of the funds to which she was legally entitled under the marriage contract. I was grateful enough that she kept away from me and let her have the money. I did indeed wonder why she needed it and what she used it for, but questions required answers, and answers meant conversation, and I wanted none of that. I gave her the money she asked for. I asked Isabella what they had found in common. "Company," she said, and was not inclined to elaborate.

Certainly I was busy; overwhelmed with work. But I sought her and often did not find her, and my own misery deepened. Her seventeenth birthday came and went. She refused to celebrate. The way she looked at me that day, as if I had beaten her, broke my heart; but she said nothing. I knew that in that look she was saying: How many birthdays? It was in her eyes. Or in my imagination.

Then I made a discovery that stunned me. About a month before I made it, two men had come to Barn House, Patton told me, "asking for Mr. Seán McCarthy." They had, he said, started with the gardeners and the groom and succeeded in reaching some of the inside staff before Patton became aware of them. He had seen them. They were anxious to find Mr. McCarthy, they said. You'll not find him here, Patton said. Who are you? he asked them. We are from the government, they said. The man is barred from this house, Patton told them.

It was none of my business. Seán McCarthy had nothing to do with me. If Hugh's friends or Dublin Castle wanted him, then let them find him. He was not here.

Elizabeth, a month later, was back at Barn House, but only for a day. Two days after she departed again to Court House, I went, for no reason that I could think of, to her apartment in the west wing. I was upset by Isabella's repeated absences from my house. It may be that I was looking for some explanation of these absences. I sat in Elizabeth's small living room, not knowing what I was looking for or doing there, perhaps like an Indian holy man waiting for a message from some other place or power. Certainly I was not alert. Nothing came to me about what I had come here to discover, and I got up to leave. I was thinking as I got out of the chair that I didn't understand how Elizabeth could endure these cramped quarters, but at once the answer came: She didn't. She spent most of her time at Court House in quarters far from cramped.

Then I saw the key, still in the lock of her bureau. Why did I turn it? I don't know. I did. That is all there is to it. I opened the bureau, and now I do not apologize for it.

On the desk in a small heap were the torn scraps of a letter in familiar handwriting; Elizabeth's mother's hand, a large childlike script. It didn't occur to me not to put them together; indeed, I began the task at once. It wasn't difficult. Nor was the part of the message I made sense of difficult to understand. There were only two pages of a longer letter. I needed only one. Mrs. McCarthy was thanking her daughter, my wife, Elizabeth, for "having kept him hidden." They are, she wrote, "very persistent in their search." Who they were, who he was, she did not say, but the two men who a month earlier had been here asking about McCarthy came back to mind.

"He" was McCarthy. "They," I had no way of knowing, but if they were persistent in their search for him and he needed to be hidden from them, they could not be friendly. It was criminally careless of her to leave the letter there. She could not have meant to. It was too dangerous for her brother. I could only suppose she was interrupted in her preparations to return to Court House and forgot about it. The torn letter went into my pocket. I called a carriage.

The girl who opened the door was a stranger to me. I thought I knew the servants at Court House. There were only three, a woman who was not a qualified housekeeper but had been elevated to serve that purpose in a house that was little used except now by Elizabeth. (It would of course be used a great deal more as the children grew and assembled their friends.) The girl who admitted me wore a small cross around her neck. Protestant girls do not do that. Christians though they be, crosses were Catholic, and some spiritual injury might come from them. The housekeeper had been Catholic, the two girls Protestant. That appeared to have changed, and I was irked. The religious complexion of my staff was a question of tactics. I made the decisions on the balance to be maintained. Elizabeth had altered it.

She was in the drawing room on the second floor, overlooking the Lough with, on the right, the gray old castle on its great rock and the left arm of the harbor that reached out into the sea. There was something about her smile that disturbed me. It was cunning, derisive . . . or was I in the mood to imagine things?

"Why did you change the servants?" I asked her without preamble.

"I prefer my two new girls."

"Catholic and from the South?"

"Both. They needed places. They have them." No concessions, no concern for my concern. A brittle, resentful—or defiant?—light in her eyes.

"You know I'm careful about this business. I can't have houses full of Catholic servants. What are you trying to do?"

"What do you want in this house?"

It was as if I had crashed my way into my own property and was accountable for that.

"Where is Isabella?"

"About the house."

"Call her, please."

"Why?"

"I wish to have her here while we talk."

"No."

I walked all the way around the room, slowly, placing my feet carefully, playacting. It is a large room. "I think," I said when I came to her again, "you know I no longer have any regard for you. You may not have been sufficiently in touch with me to know that I do not give a damn what happens to you, and if you should find yourself in serious trouble, I would not raise a finger to help you. Send for Isabella."

"No." She looked cocky. Her smile was impudently foolish.

"You're a stupid woman." I pulled the bell rope. "Bring Miss Isabella," I told the girl.

She looked to her mistress for confirmation of my order, and that was too much for me. Elizabeth gave her no help. Not all her senses had deserted her.

"*Bring Miss Isabella*," I barked. The girl ran.

Isabella came, looking humble and guilty. "Carrach?" she said nervously, and sat down, her hands folded modestly in her lap. She could not look at me and was near to tears. She, at least, was shocked by my presence and afraid of it.

"Elizabeth," I said, "now send for your brother."

The impudence fell from her face. In the corner of my eye I saw Isabella's hand clench.

"What are you asking?" Elizabeth said in a gritty voice.

"*Fetch him!*" I shouted, angry. She was driving me to fury. Isabella, too. She cheated me. She deceived me. She conspired with Elizabeth to deceive me. That was more than I could endure. Elizabeth nodded to her, and Isabella went for him.

He came, grinning. "Hullo, Carrach," he said, making a show of cordiality but with undertones that betrayed his anxious state of mind. His voice trembled in his throat. I suspect myself in emotional situations because I think my own emotions deceive me, but I was certain I heard the tremor, and he glanced in what to me was a furtive way first at Elizabeth and then at Isabella. What I saw in the glances was a call for help, or support, or protection.

"So they are hunting you," I said, no more specific than I needed to be. "Snooping around my houses asking about you." Face to face with him, face-up-to-face with him after all this time, I hated him. "Get out!" I yelled in his face. "Get out tonight as soon as it's dark. And if you show your face again in my houses or in this town or near it, I'll tell them where to find you. They will not have to come asking me for you. *I will give you to them.*"

He said nothing. Elizabeth said nothing. The harsh intake of breath on my right came from Isabella. "You," I said to her, "come with me."

Obediently she followed me from the house without even a cloak. I gave her my overcoat. Home, I took her to the library: no, I stormed to the library and she half-trotted behind me.

"Sit down." She sat down, watching me now, afraid of me or of my fury. "So you cheated me," I bellowed.

"No. No." She shook her head as though she was confused and unwilling to say anything that would expose her confusion.

"You deceived me. You conspired with that woman and her rotten brother against me. You knew he was there." I was pacing and prowling around her like a guard dog holding an intruder. "You've been seeing him there." She was pale. When she tried to speak, her lips trembled and she could not speak. "And you want me to gamble your life on your maturity and your constancy. What maturity? What constancy?" I was nearer to tears than she could possibly have known; I didn't know what she knew; only that my rage was turning to a sense of desolation, not because McCarthy had been hidden in my house, but because Isabella had been party to my wife's plan to deceive me about his presence. It was an issue of loyalty, of first choices. It was a simple intestinal thing: she was mine, she was always therefore for me, and when an issue of loyalty arose, there was, there could be, no question. She had allowed herself to be used against me even though she knew I had barred this man from my house. *"What constancy?"* I roared.

She stood up. My overcoat fell from her shoulders to the floor. She walked from the room. Tears streamed down her face. They did not soften me. There was nothing where she had been. Only the empty coat that had covered her.

Hugh and his wife visited us the following week. They came to a silent and unhappy house. Isabella was heavy with a deep sadness. It lay on the children. It lay on me.

We put on a show for Hugh and his Isabella. All it did, I'm sure, was to present to them an image of the normal; not of an uncle and niece who loved one another, but of an uncle and niece.

At dinner on their second evening, Hugh said casually, "Carrach, what do you hear of Seán McCarthy?" It was, his tone said, an idle question, of no moment. Presumably the casual pose was for Isabella. His persistent questions in his letters had not suggested a too casual interest.

Isabella surprised me. "He was here at Court House, Papa. Carrach threw him out, didn't you, Carrach?"

"Yes." There was nothing more to the conversation. Later, when we were alone, Hugh came back to it.

"You were to tell me, Carrach. Where's he gone?"

"I didn't promise to tell you, and I'm not an executioner, Hugh. I don't know where he's gone. He was at Court House. I found out and threw him out. Isabella told you all I know."

"If you should get wind of him, will you this time promise to let me know?" It was curious. He was no longer casual.

"Why?" The very mention of the fellow's name and its re-introduction annoyed me. "What's your real interest in that guttersnipe?"

"I told you. He held some Fenian funds. He disappeared. So did the funds. We'd like to find him."

"I can't be his death for mere money."

"There's more than money."

"Then I have to know what, or we needn't talk about it."

"Money is the least of it." He said it dully, and a pool of silence gathered around it. There was a cold finality in the way he said it that made me shiver. "As well as the money," he said then, "there is the matter of who told the police where to find Kelly and Deasy."

"Kelly and Deasy? The men the Fenians rescued from the police van in Manchester?"

"And Maguire and Condon, Allen, Larkin, Rice, O'Brien, the men who got them out of the van. All picked up with ease. Too much ease. We have good reason to believe he was paid for them." It was said so quietly; no emphasis, almost like small talk. It was also an announcement: a sentence of death has been passed on my brother-in-law, as a thief and a paid informer. I had no sympathy for these men now being called by the Irish the Manchester Martyrs. They had murdered a policeman in their rescue of Kelly and Deasy. The Irish have such an appetite for killing. I would not encourage them in it.

"If I hear . . ." I said.

"Thank you."

I couldn't do it. Hand a man over to be murdered by his former associates? I couldn't do it. To call it an execution—as they would—made it no less a murder. There was no harm in saying merely, "If I hear . . ." I would never hear. I couldn't do it. I would never have to face the question. If I ever had to face it, I couldn't do it.

Hugh and his wife stayed for a week. All the time they were with us I felt as though my brother had me in his eye, thinking about me. Not trusting me. The night before they left, they asked Isabella to return with them briefly to London, where they now rented a house during the parliamentary session. "I cannot leave just now," she said. She said it woodenly, like one who, at some disadvantage, wards off pressure she may not be able to withstand if she attempts to argue. Hugh pressed her, her mother pressed, I said I knew of nothing to detain her. "I cannot leave just now," she said doggedly. She grew jumpy. It was very obvious her nerves were taut. The issue, which wasn't all that important, upset her beyond reason. The pressure from us all, which was not insistent, sent her into a panic. Suddenly she stormed hysterically at her parents and fled to her room.

Departures and farewells were unhappy the next day. The atmosphere was burdened by pain. "What have we done?" her mother asked, and I could not offer any explanation.

The next day Isabella went away.

✑ *Seventeen* ✑

That first day, I did not know. How could I know? When I did not know where to find her, I knew, always in these past months, that she was at Court House.

Yesterday when Hugh and her mother left, she was disturbed. She has gone this morning to Court House. She is best left alone to recover her composure. She must now be embarrassed by her own behavior. She needed to avoid me. So I reasoned when she did not come to breakfast. I am often a great and stupid fool, and when I recognize it I am sorry for myself.

That second day I could not endure the silence. I could not any longer endure my own determination to wait. It imposed too much strain on both of us. I called a carriage and drove to Court House. All the way there I rehearsed what I would say to her.

I would be gentle. In the carriage on the way home I would say, "Isabella, if you will forgive all my stupidities, I want you to come with me to my own apartments. And stay there. If that is what you want, I shall lock the doors and we shall not emerge until tomorrow."

And she would certainly say, "I want that more than anything in life, Carrach."

And I would say to Elizabeth, "I am instructing Pollard to draw up articles of separation. Engage a lawyer on your own behalf, and he and Pollard can thrash out a settlement. But never again will you set foot in Barn House. You can depend on my generosity but not on my tolerance." I went on and on in my mind.

And I began to rejoice. Within an hour I would shower my love on Isabella and we would live together, whatever the cost . . . With passion I had never before commanded, I would pour my life into her, and if she conceived, then, by God, I would proclaim our common life from some high place. It was almost heroic.

Elizabeth was in a cheerful state of mind. "I have come for Isabella," I said.

"Isabella?" Her tone rose. She was smiling. She seemed surprised. "Why come here for Isabella?"

"Because she is here." There would be no argument with the woman.

"She is not." That sneering smile never left her face.

I searched the house, even the servants' quarters. She was not.

I raced to Garden House. She was not. She did not come home that day.

No, Hugh replied, she has not come to our London house.

No, O'Keeffe replied, she has not come to Schull. She has not come to Goleen. He was brief in his telegraphic replies. In his letter he was long and abusive. "You snatched her from the cradle and couldn't look after her, you filthy old bastard." That was the cleanest and kindest thing he said.

No, she was not with Emily in Dublin. She was not with the Forsythes in Edinburgh. No, she was not with her mother's people, the Ybarra family of Seville. In desperation I was advertising my loss to the world.

I was not right in the head. In such crises, ordinary people like myself are at a fearful disadvantage. We do not know what to do. Heroes in romantic novels know what to do. We are crippled by fear and incompetence. Where do we turn? Where now do I look? From whom do I now inquire? The terrors of imagined disaster twisted my mind. Where was she, what was she suffering, who had done her some injury, where would I find her body? The house was silent. The servants were silent. Miss Isabella was here and is gone and there is no explanation and I cannot stand and weep among them of my ignorance and my fear. Settings for dinner, sir? said Patton. One. Not for Miss Isabella, sir? No. His look to my disordered mind said: What have you done with the body? What evil has someone done to my love?

At the end of the week I went to Schull. It was a long,

long journey and crucifyingly slow. I had to threaten O'Keeffe with a stick to calm him down. Help me to find her, damn you. Take me to every house she might run to. She was not at and had not been to any of them. She was not at Goleen. She had not come to West Cork.

I spent the night in Emily's flat in Dublin, which was indiscreet and dangerous. I was too distraught to think of that; it did not appear to enter her head. But she could tell me nothing except that I was not exceptionally stupid about women—"only normally lacking in perceptions denied you by society's attitude to women. You never understood the girl. She was so committed to you, I honestly thought she would blow up if she didn't get you. Well, she's blown up, and if you want her, by God, you'll have to search. That one won't walk back into the kennel you've built for her. Find her, Carrach, or lose her."

I fled to London, to Hugh's rented house on Cheyne Walk, in Chelsea.

"I want to understand, Carrach," he said. "You're demented."

He was her father. He had to understand. He was entitled to know. All I cared about was finding her. I was reckless of censure or opinion, even of Hugh's opinion or condemnation. I paced up and down past the long windows that overlooked the Thames and did not see the Thames. I think I did hear Hugh saying, "Oh, will you for God's sake sit down and compose yourself."

I told him. I was astonished by his calm and his silence. He saw the Thames. He came to the window and looked down at it for a very long time.

"And did you?" he said at last in a voice like glass cracked by cold.

"Before God, I did not, Hugh," and when he said nothing I said, "Hugh, you must believe me."

"I do," he said. "You are you, Carrach." I could not tell what was in his voice. I was afraid he might see me in his mind like a cesspool, fouling his child. He said, "Her mother told me this would be it."

"What would be it?"

"What you've just told me, dammit. That Bella was in love with you and you wouldn't know how to handle it. She saw it when we were at Barn House. She said you were both playing uncle and niece, trying to hide it. It was clear to her.

Now, will you for God's sake compose your mind and try making sense?"

"It's damned easy for you to say that . . ."

"I'm her father, man. *I know her."* He was yelling at me. Angry with me, I knew. "Her mother was right: you couldn't understand her."

"I don't know what you mean. Of course I understand her."

"Did you? You think you understand me, but you don't. Her mother said, 'Carrach loves her but he's a stiff man. He will not do what he thinks is scandalous. And she will punish him.' Did it ever occur to you that she would punish you?"

I sat down, facing the window, facing the water. "No," I said. "I didn't." A narrow stream of ease flowed through me, a very narrow stream. I saw the river. "Do you think what she wants is scandalous, Hugh?" And as soon as I said it, I felt myself stripped naked of dignity, maturity, manhood, and my image of my responsible orderly self: I was to myself a small and defenseless boy calling for help.

He kept me waiting. I think he kept me waiting deliberately. I watched his head turning with the movement of the barges on the river: upstream now; now downstream; very slowly. "You're her uncle, goddammit, man. You're her *uncle,* not some young man who has the right . . ." He was struggling with anger and the conflict of diverging love, for his daughter, for his brother. "You shouldn't have taken her north."

That I would not endure. "You and your wife wanted me to, insisted on it." And I lied as we all lie in such confused situations. "I tried to resist the thing. You know that."

"Yes, I know that. I'm sorry. Even before we asked you, Isabella knew Bella was in love with you. We both thought it was a family crush that would die away. No, that's not true either. Her mother said it was for life with Bella."

"Then why did she let her come with me?"

"All right, Carrach, I'm disarmed by that one. Isabella is an Andalusian woman. I'll tell you what she said. She said, 'Elizabeth has abdicated, the throne is vacant, and Carrach is a good man. If she wants him, let her be happy if she can get him.' "

"But not you?"

"Not me. There's one word that's fifty feet high in my head. *Uncle.* You're her *uncle."*

"And you could never accept it?"

"With Bella, that, I'm afraid, is not the question. She doesn't wait for anybody's acceptance. She made her decision. I have nothing to do with it. It frightens me, but it's what frightens Bella that counts, when you're dealing with Bella." He asked me then, in a throaty voice as if he hated the question, "Do you love her? Do you want her for the rest of your life the way I wanted and still want her mother?"

"Why in the name of God do you think I'm demented?"

"And is what you're talking about with my child—with your niece—" and I felt the stab in it, "for so long as you both shall live?"

He's marrying us in his mind, I thought, for his own spirit's comfort; exacting guarantees to make the unacceptable tolerable.

"For Christ's sake, Hugh, why do you think I was waiting? So that she'd be sure. So that there could be no doubt in her mind."

"I see."

I don't know what that said.

"So you actually intended to live with her." He was still watching the barges: upstream, downstream, facing away from me.

"Yes," I said. "*Yes!*" I shouted at him.

"You're being punished, all right. There's no doubt about that."

No storm. No censure. Only sadness. I don't know what he was thinking or feeling. Perhaps his face was to the river to keep me from seeing murder in it.

"Try Forsythe's," he said. "Maybe she's there. I know you're being punished. Wherever she is, she's all right. She believes you've made her suffer. She's making you suffer. I know my Bella. She'll come back."

Still he didn't look at me. He turned away, toward the door, and walked. His head was down now. He opened the door and faced me. His eyes were clouded. "You'd better go and see at Forsythe's," he said. "Right away." Throwing me out? "Carrach," he said, "she's chosen her life. If she's chosen you, she won't change. So be it. There is nothing on God's earth I could do about it—not with Bella. You're her life. It's an unnatural thing. I don't understand it. But I know her. I'll say this to you: When she comes back, you'd better make my child's happiness the thing that's more important to you than your own life. If you don't, that's exactly what the price will be."

It was a threat. His voice and his face said it. All the ruthlessness of his whole being was in it. He closed the door.

She was not at Forsythe's. Six weeks later she had not come home. It was a long, long time to sustain a punishment that was prompted by hurt love. And once again I had lost my brother. I was going out of my head.

One thing made it worse. Elizabeth came back to Barn House. She did not hide in her west-wing nunnery. In her black clothes she resumed her life in the house. She came for breakfast, she used the drawing room, she dined with me in the evening. And she smiled. Not at me? Not to me. To herself, as though within her was some pleasant thought, at least something she found amusing; something satisfying; not to laugh at; only to smile about, in a private sense. I brooded on that smile. At first it was merely an irritation, but its persistence made it puzzling, then infuriating, then alarming.

Each morning she said the same thing when she came to the table. "Any word?" Smiling. Each evening she talked of Isabella at dinner. She did not expect me to talk, and I did not. It was enough for her that she should talk: Isabella, Isabella, Isabella, every evening.

Emily came in answer to my pleading. Defiantly, as an act of open hostility toward her sister, she slept in the room next to mine.

"She thinks you slept with me and found me too animal," I said.

"I know what she thinks. Maybe she thinks I'm back to try again? Let her think."

But Elizabeth was cordial toward her sister. "Help yourself to every home comfort," she said to her, smiling, smiling, smiling. It was a joke, Emily told me, from their early days, when Elizabeth had said that the wife of a rich merchant, Andrew Cleaver, looked to a local lawyer for "home comforts"—for bed without board.

She stayed awhile, calmed me a little while she stayed, and went home again. "Come often, please, Emily," I said.

"Find Isabella and I'll come and celebrate with the pair of you."

The children wept for Isabella. "When will Isabella come home, Papa?" they asked, and wept. "Please bring her back, Aunt Emily," they implored her.

It was Alasdar who was most deeply stricken. I could not understand the persistence of his grief. He was a sad and lonely boy, and once more I misread emotions. I thought he grieved for a lost foster mother.

And then, when Elizabeth had gorged herself on the grief and distracted anxiety of those for whom she had no regard, she said one night at dinner, "Carrach?"

"Yes?" I do not talk to her at all.

"Seán said I must wait two months before I gave you his message."

"That thieving informer has no message I care to hear."

"Then perhaps you will hear mine."

"The same applies. You have nothing to say that I want to hear."

"Your brother, Hugh, would want to hear it. He made his contribution."

Her face was very red. Patches of a deeper red disfigured it, like rashes. Her eyes were bright with malice. She was indescribably ugly.

"Your brother, Hugh, is a cruel man, a monstrously cruel man. You are no better. Between you, you have poisoned my life, destroyed it, robbed it of every good thing."

In such domestic situations, nothing changes; the only alteration that hatred undergoes is its own deepening.

"The poison in your life came out of your own spirit," I said.

"But you and your brother, Hugh, have one other thing in common. You love Isabella. Oh, I'm not accusing you of fornicating with the child. You keep my sister for that. But you love that child. It was clear when she was here. It's even clearer now. And nothing could please me more."

The smile on her face was so distorted by malice that it was less a smile than a mask. Now I paid attention.

"Mr. and Mrs. Hugh MacDonnell," she said, reading, or pretending to read, from a card on the table before her, "are happy to announce that their beloved daughter, Isabella, was, two months ago, at St. Malachai's Parish Church in the city of Belfast, married to Mr. Seán McCarthy, beloved brother of Mrs. Carrach MacDonnell of Carrig, and the happy pair are now living quietly where they are not likely to be found." She spun it down the table to me.

It was in her own hand.

"That," she said, "accounts for the absence of Isabella. It also compensates me for the ruin you and her father have made of my life. My brother is indeed a thief and an informer. He is an egoistical weakling, cheap, treacherous, and despicable. My sister is your common whore, and my brother is an informer. But he had enough charm and enough cunning, and was in enough need of the additional money you gave me for him, to behave for just long enough toward Isabella like a gentleman and a friend—and he earned every penny of your money. He married her, and I was midwife to the marriage. I hoped for it, worked for it, encouraged it, and in the end arranged it. Nothing in my whole life has given me so much satisfaction. It is what hurts both you and Hugh most, and it is less than you deserved."

I walked from my end of the table to hers. My head was solid stone, no thoughts, no feelings: none I was conscious of. I struck her with my open hand across the face. She toppled from her chair to the floor and lay there, staring along the line of the floor, like a corpse. I dragged her to the door.

"Get up. Go to your quarters. Do not move from them. Do not call a servant. Do as I say *or I shall kill you.*"

She rose up, first to her knees, then to her feet, shakily. It took all the control I could command to keep myself from kicking her when she was on her knees, or slapping her again when she was on her feet.

She went, scurrying like a rodent. Then I had thoughts and feelings. I was mired in Irish venom, in one of those blind Irish family conflicts of hatred and poisonous revenge and politics and and and . . . all I had done all my life to guard, safeguard, living cautiously, carefully, defensively, did no good in this emotional cesspool. Then I think I went mad.

✑ *Eighteen* ✑

I'm not sure what I did for the rest of the evening. I went
out, I know that. I saddled a horse and rode, I know that.
Where I rode, I do not know. I have the impression, like a
fragment of a remembered dream, that I sat on my horse on
the flat summit of the Knockagh Hill looking down over my
land and over the Lough to the moonlit shore of County
Down. It is only an impression. I must have stabled the
horse. I must have gone to my room. I was aware of myself
again in my room. This ugly and treacherous woman had not
only helped foul Isabella by contriving a marriage with her
brother, she had put her in danger from the ruthless and re-
lentless forces that sought the man to take his life. Now one
question pounded in my head: What does that woman hate
and fear most? What can I do to hurt her to the limit?

I went like a thief to her room. The light wakened her.

"Get up and get dressed," I said.

She leaped out of bed, full of fears. I'm sure she thought I
had come to kill her. "What are you going to do?"

"You are leaving. You're going back to Court House, and
you're staying there. You will never set foot in this house
again."

"Yes," she said obediently, barely able to make herself
heard, for she had never before seen me with the wish to kill
in my face.

I watched her dress. She had put on weight. There was
more to her in the flesh than there had ever been. I made her
walk to Court House and followed her in. It was two of the

clock. I took her to the remotest bedroom in the house, far from her servants.

"Get into bed." She was almost paralyzed by fear, but she moved backward toward the bed and groped to take hold of the covers as if to get in, fully dressed. "Naked," I said, "and one sound out of you," I showed her my big hands, "and I shall choke you to death."

I watched her strip naked and get into bed.

"No," she said, "no," when I started to take off my clothes. The very act of taking them off transmuted hatred to brutal lust, and when I was naked, I was ready. "You filthy, ugly, obscene bitch," I said as I tore the covers from her and went down on her, ramming her legs apart with my knees, driving at her like a wild boar. Hating her.

There was no thought for the safety of my parts. I went at her with brutal, hating lust, pouring obscenities into her ear, making the room shudder as I battered her belly and the bed; pouring my seed into her. "Get away from me," I said when I rolled off her.

She lay away from me, on the far edge of the bed. Not curled up, not stricken, but on her back, watching the ceiling. Not staring at it lifelessly. Her eyes were alive, moving. Her face bore no expression.

When I was ready, I hauled her, without care for any pain I might cause her, into the middle of the bed and mounted, roughly, heavily, hatefully, vengefully, and went at her again. This is what she hated; this is what she feared. And this is what I never knew before—wild, ungoverned lust. I could have beaten her with a chain and felt the same destructive fury, but the law does not protect a husband for that. His rights over his wife's body are absolute. It was my member she feared, and what it could do she hated. My member was my chain.

And suddenly her nails were digging into my back and her body was attacking mine and she moaned and writhed and came with a violence that must have shocked her small frame, and I leaped off her, unaccomplished, full of sudden and self-emptying defeat. This was what she wanted somewhere in her recesses? To be raped. This is what Emily talked about when we walked in Lovers' Lane so long ago. Elizabeth was getting at long last and as my hate-propelled vengeance what somewhere in her she had always wanted. I had heard of such women. Emily told me there were such women. This, she told me, was what her sister wanted from Hugh. I had not believed it. And now she had it—from me. Once, a friend told me, he had thrashed his son for his delinquencies until he discovered to his horror that the boy wanted to be thrashed. Sometimes the hidden places of the human heart terrify me.

She was smiling as I dressed, a little smile that was not for me.

I walked home with only one thought: That I could defeat this malignant and loathsome creature only if I destroyed her.

My actions and my thoughts made me an offense to myself. I struck at her, and my actions and her response made me loathsome to myself.

❧ *Nineteen* ❧

Yes, said a priest at St. Malachai's, they were married here.

No, said the shipping lines that carried passengers to America, no Mr. and Mrs. McCarthy sailed on our ships. That was not surprising. A hunted man would not use his own name; not till he was very far away. But it might well be safer not to be very far away? They might be in England's teeming cities.

Hugh came over to see me, in a lethal rage at McCarthy. No, he said, not in any English or Scottish or Welsh city; not among the Irish. If he is among the Irish, we shall find him. We shall find him wherever he is; the Irish are like a universal secret society; he cannot hide in Paris, he cannot hide in New York or Boston or Chicago. He cannot go where the Irish are, for we shall find him. So we shall look for him elsewhere. Everywhere. Even on his breath there was the smell of murder.

"Elizabeth knows, I'm sure, but I got nothing from her," I said. Of course she knows. She was "the midwife for the marriage." Her brother would keep in touch. He would need money, sooner or later. She would be the source.

Hugh went to see her. It was one of the most unpleasant encounters of his life, he told me. She laughed at him, abused him, was full of confidence that what she had done gave her some power over him. He was certain she was no longer sane.

"Oh, Seán's everything you say," she told him, "but he's no worse than you are and were. One thing he did that will keep him safe from you, Hugh, is that he learned a lot about you when he was among the Fenians. Small scraps he could paste together—about you. You're a member of parliament now, but you're the one who went back and forth to America getting arms and explosives for the Fenians. Do you want me to send that word to Dublin Castle? He's your son-in-law, Hugh. Wherever he goes, your girl goes, and he'll see that she's always near. If they come to kill him, she'll be there. If he has to, he'll hold her in front of him, and then where's your daughter?"

She said, "How I like watching your face, Hugh. It's frightened."

She went on like that. "I think," she said, "you owe your daughter a decent life, Hugh. You're a wealthy man, and your son-in-law never did an honest day's work in his life. Running messages for the Fenians, keeping their books for them, such as they were, and a bit of poor journalism. He can't earn the kind of living Isabella needs. Seán is a natural and incurable dependent. You owe your child a living. Seán won't provide one."

Hugh thought he saw an opening. He agreed with her. "I'll make them an allowance," he said. "I'll give my lawyer their address and have something settled on them," he said.

"Something like a Fenian gunman?" she asked him. "Send the money to me," she said. "I'll get it to them. We're in touch."

"That woman," he said to me, "I hate her. There's something dirty about her now." He went away empty. "Try to get at her mail," he said.

I am not a murderer. Sometimes I want to be. If I learn anything, I shall deal with it myself. I shall not hand him over to Hugh or the Fenians. I shall deal with him myself. If she wants rid of him. My God—if? And if not?

Month followed month followed month, and my misery deepened. There was no trace of Isabella; no word, no sign. No hope.

I had not seen that other woman since the dreadful night at Court House when I acted like a murderer. I did not want to see her. The thought of seeing her stirred up my self-loathing for that act. I told my solicitor, Pollard, to complete his negotiations with her about the terms of articles of separation. "You may not be generous," I said.

She laughed at him. "Ask him how Isabella must be feeling now," she said. "My brother is not a provider."

It was too much. I went to Court House.

"Where is my brother's child?"

She was oddly subdued. "I think we can agree, Carrach," she said. "I want to agree." There is nothing so revolting as sweetness dredged up from the long past by a woman you hate. "But Hugh cannot have *my* brother's life."

I said only, "I have one thing left to tell you. Your threats to my brother and your sweetness to me are equally unimpressive. Either you instruct your lawyer to accept the terms Pollard offers you when they meet tomorrow, or you will get nothing beyond the terms of the marriage contract. That is all the law requires of me. Take it or leave it."

"I am willing to return to your house and your bed," she said.

"That would make me sick."

"Why did you not do long ago what you did in this house?" As if that might have a softening influence on me. As if Isabella was of no consequence.

"You already make me sick."

The terms of the marriage contract were meager enough. She brought nothing to it. Court House was hers only at my pleasure. On my death it was hers only at the pleasure of whomever I left it to. She got little else for herself. Trusts tied her hand and foot.

She came to terms quickly.

"He owes me income and shelter," she told Pollard, "and now he owes respite from his brutal interference in my life. That bestial creature came here and raped me. I now owe him nothing, nothing at all. Tell him I said this: My bed is now my own. Tell him to think that over."

That is what he told me. It may have been meant to alarm me. Let her bed be her own. Let her use it any way she pleased. The thought gave me a sense of liberation.

For all practical purposes, I now had no wife: only on paper and in heaven, if such marriages as ours could be considered acceptable on earth or in heaven. It seemed unlikely that heaven could see any virtue in them. My church did not share my views on what heaven might judge to be tolerable. At times I wondered how they knew the mind of heaven. It is always easier to question the wisdom of the church when it comes into conflict with the harsh facts of a life, but on this, I question her knowledge and wisdom. The celibate can know of such suffering?

The world was fragmented. Mr. Gladstone disestablished

the Church of Ireland, and my episcopal lords breathed fire. The Irish conspirators, not only Fenian but others, committed vicious and violent crimes. The Orangemen drilled. The Franco-Prussian war raged, and the French, whose elegant confidence had assured them of a swift victory, retreated in disorder toward Paris. That man McGladdery was back upsetting my workers. His ally was still Aherne. All these were minor matters in my troubled mind. I could do nothing about the Franco-Prussian war, the succession to the Spanish throne, Fenian murders, or Orange militance. I could do something, and quickly, about McGladdery and his union. Nothing must be allowed to distract my thoughts from a search for Isabella. Get rid of every distraction.

I sent for Aherne and told him to bring McGladdery with him to my mill office. I did not feel reasonable. I did not feel tolerant. I was not quite the same man who had built a lunch room and provided tea and sandwiches for my workers after the last union foray; raised wages and absorbed the cost, spent large sums of money making the mill healthier. Yes, I was the man who did these things and saw Haggan and his family and Cafferty and his old mother off to their promised land; but with a difference. Battered and hardened, wounded indeed, with scar tissue that reminded me of the cost of life and cowardice and delay, I attended to my business the better to attend to my life. Nothing would now hinder me from attending to my life, and when I found Isabella, by God, I would live it.

McGladdery was arrogant, so I started with him. He had a broken face and a street brawler's body. He had not signed one more worker than on his previous attempt. Now all those who signed were Catholic. His few Protestants had withdrawn.

I said to him, "Change your tune. At every entrance to this mill a sign is going up. 'No trespassing. Trespassers will be prosecuted.' That excludes all but the workers, other employees, and the customers who come here on business. The orders are already in place that you in particular are to be removed, if you try to enter. The order is that your expulsion need not be too gentle."

"Now, you listen . . ." he began, gesturing with arrogance.

"*Shut—up*. You will do the listening, for you are a stupid man—a stupid papist."

"Have you gone Prod? You were a papist yesterday," with an insolent grin.

"I am one today, but not a stupid one. Now, shut up and listen, for I am talking to you as a Catholic employer about the Catholics I employ." I rushed at it, getting it over. There were more important things than these people waiting for me. "I pay the highest wages in any spinning mill in Ulster. I do not pass on the cost to my customers. I am the best employer in the linen industry in this province. I employ Protestants and Catholics. Only the Catholics in this mill have signed up with you. The Protestants you had have withdrawn. Do you understand why?"

"They're scared of you," McGladdery said.

"No, they are not. I'll tell you why they have withdrawn. Because the Catholics have signed. Because they have been organized by—Catholics. Because every Protestant in the place sees conspiracy—by Catholics. The atmosphere in this province is poisonous—between Catholics and Protestants. There is trouble everywhere—and you two are too stupid to see what you are doing. I have no great objection to unions. So I'll tell you what is going to happen. If I let your union in, my prices to my customers go up. Lisburn and Cookstown will produce cheaper and sell cheaper, and because I have admitted a union, my customers will order from Lisburn and Cookstown and this mill will close. It will close anyway, because none of my customers will buy from me if I am the first to let in a union. But before the mill closes, the place will not be safe for a Catholic to work in, because what union there is, is Catholic. When the mill closes, Carrig will not be safe for a Catholic to live in, because Catholics cost the Protestants their jobs. If you cannot see this, you are worse than stupid, you are mentally defective. McGladdery, the day I know you have strong unions in the linen mills of Belfast and the spinning mills of Lisburn and Cookstown, full of Catholics and Protestants—come back here. I'll ask you back here to bring in your union. Now, get out and don't come back." I had no more to say to him.

"I'll be back," he said. Aherne was ready to leave with him.

"Not you," I said. "I have more to say to you."

Aherne looked uncertainly at McGladdery, but he stayed. I gave him no time to collect his nerves. "This is your second stupid adventure into religious politics, and you haven't the wits to swim in the deep water you're getting into," I said, and yelled, "Buchanan."

When Buchanan came, I said, "Give this man his time,

Buchanan. He no longer works here. And let it be known why he has been dismissed. He has been dismissed for fomenting sectarian conflict in the mill. Let everybody know that. Let everybody know also that anyone who foments such conflict, Protestant or Catholic, will be dismissed. And if I see any sign of it spreading, I shall close the mill till they all come to their senses."

"Yes, sir."

I did not expect to hear any more about unions in my mill. It would not be with any help from me that the Protestant mill owners of Ulster, when they were asked for better wages, cried, "Rome," and by that battle cry of sectarian fear and suspicion kept their underpaid Protestant employees on the job at the old rate of pay.

A week after the union incident, Cassie Hyndman came again to Barn House, and again at night. She had come straight from the manse of Dr. Lyons, the Congregational minister who always read to her the letters she received from Agnes. She looked old and tired, and her weathered skin was pale.

"Are you all right, Cassie?" It was a stupid question. She was obviously ill.

"Och, aye." With the patient resignation of the poor. "I brought you this, sir. Dr. Lyons said I was to let ye see it the night afore I went home."

"From Agnes?"

"Aye. It's the bit at the bottom, sir." She was abject, like a sick woman who believes she has nothing more to give and sees no value in herself.

I didn't confine myself to "the bit at the bottom." Agnes is my daughter. Why should I not learn of her condition?

I learned also something about Cousin James. Agnes explained to her mother that the address at the top of her letter was new. (It was the only letter I had seen from Agnes, and I knew nothing about their arrangements in America.) The job at Waltham was not satisfactory. So her husband, William Morgan, the carpenter, had

> decided to take your advice and try the MacDonnells at Lowell. You were right about them. Anybody from Ulster can get a job at the MacDonnells' while there's work. William is working in the mill carpenter shop and we have a decent house in the town of Lowell.

It was all new to me. I did not know that James and his family welcomed workers from Ulster. Cassie knew about James only what I had told her in bed, many years before. She could not write, but there was nothing wrong with her memory, and it was serving her daughter in a far place. There was a certain justice in the notion that out of the bed in which she was conceived should come the knowledge that served my daughter well in the employment of her husband by my family, an ocean away.

I didn't have much time to think about that. The next paragraph was "the bit at the bottom."

It said only:

Who do you think I ran into on the street? Isabella. I was so surprised I spoke to her, and she was all over me. She asked me to give you her warm regards. It made me think she must know about me, but I didn't risk saying that. Maybe she hasn't been told? I thought she was here visiting relatives, but she isn't. She told me she was working in the Barnes Savings Bank and James MacDonnell doesn't know she's here. She asked me to visit her at her boardinghouse. She sounded lonely and she looks lonely. What happened at Barn House? Do you know why she left? I like her very much, and I could do with her as a friend, but I wouldn't risk it. I'm not ashamed to say I like Old Stuffy too, and I do understand about him. Someday maybe I'll know him. I'd like to, but not as a servant.

"She knows, Cassie?"

"I told her. She knows the money I gave her was yours."

"What did she say?"

"She said it wasn't money she needed from you. She likes you."

I got surprising pleasure from that, but it was about Isabella that I felt a wild excitement.

"Do you understand about Isabella, Cassie?"

"Aye," she said, "I do rightly. Ye'll be goin for her?" She said it sadly, wearily, and I looked at her carefully. She was worn and ill. I had known genuine affection and satisfaction with this woman when she was young and I was younger. I thought of her now with fondness. I thought of the daughter I fathered in her with fondness, but looking at Cassie now, it was hard to believe that this tired and weary woman had ever been, in bed, a burning furnace of a woman.

"Yes," I said. "I'll be going for her."

"They're sayin she married yer wife's brother."

"Yes." Sooner or later they know everything. Servants are more reliable sources of information than the newspapers. They have very large ears. And mouths.

"She married thon thing?"

"I'm afraid it's true." She was talking as if it mattered to her; as if it was her business.

"An yer married to Mistress Elizabeth. Yer lukin like death yerself," in doomsday tones, but with sympathy.

"You understand very well, don't you, Cassie?"

"Aye. Ah knowed this long time." She stood up unsurely. "There's nothin fer any of us in this life. All the right things happen at the wrong time."

"Rest awhile, Cassie. I'll send you home in a carriage."

"What would Hyndman say to that, Carrach?" But she was smiling. She sat down again. "Och, all right. Let him say. Ah'm that tired ah don't care what anybody says. Och, ah'm that done now."

"You're not well, Cassie. Are you seeing Dr. Houston?"

"Aye." But she said it cheerlessly.

We sat in silence till Patton announced the carriage. There was nothing to say. She was the mother of my daughter. Perhaps she was thinking about that. I was thinking of that, but more of the fact that I had found Isabella and was going to bring her home. I did not feel the elation of certainty. I did not know that she would consent to come home. I was afraid she would not. What did I know about her, or McCarthy, from Agnes's particle of information? Nothing.

For the first time in her life, Cassie left Barn House by the front door, and left it for the last time in her life.

I wrote one letter that night, to Dr. Houston. It said, "Whatever medical attention Cassie Hyndman needs, please see that she gets it and send your bill to me."

My groom brought his reply: "What Cassie Hyndman needs is her daughter back home and something to live for. If you can get these for her, I'll write the prescription."

In the morning, I telegraphed Hugh. The message told him little, but he was entitled to know at least that I knew where Isabella was. He was not, I believed, entitled to an informer's message about an informer: "Know where Isabella is and going to get her. Shall return via London." That left him free to speculate on whether she was in Europe or America.

Fearfully I sailed for Boston two weeks later aboard the *Sorley Boye MacDonnell*. I had made arrangements for what might be a prolonged absence from my offices. That same day Dr. Houston took Cassie to hospital in Belfast.

❧ Twenty ❧

I love Boston. I have loved the place and admired the people since the first time I came here as a youth "broadening his mind." Boston, my father told me, "is the most civilized city in the world." I love it more today.

We had an easy voyage on the *Sorley Boye,* and from the moment we picked up the pilot at Fort Independence until we tied up at Long Wharf alongside the Custom House, I was ready to disembark.

My mind was full of the fear that if Isabella was still with McCarthy, she was in as much danger from Hugh and his Fenian friends as she was from the man she married, and I was convinced she was in danger from him, for Hugh had no intention of paying him off or protecting him. If I found him, I would pay him off, so long as he would go away and stay away. I didn't care how much it cost me, but he would have to go, and go far, far away. He wanted safety and money; that much Elizabeth made clear. I could give him the money, and distance might give him safety.

I had plans and another particular concern. My father had used Brennon, the Boston house agent, on several visits to this city with Mother. I had used him myself. The shipping company had necessary banking facilities in the city. There was no problem here, and Brennon said he had a house I would enjoy. My problem was that on no account could I afford to let Cousin James know I was here or why I was here, and our banking facilities were at his bank. Uncomfortably, therefore, I had to insist to our Boston banker that James must not know of my presence. I received the banker's assurances and his puzzled glances, but he was a Bostonian. He did not ask questions. I have no doubt he wondered what I was up to that my cousin must not know about. I could not tell him that a shabby family situation that might in time involve political murder was not the sort of thing James would understand or should be involved in.

At this point, I did not know whether I needed a house for a happy ending to a miserable affair, or whether I would soon be sent on my way, and not rejoicing. But, carefully, I would be ready for success if I found it. Defeat required no preparation; it called only for my departure and the strength to endure heartache and continuing fear for Isabella's safety.

The house was in Cambridge on Brattle Street. Its grounds ran down to the Charles River. It was a pleasant house, which Mr. Brennon always referred to as "the Henry Vassall house." He kept referring to the house across the way as "the professor's house." I asked him, after some hesitation, who the professor was. Why, Professor Longfellow, he said, and for a moment my mind missed the meaning, misled by "Professor." Who thinks of Henry Longfellow as a Harvard professor? The world knows him as a poet. I took the house—for a year. It was a foolish extravagance that only a year ago would have run counter to everything in me. Now I scarcely thought of it. All my mind was in my dreams of Isabella. And my fears.

My search for the house had taken only a day. The bank in Lowell would be closed. I arranged with Mr. Brennon to find a housekeeper-cook and two maids and to lay in stores, all to be ready by noon the next day. That is one thing I admire about Americans; if there is any service to be done for which they can charge a fee, it is worth doing. They work hard and well and willingly at making money. I slept that night at my hotel. I slept badly. Excitement and anxiety harassed me. My mind spun all through the night. Did Isabella know she was trapped in a murderous situation? That she was a pawn? It was a night of vague horror.

In the morning I caught a train to Lowell from the Charles Street Station and took up my position on Merrimac Street, some distance from the savings bank; it was eleven o'clock when I first stood there. My thought, without any foundation in knowledge of her circumstances, was to spirit her quietly away from this town, and from McCarthy if she was still with him.

Yes, of course I was foolish. My feelings were those of a youth waiting to waylay a young girl who might hate him. The bank would not close till three. Isabella would not leave it until five or six. I was many hours too early. Was I going to stand here all day, watching the front door of a bank, attracting attention with my English clothes and my sinister immobility? There was something ludicrous about the thought of Old Stuffy MacDonnell being suspected by the police of, I think they call it, "casing the joint." Certainly the policeman who stood watching me, trying to appear indifferent, put the notion in my head.

Should I intercept Isabella or follow her home? My mind wavered. Where was McCarthy? Would I find out at their lodgings? Then what would I do? Fight him for his wife, like some raw youth? Engage in some domestic melodrama?

Also: it was uncomfortably hot on Merrimac Street.

I went into the bank and asked a teller to change a large bill. There were no female employees in the public office. Isabella must work in the office behind. I took my change and went back to the street.

As I may have said, and say to myself from time to time, I often feel ridiculous because there are times when I appear to myself to be ridiculous. This was one of them. At almost forty I was not Young Lochinvar (sailing) into the West. Here I was, pouring with sweat on a New England street in a New England summer, with the temperature at midday soaring into the eighties, and there are few things that reduce the dignity of a well-dressed man of my age so quickly as the inability to adapt his clothing to a change of climate.

And the scrutiny of the police. There were two of them now, one to my left and one to my right, watchfully indifferent to me. Was my imagination playing tricks?

I was too early and too hot and there was no decent hotel I could go to. James was not to know—in no circumstances was James to know I was here, or why. I was not ready to seek out Agnes. She would misread my intentions, and I could not tell her the truth. She would write again to her sick mother. But I had to do something. Go into the bank and ask for Isabella? By what name? Offer a variety of aliases for a bank employee? Say to the bank she may be calling herself McCarthy or MacDonnell? A bank employee with more than one name. I went into a large store; to stop the sweating. To think without thinking about the policemen outside. One police observer came behind me. Already I was making a mess of things.

There was nothing I wanted to buy or carry around with me, and the shop assistants knew the policeman, could see he was clumsily following me. They stopped work to watch. Their customers watched. Dressed in my best and conspicuous English, I sauntered carelessly to the street and back into the heat.

I began to add up my blunders. I had watched the bank. Then I entered the bank on a trivial errand and again took up my position on the street. There were two policemen, one scanning the street, looking closely at everyone who paused near the bank, or stopped to speak near the bank; the other still watched me from a little way off. I went into a shop opposite the bank, walked around it, and came out, never out of sight of one policeman, *never out of sight of the bank*. That was the thought that shook me. I was a fool. I went into a small café and sat in its window, ordered coffee and toast, asked for marmalade, and was stared at. The girl was some sort of foreigner. I recalled, a little desperately, that when Irish children mocked foreigners or the idea of foreignness, they chanted "Mamalada, mamalada, mamalada" (whether an imitation of Italians or Lascar seamen, I never knew), and this would have amused me had not the policeman entered the café and sat down at my table.

"When I get up," he said, "you'll get up. Very slow."

I felt like the black-clad gambler in one of Mr. Buntline's paper books of the Wild West, but I saw nothing funny about it.

"You walk out with your hands nowhere near your pockets. You get that, mister?"

I did not believe it. I most seriously believed it.

"Why should I do this, officer?" I said civilly. "I'm simply . . ."

"Because if you don't, I'll blow your head off." He was a straightforward sort of man.

"But, officer, I'm only waiting for somebody. I'm waiting for my niece."

"Sure you are."

"She works in the bank."

"Sure she does." He was chewing something. "Now, off your ass and out. Slow. Hands away. Your pals aren't here yet."

"I have no 'pals.' You are quite mistaken." It sounded so

prissy, so British. So foreign. And I was frightened now. Of what? Of appearing ridiculous?

"On your goddamn feet," he said quietly and very impatiently.

"He hasn't paid," the waitress protested.

"Right now," the policeman said, "he isn't putting his hands near his pockets."

The girl looked at me, terrified. What sort of a desperado did she see under my English clothes? I knew then that my position was grotesque and dangerous. Whom could I turn to?

It was a strange little procession. Not really a procession, a legal sandwich. They walked me slowly, with infinite watchfulness for my "pals" who might appear, and brought me to the police station. At home, I would have known I was under arrest for "loitering with intent." Here I did not know the language or my rights. I thought about consuls, and that held all sorts of complications. Explanations were in order, not consular officials, and anyway, they were in Boston. Show your papers and the thing will be done with. It was pleasantly cool in the police station, and that was comforting. Also, I was being honored by the attention of a man my two friends called captain.

With care they established that I was unarmed. They laid out all my papers and examined them with interest. Into my head came two words that kept ringing and would not leave me alone, and I could not account for this: Gulliver's travels, Gulliver's travels, Gulliver's travels. There must be some reason for this and for a sudden compulsion to laugh. I had to suppress it. It was hysteria. My friend from the café muttered, "Big, big," again and again and smiled at the others.

"Name?" he said suddenly and *"Yours!"* when I did not grasp what he was up to.

"It's all there. Those are my papers. Bank documents, passport, a lease to my house . . ." I detailed every scrap. "Who do you think I am?"

"Where'd you get them?"

"They're mine, dammit. One's a letter of credit, one's a passport issued by the British government, one's a lease . . ."

The captain took control. He too was chewing something, and with distaste I discovered it was tobacco and the spittoon was close to my chair; beside it, almost at my left foot. I had chewed a sliver of cut plug given me by a sailor in my boyhood and had been miserably sick. My stomach heaved at the memory and at the splash-plop beside my chair. The spittoon had not been emptied for some time.

"Your niece works at the bank? Hey? What's her name?" the captain asked me.

"Captain," I said, "I need to explain something . . ."

"Sure do." Plop.

"About my niece, I mean. Look, I am here in Lowell on purely family business. You see, my niece eloped . . ." Why did it sound so foolish? It was a fact.

The captain raised his head from my passport. "She what?"

"Eloped. Ran away. She married . . ."

"Jeezuz," said my friend from the café, grinning.

"It's a beauty," said the captain, handing my passport to his subordinates. "Real beauty." And to me, "Yeah, what'd you say?"

"Would you do me the courtesy of listening when I answer your questions?"

"Jeezuz."

The captain placed a chair before me and sat in it. "Sure," he said, "I'm listening." Splash-plop.

"Officer," I said, "I am the person my papers say I am. I came here trying to trace my niece, who lived with me and ran away with my brother-in-law. . ."

"Jeezuz." I had, it seemed, said something quite foolish.

". . . whose name is McCarthy. He is not a reliable man. My niece may no longer be with him. She may be living under her maiden name, which is the same as mine, MacDonnell or her married name, McCarthy . . ." then it occurred to me, "or her mother's maiden name Ybarra . . ."

"What?"

"Ybarra. Y-b-a-r-r-a. Spanish. Her mother is Spanish. All I know at the moment is that my niece works at the savings bank . . ."

"How? How'd you know that?"

"A friend here wrote her mother . . ."

"Whose mother?"

"My friend's mother." Did I make it even more involved by saying my bastard daughter's mother? God! Agnes would be in it in a moment, and I didn't want that. I looked foolish enough already. A letter from Agnes would ruin me in Carrig.

"What's her name? This friend. What's her name?"

"One of my ships is docked in Boston. Send for her captain. He'll identify me."

"Ship waiting," said the Jeezuz man.

"This friend," the captain said, "what's her name? Where is she?"

"I'm not involving anybody else in this stupid thing. If you won't send for my captain, send for my Boston banker and have him identify me. His name and his bank are on that line of credit."

"This niece? She works in the bank? She could have one of three names? Working in a bank? That's good."

"Inside man," my friend from the café said.

"Write down her three names," the captain said. I printed them in block letters. "Pick her up," the captain said, and they went to do his bidding.

Alone with the captain, only the sounds of the station were to be heard. Heavy feet fell. Splash-plop. The captain reexamined my passport. "Real beauty," he said. "How d'you keep up that accent?" and did not speak to me again till the doors of the room opened and there she was. Standing. Staring. Dumbfounded.

Joyful. She leaped on me, her arms about me, kissing me, crying, keening, "Carrach, Carrach, Carrach darling," and I held her and kissed her and for a moment forgot about the police and my silly predicament.

I heard my friend from the café say, "Niece, by Jeezuz, niece, he says. Daddy, he means."

"Break it up," said the captain, and to Isabella, "Sit down. He your uncle?"

"Yes. What is happening here? Do you realize you cost me my job, sending two policemen to bring me here?" She was not intimidated by the situation. Perhaps because she didn't see its implications.

"Pity. You always kiss your uncle that way?"

"Every chance I get. Will you please explain what is going on here?"

"Your name Ybarra?"

"My name is MacDonnell, and I shall have an explanation."

"Jeezuz."

"You elope with his brother-in-law?"

She looked at me. "I'm sorry, Carrach," she said. To the captain she said, "That is none of your damned business. Will you explain to me?"

"What's her name at the bank?" the captain asked his men.

"Ybarra."

"You also work under the name McCarthy?" the captain said.

"My husband's name is McCarthy."

"Where is he?"

"I don't know. Will you answer my questions. What is all this about?"

"Lady," the captain said, "answer questions. Don't ask them. You lived with this man here?"

"Yes."

"He's your uncle?"

"Yes."

"You ran away with McCarthy?"

"Yes."

"You don't live with McCarthy?"

"What the hell has that got to do with you? Why are you doing this?"

"Officer," I said, "will you please send for my banker? If you don't, as soon as this mess is cleared up, I'll sue you and your men for false arrest."

"Lock them up," the captain said, unimpressed. "Niece, for God's sake," he said, smiling.

"You're jailing us?" I yelled at him. "Do you know what you're doing?"

"Yeah. I'm jailing you."

"There's no room for her," one of his men said. "The women's cells are full of hoores."

"Clear a cell and put them together," the captain said. "She's his niece." That must have been very funny. They laughed for a long time; it was loud, thigh-slapping entertainment. "She eloped with his brother-in-law, for chrissake. She left her husband. She calls her uncle darling. Christ!"

"Are you sending for my banker?" I shouted at him.

"Sure. We'll get him here. Tomorrow."

"Now, by God, I certainly shall sue for false arrest. And I'll have my papers, if you please."

"Rule Britannia," said the captain. "You'll get them tomorrow. Maybe."

I had had enough even if the captain hadn't. "I'm warning you," I said, "that you are a stupid man and you are throwing us in jail for no reason, with no grounds, and most certainly I intend to bring a case against you. So think of your job, captain, and get my banker here, not tomorrow but today."

"Rule Britannia," he said again, but this time I think with less confidence. "Lock them up," he said.

Isabella said, "Never mind, darling. At least we can talk without interruption."

"That's right, darling," the captain said, but it had about it the ring of self-reassurance.

They locked us up.

My friend from the café turned the key. "We'll be real nice to you, Lily," he said, and went, laughing.

The whores were in the next cell. They hooted, jeered, yelled obscenities, but after a while wearied of it. Then into the silence one of them shouted, "How'd you get to rent a cell for a day's trick with that fancy fella, dearie?" And it ended there for a while.

"He called me Lily," Isabella said. "What did he mean?"

"I don't know. I suppose he thinks he knows who you are."

"Who does he think you are?"

"A bank robber, I think. I was waiting for you outside the bank. I'm a fool. I don't do anything right."

She took my hand.

I had never in my life been inside a prison, not even down to what are called "the cells" under the Carrig police station. As I understood it, they at least are cells, with walls and doors that shielded one from sight. These were open cages with benchlike beds along the separating bars and against the back wall. The women kneeled on the benchlike bed, their hands on the bars of our cage, and watched us. All of them were young. Perhaps what we felt was what the animals in a zoo feel?

We sat against the back wall, close together, our eyes averted from the staring whores. They no longer peered; not even smirked; they were curious about this odd pair in the next cage, a man and a woman. There were seven of them together. Some of them had been in this cage till it was cleared for us. It was surely not legal to put a man and a woman in the same cell? Perhaps legality was of small concern?

My rage boiled. It was not affront that Old Stuffy had landed in a New England mill-town jail. I did not feel like Old Stuffy. I felt like those men who in enraged frustration smash everything in their cells. I found Isabella, and within fifteen minutes of holding her in my arms, we were together in jail. I knew nothing of all that she must have to tell me, all that I wanted to hear, needed to hear. Why did she marry McCarthy, run off with him, stay silent for a year? But my immediate concern was to get her out of this cage, out of this police station, out of sight of these young whores, and away to the house on Brattle Street. I had one comforting thought: She ran into my arms.

"How'd you get to bring the fancy fella in here?" one of the whores said.

"What?" Isabella looked up. She hadn't really heard the girl.

"Don't you want us to watch you?"

"Watch us? I'm sorry, I don't understand."

"Working your trick with him? D'you not like being watched?" The girl was very young.

"We've all been watched," one of them said. "Go on. Let us see you, dear."

"I like being watched."

"Give us a show, dearie."

I was shrinking. Isabella was not. She went to the bars. "I didn't understand you for a moment," she said. "And I don't think you understand us. We are merely visitors to this town. So far as I can understand the situation, the police think we were planning to rob the bank. This gentleman is my husband. We are quite bewildered by all this. Do you think we might just sit over there by ourselves and work things out? Please?"

"Sure," said the youngest of them, "sure, missus." They stared at her and withdrew slowly, still staring.

"I'm sorry we put you out of your room," Isabella said with all her old charm and grace.

The humor of it struck them slowly, but when they saw the joke, they went wild, dancing about the floor of their cage, shouting, laughing, singing, causing uproar. Enough uproar to bring my friend from the café walking along the corridor.

"Shut up!"

They were silent, standing where they froze.

"Keep it quiet, you dirty bitches," he said.

The youngest girl was far back in the cage. "You didn't call me a dirty bitch when you put me down and got yours in here last night," she said quietly, and the uproar began again.

Isabella retreated to the bench-bed and sat down beside me again. We couldn't talk. In this noise we couldn't hear. They were making the cage bars ring, beating them with their shoes. They kept it up till the policeman went away. Then they seemed to wilt, slumping on the bench-beds. Two of them lay down together, their skirts pulled above their waists.

"Turn around, Isabella," I said. This is what my coming had brought to her?

"Don't talk," she said, "think about home."

At nine the girls were asleep, on the floor, on the bench-beds. Isabella was asleep lying against my back as I sat on the edge of her bed. It was all the shelter I could provide without lying down beside her, and that we did not want in this place. The commotion in the corridor was sudden and frantic. I recognized one voice, that of my Boston banker. I shook Isabella awake. He came, trailing like buckshot pigeons the captain and the two policemen and a man I had not seen before. My banker peered through the bars at us and then at the girls in the adjoining cage.

"My God," he said grimly, "you, captain, are in trouble. Real trouble. Get this gate opened."

We were out. The second man was the bank's lawyer. "Don't sleep too well, captain," he said, "unless it's on a clipper bound for China." He was smiling like an angry dog.

"It was an honest mistake," the captain said.

"And your last."

All the way to the house on Brattle Street the banker apologized, grimly; ashamed. He even appeared to forget Isabella, which was difficult to do: she was with me in a cage; he had never seen her with me before. He was a gentleman. "Scandalous," he said. "Disgraceful," he said. "Unforgivable," he said.

"This is my niece, Isabella MacDonnell," I said out of hearing of the whores. "I came here to find her."

"Ma'am," he said, and bowed crisply in her direction. "Find her?" he said in my direction.

"Yes."

"Those were whores in the next cage," he said, horrified into an unfortunate association of ideas.

"Kindly souls," I said, trying to counter his unuttered questions.

He was a gentleman of Boston. It was the only question he asked. He was relieved when I said, "And no charges against the police. I've had enough trouble."

"No," he said. "Good," he said. "Explanations are sometimes difficult." He was careful not to look at me.

At the house I said to her, leaving her in no doubt that the waiting was over, "Come straight to bed."

She said, "No."

Very firmly. "That will have to wait," she said.

✑ᴥ *Twenty-one* ᴥ✑

There she was, her back propped against the side of the fireplace, sipping warm milk, a mystery to that stranger, the
cook-housekeeper. So much younger than myself (she was
almost nineteen then, and not far from twenty-one years my
junior), and with only the clothes she stood in when we
reached the Vassall house, Isabella was Mrs. MacDonnell
who had lost all her baggage and must tomorrow go into Boston and be outfitted. I did not like these cheap deceptions.
They made me uncomfortable. But bathed and refreshed and
wrapped in my robe, and the new servants in bed, it was time
to talk, she said.

"Well," I said from the armchair to which she directed me,
well out of arm's reach, "why did it happen?"

"You made it happen, Carrach," she said. And this is what
she told me.

"I waited, Carrach. I told you I would wait for a while. But
the longer I waited, you grew less like a lover or a husband
and more like an uncle. When the Forsythes were with us, I
practically shouted from the housetops that I was yours, we
were ours, I was your wife, your mistress, anything you
wanted, and what did you do? You sat up beside me in your
bed and gave me a pompous lecture about becoming 'damaged goods.' My God, Carrach, that night do you know what
I wanted to do? I wanted to crack a full chamber pot over
your thick head. Even when Rob Forsythe wrote to you
asking leave to come and offer marriage, what did you do?

You referred him to Papa when I wanted you to be furious and tell him to drown himself in the Forth. Why do you think I showed you his letters? To make you do something. You did nothing. You were Old Stuffy! In the end you made me despair. *You didn't need me, Carrach*.

"Oh, I know I was stupid about McCarthy. He was cunning, Elizabeth was cunning. They worked hard and carefully on me. And I was very young. I admit that to you, Carrach, younger than I knew. But none of their cunning would have worked if I hadn't given up hope that you'd ever really love me.

"And McCarthy needed me. He's a weak man. I needed to be needed. I think it was his weakness and your coldness together that did it. And my foolishness. They told me Dublin Castle was after him, not the Fenians. I had no reason not to believe them. But you knew, and you didn't tell me.

"So I married him. At least, I thought, if I can't have the man who says he loves me, I'll have one I can help. I didn't know till then that it's the weak who get vicious when they're at their weakest. That man wanted me because he thought it would mean Papa's money and his protection from the Fenians. In time he told me that.

"I slept with him."

"I don't want to hear," I said.

"That won't do now, Carrach. You are going to hear. I was his wife, I lived through that. It's part of what I am now. I'm no longer a girl, and you will listen to me.

"I hated it. I couldn't love him. He knew I hated it. I couldn't hide it. In time he did it with a knife at my throat. I can scarcely bear to think of the horror of it. I was very afraid of him, Carrach. He was always boasting, brandishing his knife, crying, abusing Papa, demanding that I write to Papa and get his protection. I wouldn't do it, and he got weaker and more vicious. But it was the day he tried to beat me with his fists that I had enough. He wasn't even good at that. I beat him when he tried it, and he wailed himself to sleep. Then I packed what I needed, took half his money—your money it was, from Elizabeth—and left him.

"You remember Leonard Jerome, the man Patrick Forsythe talked about? He has a private racetrack, and I thought horses were all I knew. I went to his Madison Square house to ask for a job at his track. I was lucky, for his mistress, Fanny Ronalds, was there, and though he refused, the idea of a girl stableboy amused her and she made him give me a job.

"I lived above a loosebox in a room that was reached by an outside stair. I knew McCarthy would search for me. He worked for a German, a man called Kimel, who ran a liquor store. It was the only sort of thing he could do. So when I found an old pair of spurs with Mexican rowels in the room, I wired a six-inch hand grip to one of them and kept it by my bed.

"One night I was awakened by somebody working at my door. I wasn't going to lie there till they got in, so I put on my trousers and a shirt and with the spur behind my back, opened the door.

"He was there.

"He pleaded at first. They would find him, he said. Yes, he stole their money, but he didn't inform on them. I had to come back. I had to write to Papa. We would go west with Papa's money. Far away. We'd be safe out there. Then he threatened. He'd write to Dublin Castle and tell them about Papa's arms buying. He could give dates, places, people. I knew he couldn't. I was with Papa on some of his journeys. I knew more than McCarthy ever could. They could never prove anything against Papa.

"Then he charged into the room with the knife he loves so much. My spur caught him on the cheek, and the big sharp rowels went in. His blood streamed out. I was afraid. Very afraid. I kept on hitting, and he kept screaming and backing out of the room onto the platform and then back onto the steps, and all the time I was lashing him with the spur. He rolled down the steps to the bottom.

"The stableboys were out, standing down there.

" 'What do you want done with him?' they asked me.

" 'Take him to the road and leave him there,' I said.

"But the trainer heard about it in the morning.

" 'I can't have it,' he said, 'you're going.'

"Mrs. Ronalds gave me a job in her kitchens, and he came again, and I didn't have my spur. It was in the attic. This time I used a butcher knife, and he ran. But I was fired again. That time he shouted that he'd kill me when he caught me.

"I had five different jobs after that, and he found me at four of them. I left the fifth because I was getting so nervous I was sure he was always behind me. I was working as a translator in a New York stockbroker's then. I went to Lowell because James was there, and if I was in real trouble, I could run to him. Then one day I saw Agnes on the street.

She didn't see me. So I watched her for a while, not sure what to do. McCarthy was lying around me as if he was always there. He was always there in my mind, and I had no peace. I was always afraid. Not just of McCarthy. It was Papa too, and his Fenians. And Elizabeth. And what was I? They were all in it and over me. I was only a woman caught among them. There was only you, Carrach, in the whole world. I waylaid Agnes one day and pretended she saw me first. I wanted her to tell her mother she saw me, and I was sure she would. If she told Cassie, Cassie would tell you. I was crying out for you, Carrach. I told you once, you're my rock.

"But I didn't know you would come. How could you love me after all this?"

"I love you, Isabella. That's all the talk we need. It's bedtime."

"No."

"There's more to tell?"

"In a way. I want you to understand me, Carrach."

"Don't I?"

"You don't know me anymore. In this time I've learned to survive. I won't give that up. I can never be a decoration. I learned to defend myself. I've learned to support myself. I know what all that feels like now, and I can't go back on it. Here, I learned about some of the women of Boston. They're free women, like Emily. They do things, they are somebody. They're *something*. They have views. They work. They advocate. They fight for things. I want to *be* somebody."

"You are somebody."

"Not yet. But I'm going to be. I'll go back home with you, Carrach, if you'll have me. I love you, more now than ever before. But I'll not wait for anything. I'm not going to be a decoration. I'm not going to be a kept woman. I'm yours. I want you to be mine. But to be ourselves, Carrach, and not to be afraid or dependent or obliged. To love one another but to be ourselves, to be somebody, each of us, together. Do you understand, Carrach?"

"I understand."

"And I'm not to be a chattel? Not a kept woman? Not waiting as if my only use was to love you?"

"Not any of that."

"I have one more thing to tell you, Carrach. I ought to have listened to you. You were right about us. I was too young."

"My God! You tell me that after all . . ."

"It's bedtime." I had never seen her smile as she did then.

Till those few hours in that night came to pass, there had not been enough moments or hours or days or years in my life that, added together, made up a fragment of this joy and meaning. West Cork came back to me, beating like my heart, and I took her strength and courage and independence and love again and again, as a warrior eats the heart of a brave adversary, to make that bravery his own. In that bed was my life's beginning.

And we awoke in the morning and rose to face the day like warriors?

No. We were tired out and slept late and loved again and rose at noon and dined and went into Boston to buy Isabella a new wardrobe. Life was suddenly on an even keel.

It was then that I told her about Cassie and Agnes.

"When that happened," she said, "I was in my mother's womb. It is none of my business." She thought awhile, and I was afraid it might become more to her than I wanted it to be. Then she said, "But Agnes is your business. Why don't we go to see her?"

"Not yet. Not yet. I want to, but not yet."

I hadn't yet eaten enough of her heart to give me her kind of courage. But even then I knew that, being what I am, the time would have to come. I always had to clean the slate.

Twenty-two

With panache, Isabella went about preparing to be somebody. She won access to Henry Longfellow by speaking in Spanish to the maid who opened the door to her. Longfellow speaks eleven languages and was sent for to rescue the maid, and a brief friendship began. After a few days of mutual readings of the poet's verse and Isabella's Spanish translation of "The Village Blacksmith"—which he judged to be "admirable" but, though he had once been professor of modern languages at Bowdoin College and though his translations introduced European literature to most Americans who wanted to know anything about it, Isabella found his Spanish "shaky" and his white hair and beard "like those of Merlin of Camelot"—she had from him a letter of introduction to Elizabeth Peabody.

While this was going on in the house across the way, I established that McCarthy was still working for Kimel, the liquor-store keeper of Providence. I made my plans to see him, and Isabella's plans, or the plans she hoped to make in her new kind of independence, fitted mine very well. I wanted her in some safe place while I was away. She intended to use the Peabody sisters to teach her something useful and to furnish her safe haven.

So we went to Pinckney Street on Beacon Hill, where the sisters had their school, and Isabella presented her letter from Longfellow.

Mary Peabody Mann was the widow of the famous educationalist Horace Mann, who had chosen to be president of the then new Antioch College in Ohio at two thousand dollars a year, rather than governor of Massachusetts. He died in Ohio and his widow came back to New England, and with her sister Elizabeth opened a bookshop and a publishing house. Both enterprises failed, but nothing dismayed or deterred these women from their purposes. Isabella was full of admiration for them, and here they were.

Elizabeth was the talker, the lecturer, the most prolific writer, the most persuasive advocate of the sisters' great passion, a new kind of education for the very young. The kindergarten, they called it, after the teaching of some German fellow named Froebel.

"Ah, all the way from Ireland, my dear," Elizabeth said, and her heavy face sparkled, "to learn about kindergartening?" She looked benignly on Isabella's eager face and said, "Yes, my dear, you must take up kindergartening."

It was news to me that we had come all the way from Ireland to learn from the Peabody sisters about kindergartening, but that is what Longfellow's letter said, and it was presumably what Isabella told him. I did not dispute it. Elizabeth Peabody gathered Isabella to her as a hen gathered her chickens under her wing. It was well known that she was the mother hen who saw a kindergarten teacher in and of her system in every pretty girl. With a growing sense of wonder, I listened to them talk and doubted that Elizabeth Peabody had ever before been outtalked or outcharmed.

"When I know what I'm doing," Isabella said, "I shall turn one of our houses into a school—a Peabody kindergarten. But first I must be prepared. So we came here to learn from you."

Elizabeth Peabody was familiar enough with young women who wanted to learn, but clearly not with young women who spoke of their houses.

"Yes. Your houses," she said. "How many houses do you have?"

"We have three. The dower house is the most suitable. It is called Garden House. What I want to do is bring Catholic and Protestant children together in a school of the sort you are conducting here."

How long had she been thinking these thoughts? They too were news to me.

"I had heard," Miss Peabody said, "that Catholics and Protestants do not mix in Ireland."

"They also kill one another," Isabella said, "which is tiresome. Somebody must teach the Irish to love one another."

"Indeed, yes," Miss Peabody said, "very—tiresome. And indeed someone must teach them to love one another. Have you thought of the possibility of defeat?"

"Defeat? What is that?"

Elizabeth Peabody laughed and embraced her. "It all costs money. Have you thought yet of finding wealthy sponsors to finance such a school?"

Isabella glowed. "I brought mine with me," she said, and smiled at me. "Now, will you teach me?"

"Teach you, my dear? Can you find me a dozen like you? With handy sponsors like yours? I take it you do not yet have children of your own?"

"Three."

"Three?" Astonished, Miss Peabody was guessing birthdays in her head.

"And I must not be away from them for long. When may I begin?"

"Three?"

"So far."

"How old, my dear?"

"You're speaking of the children, of course. Young."

"So I should suppose."

"When may I come?"

"Tomorrow. For the first few days, perhaps a week, you must live here in the school. Three, so far?" And with wonder, "Do you intend to have more?"

Isabella turned her most brilliant smile on Miss Peabody and took my hand in hers. "Well, you know," she said, "when you love fortissimo, it's impossible to know what's going to come of it. Don't you think?"

Mary Mann, the shy sister, had not spoken. Mr. Longfellow said she had loved Horace Mann "fortissimo." She studied Isabella all through the conversation. Now and then she smiled with open approval. Now she laughed. "I think, Mrs. MacDonnell," she said, "your school must be a great success. Come and see ours."

In our hired carriage on the way back to Brattle Street, Isabella was gleeful. "I am a wicked, wicked woman, my darling Carrach," she said, "but I mean every word I said to them. How will you like living with this new woman?"

"If my strength holds out, I'll love it."

"I feel dreadfully fortissimo. How do you feel?"

"Doubly fortissimo." I told the driver to hurry.

Next morning Isabella moved into the school on Pinckney Street, safe in the arms of the Peabody sisters. I set out for Providence with ten thousand dollars for McCarthy. A glorious feeling of invincibility floated in my head. I had Isabella and I loved her recklessly. Fortissimo. All was as I had dreamed of it. I was what I wished to be and never had been.

"What if I get pregnant, darling?" she said the afternoon before when we returned from the Peabodys'.

"You'll get fat," I said, and we laughed. It might have been the joke of the century.

"More fortissimo," she said.

Day and night, at home or abroad, each moment was a kind of ecstasy, of the spirit, of the body. Happiness was a great cry of jubilation. In a way it was West Cork again, a world beyond our world. By some accident we might run into Cousin James in Boston. So be it. Recklessly, we didn't care. It is said that men of my age are subject to such excitements, by which they ruin their lives or emerge wiser but gloomier. No such thought touched my mind. Old Stuffy was dead. I saw no possibility of his resurrection.

That was my mood when I found McCarthy. I followed him to his lodgings. He had moved from the cold-water flat he and Isabella had occupied, and I thought with disgust not only of Isabella having had to live there but of what he had done to her in that place. There was nothing for it but to go boldly into Kimel's liquor store or wait, this time with some sense, and follow him home.

His new place was more respectable, in a working-class home. The woman who came to the door was of my generation, clean, neat, and handsome, with an unfinished look. "Yes?" she said.

I asked to see Mr. McCarthy.

She did not reply for a moment, but examined me from head to foot. "Who?" she said.

"Seán McCarthy. I'm his brother-in-law."

"Oh." She was relieved. "I'll see if he's in."

In a house this size, it was scarcely necessary to look, and I was no more than a minute behind him when I knocked on the door. "He's in," I said.

"Oh."

"May I come in?"

"I'll get him." She closed the door. McCarthy opened it. He cannot have been far from it.

"Carrach!" he cried with simulated pleasure, and seized my

hand. The woman was behind him. "Come on in!" He led me to a tiny parlor. The woman came with us.

That was interesting enough. Landladies know their place. This one had an unusual place, at least in relation to McCarthy.

"Will I get coffee?" she asked him.

"That'd go down well," he said, and she went off to get it. "Well," he said, "what d'you want here?"

"First I want that woman out of the way. I have things to talk about you'll not want her to hear."

"How would you know what I don't want her to hear?" It wasn't defiance or hostility. It was a complaint made in a complaining voice, and he looked down at his feet. It was: What do you care about me?

"Money," I said. "You wanted support. You're going to get it." That told him very little; enough to interest him.

He stared for a moment. Then he smiled. "What support?" Cups rattled on a tray outside the door. "Wait a minute," he said hastily, and opened the door.

There were three cups on the tray, and I had no intention of negotiating third-party obstacles. "Mrs. . . .?" I said. "I'm afraid I don't know your name."

"Wilson," she said, pouring coffee, "Muriel Wilson." She handed me my cup.

Let him talk his way out of the thing when I left. I said to her, "Mr. McCarthy and I have some family business to discuss. Do you mind if we take our coffee to his room?"

She didn't reply and didn't look at me. She looked at McCarthy. There was no expression on her face, and for the first time I realized that she was less intrusive than dependent. And dull-witted. McCarthy nodded to her and took his cup.

"We'll only be a minute." He said it kindly, and I thought I saw something or understood something in him. He was afraid of Isabella because in everything he felt inferior to her. He felt superior to this slow woman, and in his own weakness could afford to be kind, maybe even tender toward her in her evident dependence. She nodded submissively, and we went upstairs without her.

It was a woman's room, there was no doubt about that. "Why this room?" I asked him. "Why not your room?"

He shifted his feet uncomfortably. "This is my room."

"When did you start using talcum powder?"

He shrugged himself into some appearance of defiance. "You were talking about money," he said. "What money?"

I took the money from the case I carried it in and counted it out slowly on to the marbled washstand. "Ten thousand dollars," I said, and put it back in the case. I thought his mouth watered. "Now we'll sit down and talk." I sat on the edge of the bed. He sat on the one upright chair in the room. His excitement kept him silent. He did not take his gaze from the case. I pulled down the pillow nearest me. There was a woman's light nightgown under it. I pulled down the other one. His nightclothes were there. He was watching me now, swallowing hard.

"You sleep with her."

"My wife left me."

"So you have a substitute. Do you need to put a knife to this one's throat?"

"That's a lie."

"You stole from the Fenians and you sold the men in Manchester, and for that they'll kill you if they catch you. Don't deny that you sold them," I said as he opened his mouth. "I do not intend to sell you." I was not going to say to him the things I desperately wanted to say; to shout at him, abuse him; then beat him. I did not want his mean mind brooding on the insults or the abuse, or festering over the beating. A simple bribe would not insult him. A clear and sure escape from the reach of the Fenians would surely please him?

"I do not want Isabella's husband to end in an informer's grave," I said, "and you have no cards to play against Hugh." He was gazing at the case again. "And California would be far enough away. But you have a choice."

"What choice?"

"You go west with ten thousand dollars in your pocket, or I set Pinkertons on you and they will keep you in sight wherever you go and keep me informed and I shall inform the Clan na Gael and call off Pinkertons. There would be no witnesses. That is your choice."

His hands writhed together on his knees. His eyes were wide open. In a peculiar way, his scalp moved backward and forward as his eyes opened wide and his eyebrows moved up and down. I had never seen in him any such signs of distress, if that is what they were.

"My wife . . ." he began.

"Is not your wife. That, you agree to. You will never for

the rest of your natural life come near her again. You will not try to communicate with her again. You do not have her. You cannot have her. You will put her completely out of your mind. There are no options. You disappear—off the face of the earth. You never reappear . . ." My voice was rising, my control loosening. I seized myself.

His hands stopped working. The strange movement of his scalp and his eyebrows came to an end. He was not sitting erect now, but slumped like a very tired man or one on whom a great tranquillity had descended.

"Is Mrs. Wilson a widow?" He nodded. "Will you take her with you?" There was no response. "I have Pinkertons alerted. I shall not wait. I do not intend to negotiate with you. You agree or you do not, and whatever it is to be, it will be decided now." He did not speak. His breathing was deep and even.

"There is a cheaper way to deal with this," I said, going beyond the mandate I gave myself. "You are living with this woman. A divorce would cost much less than I have in this case."

"My wife's a Catholic," he said indifferently.

"The Fenians would cost me nothing," I said, "and your time is running out."

He puzzled me. His passivity had begun to disturb me. I could not read it. It was passivity, not tranquillity; it was, it began to appear to me, the state of nervous recuperation into which I fell myself after some intense strain that had drained me of my inner resources. He was rebuilding himself. Slowly he sat up and smiled at me.

"Yes," he said.

"Yes what?"

"I agree."

"You have no doubt about the terms. You simply disappear off the face of the earth."

"I agree." His face sweated. He wiped his brow on the back of his hand and stood up. His smile softened. His manner was servile. He picked up the woman's talcum bowl, and it slipped from his sweating hands and made an off-white heap on the floor and a small cloud that settled about him. "It broke," he said without concern; with a little amusement. "She'll clean it up." It was a small assertion of a manlier self. "I agree," he said again. "The money?" He pointed to the case.

"I want to hear a lot more than that," I said. "I want to hear that you know exactly what you're agreeing to."

"I'm to disappear off the face of the earth, never to come near, write to, or think of my wife. To all that, I agree."

"West. Australia. As far away as you can get."

"Farther," he said, revived, smiling, obsequious, full of the smiling soft answers of the Irish. "How is Isabella?"

I opened the case and took out the money. No answers to any questions. His hand was held out. Then both hands. I put the money on the washstand and opened the door. He scooped it up quickly and closed the door again. "Just a minute, old brother," he said, and opened a cupboard and packed the money at the back of a high shelf.

"I agree to everything," he said again with unnecessary fulsomeness. "Tell Isabella not to worry. She's free as a bird. There's a nice little Irish poem about that, but I forget it. Never mind. I agree to everything, and that's the God's truth. Are you well yourself, old brother?"

I opened the door again and called downstairs, "Mrs. Wilson, can you join us for a moment?"

"What the hell now?" McCarthy said, and grabbed my arm. I shook him off. Mrs. Wilson came, hurrying. She looked only, and with questions, at McCarthy.

I picked up her nightgown. "I see you sleep with my brother-in-law, Mrs. Wilson. So take very good care of him. Go with him on his travels."

She mistook it, I'm sure, for family concern, and smiled and nodded. McCarthy did not misunderstand. Some Catholics cease to be Catholics when the restraints of their church make life unendurable. He was paid off. He could still be divorced.

He said meanly, "He's married to my sister and she doesn't sleep with him. She says he has a prick that was transplanted from a stallion. If he comes near here again, give him the door."

Mrs. Wilson said gently, "Oh, you didn't drink your coffee."

I wandered in the station, waiting for my train. I was ten thousand dollars poorer, and not at all certain now of what I had accomplished. There was nothing stable about the man. He was insolent, frightened, obsequious in turn. He smiled and sweated and promised, and was treacherous to his friends. Why not to me? The prospect of his treachery and of any action it might force me to take in our defense made me feel sick.

When I took my seat and was settled, I looked down the platform. The colored man who had shown me to my seat was looking in my direction and talking to McCarthy, who mouthed something at the window. It looked like, "Have a good trip."

To Boston, of course. The colored man who saw my ticket could tell him that.

✑ Twenty-three ✑

It was only a few days later, when Isabella was engaged on some enterprise with the Peabodys, that I walked alone in a cold wind down Marlborough Street toward the river. I walked briskly. The figure ahead of me walked briskly and shocked me. He turned into a doorway and was lost to me. I ran. He had turned into number 140. I ran up the stairs, but he had disappeared. From the top flat down I checked the names on the doors. The top floor was Polish. The second floor was O'Houlihan, the ground floor was Mansfield. I climbed again to the second floor and knocked. A young woman opened the door.

"I should like to see my brother," I said.

"Your brother?" she said. "Well, who's your brother?" She was as Irish as the bog.

"Hugh MacDonnell."

"Wait a minute." She closed the door.

Hugh opened it. "There was always a chance of it," he said with his lunatic grin. "Come in."

I didn't see the young woman again. I heard voices, but when Hugh closed the living-room door they were shut away. "This, I take it, was an accident," he said.

"I saw you on the street."

"And followed me."

"I didn't have far to follow. It was this street. I take it you're on parliamentary business?"

"In this country? No, I'm not on parliamentary business."

"What are you doing here?"

"Carrach, we meet three thousand miles from home and you question me like this? I thought you'd simply be glad to see me."

"So what are you doing here?"

"Money raising for Parnell."

"Who came with you? Tim Healy?" They always did it in pairs.

"I came alone."

"On private business, Hugh?"

"Yes." He said it resentfully.

"You could have told me you were coming. I have a house where you could stay. You'd have seen your daughter."

"I didn't have your address."

"I sent it to you."

"I left soon after you did."

"In fact, you followed me. Everywhere?"

"Not everywhere. Only to Boston."

I almost said, Not to Providence? and caught myself. I said, "But you know where I live?"

"Yes." He didn't look at me. He hadn't expected to be caught, but caught, he tried to laugh it away with his lunatic laugh.

"It's McCarthy, isn't it?" There was no point in pretending. "You knew I'd found Isabella. If I had found Isabella, I would find McCarthy, and if I found him, you'd find him. Isn't that it?"

"Not me."

"Them."

But his patience was exhausted. "Look," he said, angry. *"She is my child."*

"Murder by proxy. Is that it?"

"They have good cause."

"And you have good cause? Well, you won't find him. I paid him off. He's gone."

"How much did you pay him?"

"Ten thousand dollars."

"He'll be back. That's not enough for a wife, not to him. You don't know men like him. Carrach, he sold men. You're an innocent. He's just begun on you."

"And when he comes back, you'll be there?"

"Not me."

"Why not you? You have cause."

"Because I don't need to."

"But if they weren't there, you would be."

It took a long time. Then he said, "Yes, by God. Yes."

What was there to say to him? This was Hugh, my brother, whom I loved. I didn't feel anger. How could I feel anger when I had felt more than once that I could kill McCarthy myself? But to be here to do it, or see it done—that was another matter, another sort of mind, another sort of life. This brother was the Eagle of my boyhood, Black Hughie, the sea marauder, the Viking, the Highland gallows tribe whose delights were the sword and conflict.

He stood there staring at my disconsolate-looking face, and his own face was hard. "You don't understand, do you, Carrach?"

"Yes, I understand. It's my stomach that's weak, not my understanding."

"You should thank God for that."

"You mean, you sometimes tremble?"

"Maybe more than you do."

"I'll go," I said hopelessly.

"You'll not tell her?"

"Oh, no. She's endured enough. I won't saddle her with this."

He put his arm about my shoulders. "Don't cast me out," he said.

"You know," I said, "Hugh, you know."

What was it Mr. Longfellow said? That the Irish would come roaring out of their ghettos to devour us?

And to devour what? We wandered a little in our months in Boston. One of our wanderings was with Elizabeth Peabody to Portland, Maine, where she was to lecture. On that trip we visited a community workshop where farmers and fishermen, of whatever church and prevented from working by snow and winter storm, joined together to hand-make shoes. They hired a reader to read to them while they worked.

"The farmers and fishermen of New England," Elizabeth said to us, "are better qualified than almost all the incumbents in the Senate of the United States." To devour that.

"Civility," Isabella said.

"That is what it is," Elizabeth Peabody said. "That describes our New England farmers, fishermen, merchants, and scholars—civility."

"If I were not so determined," Isabella said to me, "I would say to you, Carrach, let us stay here."

Several times over these latter days, Isabella called me to

an upstairs front-room window. Look, Carrach, yesterday two men were pacing up and down between Longfellow's house and ours. There they are again. It was true. They were flapping their arms, stamping, blowing into their gloves, blowing on their hands. Four times, with days between, she called me and there they were. Not, so far as we could judge at this distance, always the same men. We could not tell what they were. I was not much concerned about what they were. We were in a strange country; they could mean something or nothing. To us, nothing. They have nothing to do with us, I told her. But I looked out more often and kept my thoughts to myself.

Then she called me again, from a landing window. Two men from a carriage were talking to the foot stampers. They turned our way. They walked toward our house. "They're coming here," Isabella said.

I sent her to the drawing room and went to meet them at the door. In these odd circumstances it was well not to let them have talk with a servant.

They were Irish. There was no mistaking the look. The Irish look is as distinctive as the Slavic or the Jewish. Put whatever elegance you please over the body, the face makes its own announcement.

"Mr. MacDonnell?" the bigger of them said. They were both big, burly, making their coats look too tight for them.

"Yes." I could see Hugh like a ghost behind them. He was a member of parliament in London and still a Fenian at heart.

"We have a letter of introduction from your brother, Hugh." Of course. The universal conspiracy. It wasn't Catholic; merely Irish. Orange or Catholic. There was no point in keeping them standing in the cold. It was in any case ill-mannered. They did not hand me the letter. Their immobility announced I would get it after I asked them in.

In the drawing room they handed it over. No introductions till I had read it. Isabella nodded cautiously. They sat down without removing their coats. I read the letter.

My dear Carrach: The bearers are West Cork men now living in Boston. They will introduce themselves. If Isabella is with you—which pray God is the case—she can establish their knowledge of West Cork by sharp questioning. Please give them all the help you can. And please bring my child home. Give her our love. Your devoted brother, Hugh.

My child? I looked at her and thought of her in bed and saw no child. She took the letter. Had they read it? No, they said. Yes, I was quite convinced.

She looked hard at them. "I have no questions," she said. "I have seen that one," she pointed to the smaller of the pair, "at home."

"Sullivan, missus," he said. "From Ballydehob."

"Powers, ma'am. From Bantry."

McCarthy hadn't come as Hugh was sure he would. He couldn't wait forever. So he would try to hurry it? I wondered whether he smiled when he wrote this letter, or whether he had doubts about his tactics. He had no doubts about his purpose. McCarthy was to be found, by any means.

"Take off your coats." She took them.

"What help does my brother expect me to give you?" I asked them.

"It's in the matter of McCarthy, beggin your pardon, missus," Sullivan said. "You're here, but where's he?"

"I left him."

They looked at one another. Who goes next? Powers said, "Where did you leave him, ma'am?"

It seemed wise to me to establish the ground rules. They were not going to harass Isabella. But I had no need to worry. She said, "You gentlemen are interested in McCarthy because of the Manchester affair . . ."

"No, no, ma'am. Nothin like that. He's just a fellow Irishman new in a strange land. We want to help him." It was Powers looking pious. There is something comic about big pious men.

"I've no doubt he deserves your 'help,' " Isabella said. "But don't ask me any more questions. I won't answer them. I am not an executioner."

"That's a scandalous thought, ma'am," Powers said. "We would never ask you . . ."

"Don't." She sat back, folded her hands in her lap, and set her lips. It was the last word they got out of her.

"Then I'll have to ask you, sir," Powers said.

"I'll tell you what you need to know," I said.

"We need to know it all," Sullivan said.

"In that case, I'll amend that. I'll tell you what I think is all you need to know. I have seen McCarthy. I have paid him the sum of ten thousand dollars to move far away—disappear off the face of the earth is how I put it to him. He has agreed to go and not to return."

"Where was this you saw him, Mr. MacDonnell?" Lightly. Innocently.

"I am not an executioner," I said.

"Are you serious, then? Are you tellin us you believe the man? After all you know about him?"

"I'll wait and see."

"You're not scared for the young lady, then?"

"I can deal with that, thank you."

"It's not the sort of thing you deal with, Mr. MacDonnell. We can save you the trouble."

"I have nothing more to tell you."

Their faces were set. They had expected more from Hugh's brother.

"I mean no offense, sir," Powers said, "but you paid a paid informer to get away."

"No, Mr. Powers, I paid a blunderer to remove himself from our lives. What I did about McCarthy has nothing to do with your reasons for seeking him out. You want him dead. I will not be your tool. That is what I'm saying to you."

"Your father won't like this, ma'am," he said to Isabella. She did not reply.

"Split the difference, sir," Sullivan said to me like an auctioneer.

"What does that mean?"

"Well, was it in Boston you saw him?"

"No."

"How many miles from here? In what state? You could tell us that much?"

"No."

"You've got the great faith in human nature, Mr. MacDonnell," Powers said, and got up.

"No. I have very little faith in human nature."

"You're right. You're right at that. McCarthy's the proof."

Sullivan got up. We all stood up. Isabella brought them their coats. They put them on and lingered. There was more to say.

"He'll come to you for more pay," Sullivan said.

"Perhaps."

"Does he know where you live?"

"No."

"If there's money in it for him, he'll find you."

"Perhaps."

"He'll come here."

"He might."

"Well, then, Mr. MacDonnell, I'll tell you this," Sullivan said, and stuck his hands deep into his coat pockets and looked, not at me, but at Isabella. "If he comes, we'll let him get in. And I don't think you, missus, will be too pleased about that, or you wouldn't have left him. The question is, then—will we let him out once he's in? How long do you want him shut up here, missus? That's goin to be a very disturbin time for you. Maybe you'll say you'll call the police to get him out? Well, now, there's plenty of Irish stevedores here, plenty of Irish upholsterers, shopkeepers, bootleggers, hoores, and gamblers. There's not many Irish doctors or lawyers—yet. But the police, now? Callin the police would be like callin the Clan na Gael. They would come here, they would escort him outside, they'd keep him in till it got dark, they'd send somebody to tell me he'd be walkin out of their station at such and such a time, and we'd be there waitin. Missus," he said, *"he got paid for hangin three men."* They walked out of the house.

I don't think we spoke for a long five minutes.

Isabella said, "Carrach, are they right? Will he come back for more?"

"I don't know. I don't know. Maybe. He's the kind."

But we were happy. Sublimely happy. How we laughed at the amount of Auld Alliance Scotch already being sold, and how quiet we were about who owned a large part of it. And because we were so happy, in spite of occasional gloom we were optimistic. It was impossible to be among these Bostonians and not believe that evil could be circumvented or transformed into good. Even in Ireland. We had our moments of invincibility. And the joy of constant anticipation at any hour of the day or night.

Once we went with Elizabeth Peabody to New York. We were charged with her care by her sister Mary and to see that she wore her new black silk dress and not her old worn black silk dress. She was not to be allowed to wander the streets alone talking to wicked strangers or walking into traffic. Then, having enjoyed our marvelous charge and the people she brought to meet Isabella, we returned to Brattle Street, hurrying to be alone again. We could never be alone enough.

"Mr. Seán McCarthy is waiting to see you in the study," the cook-housekeeper said.

All joy, all anticipation, all optimism died. Hugh's messengers were right.

He was not in the study. He was not in the drawing room. We found him in our bedroom, lying on our bed. Over the end board of the bed were draped Isabella's nightclothes and mine. He did not get up.

"You were saying something about divorce, brother Carrach," he said. His narrow face was the ugliest I have ever seen.

Old Stuffy was dead. With violence I threw McCarthy from the bed. He rolled across the floor.

"That will be expensive," he said on his knees.

"Leave us," I said to Isabella.

"I'll stay." She closed and locked the door.

I intended to beat him. The servants would hear it, but I cared nothing for what they heard. I cared nothing for what anybody heard. But first there was something I wanted to hear: something that for the rest of my life would allow me to justify to myself what I intended to do.

"How did you get here?" I asked him.

"Up the riverbank along the bottom of the garden," he said, looking smart.

So they hadn't seen him come in. That involved me in more positive action than I wanted to take, but now, before God, I would take it. When I was ready. "What do you want?"

"Talk," he said, and got to his feet and pulled up Isabella's chair.

"Don't sit down. Stand just where you are and don't move. And do your talking." I dragged the chair out of his reach. "And be very brief."

"You're sleeping with my wife," he said.

I wanted to beat him then. The thought that he could degrade all that we were to one another in this room, in this house, and reduce it to one dirty statement, blinded me with rage. She was not his wife. Damn the church, damn the law. A girl's mistake or her haste or her foolishness did not and would not be allowed to reduce her for the rest of her life to the level of this creature's legal chattel. Nor would I talk to him, or about Isabella to him, as if he had rights in her or near her. As if he had the right to talk about her at all.

"Say what you came to say." I took off my jacket and threw it on the bed.

He watched it fly and fall and wiped his mouth with the tips of his fingers. "You can tell who you like where you think I am," he said. "You can do what you like. Get all the good you can out of beating me. But I have money now, Carrach, and I can move. They'll not find me." A little flame of courage or anger blew in him for a moment. "I know now what I need to know. You came and shit on me. You, you hypocrite, talked about me sleeping with Mrs. Wilson while you were getting yours with my wife. Then you paid me off like a hoore master—for my wife. You bought her from me. And you didn't pay me enough." His own words fired his anger or his courage. "You didn't pay me enough for her, and you're going to pay my price, not yours."

He was leaning forward, almost crouching. His face was distorted. He was screaming at me. It wasn't courage, it was fear. Once he saw that his reappearance had not frightened us, this was the only way he could say what he had to say. As a blackmailer he had no skill. As a man he had no courage. No doubt he wandered the house when he came, and found this room and made his small discovery and felt it gave him power. Power over Old Stuffy. Not power over me. No doubt in Providence he brooded alone on the money I gave him and on how much more I could have given him and how much more he ought to get. Alone, using his own judgment, he drew his own isolated conclusions. He knew the Fenians, but somewhere in the isolation of his own mind he decided to steal from them. No skill, no courage, no judgment. And all he got now for his shouting was silence. He looked to Isabella, who stood by the door, her face pale and grim like a woman fighting back nausea. He looked to me, and I do not know what he saw. If he saw what I felt—he saw nausea.

"You're going to keep me, Carrach. I came here a week ago. I've been searching for you all week. I found your house this morning, and when I knew you were sleeping with my wife, I wrote a letter, down there in your library. I sent one of your maids to post it to Mrs. Wilson. It's to Elizabeth, Carrach. I wrote another one and put it in the same envelope. It's to Hugh, old brother. And if I don't get what I came for, they'll both go. I sent her others, old brother. To your clerk as well. To your Orange butler, Patton. To some of your neighbors. I wrote a dozen letters while I waited for you. If I don't get what I came for, they're all going. One by one. Think of the talk, Carrach. Old Stuffy went to America on a visit, and what was he doing there? You can hear it in the lodges, can't you? But I'll be moving. You won't find me. They won't find me. I have the money to move."

"While it lasts," I said.

"You'll make it last, old brother."

"How can I do that if I can't find you?" It was less than he expected, quieter, maybe more submissive than he expected. It encouraged him.

"This is a very fine house, Carrach." His head was cocked, his eyes roving. He was grinning. He had me. Everything about him said he knew he had me. "It's a rich man's house. How long did you take it for? How long are you going to stay where you think you're safe, taking the wife you bought from me to bed? You're a very rich man, old brother. You want to keep her?" He nudged his thumb at her. "You want a lot of time to enjoy her? Then pay the right price for her, old brother."

I was no longer thinking of the squalid things he had to say. I was thinking that if he called me old brother again, I would throw him through the window.

"You haven't much to say, have you? How much? Is that what you want to hear?"

What I heard then was the key turning in the lock. Isabella opened the door. "Get out of my house," she said to him.

I closed the door and locked it and gave her the key. "Oh, no, no, no. He's not leaving yet. He has more to say. I want him to say it, all of it. Then, he will leave the house. That I promise you. I have a price too. It goes up with every dirty word he utters, every threat he makes. Let him drive it up. High. Very high. Then he can leave." I said to him, "What's the highest you can push it, Seán? How high do you want to push it?"

I had never in my life felt like this before. It was anger, I know that. Rage? Fury? The words don't matter. It was cold, as ice is cold. There was no pulse in it. There was no feeling in it. It was a cold and settled intent, and I wanted him to justify it to the last fragment of my endurance and hers. I looked at the man, and he was no more than a weasel in one of my fields threatening my boots. To be dealt with. So.

He did not understand what I said.

"What price?" he said. "I'm the one who'll talk price."

"Of course you are." He sold more than a half dozen for

money. They were enemies of all I believed about Ireland, but he sold them. Three of them hanged by the neck till they were dead, and he sold them to the hangman. There is a right to life till you take a life. I could not now raise my voice. "Of course you are," I said again, and watched him misread the sound. His self-deceiving judgment told him I was afraid. It told him I was so afraid I could speak only above a whisper, and the thin face sweating from nervous strain declared his mounting confidence. "What price?" I said.

"You're going to support me, Carrach."

"What price?"

"For the rest of my life." It was glee, or hysteria.

"What price?"

"Think of all those people reading my letters. Tomas Carrach, the proud, correct, and honorable MacDonnell, coming all the way to Boston to fuck his eighteen-year-old niece, the wife of his own wife's brother. That's what my letters say, Carrach, and they're all on their way to Mrs. Wilson. That's what they'll read about you. Robert Garrett, Hugh MacDonnell, Elizabeth MacDonnell, Patton, Buchanan. The talk, Carrach! What will they call her, old brother? The Boston whore? You don't want that, do you, Carrach?"

"What price?" He had settled my price long ago. Now he made it irrevocable.

"Oh, you want to pay now, all right, don't you? But there's one thing you'll always know, old brother, and it will eat your guts out. You'll be keeping me, but you'll never be able to forget that I got into her first."

It was enough. Nothing he could do now, say now, could save him. I could have killed him myself, there, where he stood. I expected Isabella to unlock the door and run. She did not. She moved slowly, so slowly that apart from a glance when she took her first step, he paid no attention to her. I did not know what she was doing or going to do.

"What price?" I said. "If you want it, get to it."

She was behind him now, at her dressing table. She sat down. By her right hand was a tray, and on it a carafe of water and two tumblers.

"You're going to settle a nice little fortune on me, Carrach."

"How little?"

"Fif . . ."

He heard her move as she pushed over the stool and swung. He spun, and the carafe caught him, not where she intended it to, on the back of his head, but on the upper left arm. All her strength was in it. The crack as the arm broke was like a gunshot from somewhere else in the house. His scream must have been heard by the watchers on the street, if they were there. He toppled to the bed on his right side and lay howling and moaning and whimpering. We stood aside to watch him. The servants did not come knocking. They were, no doubt, in the hall listening.

"Pain?" I said.

"Holy Mary, Jesus Christ," he wailed, "Mother of God, Christ, Christ . . ."

"You've never done anything but cause pain," I said, and Isabella, her face without expression, put down the carafe, brushed indifferently at the water on her clothes, and went to sit down.

I hauled him to his feet and dumped him in a chair. His arm dangled, and he made sounds of sick anguish. "I have news for you," I said. Pain robbed him of his triumph, of his manhood, and I almost weakened. Even a gut-shot rabid dog is a pitiful sight. But I thought of all he had done down the years and all he had said in this room about Isabella. I had more sympathy for the dog. "The Fenians have been here."

"No." He was moaning and whimpering now, and I think not really aware of anything I said.

"Did you hear me?" I said. "The Fenians have been here." He heard me.

"No, no, no," he said.

"They have been watching the house for days. They are waiting for you outside, on the street."

The effort he made was Herculean. He dragged himself upright and grimaced with every movement of the broken arm. "Carrach," he said, and marshaled himself against pain. "Carrach, don't let them." He was truly pitiful.

"Did you write the letters?"

"Yes."

"Did you post them to the Wilson woman?"

He twisted himself and cried out. "In my pocket. Take them, Carrach. Get me out, please. Take them, Carrach, and get me out."

"The front door."

"The back. In the name of God, the back. Christ's pity, Carrach." The name seemed inappropriate in this creature's mouth.

I took the letters from his pocket and put them on the bed.

I went through his pockets, and he sat with the face of a dog in pain. My money was in every pocket. "You took the money and ran out on that poor woman Wilson?" I put it back.

"She wasn't . . . she didn't . . ." But his invention was weaker than the pain, and he howled. Then, "Yes," he whimpered.

"You're really not fit to live."

"Let me, Carrach. I'll go. Honest to God I'll go. You'll never set eyes on me again, as sure as God's my judge."

"Unlock the door," I said to Isabella. She did.

"He's leaving by the front door," she said.

"No. The back. Find his coat." I couldn't deliver the body to them. Not even this one.

I took him downstairs and put his coat over his good arm. He would most likely fall down in the snow and freeze to death or stumble into the Charles River and drown. "Wait for me in the drawing room," I said to Isabella, and took him to the back door. "If I ever see you again in this life, McCarthy, even at a distance and when you don't know you're near me, I'll kill you myself."

"Honest to God, Carrach, you'll never see me. I'll go far, far, far . . ."

"Start going."

Hesitantly, like an old man, he went down the steps into the snow. I watched him stumble down the white slope toward the river. The moon was bright, the snow white, the trees and their shadows stark and black. I watched three men run from the trees in Mr. Longfellow's long garden. I saw McCarthy try to run, stumble, and fall; I heard his scream. He fell on his left side. The men came running in the black-and-white landscape.

Like the landscape of the Irish mind, I thought. I closed the door.

Isabella said in the drawing room, "He'll come back, Carrach."

"No," I said. "No."

She looked at me and looked away and said no more.

"It's bedtime," I said.

"Not in that bed," she said, "and not tonight. That man pollutes everything he touches and everything he speaks of."

Not now, God help him. But I said nothing.

✍ Twenty-four ✍

We spoke now of "the children," and it brought a wonderful feeling of oneness. It was in our cabin on the New York–Liverpool steamer—stable and luxurious travel after sail and the *Sorley Boye*—that Isabella let me into a secret she had harbored for two weeks. It was a belated Christmas gift for her parents.

My God, what joy we anticipated for the years ahead. I felt it in my marrow.

We hurried to London to see Hugh and his wife; not to sleep in his house but at a hotel, for we were not to be separated. It was a quick visit, then to the Holyhead–Kingstown boat to see Emily, for Isabella had plans for her also. The telegraph wires sang with our hearts and heads. These were delirious days for us.

Hugh's happiness at seeing his daughter overcame his painful scruples about her relationship to me. His wife was all over me with warm affection, binding us all, I suppose, into a secure and united future. My own sense of family responded to that.

A number of Irish members of parliament lived at Hugh's house. Happily, all of them were home in Ireland for the parliamentary recess. He "sheltered them," he said, "in the attics" because they were poor and maintained families in Ireland and could not afford two homes. The parliamentary recess meant that we did not have to meet them. He had two servant girls, brought with him from Goleen. They slept below stairs to protect them from the Irish members.

We had a happy family dinner, the four of us. There was wine and laughter and good feelings, and Isabella was so happy I was persuaded that she must soon fall from her chair or fly in pieces about the room.

"Papa. Mama," she said, "I have brought you a present that will last you all your lives."

She stood up and turned about. "Look hard. See if you can guess where I've hidden it."

I could see it, but only because I had been told where it was. Her mother could see it. "Ayeayeayeee," she said, and, "Ayoayoayoooo."

"Not me," Hugh said, "I can't see it."

Isabella sat down. "You'll see it next month."

"I want to see it now. What's a Christmas present in spring?"

"Papa, I'm pregnant."

Hugh sobered quickly. "What are you going to tell us about your life in this past year?" he said. Perhaps paternity could be established by the calendar?

"Nothing. It is my life." Her gaiety did not leave her.

"What are you going to tell us about the father of this child?"

"That you know him. That is enough. It is my child. Papa, I love you. I love you most dearly. I shall love you till I die. I shall love you no matter what you do or say." She went to him, put her arms about him, and kissed him. "But I would advise you to be happy at my happiness, or I shall make your life one long misery." She went back to her place. "Do not judge me, Papa. The baby is mine. You cannot have me without it."

"Carrach?" he said.

"I believe every word she says, Hugh." I was a little light-headed. "I shall say only what Isabella allows me to say."

"What do you allow him to say?" He was remarkably composed.

"Whatever he pleases."

They all watched me, but it was Isabella who mattered. She had not made a point of acknowledged paternity. We did not discuss it. Frankly, I question whether in our excitement either of us had thought about the matter. I certainly had not. I wondered now what she really wanted, and her face said nothing.

"Mine," I said. "Ours, Hugh. I'm not sure what your relationship to the child will be, apart from grandfather. As my son or daughter, are you also its uncle? There is also the church. Degrees of consanguinity come in here, don't they? And to tell you the truth, and you may as well hear it at your own table, I don't give a damn, not about the church—or anything."

That is what Isabella had been waiting to hear. "Nor do I. You, Mama?" she said.

In some ways, Hugh's wife was like his imprint. She lived in his shadow, but I had the notion, the more I saw of her, that she governed my brother more than he knew. I wasn't sure of that. Maybe he knew? Maybe the modification that was going on in his mind and spirit—and it was certainly going on—was her quiet work. It was not possible for them to hide their mutual devotion. They made no effort to hide it. It was the devotion that belongs to an old, not-yet-burned-out but quietened passion; a mutual dependence. The question was: Who was most dependent, most influenced by the other? At times they came to remind me of Father and Mother and their devotion.

She said, "You were your father's heir, Bella. Not now. Come and kiss me." Her smile answered all my questions. "Have a son. He will inherit."

"And if I have a daughter?" Isabella said, holding her.

"She will inherit," Hugh said. "What we must think about is registration."

What danger there may have been of a storm—and how could I be sure there had ever been such a danger?—had passed. I should not be at all surprised to learn someday that all this had been discussed between them while I was in America, all settled, all positions taken and modified, all agreements reached.

"Ring for more wine," Hugh said to his wife. "The child will be born here. Registered here. Daughter—or son—of Tomas Carrach MacDonnell and whatever he does for a living. Are you officially a flax spinner or a sailor, Carrach? Or do you put down 'Gentleman'?" I was not expected to answer. "Daughter or son of Isabella Marimar Juana Medina MacDonnell . . . The name's the thing. MacDonnell . . ."

"Spinster," Isabella said. "Isabella MacDonnell, spinster. You have to put that on the registration paper."

"The child will be quite real, dear," her mother said, "the rest is paper."

"Who's worrying, Mama?"

"I am." Hugh had his head into family business. He had

turned his back on it in his twentieth year; now he took it over. "Carrach, you'll have to make some sort of generous settlement on Bella, for her protection . . ."

"Mind your own business, Papa."

"I'll look after the boy."

"Child, Papa. Boy, girl, wait and find out which."

"This is my business. You are my business."

"I am my business, Papa."

"A trust fund, Carrach."

"Mind your own business, Papa."

I drank more wine. This was family. This was what I had needed all my adult life, and at forty it had come at last. This was acceptance, one of the other, without malice or distrust or suspicion; this was home. I was a very happy man.

I drank more wine.

"A trust fund, Carrach?"

"I am very happy, Hugh," I said. "I shall discuss all this with Isabella when we get home. At the moment," I drank more wine, "you will tell us how your Irish are doing at Westminster."

"That is your business, Papa."

I drank more wine. It was a wonderful evening.

The wine talked of Ireland, of Ulster, of politics, religion, England, America. It rhapsodized on Boston and its civility and all the thoughts that formed in my mind while we were there came rolling off my tongue: I was no longer passive. I was going to take a public role in the life of my province, and no one would be allowed to stop me. Ulster, I said, must be separated from Ireland until Ireland is advanced enough to be an equal partner with us in industrial development.

"We shall not surrender any part of Ireland," Hugh said, "we shall have it all."

I talked of the judgments of honest men from many parts of the world who saw Ulstermen as different men and a different nation. We must reconcile our differences, I agreed, you must develop your skills, including farming. You must be like the Danes. The world that is coming is a world of machines, but men must still eat. You must help to feed them, but your agriculture is primitive and wasteful. My long-hidden thoughts poured out. We were brothers. We loved one another. We did not agree. But I meant what I said. The change in my life was real.

"You want to be King of Ulster," Hugh said, hearing only the talk the wine made. Home Rule, for him, was the solution to all our troubles. "But kings in Ireland have never been secure. Every Irishman knows that he and he alone would make a better king."

We left very late for our hotel. We were a family again, as we had been when we were young.

While Isabella was alone for a moment with her mother, no doubt receiving maternity advice, Hugh pressed a bulky envelope into my hand. "This, I think, is yours," he said. "Look at it later." I stuffed it into my overcoat pocket.

I did not think about the envelope when we got to the hotel. We were much too happy. I was packing in the morning when it came to mind and I opened it.

In it were nine thousand American dollars. We were on the Holyhead–Kingstown boat before I was able to drive the crawling sensation from my skin.

One night at Emily's, then home. "My God," she said when we were going to our room that night, "you're living in sin."

"It's lovely," Isabella said. Her laughter was music to me.

When you are forty, other people's happiness in your happiness enlarges all things good. All that evening they talked together about Isabella's plans. Emily argued. Isabella explained, enlarged upon, advocated, persuaded. Her enthusiasm overwhelmed. While Carrach is making himself King of Ulster, you and I shall tame the passions of his future subjects, Emily.

"You need us, we need you, darling Emily," she said.

"Why do I need you?"

"Because you need someone who will sell your pictures. Carrach will sell your pictures. He'll begin by buying them, and when he does, others will."

"Others do now."

"But not enough. Papa will buy your pictures and hang them in his house in London. People will see them and want to buy from you. Blue Irish landscapes will be the rage in London. People come to see Papa from France and Spain. Blue Irish landscapes will become the rage in Paris and Madrid."

"That will come anyway."

"Emily dear, will you please tell me how I can run a kindergarten alone when my belly is bigger than Robert Garrett's?"

"That's the first good argument you've used since you started. I'll come. Carrach?"

"Yes, Emily?"

"You will buy my pictures?"

"Yes, Emily."

"And help sell them?"

"Yes, Emily."

"I'll come. Give me a week to clear up here, and I'll follow you."

"Emily, when you come, you'll have my old room. I'll be in the room next to Carrach."

That was when Emily, who had already rejoiced over Isabella's pregnancy, said, "My God, you're living in sin!"

And Isabella said, "It's lovely."

To me it was wonder and joy every step of the way. Isabella carried my bastard child, and the people I loved best and who loved me rejoiced in it. It was, surely, delirium?

In bed, I said to her, "What ever happened to that independence you talked about in Boston?"

"Darling Carrach," she said, wrapping herself around me, "between two people who love one another, independence is a collaboration. Don't you think?"

Alasdar and Morag and Kitty. How they had grown. The same delirium was in them. Alasdar clung to Isabella with a ferocity that alarmed me and delighted her. He would not let her go. He chanted and held her.

"Isabella, Isabella, Isabella," he chanted, and would not give way for his sisters.

"Alasdar, you beast. You selfish beast."

"Alasdar, she's ours too. We want to kiss her, you bully."

He paid no attention. The girls climbed on them, on Alasdar's back, on Isabella's back, and bore them to the ground. They were rolling on the floor again as they had done so long ago when we first came back from West Cork, and now I was afraid for her belly and the child. "Watch the baby," I said, "be careful of the child, Isabella." But she would not take care. She was home.

"My lovely, lovely children," she said, and wept over them.

They tore through the house yelling, "Isabella's home, Isabella's home," though they knew every servant in the house knew it, and most of them had peeped and dared to come to the fringes of the hall to see her and smile at her and, where they were close enough, say welcome home, miss. And I did not realize I had told the children anything in my concern for Isabella and the child until Morag danced around the kitchen holding Isabella's hand and singing, "Isabella is having a baby, Isabella is having a baby, Isabella is having a baby."

What did Patton think? He did not call her Miss Isabella. He said, "Nothing could have made me happier, ma'am, than to see you home again."

"Ma'am." What did he know or think he knew?

The children had been in bed for hours. We sat by the library fire, home and deeply contented. Patton came himself with our glasses of warm milk and Jacob's cream crackers. It was his way when he had gossip for me.

"What news have you for me, Patton?" I said.

"There isn't much of anything, sir," he said. "While you were away, a gun was stolen from the gun room. It's gone entirely."

"Not the staff?"

"No, sir. We've made sure of that. It wasn't anybody in the house."

"Have you tried the gunsmith?" The gunsmith was also the butcher in Carrig. He was talented with guns and had attended to mine for many years.

"We have, sir. He said it was there the week you left, and when he came back two weeks after, it wasn't there."

That was worrying. In this house, guns do not disappear. Nothing disappears except meat from the larder. But we were home. That was all that mattered. I put the gun from my mind and forgot about it entirely.

And so, what I expected to be and planned to make the richest and the best and only exciting years of my life began. Life and the things I had determined to do, or to try to do, I set about with will and confidence and optimism.

Isabella and Emily opened their school. Parents allowed their children to come. My spirits soared. Signs and portents.

Tomas was born in 1871 at Hugh's London house, an easy birth to great rejoicings.

He grew, and so did Alasdar. At the age of twelve, in 1874, Alasdar went off like a sad hero to board at the Royal School, and that was anguish for us all. "I read of you in the papers, Papa, and long to come home," he wrote.

Cassie Hyndman died, and I went with Isabella to her burial at the North Road Cemetery.

That day, too, Hyndman was black with what I supposed to be grief.

"What do *you* want here?" he asked of me.

"I'm saying good bye to an old family friend," I said.

"Aye. God damn your soul," he said, and walked away.

It had to be put from mind. There were problems with Elizabeth, of course. We knew now that Elizabeth, who was lost without trace for more than two months, had been to America, searching for Seán McCarthy. The Fenians in Boston told Hugh she had hired Pinkertons to find traces of me and link my traces to McCarthy. We doubted her sanity, for a card came to us in her hand, posted in Boston but signed, "Seán McCarthy." Only a woman not in her right mind would have done that. There was a blackness about it that frightened us which, I suppose, it was meant to do. There was one other thing, more immediate and in a way more puzzling: young Harold MacNeice, the youngest brother of the sitting Member of Parliament for Carrig and a Unionist, had taken to calling on her at Court House. Why? we asked constantly. Through the servants we learned that he came at first only in the afternoons, but soon in the evenings and after time (it was being said) in the night, leaving in the small hours. Sex seemed improbable, but I remembered that dreadful night I took her to Court House and in a rage I regretted, raped her. I remembered her face as she lay there—she enjoyed it. Emily was right about her; underneath all that righteous loathing of the marriage bed was an obscene lustfulness and perhaps she had found what she wanted in young MacNeice? But what had he found that he wanted? Pinkertons report on my visit to America to bring Isabella home? What had they found, and if MacNeice could get it from her, what use would he make of it? But these were hidden things. We could not know their meaning or their consequences. We had to put them from our minds and get on with our lives. My life was roaring forward, and now Robert Garrett was with me. There would be others to join us. We could in time bring sanity to Ulster. Serve everyone's self-interest, and all men will profit, and agree. Melodramatically and rather uncharacteristically, I'm afraid, I said to myself one day, *"Let life roll forward . . ."* But however unlike me that might be, it was our state of mind.

Part Two

Alasdar Carrach MacDonnell

For
GORDON and MARY ROBINSON

✑ One ✑

They sent me away to the Royal School.

For a while I was subject to irrational resentments. It was Father's doing, I was certain, and every kind of poisonous suspicion filled my mind. He wanted me out of the way because I loved Isabella. (I knew there were varieties of love, but at that time I didn't know that mine for Isabella would affect anybody but myself and Isabella.) She agreed to my going. She had no choice but to agree. I made no allowances for that. I made no allowances for anything. Our old priestly tutors had been good enough for every son of the family through generations (how we come to change our minds!), but I had to be sent away to school because of something Father called "preparation for a different world." If he wanted me in shipping, why didn't he simply order me into his shipping office and on to the sea? Isabella was the reason. If he wanted me in flax spinning, why didn't he put me in the mill? Isabella. I didn't want to be in either, but that made no difference to my anger. Why didn't Isabella fight to keep me at home? He was the reason. She had to please him. Till the very last moment I believed she would fight for me and win, so I was not particularly troubled; nervous but not troubled. She did not fight. She discussed. They always discussed. They were always discussing. She did not really try to win. She let him send me away. The shock was devastating.

Yet when my anger died and resignation set in, I had learned some things about myself. One was that I was a jealous and resentful boy, and I was half-ashamed. Another was that I was a weakling, for when they came with me to the Royal School I knew that what I really could not face was separation from either of them. I was presented to the headmaster and said, Yes, sir, Yes, sir, Yes, sir, to everything he said. You will be happy here, MacDonnell. Yes, sir. You will make enduring friendships. Yes, sir. Most of what he said I did not hear. But ill-mannered as it was, I did not look at him. I looked only at them as though their departure from this place would open up the pit.

I was envious that he could be with Isabella and I could not. Perhaps it's strange, I do not know, but there was not in my mind any jealousy of the fact that he would sleep with her, make love to her, hold her in the night. That sort of thing never entered my head. There was my half-brother, Tomas, to prove that they did these things, but I did not think of them. It was her presence that he would have and I would be denied.

I walked with them back to the school gates. The headmaster had other thoughts and gave other directions, but Father did not choose to hear them. "Thank you, Headmaster," he said, as one speaks to a servant who has stepped beyond his station, and "You, my boy, will walk with us to the gates," and to the head, "Good day, sir." Isabella took my hand. I was a weakling. I wanted to weep. I must not weep. When we drove away from Barn House, young Tomas said like a miniature of Father, "Bear up, Alasdar." My sisters wept adequately. I said nothing. I could not smile.

At the school gates, Father said, "Now you must go back." It sounded like abandonment at the poorhouse. He shook my hand. He was calling on me to be a man. He said, "Work hard, my boy." But Isabella took me in her arms. I had been numb, and suddenly I was burning. She held me close. I felt her breasts against me and her belly, and rose. It was a mixture of lust and the need of a mother, I suppose. Whatever was in my mind was desperate, not dirty. I pressed hard against her and clutched her to me, and she whispered, "Don't crush me, dear." Did she think it was dirty? I broke from her and touched Father and ran. I did not look back. I turned only at the end of the avenue by the school steps. Father had passed out of sight through the gates, no doubt tall and stiff and manly. Isabella was still there watching me. I wanted to scream in my despair. Instead, I ran inside making incoherent sounds. The headmaster was watching from the secrecy of the hall. "Now, now, now, MacDonnell," he said from the shadows, "be a man." If I had had a club in my hands I would have battered him down. What did that pompous insensitive old bastard know about us? Any of us? About Isabella and me? He was nothing but my jailer, the head jailer. Be a man, be a man, be a man. I heard it in my head. God damn you, God damn you, God damn you screeched along my nerves like metal on metal and drove down his flat voice. He was the only substitute I had for Father.

❧ *Two* ❧

What did I learn at school? Academically, almost nothing I would not have learned as well from a scholarly priestly tutor—perhaps less. I did learn, however, in three distinct fields what I would certainly not have learned at home.

I was the only Catholic in the school, so I became almost terrifyingly skilled in the manly art. Practice, and a smoldering rage that never seemed to dampen, made perfect. The practice gave me skill, the rage, burning somewhere deep in the bottom of my belly, gave me attack. The bullies all wanted to pound me. To bloody MacDonnell's papish face and bruise his Roman belly became a goal. Come out to the woods, you dirty pape, they would say, but my friend the chaplain, a strange man who chewed tobacco and picked his nose, taught me: Fight not by invitation but for cause only; then you are always right. So I fought insult or attempted injury, and when I reached the upper school, big, strong, and in a secret sense always angry, the invitations to the woods were at an end and the insults were from tongues tripped by frustrated prejudice.

But there was one large stupid bully in the sixth on whose great hulk I practiced with something like joy. He was a head taller and a lot heavier and his favored victims were small boys in the lower school. After every bullying I sought him out, taking along a few companions as witnesses. His name was Livingstone. His father was an Orange henchman of Lord Enniskillen's, an ardently servile licker of Ascendancy arses, and there were few Orangemen in the school. Orange-

ism was too vulgar for most of the partly civilized families of
the students. I taunted Livingstone into fighting. His big stupid face would stay still and expressionless till my taunts
reached. his Orange father: What is he, Dead Brick? I would
ask him. Is he one of Enniskillen's grooms? Does he wipe the
great man's arse? The taunts sank lower, and his face livened
like a stirred peat fire, slowly, almost as if he at first did not
understand. When Enniskillen gets horny, does your father
lend him your mother, Dead Brick? Then he rushed at me,
flailing. I used his body for practice. Pound the body, my
friend the chaplain said. You will mark his face, and the
Beaks (masters and prefects) will see, and anyway, you will
crack your own bones on his thick head.

I had friends, of course, but my great friend was the
chaplain. It was from the Reverend Mr. James Calder, who
also taught English in the upper school, that I learned most
of what set the unrealized dreams of my heart. He was a
great teacher. (I know little about teachers, great or small,
but to me he was a great teacher.) You have the gift,
MacDonnell, he said. Learn to see, MacDonnell, he said. See
everything, MacDonnell. What will you be in, MacDonnell?
Spinning or shipping? Neither, if I can help it, sir. Tell me
about your mother, MacDonnell. I do not know my mother,
sir. Then tell me about your cousin, MacDonnell. My cousin,
sir? I did not think of her as my cousin. What was she?
Mother, the loved, my friend? I mean Isabella MacDonnell,
my boy. Yes, sir. Then I would talk about Isabella; sitting in
the woods, snapping twigs, scattering the pieces, talking, talking, talking of Isabella. He listened with patience and tact.
You are in love with your stepmother, he said, finding an acceptable role for Isabella. Yes, sir. That is very dangerous,
MacDonnell. It could be tragic in its consequences. No, sir. It
is merely hopeless. I know what that means, he said.

Of course Isabella's kindergarten collapsed. That was another hopeless enterprise. If the Protestant infants did not
corrupt the Catholic infants, then it was the other way
around. The school lasted for less than a year, and both sides,
under the guidance of their priests and ministers, saved their
infants from mutual and eternal damnation.

It was the death of the Garden House kindergarten that
led to the birth of *Ulster*, a magazine that avoided all political debate but was slanted in everything it printed to demonstrate that Ulstermen were a Scots-Norse-Irish mixture but
not Irish. Emily and Isabella started it, in debt to Father. It

roared out of debt and into prosperity in a very short time, illustrated by Emily, edited by Isabella, produced by both, and
was as popular in the South, where it was not understood, as
it was in the North, where it was merely enjoyed and, very
likely, had no political effect whatever. They found contribu-
tors everywhere, scholarly men from Scotland, local histori-
ans from every corner of Ulster, men and women who knew
the distant and recent past and the lost characters who had
once given color and excitement to the land.

The chaplain was one of their most enthusiastic readers.
He sent to Garden House, where the magazine was produced,
a story I had written for his class. It was about two great
warriors from Ulster's far past. I had invented both of them.
What pleased the chaplain about it was not my invention but
my observation. I had given my warriors the personal habits
of two of our masters, both fanatical sportsmen. Isabella
printed it. Emily illustrated it, and from photographs sent by
the chaplain drew heroic portraits of the masters. The thing
was a sensation in the school. It was condemned as a disgraceful hoax by a professor at Trinity College, Dublin, who
brought his solemn authority to bear on the nonexistence of
my two great figures. One of the masters wrote the professor
to say that he was indeed mistaken, for "I at once recognized
myself and my colleague and we have no doubt that our
characters and accomplishments are as the author portrays
them." Isabella printed an editorial note to the effect that
henceforward fiction would be labeled as such and that humor would be labeled, but only for humorless professors. I
was launched, in a small way, and became a regular con-
tributor to *Ulster*. The chaplain edited all my contributions
before they went off to Garden House. He could not edit out
the family situations I sometimes included in my ancient
tales. Isabella did that. They were there, messages to be read
and removed. Sometimes they were, and very clearly,
messages of love. But she did not mention them in her letters.
In time the chaplain said, "I find the omissions in the printed
texts very interesting and instructive, MacDonnell. I think
you should in future edit them yourself." That sort of advice
he always offered gently, usually walking in the woods, looking up into the foliage.

And at the Royal School, the third thing I learned about
was sex. What I learned did not help me much when I went
to Trinity College. It came as a shock and stayed too long as
an obsession. I learned first, in lower school, from our busy

informants and mockers in upper school, that a Jewish woman's sexual organs differ in one important respect from those of a gentile woman. The gentile female cavity, we were assured ("the crack," they called it), "was slit from north to south. The Jewish from east to west." We believed them. We learned of the sexual diseases spread mainly by serving women in taverns. "You young fellows must be careful when you are at last allowed to walk in the town. If you catch it, the cock first turns black, then swells up to an immense size, very difficult to hide. Then it bursts." The cock of a former minister of the Presbyterian church in the town, they told us, burst while he was preaching a powerful sermon in praise of the Seventh Commandment. The scandal was such that he had been forced to leave the Presbyterian church and become a priest of the Church of Ireland, where such things were better understood.

We were not, as so many suppose, subject to the sexual attentions of older boys, only to their corrupting humor that filled our minds with hopeless fantasies relieved by masturbation (night after night the dormitory bedclothes rustled) and vigorous sport. A healthy mind in a healthy body, our younger masters said on the playing fields, and then went to their lodgings and their younger wives. Even Catholic priests have an easier time than we have in this monastic settlement, the upper school told us. Watch the wicket gate in the convent wall at eight o'clock any morning. After breakfast we put glasses on the wicket gate and watched the convent down the hill, and the priest came out, after celebrating Mass. He serves so many every night, they told us. And this one they all believed, for they were Protestants. I believed the one about the Presbyterian minister because I was Catholic. Dirty sex grew enormously in our minds. Religious scandal also, according to our prejudices.

My sexual obsession was secret. In upper school I damned the sport (to which I had listened at first in shock, then in secret greed) of feeding the lower-school boys with dirty tales. I fostered in my secret head fantasies about the wives of the younger masters. With no knowledge of how the thing was done, there were no limits to my achievements in bed or in the bushes with Mrs. Mary McCartney and Mrs. Grace Gibson and Mrs. Brenda Kyle, and one of the flattering satisfactions of this sickness was that when the variety of my first triumphs as a skillful seducer became monotonous, I stopped seeking or seducing them and was seduced by them. They sought me until, in time, so great was their lust for me that only my nod or a raised eyebrow sent them to the woods, their skirts and their bloomers flying in the branches. I invented the lustful pleasure with which they called me to their vigorous service, and it was always vigorous and they were always grateful. But to my upper-school friends I was righteous, censorious, indignant.

It was in upper school, when our nights were less public and our quarters more secluded, that we "went over the wall." There was a serving girl in the Angler's Arms on whose services I had set my mind. She was a jolly soul, an older woman—perhaps twenty-five years old?—handsome in her way, always kindly when we crept down to the town for a glass of beer, always one to give us a warning nod when a drinker likely to report us came into the bar. Before he could reach the school we were back in bed.

I laid my plans for Molly with some care, and the waiting was anguish of a sort, for she took over my fantasies and drove out the masters' wives. Often I came over the wall alone and talked with Molly at the end of the bar. I left before closing and waited for her in the dark and walked her home to a small cottage in a quiet lane, then left her, suddenly speechless when the field behind the cottage and the time for action were all at hand. I followed this futile routine even when several of us planned to go over the wall. The others, I was confident, knew nothing of my walks with Molly, but supposed I had gone carefully back to school. She took my arm one night, cuddled close, gave me what I believed to be encouragement, and I could not make my attempt. I didn't know what to do. So she kissed me. "You're a big strong one," she said, "but you wouldn't do anything." It was a challenge, I knew that much. She was daring me to get on with it. It was loss of control that brought me to the point. And loss of breath. "I want to touch your breasts." I got that much out, for breasts were a tantalizing mystery, and in the woods young masters' wives always wanted to show them. "Have a good feel," she said, and put my hand under her blouse. From that point there was no control at all. She unbuttoned my trousers and took it out, and when I should have been leading her to the bushes, my feet were anchored to the ground, her big breasts in my hands, my loins pumping into the palms of her hands, and in an instant it was over, stuttering ecstasy suddenly wilting, and I stood exhausted and drooping and she stood back from me, laughing, drying her hands on the uplifted tail of her skirt. "You're easy satisfied," she said, and the laughter crushed me. It was not hers alone. Wilde was there, and Livingstone and Conyngham and Montgomery, only a few feet away, laughing and chanting, You're easy satisfied, and I ran, still dangling, into the fields; shame, humiliation, and then wild rage drove me up the hill, with their lunatic hooting and her cackling still in my ears halfway to the wall. In the morning, Say anything and I'll kill you, I threatened them. I ought to have said it the night before. They had already told the tale. Molly's Toss-Off they called me after that.

I had no more schoolboy fantasies. I was afraid of fantasies. Who might see them in my head? My righteousness had no more ground to stand on. The four voyeurs had frequent knowledge of Molly in the bushes at, they said, a shilling a time and flip a penny for who goes first. They had arranged it all with her when she laughed with them about our "secret" virginal walks. It had been their intention to come on me, active on Molly in the field. It was her part to bring me to action. For that they paid her four pence each.

"Clearly," said Wilde, "you didn't know how to proceed with the business, did you, my dear fellow?"

His ruin delighted me.

❧ Three ❧

Home at Barn House on short or long holidays, the Royal School became unreal. Is it a trick of the mind? I could scarcely recall anything that happened there; it was all almost hidden behind a cheesecloth curtain. But the effect of our pseudo-monastic life in the place remained. I could not hear Wilde's laughter, but I had handled Molly's breasts. That was knowledge. I examined women now: in the village of Eden, in the streets of Carrig, Emily ("Get your hot eyes off me, you dirty schoolboy," she said), my sisters—and Isabella. When Isabella rode in her Spanish *zahones*, the leather riding breeches, I had to ride away in case Father should notice how I examined her. But half-brother Tomas noticed.

"Alasdar, why do you look at Mother that way?" he asked me.

"What way?" I asked him. He could never tell me. Not yet.

Most of the time, however, I thought myself quite balanced. I had little real interest in politics now, but during these school years I was taken out of school to go to London, sometimes with Father and Isabella when he had business there, sometimes with Isabella alone when she went to visit Hugh and her mother. It was all part of Father's preparation of me for the new world that was coming, and I was required to sit in the gallery of the House of Commons and watch the antics of Hugh's colleagues as they disrupted the business of the House.

On these visits to London we stayed sometimes with Hugh, but since he housed several Irish members who could not afford their own lodgings—the maids sleeping below stairs to protect them from the members who slept in the maids' quarters in the attic—more often we used the London house of Lady Margaret Somerville.

Lady Margaret in time played a large part in my life, a part that in those schooldays I could not have imagined. She was the second wife of an immensely rich old man, Sir Michael Somerville, who had been paralyzed in the third week of their marriage and spent years slowly dying. He had been my grandfather's intimate friend. Before her marriage to Sir Michael, she had not known us. But since both Sir Michael's marriages were childless and his relatives very distant, Lady Margaret, Isabella said, wanted to preserve a family connection and took Grandfather's family to her heart. She drifted into and out of Barn House—no, a woman of her dimensions could not be said to drift, she barged—but once she was in our lives she stayed and we loved her. I came to know her better than anyone else in the family, but that is in the future. Often she came to be with us in her London house. "She is queer, kind, and lonely," Isabella said, "and you must give her a great deal of attention." Aunt Margaret, we called her. She was at first very old. Like Father, we thought. When we came to that conclusion, she was, in fact, thirty-two. When Sir Michael had his stroke, he was seventy-three. Father—in her absence—called Lady Margaret an old man's darling. Lady Margaret spoke of Sir Michael as "poor old Mickey."

There was a special benefit of these visits to London as the years passed. I often had Isabella to myself. These were hours of adolescent pretend. She was mine then. She walked the streets with her hand in mine. When she smiled it was for me. I do not know whether, when she kissed me, hugged me, smiled at me, and walked laughing with her hand in mine, she knew what she was doing to me, or to the future. Sometimes I believe she did. Sometimes not. I have never been able to think clearly about Isabella, only to love her. All that mattered was that often she was there and often Father was not.

Sometimes she asked me: What are you writing now? I told her, often showed her. Good, good, she said. She alone knew I did not intend to be a shipper or a spinner. But she kept this to herself. She smiled at me. We have a secret, she said. It was not a great secret, but to me it was as if we lived a little together in a world nobody else could inhabit. And I was sixteen then.

She was more and more deeply involved in Father's business affairs, immensely competent and a quick and shrewd learner. Energy for everything came from some deep resource that seemed to be limitless. Nothing was neglected. She governed Barn House, spent days each week on business affairs, loved and cared for Kitty and Morag and young Tomas and made them all feel they were the center of her life; and there was *Ulster* at Garden House. Old Pollard came first to her before he brought his legal questions to Father. After several good years, linen was declining again. At dinner, she discussed with Father, and with us as though it was her purpose to teach us something, how to choose the time to get out of flax spinning and into something with a certain future. Food, she said, people will not always need linen but they will always need food. The Americans are preserving food in tins, she said. We must study that. It was dinner-table talk, intended, we believed—Father knew better—to make us think of where our comforts came from and what must be done to earn and keep them. It was also—we did not know—the pattern of the family's future, our almost immediate future. Young Tomas listened solemnly and chimed in with the air of a miniature industrialist. Father smiled happily at his interventions, and Isabella said, "Very well said, darling," and smiled at me as if to say: Don't worry, there's a MacDonnell to do what you don't care to do. So indifferent were the rest of us to the source of our comforts that none of us, in the midst of Isabella's talk, remembered that she took us into Scotch whiskey and its spectacular profits. At this time also, she took the MacDonnell Line out of sail and its impending losses.

The tall ships went in my seventeenth year in 1878 and with them the romance of the past. They had seen the War of 1812, the American Civil War, the Indian Ocean, and the China Sea. Father had sailed in them, Hugh had traded in them. I would never know them. I did not want to. Travel for me meant Europe and America and the comfort of steam. Hugh's wandering exploits did not attract me. Nor did the ships that replaced the sails—four tubby coasters that henceforward would carry coal to Ireland and whatever they could find to Europe. Father entered into partnership with Charles Legum of Carrig, a Protestant, a coal importer, and known to us as Rubberface because he had one of those mouths that disappeared into his face when he smiled.

To celebrate this descent into the modern world, we went

to London for a month. Lady Margaret loaned us her house but did not come with us. Sir Michael was too ill, she said. It was to be a month of theaters and galleries for Kitty and Morag and Emily and Tomas, the House of Commons and the politicians for Father, and bookshops and sightseeing for Isabella and me. It was also to be one of the most sickening experiences of my life. I was almost seventeen, I was a man—almost. I intended to behave as one and make myself perfectly clear to Isabella. She was certain to understand.

I was suffocating with excitement when I left the house alone and made my way to the jeweler's with one of Isabella's rings in my pocket. I chose a ring, paid for it, and left the message to be inscribed inside it. A week later, when Father and the others had gone on their various excursions, I called Isabella to the drawing room and gave her my gift.

I had rehearsed it all again and again in my head. I had written the dialogue many times in many ways. Every gesture, every look in her eyes, the movements of her hands and face were known to me. And when she had taken my gift and read the inscription, she would embrace me, kiss me, and as we walked out, we would fill London with our laughter.

I put the little box in her hand. "It's a message," I said.

"What is it, my dear?" but her face said she knew. It was not the face I had prescribed in my rehearsals.

"Open it." I was already sick with apprehension. "I love you, Isabella," I said, trying to recover lost ground, trying to push away the uneasiness in her eyes.

"I know you do," she said, "and I love you. We have always loved one another."

That was not right. It was not the right talk of love. It was merely family talk. She opened the box and took out the ring.

"It is very beautiful," she said, and her smile was not her smile.

"There's a message inside it."

"Oh?" It was an uncertain Oh, the Oh that says, I know there is and I do not want to see it. She took the ring to the light of the window and turned it as she read. Her face was not cold; it was sad and a little frightened. The inscription said, *I shall love you always. A.* She put the ring in the box and came back to me and pressed the box into my hand and closed my fingers over it.

"We must talk," she said, and walked nervously to the door and turned and came back. "Alasdar," she said, "we must talk." She did not know what to say, what to do, how to begin, where to begin. There was nothing about her of the strong, wise, beautiful woman I had always believed her to be. I had never seen her so weak, distraught, and confused.

"This is all my fault," she said impatiently. "I am a stupid woman."

"You are not." I could not allow her to accuse herself of anything, though what I was denying I had no notion.

Opposition from any source for any reason seemed to gather her together. The nervous hands settled by her side, clenched but still, and she faced me, looking very stern. "Alasdar, this is my fault, and I shall not be contradicted." For the first time in years I heard the echo of her Spanish accent that had been lost in its familiarity. "I know what you mean by that ring. I have known all along and chosen not to pay attention. You and the girls and Tomas and your father are my family. You are all my security. I could not live without you. I love all of you, and you in a very special way—but not in that way. That way, I love your father and your father only. Oh, do you understand?"

Oh, yes, I understood. But my head was frozen and I could not speak and I knew as she spoke that I had always known this was the way of it. But there was no help in that. A kick in the stomach still hurts and sickens, however well-deserved.

"How could I explain that inscription to your father?"

My tongue was locked. I was gaping, that was all, like a dog that came for a pat and got the whip.

"I shall not change my ways with you. Wouldn't they all want to know why? But you must understand, Alasdar," she said, as if some new and helpful thought had come to her, "I am your brother's mother." Then, desperately, "I don't know what to say to you. I know I'm hurting you. I thought if you were off at school it would die away . . ."

That was what came back later. She was still talking as I rushed from the room, and I heard her calling, "Alasdar, Alasdar," on the stairs and at the door as I ran down the street. I had no thought of where I was running, but disembarking from the boat at Kingstown, I began to be conscious of some sort of intention. I was running to Goleen.

But having paid my fare with the money I had in my pocket, I could not run farther than the dock at Kingstown. I hadn't a penny.

Lady Margaret was the answer, and I did not want her company or any company. But I walked to Dublin. It was raining. It was always raining. I reached her door in the late afternoon. My city shoes blistered my feet, the rain ran down my face, it stuck my clothes to my back and my trousers to my legs and drained into my shoes. The servant girl who opened the door on Upper Temple Street, next door to Parnell's town house, said, "Merciful Jesus, sur," and ran for her mistress and left me in the rain at the open door.

Lady Margaret found me dripping in her hall.

"Holy God, dear boy," she said. "Hot baths," and rushed me to her room.

My bath was drawn in her own bathroom. She bustled, brought me one of Sir Michael's dressing gowns, and left her room. I sank into the hot water. We had not talked. She had talked. "Clothes off, you poor dear. What in God's name have you been doing? Why aren't you in London? Mustn't get pneumonia, must we?" Incessantly, even while I stripped. "Must I leave you now? I suppose so." And she left me. Isabella, when we asked her why Aunt Margaret talked like a drill sergeant, said, "To protect herself." Once we thought that meant it made her sound like a man who could defend himself.

I was lying up to my lower lip in the warm water, wondering how I could broach the question of a loan, when she strode back into her room and into the bathroom. Astonished, I was half upright and fully exposed.

"Everything all right?" she asked.

"Yes, Aunt Margaret." My hands covered me rather late.

"Don't be silly, dear boy. Lie down."

I lay down, my hands only momentarily withdrawn from my parts.

"Good. Have a long soak."

I had nothing to add. She paused at the door. "I'll say this for you, my dear," and she looked, grinning, at my defenses, "you're splendidly equipped. Yes, splendidly."

What did I think? I didn't think. She was Aunt Margaret. She was a mannish joker. She was funny. I was ridiculous. She relieved my gloom a little and made me self-conscious when I joined her for tea, Michael's dressing gown shielding my equipment from her laughter and her eyes. "Be sure to keep that thing closed," she said, "I'm easily shocked." She loved her own jokes. "And now, what's it all about?"

I was foolish, and now quite alarmed at my own behavior. She was "family." I told her.

"Dear good Isabella," she said. "You poor dear boy. It won't do, you know."

"No."

"It means the wrong sort of trouble."

"Yes."

"Tell me right out. Don't be shy. Don't be afraid. I'm only old Aunt Margaret. Have you ever done it?"

"Done?" It was too surprising to be at first understood.

"It, I think it's usually called. With a woman, dear boy, or a girl?"

"No."

"It'll happen," she said, "but not with Isabella. Eighteen's time enough." It was matter-of-fact, like learning to ride a horse. Everyone learned to ride a horse, first a pony, then a horse, then a woman; the pony at three or four, the woman at seventeen. There was nothing I could think of saying. "I'll think about it," she said, "but don't dare think another thought about Isabella." She rang for her maid to clear the tea things. "And now," she said, "you haven't a penny in your pockets. I'll lend you some money."

At Schull, I borrowed a horse from Seamus O'Keeffe.

"Jesus, boy, you're a right spectacle," Seamus said, and loaned me a coat. "Is there trouble in the nest?"

Was it so obvious to those who knew us that the very composition of our family inevitably meant "trouble in the nest"? My malignant mother shut up in Court House, Father and Isabella living as man and wife at Barn House and producing a son. There was my uncle, Isabella's husband, Seán McCarthy. Where was McCarthy? Dead? Somewhere in America? Why did he not come for her? Paid off? *I am your brother's mother*, she said, and as I rode to Goleen, for the first time I thought of it that way. She was talking about incest, was she not? But it made no difference. I loved her and there was no cure for it, and that was that. But yes, it made a difference. This was her landscape. This country I rode through was where she ran wild on her father's horses when he brought her first from Spain. This was why I ran blind to Goleen, and what I had half-consciously known to be unattainable and now consciously knew to be always beyond my reach became a great greed for Isabella. Not to be satisfied, but a greed. I was almost seventeen. It was an age to feel suitably tragic. It was to be my business in life, was it not, to "look life squarely in the face" and record it? Tragedy and all, including my own? I looked us squarely in the face and did not know enough to see anything clearly. Isabella was not my mother, though from her sixteenth year she had brought me up. She was my cousin. She was Father's niece. And this one came out in my head with a rush, as though I did not want to look it squarely in the face—she is Father's mistress and Tomas is their bastard.

But it made no difference. I could think of our house only as a place where love ruled. I could think of our family only as a community of love. Their love crowded me around. The girls, Tomas, even odd Aunt Emily, my ugly mother's eccentric sister; Isabella and Father. Even, I felt now, Aunt Margaret, funny, kind, and most certainly understanding. They were the strong shell of a cocoon of love, and I got down from Seamus's horse and lay in the grass and wept for myself, for I could see no wrong in my greed for Isabella.

And when I was done with my weeping, I mounted and rode. And now I had a different mood. I felt triumphant. I savored greed for Isabella. It was a strong thing in me. If ever the time should come when it was possible, I would have Isabella. I was the heir. To everything.

And I felt no jealousy of Father. He was sexless.

I would not be young again if all the crowns in Europe were offered for my head.

Seamus O'Keeffe rode out to the house a week later.

"They're hunting for you," he said.

"Who's hunting for me?" I would not admit such a need to anyone outside the family.

"Your family. Hugh telegraphed me to ask if you were here. I said you were."

So Father had not asked. Hugh would come in his stead. All week I had wanted Father to come; like a baby, I suppose, wanting to be sought. The young suffer more from their unschooled emotions than seems fair. Are there no other ways to learn?

But it was Father who came. He came alone when I was not at the house. He found me propped against the great rock on the shore of the cove before the house. I heard his step and knew it, and fear and joy together shook my heart. He sat down beside me. "Are you well?" he said.

"Yes, sir."

He was looking out across the bay, not at me. His silence was long. I had nothing to say. What could I say? I did not know what I ought to say. Father was here. He came.

"If you had not run away," he said, "I would not have had to know why. Will you remember that?"

"Yes, sir." I stared at the stones under my feet; he looked out over the bay.

"Do you feel like riding?" he said. That was all. Do you feel like riding? He was immense. Immensely kind. Immensely good. Endlessly forgiving and understanding. What was it our old priest, Father Mackay, was always saying? "And underneath are the everlasting arms."

"Father," I said, incoherent and childish, my eyes tight shut to hide tears that leaked to my cheeks.

"Don't," he said. "There's no need. Everything passes. We'll ride together."

But this would not pass. I could not tell him that.

❧ *Four* ❧

I went up to Trinity in the autumn of 1879.

Isabella agreed that they should go with me no farther than Carrig station. Let him fly alone, I heard her say to Father. But he had business in Dublin, or said he had, and we stayed with Aunt Margaret.

I knew a lot more about Lady Margaret now, for Isabella said I would see a lot of her and must be very kind and thoughtful and humor her. Life is difficult for her, she said, and tried to explain, for I could see few of the difficulties that might confront an enormously wealthy woman who had a secure place in her society.

Our family is my security, Isabella said, but Margeret's is only her money. Sir Michael married a plain big girl who hadn't been picked up in the marriage market. In spite of her claims that she came of ancient Irish stock from the loins of Irish kings, she was the only daughter of an impoverished English squire who had always ignored her. But she was strong, healthy, and perhaps a breeder, and Sir Michael wanted an heir to continue his name.

He set vigorously to breeding his new wife. His first wife must have been barren, Isabella claimed, because in his latter years with the woman, Sir Michael did everything in his power to restore Ireland's shrinking population. "A lot of his servant girls took their unborn babies to his London house and got generous settlements to take home to their fathers' farms." He set about Aunt Margaret too vigorously in his seventy-third year and three weeks after the wedding had his stroke. At night, the women of Lady Margaret's society said, smiling, and not in his sleep.

"The women laugh at her, behind her back, of course. She has a brain, and men like to talk with her. Women with brains are not loved by other women. She knows all this. She is outrageous with them, and her money protects her. When one of the Townsend women from the Skibbereen country laughed at her openly, Margaret told her she would buy her husband's mortgage and evict her "from that fine house you can't afford to live in." That story went the rounds, and since most of them have mortgages, they became very careful of Margaret Somerville. But she hates them. She's a very lonely and a very loving woman. A wasted woman."

I had always thought of Aunt Margaret as plain. Isabella and Father spoke of her as plain. So in her house now, I examined her. Gangling she certainly was. Gangling? She walked firmly, like a big man and without any effort to be feminine in her movements. But the more I watched her, the more it seemed to me that with a little effort at grace, she would be statuesque. I began to find what they called her plainness pleasing. She had beautiful eyes that in repose were sad, and in debate hard. She had a large nose and a wide full mouth, her bosom was ample but for her size not excessive, and her body was proportioned like the bodies of those ancient ladies one sees on Greek friezes. The more I watched her, the more I was convinced that she was physically a rather glorious creature. But she moved not at all like a gracious hostess but like a rambling horse, from sideboard to fireside, from fireside to sideboard, pouring drinks for Father. "Your talk is always more fun when you're a little tipsy, Carrach," she told him.

And, a little affected herself, she assured me, "Alasdar, my dear, I think you look splendid, splendid, mounted." We had not been talking about riding. She changed directions capriciously.

"I hope you don't mean stuffed, Margaret," Father said.

"On a horse, dammit," she said.

We always had to see Sir Michael. We had to see him now. He had not been out of bed for seven years. "He's going this time," she told us.

He had withered almost away. I thought of a leaf that had for years been confined between the pages of an unread book. He looked transparent. I could almost see and I could certainly imagine as I looked at him the rice-bone structure of his fragile being. A light movement of air around him might turn him to powder.

He did not speak. He no longer could. He looked only at Father. A glazed hand that was pale, pale blue on the dark blue cover of his bed crept toward Father's hand and touched it and settled helplessly on the bed. I think he smiled faintly. Yes, I think he was trying to smile.

We were taken quickly away, and the figure of a woman who had dissolved at our coming materialized again at our going and did not look glad to see us come or go.

"Nurse," Lady Margaret said. "Always with him. For years now. I call her the Proprietor." We knew that, but that dealt with that. She had a precise way of fixing perspective and hiding pain. I never saw Sir Michael or his nurse again.

In the drawing room, the painful business of Sir Michael having been disposed of, she gave her attention to me.

"While you're at Trinity, this house is home. Remember that. Night or day. At any time. Come. Stay. College rooms are stables. This is your Dublin home. Is that clear?"

"Yes."

"Don't expect me to mother you."

"Of course not."

"I have no talent for it."

"I won't expect it."

"We're friends. Friends. Frank and open friends. Is that also clear?"

"Very clear."

"Emphasize it for him, Carrach."

"He understands English quite well," Father said.

"We shall have some fun together," she said. "I could do with some fun."

I could not imagine what sort of fun Aunt Margaret could have in my company except that together we had always laughed a lot.

Those few days at the Somervilles' were the beginning of a clanging and clamorous year.

It began for me on the night before we left the Somervilles' house and Father went home and I went to my college lodgings. I met Charles Parnell that night. He was the young man Isaac Butt had earlier tried to persuade to run for parliament. Father and Hugh were then quite confident nothing of the sort could ever happen. Young Charles Parnell was too cold, too remote, too arrogant, too much the ruthless wencher—it was said—and too contemptuous in his bearing to be acceptable to any Irish electorate under any label. And the history of insanity in his family was too well known. But now he was in parliament at Westminster, and Isaac Butt, the old Irish leader, was wallowing in drink and debt and the beds of barmaids and Parnell was the leader of the Irish Home Rule members who made parliament mad with their tactics.

And here he was in Lady Margaret's house, come to dine with us.

The night before, she warned Father, "Butthead Parnell wants to meet you. He'll very likely say nothing and stare at you. He stares at people."

He got his name Butthead as a boy because of his less-than-endearing habit of charging with his head the exposed stomachs of all who disagreed with him. He could not endure dissent from his opinions.

He did indeed stare. His mother, his sister Fanny, and his brother John also came to dinner. Carefully, as Lady Margaret predicted, Charles counted the company. It did not add up to thirteen. He could safely sit down at table. Charles Parnell was as superstitious as any Irish peasant or lady-in-waiting at the Viceroy's court. His sister Fanny recited her patriotic verses at table and was not, I was sure, right in the head.

The occasion was obviously prepared. Parnell wanted to study the Catholic who with the Protestant Robert Garrett for several years now had been making such a political stir in the North. John Parnell asked the questions, made the conversation; Charles came to listen and to stare. Obviously not to eat or drink. He refused the wine and scarcely touched his food. He studied Father like a painter brooding on the planes of a sitter's face. Now and then his mother said, "Eat, Charles." He did not hear her. His absorption was absolute. Lady Margaret was bored, irritable. For no reason that I could see, she said to Parnell, smiling, "Salt, Charles?" Any need for salt on anything was long behind us.

Parnell rose at once in evident distress and left the house. Without a word. Immediately after dinner, his mother and sister and brother excused themselves with unseemly haste, and we were alone.

"Pass Parnell the salt and he leaves," Lady Margaret explained. "He's as superstitious as a Zulu."

"But why did you do it?" Father asked her. "His stare is more accomplished than his sister's verse."

"I wanted them out. They make me shiver," she said. "John's the only sane one among them." But she was a kindly woman. "Charles wanted to meet you, Carrach. I arranged it. I endured them for as long as I could. One at a time they're barely tolerable, but together they make my house feel like a lunatic asylum." She paused for only a moment. "And his father played cricket." She said it vaguely, maybe searching for the ultimate evidence of imbecility. "He got wet at a cricket match and died of pneumonia at the Shelbourne Hotel." Getting wet at cricket and dying of pneumonia at the Shelbourne were surely additional evidence of imbecility?

That night Lady Margaret said without a context, "Charles Parnell despises the Irish because he is an Englishman. But he hates the English because they treat him like an Irishman." It was left in the air without enlargement.

Father said only, "He is an interesting man."

In the morning I went with him to the station. He took me in his arms. He had never done such a thing before.

"Work hard, my boy," was all he said.

I felt a surging flood of anguish that I did not understand. I could not watch him walk up the platform to his compartment. Perhaps he looked back and I was not there?

I had rushed to my lodging.

❧ *Five* ❧

I had been ten days at Trinity, made small acquaintance with lecturers, even smaller with lectures, none at all with books, and taken tea three times with Aunt Margaret, when Murphy, her coachman, came for me. She always sent him for me, which was motherly enough. I always went.

"Now," she said, and sat down by her sitting-room fire. "Now," she said again, and nervously smoothed her skirt against her thighs. "Poor Mickey died this morning." And after a long breath, "It had been a long wait."

I said the things that must be said and felt nothing for poor Mickey but felt for her, poor Margaret.

"Yes," she said, as though talk of sadness wasted time. "Murphy will take you back to your rooms. Bring a few things you need and stay with me. I will not be without a friend in this house with his corpse. He has been dead for so many years, but not like this."

I agreed readily enough. I would not have to meet the corpse.

"I have telegraphed your father. They will all come. It will be St. Patrick's Cathedral. It will be false and futile. The dean will say fine things except that he married me to breed me and I married him because nobody else wanted me. The town will come, and when it is over they will make great sport of me in their drawing rooms. I must have friends near me."

She was sad and angry and—I could feel it across the fireplace—afraid.

"I'll be back quickly," I said.

"Yes. Very quickly."

I was closer to tears than she was and filled with a sad fondness for her. I kissed her cheek hastily and awkwardly, and she caught me there.

She almost smiled. "Yes, yes," she said, and held her cheek for me. "Again," she said, and I kissed her again. "My fine dear Alasdar," she said, and let me go. "Hurry back to me."

Yet it was not a melancholy house for the four days that followed. Her friends were there. Her "family," she called us. Aunt Margaret was far from gay, but she was cheerful enough except for the hours before the service at St Patrick's, which she dreaded. I sat beside her in the church, and she clutched my hand, closing her own strong hand over it and relaxing her grip and holding tight again. Yet when we left the church her eyes were hard. Angry, I would say, and she received coldly the submitted sorrow of those who approached her. Thank you, thank you, thank you, she repeated with distance, but to the wife of the Viceroy's equerry she said in a loud voice, "Elizabeth, my girl, one of the bones in your stays is broken," and led us to her carriage.

"Was it?" Morag asked her in her carriage, for she wanted us to ride with her.

"Of course not, child," she said. "I meant one of the bones in her head," and her smile wiped out the morning that had passed. At that moment she looked quite young to me, and I laughed. "My very dear Alasdar," she said, "hold my hand all the way home."

And at Upper Temple Street the orders that bewildered her staff were carried out and champagne was carried in.

"Now," she said with her large feet set apart and her glass high, "drink to it. Let it begin."

"Let what begin?" Isabella asked for all of us.

"My life, goddammit. It has been suspended since birth."

We drank to her life and were puzzled, and also, perhaps, a little embarrassed. It was a confession and a plea as much as a declaration about a future, and if the future was a mystery, the past was not. It was what she said in effect about the past that embarrassed us. We knew it and were made uncomfortable by it—but only Aunt Margaret herself declared it.

Kitty, at fifteen, was in the early stages of one of her religious attacks which, Father said with tolerance, made her more Catholic than the pope. She had not been to the church. Some Protestant infection might have undone her Catholic soul. "Aunt Margaret," she said with all the impertinent solemnity of the young, "you must turn now to God."

Aunt Margaret bent and patted her head. "I understand," she said, "that he gives consolation to desperate virgins. I was deflowered in three weeks of determined rape. I called. Where was he?" Her smile was very bright but her eyes were wet. She was sorry. "Forgive me, dear," she said, and went to her room.

I walked that night with Isabella. She asked me to, and that delighted me. We had not walked alone together since the disastrous day when I gave her the ring. "Margaret is a little unhinged," she said. "Will you stay with her for a few days more? She'll be a trial, but be patient."

I promised. To be needed by an older woman made me feel important. Or perhaps merely useful? In spite of the circumstances, Isabella was happy. Away from the house she sparkled with happiness and linked arms with me and took my hand in hers. I had not been happier for months. "I have something to tell you," she said, and didn't tell me for another half hour. When I asked repeatedly what it was, she said, Presently, and, Only Papa knows, and, The girls will not be told till we get home, and suddenly, as we looked in a shop window, "You're going to have another brother or sister."

We had not been talking. I was not listening. But I heard. I thought I knew what I heard. I said, "What did you say?" and my stomach knotted.

"I'm pregnant," she said plainly.

I looked again into the shop window. Her reflection stared at me with dismay. I said, "Congratulations."

"Alasdar," she said pathetically.

"I know. You are my brother's mother and the mother of my next brother or sister."

"Please, my darling. Please?"

"We must be going back."

"Oh, God, Alasdar."

"Come."

We did not speak again. I was ashamed of that and wanted to change it, but nothing would come. I left her at the door and went walking alone. Everything I felt and thought was irrational and unreasonable. The very fact that I felt numb was, I knew, stupid, juvenile . . . I told myself so. It made no difference, for something was at an end. The sly self-deception of all the years was at an end. Father was not sexless. They did it. His hand was on her naked breast as mine had been on the breast of the barmaid at the Angler's Arms.

I walked till after midnight. I cannot say that by then it was a relief to know that my idealization of their life was over. Idealization? By then I had rejected the notion of idealization. I had merely not wanted to know, had not allowed myself to know, that Father was like any other man and lusted after the woman he loved, who was the woman I loved. I also lusted after her. That, I had invested with purity. That, at least, I was cured of. Perhaps only by its futility?

The girl who opened the door said, "Lady Margaret wants to see you, sir."

"Where is she?"

"In bed, sir." She seemed as surprised as I was.

Aunt Margaret was sitting up in bed, sheltering under a quilted bed jacket. "It's been a day," she said, and patted the bed beside her. "Would you like to live it again? Hope for something different?"

"Hope for what?" I sat down close to her, grateful for her company. Grateful for her. There was something about Aunt Margaret that spoke of safety. What was it? Something; I couldn't have analyzed it and I didn't examine it. One could say anything to, do anything with Aunt Margaret. She was never surprised, never shocked, never censorious. I said, "She told you?"

"Yes. And of course you think you're the one who should be making her pregnant?"

"No! No, that isn't so. I'm stupid."

"Far from stupid. That isn't the problem . . ."

"I'm a fool."

"We're all fools. There's only one trick to life, darling Alasdar—choose the kind of fool you're going to be. Your father and mother were fools, married fools, and miserable fools. Your father and Isabella are fools. Unmarried and happy. Have you any idea how much the happiness in your family is a consequence of their kind of folly?"

"Yes."

"You're not censuring them at this late date?"

"No."

"Have you any idea how desperately women want to be pregnant?"

"How could I?"

She stretched down in the bed and sank on her pillow. "God, Alasdar, how I want to be pregnant."

"You?"

She sat up in a rush. "Yes, me, by God. Do you have to sound so astonished? Old Aunt Margaret. Is that it?"

"You know it isn't. I don't know what I mean."

"They're going home tomorrow."

"Yes."

"I want to get out of this house for a few days."

"I can understand that."

She was grinning at me mockingly. "Would you," she said, "like to take a little trip with dear old Aunt Margaret? To London, perhaps? For a mental-health cure?"

"Not London." It was in that house that I offered Isabella the ring.

"No," she said, "that was where you ran from." Aunt Margaret sat there reading my mind. "What about Wicklow?"

"I'd like Wicklow." She had two small estates, one in Wicklow, one in Mayo. I had never been to either. Neither had Isabella.

"Wicklow," she said. "Friday until Tuesday. I think what we both need is a radical change in perspective."

It didn't seem to me that the short journey to Wicklow would effect much of a change in either of our perspectives. I was wrong about that.

She said, "Today, that God of Kitty's and the dean turned the key in the gate of my cage. I'm coming out of it. It's time you got out of yours. Kiss me good night and go to bed." She offered me her cheek.

I kissed it, less hastily than I had done only a few day ago. There was a great warmth in my heart for Aunt Margaret. She took my face in her hands and kissed me on the mouth. "There, now," she said, and let me go. I liked the touch of her mouth. If I had dared—she might have misunderstood me—I would have kissed her again on the mouth. "Go to bed, she said gently.

I went to bed. I could taste her lips. It was a pleasant taste. I was glad Aunt Margaret was "family" and my understanding friend.

She seemed to have forgotten poor Mickey.

Till Friday I was busy and scarcely saw her. She was, she said, "doing some needlework to keep her mind off things." But in those few days I stumbled on my great scheme. First,

I attended a lecture on Count Tolstoy, who was the rage. It moved me quite deeply. I read in the papers a number of stories about the plight of evicted peasants and their families. One told of a sick man who sheltered his family under an upturned boat on the Atlantic shore. He died of exposure. His wife moved their children back into the hovel from which they had been evicted and was now in jail for having done so. The children were "on the roads," begging for their bread. From Michael Davitt's Land League people I got the number of evictions so far this year. One thousand two hundred and forty-nine. Households, not individuals. And it struck me that Ireland was the last place in Europe where serfdom survived.

It was not the fulminations of the politicians that interested me, though they were interesting enough. It was the idea of serfdom here, at home. It suggested an era of enslavement that had already ended in Russia before I was born. It was the suffering of the people that interested me—and the coldness of those who ordained their suffering. There was a great book to be written, if I could learn how to sustain a long story. But I had no story, and not knowing how such things grew in the telling, I fumbled around in my mind for one that would come whole, without rent or seam. It was the major excitement of my week till I got to Wicklow, but unlike the weekend in Wicklow, it did nothing to shape the course and content of my life. I hoarded my scheme and my excitement, but at table, when I did see Aunt Margaret, the excitement showed through. She misread it. "You're excited about going to Wicklow?" I confessed to it, and it was in a sense the truth, for I intended, when we got there, to explain the whole thing in detail and ask for her help. She must have in her head all the ingredients of the story that would not come. And on Friday morning we went.

Her Wicklow house was not large, but it was pleasant and well-proportioned, on a small estate. I held my tongue till we were cozily settled, and while we took tea before a warm fire and I could see that her mood was one of unusual contentment, I poured it out, at first in abundant factual and secondhand detail, groping as I talked for my story which would not come.

It was a discouraging experience. She listened. She lay back in her chair and closed her eyes and now and then smiled and opened her eyes and looked at me fondly, and as my confidence wilted I read in her twinkle that had so often encouraged me: *How young he is.* And when I finished, limping, she said, "Splendid, Alasdar, splendid. First you must smell an Irish serf. The truth and the story are in the smell." She was still smiling, but her eyes now had a peculiar glitter that was not amused. "Did you know that half the odorous serfs of Ireland live on private charity?"

"No."

"Then you must see and feel and smell. Are we going to talk frankly to one another?"

"I want to, but I'm beginning to feel I don't know enough to talk about anything, frankly or not." I was feeling low.

My depression seemed to cheer her. Later, when I was sane enough to think about the thing, I wondered whether my initial depression was necessary to her purpose.

"That's not the way to see it," she said. "You're chained to your youth, that's all. I've been chained to my experience. Maybe to the serfs we'd look an unlikely pair of prisoners, but that's what we are. Do you know what I mean?"

"A bit." I was feeling very humble, and the reference to my youth didn't increase my confidence. "But while you're young, how do you unchain yourself from your youth? It goes on till it's over."

"You unchain yourself with a bang," and she slapped her cupped hands together with a bang.

It came to me then, and suddenly, that I was here to learn, that we were here together, away from the eyes, ears, and noses of everybody we knew, and there was nothing we could not talk about, nothing that could not be said. It wasn't quite a sense of conspiracy between us, but certainly it was a protective sense of our isolation together. I felt very close to Aunt Margaret, closer than I had ever done—it was a pleasant sense of dependence—which was fortunate, for at once she stamped her foot on my most cherished and most persistent obsession.

"You can't write your opus till you do that," she said. "You'll write it, of course, you'll write it." She rushed in quickly with that, waving a big reassuring hand at me. "But first you'll have to see and smell these serfs you want to write about, and for that we must make a pilgrimage." We. There was a partnership. "Connaught's the place," she said. "We'll go over to my Mayo house. That's the place to start. And of course—are we going to be frank, Alasdar?"

"Please."

"What real hope do you have of using that splendid equipment of yours on Isabella?"

Maybe it was the way she put it. Maybe it was this sense of closeness and isolation together. Maybe it was her second scandalous, grinning, and open reference to my splendid equipment. Whatever it was, I was laughing. "None at all," I said.

"So you'll let it hang there useless for the rest of your life?" She was laughing. She was walking over my obsession with her large feet and her laughter, and I didn't mind at all. I was entertained, not least by the fact that it was not now hanging, though it had no conscious target.

"I suppose not," I said, and was astonished that so quickly and easily dear Aunt Margaret could bring this exquisite sense of release.

"Am I a scandalous old biddy?"

"You're a darling."

"Well, I'm leaping out of my prison with a resounding bang. We'll have to think of getting rid of your youth." *We'll.* "While you're tied to a hopeless fantasy, you'll stay in prison. Now, what else is there to talk about?"

With Aunt Margaret, there was never a scarcity of things to talk about. She talked about herself and Dublin society till laughter hurt. There was a wicked joy in her malice. "While poor Mickey was up in his room, I had to hold my hand," she said. "No more. No more." She told me whose wife was whose mistress, which child might have been fathered by whom on a weekend in the country ("while pompous Sir John Strong was out riding Lord Enniskean's horses, his Lordship was upstairs riding Lady Strong, who had been 'feeling faint' till Sir John was out of sight of the house"). How do you know such things, Aunt Margaret? Surely they're secret. Ah, I am always kind to servants, she said, and a good servant always knows how many slept in a bed. And Emily Strong is too stupid to know how to remake a bed.

She was more outrageous when she got to the family of the Viceroy, the Duke of Marlborough. He is a good man and doesn't deserve his sons, but why are all the Churchills popeyed? she wondered. Do you know how Randolph Churchill got syphilis? He claims that he got drunk at a student party—was it Oxford or Cambridge? but he's so undereducated it doesn't matter—and his friends put him in bed with an old hag. But if he was so drunk that he didn't know, how could he perform? He hired a whore and she wasn't clean; that's what I think. And Randolph is in Ireland as his father's unpaid secretary because he fought with the Prince of

Wales, who was trying to get Jennie Churchill to bed. He'll get her there, he'll get her there, she assured me. That snob won't be able to refuse the Royal Cock.

She was full of comic anecdotes, and her malice had a personal cutting edge that rang in her voice. She rejoiced in the story of the embarrassments that attended the changeover of Viceroys, Lord Abercorn for the Duke of Marlborough, for Marlborough's heir, Lord Blandford, was married to Abercorn's daughter and was sleeping with a Lady Aylesford. Blandford's wife was an incurable practical joker and liked to place buckets of water on top of slightly open doors. When this Lady Aylesford scandal broke into public knowledge and her pregnancy was attributed to Blandford, Lady Blandford herself served him breakfast one morning. When he lifted the cover, there on his plate lay a naked pink baby doll.

It was early evening now, but she said, "And now we must go to bed. The needlework I was doing—I must show it to you. Later. Go to bed now."

Obediently, I went to bed, too exhilarated by an afternoon and evening of talk and laughter and close companionship to be ready for sleep. This was a new and different Aunt Margaret, and with the family far away, I liked this one even better than I had liked the old one. I had never had fun like this with a woman of any age. I was chuckling at Jennie Churchill's prophesied and snobbish surrender to "the Royal Cock" when Aunt Margaret opened my bedroom door.

"You're not asleep?" I had not had time, and I had no inclination to get to sleep. "Good. I have something to show you." She closed the door.

She was wearing one of her magnificently decorated shantung dressing gowns. "I told you I was an accomplished needlewoman," she said. "Do you like this?" She strutted about, like a proud seamstress.

I sat up, quite astonished. "Did you make that?"

"Good God, no. Have you enjoyed the day, Alasdar?" She sat down on my bed.

"Immensely."

"So did I. It's been a good day. You're a good companion."

"So are you, Aunt Margaret."

"Please don't call me Aunt Margaret anymore. I'm not your aunt. We're friends. Good friends. I've never had a good friend I could talk with the way we talk." And, "It's been a good day for me."

"And for me." She was lonely. She was showing it. No, she was simply not hiding it from me. I did not feel like a youth. I propped myself up on my pillows, ready for another bout of talk. "What were you making in the sewing room? You said you'd show me later. Show me now."

"You'd like me to?" She stood up. "You're quite sure?"

"Of course I'm sure. I'm curious."

"And you won't be scandalized?"

"How could I be scandalized?"

"I made this," she said, and dropped her glorious gown to the floor.

What she stood in was red. What was I to say about it? I was swallowing too hard to say anything. Red? It was scarlet. It clung. The bodice was cut in a wide V from her shoulders. The V was so wide that its edges were held precariously in place by her nipples. As it was, the purplish bases of her nipples were showing.

"It will be cool on hot summer nights," she said, and turned about. It clung to her hips and her thighs, and as she turned to me again, to her belly. "Do you like it?"

Aunt Margaret died in my head, before my eyes. God, what a glorious woman. My equipment ran rampant. I was light-headed.

"You don't like it?" she said. "You don't say anything." Her eyes were full of laughter.

"Yes," I mumbled. "Yes, I do."

"What do you like about it?" She walked back to the bed, and her breasts moved in their insecure covering. She sat down close to me. "What?" she said, smiling. "Tell me what you like about it," and leaned forward a little.

One of them was out. My hands closed hard, gripping my thighs to keep myself from reaching. I could see only that gently moving mound.

She looked down at it. "Well," she said, and tucked it in again, but she was still smiling. "What does that matter? It's so nice that we're alone. Now, answer my question."

"Truthfully?"

"Truthfully."

"You."

"My darling Alasdar," she said, and pressed me down to my pillow and kissed me on the mouth, a long slow gentle kiss, and as she rose from me, both of them were out and I took them awkwardly. "This way," she said, and cupped my hands around them. "There now," she said, and drew my hands away and leaned over me and brushed them against my face. "Doors are opening," she said, and stood up and put them away. "Sleep well, Alasdar," she said, and bent to pick up her gown, and they were out again. She did not put them away. The thing had fallen from her shoulders, and she was bare to the waist. She did not put on her gown. "Sleep well," she said again, and opened the door.

"Aunt Margaret," I bleated.

"Sshhh." She put a finger to her lips and closed the door. Sleep well, for God's sake? At dawn I did.

We rode on Saturday, inspected the well-kept cottages of her tenants, and I had trouble with my tongue. She was happy. Her smiles were sidelong. She talked the business of the estate, which was the envy and admiration of her neighbors' tenants and an irritation to the landlords. Her rents were low. Poor Mickey's money came from industry in England and Scotland. "I don't do it to spite them. I do it because I care," she said.

I had no mind for estate matters, or for anything else but the living and pulsing memory of the night before. When my splendid equipment made things difficult in the saddle and I shifted about in search of comfort, she knew and gave me her sidelong grin and said, "Should we walk?"

But she did not touch me all day, and at table was sedately circumspect and made me talk of flax spinning and coal boats and Trinity and Morag and Kitty and Tomas and Emily while her servants were near. Family covered us like a canopy. And I called her Aunt Margaret and told stories of Emily's eccentricities, and under every word I spoke there was a long continuing thought and surging impatience. Tonight, tonight, tonight. It rang in my head like a bell, and after dinner she told her houseman, "I shan't need you again till morning, Riley." All I had to do was wait.

At eight she said, "I'm going to bed. What are you going to do?"

I took the bull by the horns, if that is the way to put it. "I'm going to bed to wait for you," I said, and meant it to sound commanding.

"I'll come—but only for a moment."

She came. I was naked and as wild as a sea gale. I didn't wait on her enterprise. I took the thing from her shoulders and pushed her down on the bed and kissed her eyes and her mouth, her throat and her shoulders, and she lay passively

and smiled when she could and said, "That's nice," when I
took one of her nipples between my lips, and her own hand
wandered, and when she found what she searched for, she
said, "My God, darling Alasdar."

"What's wrong?"

"Nothing's wrong. I didn't know how splendid it really
was," and she pushed me away and got up and ran to the
door.

I watched in dismay, kneeling on the bed. "Aunt Margaret,
for God's sake," I cried to her.

"Aunt Margaret my foot," she said, and closed the door.

It was not to happen twice. By God it was not to happen
twice. I charged about my room, trying to make my courage
match my frenzy, and ran next door to her room. She was
standing, naked, before a heaped turf fire. "I was so certain
you'd come last night," she said, "I wanted you to come to
me." I was all over her as clumsy as a farm hand. I rushed
her to her bed, and she was laughing. What I did not know
how to accomplish, she accomplished for me. It was wild and
violent and over in seconds.

"Wonderful, wonderful," she said, "but brief. Now, lie
there for a little and we'll begin again, and this time, slowly,
slowly."

It must have been midnight, when her arms and thighs
were holding me savagely, that she whispered, as though not
to be overheard, "And nobody knows but us, darling Alasdar.
My darling Alasdar and old Aunt Margaret alone in their
own world."

I knew it was three and the often-fed fire nothing but
warm ashes when she said, "By God, we are smashing down
the doors," and put her arm across me and went to sleep.

In the morning she sat up and looked at me. "And you,
dear, dear Alasdar, were midwife at my birth."

✍ Six ✍

I worked. She made me work. She worked with me. But the only time I was allowed near her house was at the weekend. "Hunger makes ready for great feasts," she said, and the weekend feasts were gargantuan. They were also addictive. My feasts with Aunt Margaret were as necessary to me as sleep or food. Very soon they were a right that I exercised with authority. It did not occur to me that a pattern was being built into my life. "My God, darling Alasdar, but I love the weekends," she said again and again. "How happy I am then." She looked younger, had more grace. I had no sense of sin or guilt. "This is ours, darling," she said. "Nobody knows but us."

From Trinity she brought learned men to dinner and made them talk, always on my subjects, always on Friday; our private seminars, she called them; she sent them home at ten, "not to shorten the night." Emily came to Dublin three times before Christmas selling pictures and stayed with Aunt Margaret. Always at midweek. I was asked to dine with them and sent away early to my rooms. "I see a lot of Alasdar at weekends," Aunt Margaret told Emily in my presence. "We visit churches and go for carriage rides," and her face was innocent of all guile.

Father and Isabella came twice and stayed with Aunt Margaret. They came at weekends. "Alasdar must be with us," she would write to Isabella. "I have asked him to stay." Very late at night she came to my room. "Gently and sweetly and only once," she said, "these are family nights." Then she would not leave till dawn, and it was gentle and sweet and conspiratorial and more than once. There was something immensely pleasing about delighting Aunt Margaret in bed—in the varied ways she had taught me—after long evening conversations with Father and Isabella and while they slept at the other end of the house. When I said so to Aunt Margaret, she said, "But it's in the family, darling." She seemed to believe it now. I was coming to believe it. "It's so comfortable this way," she said.

It was comfortable also when we drove to Phoenix Park and walked apart, Aunt Margaret and Isabella together, Father with me.

"You're getting along with Margaret?" he asked me.

"Very well. She's been very kind."

"She tells Isabella you've formed a kind of scholarly partnership. Tell me more about that."

So I told him how hard I worked, that Aunt Margaret was my taskmaster, that we read and discussed the books relevant to my courses, that she brought learned men to dinner on Fridays, including some of my professors, who were flattered to be asked, and trapped them into conducting seminars on my subjects.

He laughed at that. "And," very carelessly, "of course you have other friends?"

"Oh, yes. I see them during the week. Aunt Margaret keeps her weekends for me."

"You stay there?"

"Often." In openness was the best security. There was only one thing he need not know. "It's family. I'm very fond of Aunt Margaret, sir."

"Good. Good. Be very kind to her."

"Yes, sir."

He was looking at me with a speculative eye. "And other houses? Young people? Your letters tell us nothing about that. Young women, perhaps?"

"I haven't had time. I work very hard."

"Yes, you said that. Margaret said it also."

"And about young women. I haven't felt any interest. Perhaps later."

"Yes." Then he looked over toward where Aunt Margaret and Isabella were walking and in what looked like intense conversation. "But it's unusual in a MacDonnell. Doesn't Isabella look well? Showing a little now."

So that was it: a circuitous probe into the prospect of an emerging alternative to Isabella. "Oh? I hadn't noticed, sir."

Then I walked with Isabella and he walked with Aunt Margaret.

"Aunt Margaret thinks you've grown up to be such a splendid and a darling young man." Her arm was linked in mine. "You're not getting bored with her weekends?"

"Aunt Margaret couldn't be boring."

"I find her eyes quite fascinating when she talks about you."

"Her eyes?"

Isabella stopped me and faced me and took my hands. "Yes, her eyes. Aunt Margaret's in love with you."

"Isabella," I said with the full weight of my new and flowering manhood, "I hope you'll never say a silly thing like that to Father."

"Of course not, you lout. But it's true."

In a strange way I was glad she said it. I was glad she thought it. I didn't believe it. Aunt Margaret was loving. She was generous. She was kind. She was amazingly loving. And she was overwhelmingly lustful, and whatever the reason or reasons for it, she got the same exciting satisfaction that I got out of the fact that, blood or no blood, she was in all other respects one of our family and I was ravished by her and ravished her at will and in secret. "Aunt Margaret my foot," she said on that first delirious night, but at the height of our ecstasies I still called her Aunt Margaret, and sometimes she asked me to. The very thought of it had erotic overtones for both of us. And perhaps I wanted Isabella to know. I did not want to tell her. I was not in the least tempted to tell her. I wanted her to think, to wonder.

I said only, "If the baby is a boy, which of the men who love you will you name it after?"

"Alasdar," she said, "because you are your father's son, and for no other reason."

They were approaching us again, and we walked again. "I told you when you left for Trinity, 'Fly,' she said quickly. "For God's sake fly, Alasdar. Find your own. If you're offered a gift of honey—take it for a while."

She was angry with me. But she was putting her stamp of approval on what had happened or on what she thought might be about to happen. "She's never had a day's joy in her life," she said angrily.

Isabella was capable of explosive anger. I had seen it at Father's political meetings when heckling touched a low level. Or once when she came on a hired man abusing a horse, and flailed him with her crop. I had never forgotten the day in Eden village when she was sixteen and raked with her nails till he ran bleeding from the scene the face of the bully who tripped me as he passed us. Such rages were followed by a euphoria that sank slowly into depression. Now she seemed alive with energy.

"Margaret," she said, and kissed Aunt Margaret, with Father out of earshot walking purposefully to the carriage, "take this lout of ours in hand and teach him more than history."

"Well, dear, where do you suggest I should begin?"

"Mayo would be ideal."

Aunt Margaret looked at me. "What a perceptive suggestion. Alasdar, my dear, didn't we think of spending some time in Mayo . . . to get the smell of serfdom in your notebook, wasn't it?"

"It was." I followed Father to the carriage. Their eyes, I'm sure, were boring holes in my back.

But we didn't go to Mayo. Not then. Our Friday dinners underwent a change that was gradual enough to be at first lost on me. Our learned men had company. With them now came one or two or three politicians of different stripe. Poor old Isaac Butt, the former leader of the Irish members, was the first. He was a man of great erudition, an advocate of immense skill, a man of charm, a drunk, and a bankrupt and about to die. I took no part in these discussions. Tories, Whigs, and Home rulers of some polish came to dinner together, and Aunt Margaret intrigued me by the skill with which she led them to talk of things she wanted me to hear. Afterward, in the bedtime lulls, we talked about them, and my mind built up an image of the complacency of the Tories, the nervous hesitation of the Whigs, and the earnestness and idealism of the Home Rulers. Perhaps it was my gradual introduction to the realities of life in Mayo and the smell of serfdom. So I came to believe.

I began to think so when, before the Christmas holiday, the last of our Friday-night guests came to dinner. He was the transition from Isaac Butt, the passing leadership of a less ambitious Ireland, to the violent resolve of the Irish serfs to see some reform in their condition. It was reasonable enough to see in this transition the sowing in my mind of a point of view. What I could not be expected to see—and neither, I insist, could Aunt Margaret—was the digging of a pit.

The man's name was Michael Davitt. There could not have been anyone in the country who did not know it. There were a great many who hated and as many more who feared it. He was the leader of the Land League, the leader, in effect, of the revolt of the serfs. Aunt Margaret made no subtle attempt to lead his talk in any direction.

She said, "Michael, tell Mr. MacDonnell what you are doing and why." They were already on familiar terms. She had never spoken his name to me.

One-armed, gaunt-faced, and in his way handsome, his impact on me was devastating. So was the story he told me. He was not dismissed at ten. He left at midnight. She put a paper parcel in his hands.

"What was in it?" I asked her.

"Money," and she did not tell me more, but her smile was fierce. "Take me to bed," she said. "Tonight I need you like a madwoman."

She had been gentle and sweet and fierce in love, all in one night, and often. Now she was savage and insatiable and for the first time whispered to me the wild lustfulness that drove me to match hers with my own.

On Monday, a letter from Father: "Isabella thinks it would be kind to ask Aunt Margaret to spend Christmas with us. She has written to her in this post. It would seem sensible that you travel together."

Aunt Margaret said cheerfully enough, "We'll have to starve for a while, but after Christmas we can go to Mayo. After the famine, the feast." And the smell of serfdom.

Disaster scarcely hesitated.

We were in a boisterous mood at Barn House. No doubt our household was the subject of a good deal of talk in the countryside with this second pregnancy while Mother shut herself away in the dark at Court House. But that woman was generally loathed, and Isabella was as generally loved. There had always been talk, especially among the Orange, much of it bawdy. We had, when we were younger, given it no thought. Now, for reasons that I only vaguely understood—but one of which obviously was that we were older—we were conscious of it as part of the texture of our lives and I think there was in us that Christmas something of a siege mentality, an unexpected mood of defiance. That was what made the household boisterous. Even the servants seemed to be in a battlement state of mind, and Patton, growing old, exceeded all the obligations of a butler and behaved toward Isabella like a doting old nursemaid. For ourselves, the young ones, we were conscious now that, as Morag put it, "Our household is not quite orthodox." Morag talked in smiles more than in words. I think she practiced them before the looking glass. Her smile when she said we were "not quite orthodox" was an elaboration that said: Quite peculiar. We accepted our peculiarity as a right and a destination. It could hardly serve Father's political intention, but he was, or he appeared to be, utterly indifferent to its possible effects. He was a good man. That was his reputation among all but the most rabid Orange. He was a just employer, he paid good wages; he was a good landlord whose tenants respected him and were loyal. Isabella was a good and lovely woman, even "a darlin girl," and Emily, who made familiar friends with everything that spoke, was "queer" but good. The rest of us lived on their capital.

We had a game of our own invention called Rugpolo. It was not played on a rug but on horses. All we needed were a few rudimentary rules, polo sticks, an egg-shaped Rugby ball painted white, and our horses. We played it on the shore at Eden, always at night when the moon was full and the tide out. The ball was unpredictable. It capered about on the wet sand like a demented goblin, and the village tenants came out to their backyards to watch us play. They stood by their back doors, silent and bewildered at so much energy, so much trouble and so much danger being spent on so much folly. But they were not surprised. We were like that.

Patton, when the moon was up and he knew of our intention to play, with respect but great concern urged Isabella not to take part. Let Lady Margaret take your place, ma'am, he implored. The . . . the . . . the . . .

"The what, Patton?" Isabella said.

"The baby, ma'am, and I beg your pardon."

"There is no danger to the baby, Patton, and I'm grateful for your concern."

"Yes, ma'am."

"I'll be very careful."

"Yes, ma'am."

"You're right, Patton," Aunt Margaret boomed at him. "If I were pregnant, I wouldn't go near a horse."

"Yes, ma'am." Patton retreated quickly, not from Isabella's refusal to heed him but from the thought of Lady Margaret's pregnancy. Isabella pregnant was not strange. She was the mistress of his household. The thought of Aunt Margaret pregnant was more than he could face. She was an Amazon.

I think we played that night not with good sense but with our siege mentality, dangerously, defiantly, maybe to say to our spectators lurking in their shadows that we were indeed not as other men are.

Isabella and Tomas always played on opposing teams. Isabella was sister to a horse. Tomas, at eight, was a wild and superb young horseman, taught and disciplined by his mother. Time and again as they outplayed one another for the capering white goblin, Father yelled to Isabella to be careful. But even more than the rest of us she wheeled and cut with a kind of madness and was never dangerous and always in danger.

Only one man stood at the end of his garden and watched with an intentness that was anxious concern for the players or the hope of disaster. He was the widower Hyndman, the late Cassie Hyndman's husband. Each time we played, Hyndman was at the end of his garden standing by the post of his clothesline, a lamp hanging on the post and his face half shadow, half gold in its light. We had to ride past him up the opening to the village street. His eyes did not turn from Father's face. It was always the same, a glowering and malignant hatred.

Isabella led us to the paddock, where she had set up jumps for Tomas. He wanted to jump by moonlight. No, Father said. No, Aunt Margaret said. Let him jump, Isabella said. Let him fly. The moon was high, the light clear, his first round perfect.

"Higher, Mama," he pleaded.

"No higher," she said, "one more round and no more."

He took the beast around again. It was a difficult animal. Tonight it was under control. It took the first part of a double fence with ease, and a cloud covered the moon. The horse missed its stride, bucked, threw Tomas over its shoulder and crashed the fence, still going. Tomas's foot was in the stirrup. Fence bars crashed down on him, and the terrified animal dragged him. We all kicked our horses, but Isabella reached him first and hauled the horse down as she flew from the saddle. Tomas's horse tripped on the reins and rolled. He rolled on Isabella.

For Tomas, the price was less than any of us expected: a

broken wrist, a broken rib, a slight concussion, and a multitude of bruises.

There was no baby in Isabella now.

That was the first of her long silences.

❦ Seven ❦

Christmas came and went. There was no Christmas. Isabella did not speak.

Night and day Father sat by her bed and she did not speak. When she was able he walked with her on the lawns and in the gardens and she did not speak. When her maid tried to put up her hair, she pushed the girl away. She walked about the house, about the lawns, about the gardens with her hair down, and her eyes were dead. When they came to life, it was with a wild and desolate look, but she did not speak. She went often to look at Tomas in his room and neither spoke nor wept.

The servants crept about the house, whispering. It might have been a church or a morgue. The rest of us spoke softly, watched helplessly, and despaired for our impotence. Father grew haggard and was burdened by undefined guilt. Emily and Aunt Margaret ran the house and conferred in one another's rooms.

And in the library the first voices were raised. We were sitting about in gloom, reading or pretending to read. Kitty began it.

"We'd better stop pretending and face it." A warning voice about nothing, it seemed.

Irritably, for Kitty had been religiously trying for some time and called on us constantly to face something, Morag said, "What do we have to face this time?"

Kitty said, "I am entering. Someone must make atonement."

"Go to your damned convent," Morag shouted, "and make atonement for what?" But she knew.

"For Mother, for Father, for Isabella, for Tomas—and for the one that died," Kitty intoned. "It has been sin, sin, sin from our very beginnings, and God has passed judgment." I think in her religious fantasies she saw herself as the abbess of an enclosed House forever calling her rebellious charges to repentance.

Morag slammed her book to the floor and flew across the room. She stood over Kitty and said in a guttural whisper, "My arse."

Kitty was neither moved nor intimidated. "And you, Morag," she lamented, "you'll not escape. You're making up to that Garrett boy again. Do you want a husband who is foredoomed to hell? Is it a mixed marriage your heart yearns for?" She intended to say more, and her mouth was open. "Your soul is . . ."

"Keep your dirty little tongue off my soul. What I want, you pious brat, is a man in my bed. How does that sound to you?"

"Filthy. Don't you dare speak to me like that." At fifteen it is not easy to be an abbess.

"Don't you dare say one more dirty word about any of us. Not Papa. Not Isabella. Don't ever speak like that about Isabella or her baby, or by God, Kitty, I'll punch your sharp little face." I had never seen Morag in a fury. It was her custom to smile at Kitty when piety overwhelmed her good sense, a smile that spoke of her own tolerance and Kitty's imbecility. Now she was clenching her fists, pumping them up and down, burning to strike, when it was not in her nature to do so, and rising and falling on her toes. "Ohhhh . . ." she yowled, "why, why, why do priests' little women have such dirty minds." It was not an inquiry but a preface. "I'll tell you why, Kitty my girl, and it should begin to worry you. Piety like yours is nothing but smothered lust. You're a frightened little biddy. You're afraid of what you want. Well, let me tell you, I'm not. And I'll tell you this: You'll be the first to marry. And I'll tell you why: Because you'll not be able to wait for it. You in a convent? In a week you'd be over the wall, chasing a pair of trousers. Do you know what your real trouble is? You don't condemn Isabella because you think God's judging her, you judge her because you envy her. What do you think of that?"

"Filthy filth filth." Kitty screamed, and her own fury sprang her to her feet.

They were nose to nose like two bantams in a pit, and none of us saw Emily at the open door.

"And edifying too," Emily said, and shock swung us all to face the door. "How we Christians love one another," she said. "Isn't it fortunate that some of us love Isabella? Your father, for example, who sits with her and walks with her night and day till he can scarcely sit upright at table. But you, Kitty, whom do you love . . . ?"

"Don't you dare say I don't love Isabella."

"Don't you dare, don't you dare, don't you dare. Don't you dare me. You'd think to hear you sometimes that God sent you to this family to be its scourge. I know whom you love, Miss Kitty—you love Miss Kitty. Or maybe you really hate her. It's hard to tell sometimes." And sharply, "Go to your room."

Kitty was weeping. Loudly. Morag shed quiet tears. Kitty went to her room, heartbreak in every dramatic movement.

"And what came over you?" Emily asked Morag.

"Kitty did. The things she said . . ."

"I heard the things she said. I heard the things you said. Don't say them again—even if they are true. Now, go to Kitty and kiss her."

Obediently Morag did as she was told, and Emily turned her attention to me. "And what are you doing?"

"Shaking. I never saw a quarrel in this house."

"Aunt Margaret's moping in the conservatory. She wants to talk to you."

I didn't want to talk to anybody but Isabella, and that would not happen. "What does she want?"

"Oh, I know what she wants. Maybe she's getting it. But I don't think she wants it in the conservatory. You're your father's son, all right, Alasdar. Aunt Margaret's your Cassie Hyndman—with jewels. Off you go to her."

Her censure was in her face, but she gave me no chance to lie to her. She slammed the door.

Aunt Margaret was not in a pleasant state of mind. Irritably she plucked the blooms from some of Father's beloved exotic plants and threw them on the floor. I had never liked the place. It was hot and humid and not the setting for what looked like the prelude to a difficult meeting. I had never seen or heard a quarrel in the house and was uneasy, and I had never seen Aunt Margaret in an unpleasant state of mind and was alarmed.

"Where is Isabella?" she said abruptly.

"In her room. What has you in this state?"

"What state?"

"Cross."

"Hysteria," she said. "I want you to come with me. I'm going to talk to Isabella."

"While you're cross?"

"I can't do it if I'm not cross."

"Then I don't want to come with you."

"You've never objected to going to bed with me."

"That's not fair. It's not the same thing."

"How right you are. Going to bed with me is pleasant and easy. Talking to Isabella is unpleasant and difficult."

"Talking about what?"

"Herself. Come with me. We'll both need you."

I went with her. Isabella was sitting by the window, staring at the lawns. Just staring; she didn't appear to be watching anything. She paid us no attention.

"Isabella," Aunt Margaret said sharply.

Isabella did not move, did not look, did not appear to hear.

"I am going to talk to you, and you are going to listen," Aunt Margaret said firmly. "I know you hear me. You will not like what I have to say. I don't care. Since nothing love tries seems to move you, I'll try frankness. You're behaving disgracefully. Whether you know it or not, your behavior is hysteria. You're not thinking of your family. You're causing them to suffer. I'm not at all sure you're not enjoying their suffering . . ."

"Aunt Margaret, please," I said feebly.

"Do be quiet," she said. "Isabella, pull yourself together and go back to your family and your work. Who can do anything useful while you keep this up? Nothing can be done. All because you're determined to have everybody's loving attention every hour of the day and night. *You are killing Carrach, girl. You are killing Carrach . . .*"

Isabella rose. Her eyes were wild. She did not look at Aunt Margaret but at me.

"Take this woman back where she came from," she said. Her voice was soft and full of raging venom.

"Isabella, talk to me," I said, and held out my hands to take hers.

"Keep your hands off me," she said. "I will not leave this room till she leaves the house."

"We'll test that," Aunt Margaret said, grinning. "In two days you'll be back with us."

In two days Isabella was still in her room. Father knew what had happened—Aunt Margaret told him—and his failure to offer any criticism was qualified by his reserve. "Perhaps," he said, "perhaps," to her explanation. But Isabella talked to him in her room. When I went to see her, she said, "Take her away," and would not let me touch her.

"Maybe, maybe," Father said, and was a little encouraged. "But take Aunt Margaret home. This will pass now."

The day we left, I tried again to talk with Isabella. "Take her away," she said. But she let me take her hand.

"She was trying to help, Isabella," I said.

"And you think the truth is helpful?" She cried then and did not kiss me good bye. "Take her away," she said.

Father didn't come to the station. He would not leave her side. "This will pass," he said, but there was no confidence in it. The children—as I now thought of all three of them—saw us away.

"Treat her as though everything is normal," Aunt Margaret advised them. "She'll be back soon."

Morag said grimly, "Aunt Margaret, everything is not normal."

It was three gloomy weeks before I heard from Isabella. I saw very little of Aunt Margaret, as much by her will as my own. A little healing now, my dear, she said, we're all too sad. And when Murphy came for me the day Isabella's letter arrived, I knew she too had heard from her. My letter was brief and sad, but that it came at all was cheering. "Help Aunt Margaret to forgive me, darling," it said in part, "and tell me, for I need to hear it, that you forgive me. I did not mean to be unkind."

She wrote to Aunt Margaret:

I cannot dwell on it, for it makes me sad, but I hated you for speaking the truth to me. I know now why you did it, and I ask most humbly for your forgiveness, my dear, dear Margaret. I must be very careful and very stable, for there are things I now know about myself that I did not want to know . . .

There were things we all now knew that we did not want to know. Mayo can wait, Aunt Margaret decided, for who knows what the next letter may bring? Things waited, for even when on my first weekend in her house a month after our return to Dublin, and she called me to her room to talk to her while she lay in her bath, she asked for nothing and I offered her nothing.

For the next month we heard from Isabella twice a week, each letter more cheerful than the last. Poor darling Isabella, restoring us to herself, and herself to us. When Father wrote that "Isabella is her old self again," and Morag wrote that "Kitty is out of her religious attack and everything is as it always was," we both felt normal.

"Mayo?" Aunt Margaret said.

"Mayo."

The house near Lough Mask is larger than the house in Wicklow. Aunt Margaret's apartments overlook the Lough, which is long and narrow. It is unkind country, that. The wind blows. All over the province of Connaught evictions were high in 1880. An economic depression afflicted Britain and affected Ireland, and the weather was wet. The potato still stood between the tenant farmer and hunger, and there was an ignorant callousness in the question being asked in English newspapers about the Irish peasantry: "Why do they not improve their land and grow more than potatoes?"

During our drive to Clew House, Aunt Margaret surprised me by naming the tenants in the miserable cabins we passed. That is Callaghan, she said; that is O'Casey; that is O'Flaherty. Four acres, six acres, eight acres. Enough to feed a pig. That is Donovan. Twelve acres. "What else will it grow but praties?" she said, not to me but the driving rain. The turf stacks were sodden, the holes waterlogged. "They are cold," she said. "And hungry." General "Chinese" Gordon wrote to *The Times* after a visit to his native land, "I may say that from all accounts and from my own observations, the state of our countrymen is worse than that of any people in the world, let alone Europe." Aunt Margaret quoted it from memory, and angrily. Once she stopped the carriage to look out on the burned-out remains of a cabin. "That was a Joyce," she said. "In the poorhouse now, the lot of them. There are still too many people in Ireland and too little good land. Did you know that fifty men including Hugh own almost half of County Cork?"

"I didn't."

"Did you know that Townsend takes eighteen thousand pounds a year in rents around Skibbereen and still has a mortgage on his house?"

"No."

"Did you know that I bought the mortgage?"

"No." I couldn't tell her I knew the story but not that she had carried out her threat.

"That keeps his mouth shut," she said with a gleeful grin.

It was then that I first began to wonder whether her anger over the plight of the O'Caseys, the O'Flahertys, the Donovans, and the poorhouse Joyces was sympathy for them or near-malignant hostility toward their landlords. I ought to have seen it sooner. When she talked with Father, her talk was all hostility toward her kind. "Be careful, Margaret," Father said again and again. "They don't forgive."

"Neither do I," she said. "I know all about 'the old man's darling.'"

I didn't then wonder if now—if they knew—they would call her a young man's darling. I suppose addicts do not think about their habit, and Aunt Margaret was an addiction. My first woman, my wild excitement, I could not do without her when depression about Isabella cleared from my mind and released my equipment from its passing impotence. Even while she talked on our drive to Clew House, I was full of the pleasant excitements of anticipation. I had been without it now for almost three months.

"It's been almost three months," I whispered to her.

"We'll have three months' worth in one night," she whispered back; then, loud and bitter, she said, "Look at those bogs. The Irish Secretary refuses to establish fuel depots to compensate for the state of the peat bogs because the peasants are finding enough fuel to light bonfires. He says, 'Give them grass seed, not food. Let them grow cattle and horses.' Bonfires, by God. *Under him*," and her fingers dug into my thigh. What was she really thinking about, the Irish Secretary, or the serfs, or what was to come? "By God, Alasdar," she said, and her fingers dipped higher, "I'll give money to Davitt and his Land League even if it takes every penny I've got to bring reform."

But my mind was on her loins, and I made talk like a wooden man. "You've never told me how close you are to Davitt."

"As close as the money he needs can make us, that's all. I

have it and he needs it. You see. I trust you." It was like a challenge. She was a conspirator of a sort, and I was a trusted part of her conspiracy.

"Aren't you afraid Dublin Castle will find out?"

Her hand was where I wanted it to be. "I'm no longer afraid of anything," she said. "Not of anything." She was laughing. Her own anticipation was high. That was how I read it.

"What am I going to see here?" It was difficult enough to speak, let alone think of things to say.

"Me," she said, and made me lurch. "And you'll smell things in the next few days. Davitt told me."

"What things?"

"Tomorrow is time enough. Today, the feast after the famine."

We were there. "Let them hear plenty of 'Aunt Margaret,' " she said. In her apartment she said, "Joy and then revelations. That's what we're here for. First the joy, then the revelations. In the right order they'll do us both good." Her mood was jubilant. It was late afternoon and already pitch dark. "Here, we're far, far away from everyone and everything." It was a promise. "Very early to bed," she said. "There is nothing to do in Mayo after dark. Except joy in the night. Or night and day. In this house the arrangements suit us very well." She had never been so excited by the prospect before us.

Her own apartment was in the east wing of the house overlooking the Lough, and the turn of a key shut it off from the rest of the house. "Even at the door of this apartment, they hear nothing," she said. I took her word for it. How was I to know otherwise? And we were going to bed, not to a riot.

Bridie, one of her girls, came to my room with an extra scuttle of peat, brought in from the stables and cut long before the rains.

"Her ladyship says you might be cold, sir," she said. "Would you be slow with the peat? There'll be no more cut this year, by the looks of it."

I heard Aunt Margaret call to her as she left, "We'll not need anybody again tonight, Bridie." In a moment she turned the key in the apartment door.

The night Davitt dined with us was as nothing to this one. It began very quietly, even tenderly. She came to me naked and in my eyes was glorious. No, not in my eyes; she was glorious. Her long hair flowed over her shoulders. She kneeled between my knees and found what she wanted.

"You wonder about me, don't you?"

"No." I was in no state of wonder.

"You don't wonder why I do this?"

"You like it. There's no need to wonder."

"Like it? I love it. All the dry years with poor Mickey. There were times when I could think of nothing else. When we started, all I wanted was this. Do you know what's happened?"

"Tell me."

"I don't know anything about other women, but I think when a woman is mad with love for a man there is nothing, nothing," and she said it with whispered intensity, "she won't do to show him. Alasdar."

"Yes?"

"I am twice your age and mad with love for you. Come and let me show you. Don't talk," she said, "come and let me show you. I can't help it. You'll see tonight what's raging in me."

I didn't talk. I heard what she said. I understood what she said. I did not believe what she said. A woman who does it often with the same man, one of our Royal School seniors instructed us, has to believe she's in love with him or she can't enjoy it, so she makes herself think she's in love with him and puts everything into it. I think that was what I thought then, and that was unwise. "Come to bed," she said, "and get to know what I am."

My addiction was crying out. If she had told me she was really my mother it would have made no difference. We have broken down the doors, she told me more than once, but she had built for me an oaken door and I loved it, needed it, craved for it. No man was ever a more willing prisoner of a woman twice his age, and I felt as free as an eagle. If she made herself think she loved me, the better for me. If she had even more to show me than she had shown me already, I wanted all of it. "On your back, Aunt Margaret." *Aunt Margaret, Aunt Margaret, Aunt Margaret* sang in my head, and all the learned men and all the politicians and Davitt at the dinner table, correct and civil, and Barn House and all the family raced in my head like envious spectators I wanted to laugh at, and under me she was chanting *Aunt Margaret, Aunt Margaret, Aunt Margaret* and consuming me with language and lust and lustful laughter. But of all the lustful things she said that night, none had the effect of *Aunt Margaret*. Until, in the deep of the night with her lust undiminished, she pinned me on her with her great thighs and her strong arms and cried out, "Merciful Christ, my darling, if you were my son it would still be this."

I did not understand. I didn't care. The effect on me was a new and explosive charge of lustful energy that lasted till the dawn.

In the afternoon, when we rode in the rain to visit her tenants, followed by a cart loaded with foodstuffs for them, I was sane enough to think, to recall and ponder meanings. They came to me suddenly, all in one piece, but even then, my addiction shielded me from any alarming thought. Why me? I asked myself while she talked to me about being a good landlord and I did not listen. Because I came along, young, strong, and with splendid equipment, just at her right moment? No, it wasn't that. And however much my sense said my theory was too elaborate, too complicated, I was sure it was true. There was Mother, shut up in Court House, a woman who had, as she by one means and another let everybody know, refused her husband's bed. There was Father, who had taken his niece to his house and his bed. There was me, who all through my youth had loved my cousin and substitute mother and longed to bed her. But there was "Aunt" Margaret, old enough to be and often acting like another substitute mother, and when her moment came, frustrated and burning, the right incestuous link was there. "Merciful Christ, my darling, if you were my son it would still be this." Was it family she needed? Was she somewhere deep down afraid to burn away her lust on some unconnected "stranger"? I was far out of my depth. I could take my thoughts no further. She didn't allow me to.

"You're not listening," she said.

"No. I was thinking."

"About what?"

"You."

"What were you thinking about me?"

"I'll tell you tonight."

She was happy. "I'll wait," she said, and I gave my attention to her talk and her tenants.

At each cabin the three men with the cart unloaded one sack of potatoes, one side of bacon wrapped in sacking, a large bag of oatmeal, a large bag of tea, salt, and tins of condensed milk. "This tinned milk," she said at each house, "is very thick and very sweet. Put a spoonful or less in your tea."

She was crisp, aware of her authority. Not like Father, who spoke to his tenants as neighbors. But they were not like these people. They stood in family clumps at their doors, fathers, mothers, and barefoot children; they were her serfs. Her power over them was absolute. They could, if they had the spirit, improve her property—and be evicted from it without care or compensation. No law made these people her property. No law provided them with protection against being treated as her property; they were there and disposable at will like other goods and chattels.

But their thatches were good. Their cabins were sound. There was no evidence on this estate of the condition reported by one tenant when questioned by a magistrate about the ventilation of his cabin: "Ah, there's no question the ventilation's fine, yer honor. Yerra, the wind blows through the place from end to end and the rain comes in after it."

They received her benefactions in a silence like dumbness. The children stood apart, shy and withdrawn, their hands to their faces. Small eyes followed every movement, birds' eyes, darting. The women stood behind their forelock-snatching husbands, watching and smiling and nodding and making small bowing movements. Movements appropriate to serfdom. Obsequious gratitude, with the greediness of burdening anxiety and temporary relief in their darting eyes.

"May my nephew see your house?" She asked permission, always. They gave it, always; hesitantly. What is a poor cabin to a Gentleman from the Big House? Are there smells you don't notice and the Gentleman will? Is your cleanness dirt to the Gentleman? Don't people like Herself and the Gentleman have servants always scrubbin and polishin? They followed us in as if we were doing them an honor they distrusted.

"Hanrahan made that settle himself," she said, pointing to the wooden sofa that when the hinged seat was lifted was also storage space. "Isn't it a fine thing?" And Hanrahan bobbed with pleasure.

She was crisp, as a superior may be, but in her fashion she was careful of their dignity. She thanked them for our admission more effusively than they were able to thank her for the food they couldn't buy. She did not mention in Hanrahan's presence that she had provided timber and the tools with which he made his settle. Where would he get them otherwise; how pay for them? She mentioned it only to me. I, naturally, ought to know. No doubt Hanrahan knew she would tell me. But not in his presence. As I say, she was careful of their dignity.

"Would you like to live like this?" she said before we made the final delivery to her own tenants.

"No." Only a fool would need to elaborate on that.

"Did you know that half, half, *half* the people of Ireland live on private charity?"

"Yes, you told me."

"In the old Gaelic days at least they had vigor and pride."

"I couldn't live in the best of those places."

"My properties are the best in the county," she said. "Now I'll show you something else. Then ask yourself: How sharp a blade should your great book have and what should it cut?" I had not thought of my "great book" for months. Her eyes were wet. How many women and what sort of women were hidden from sight inside that glorious body?

The provisions were not exhausted. "Who gets what's left?" I asked her.

She pointed to a house in the distance. "That is Lough Mask House," she said. "Lord Erne's agent lives there. We'll make a few deliveries where he can see us and see what happens. I know he's there."

But first she determined that the men with the cart were willing. She rode past the cart shouting her question and made me think of Wellington at Waterloo. "Are you willing to make deliveries to Lord Erne's people as long as the food lasts?"

The driver slapped the horse's back with his reins. He didn't speak. Aunt Margaret smiled and rode before her baggage train. She was grinning, and the grin looked more aggressive than cheerful. "I'm not an incendiary," she said, "but I've always wanted to burn Lough Mask House to the ground. And by God, some day I might."

We kept it in sight, and she kept us in sight of it. "You didn't miscalculate on food," I said, "you intended to take some over there."

"Of course." There was militant wickedness in her grin. It pleased me, not because I understood it; perhaps because it made her look quite youthful; perhaps because it had in it the exhilaration of deliberate provocation offered to an undefined enemy. But she offered no further explanation.

"Why are you butting in on your neighbor's ground?" If it wasn't offered, I could ask for it.

"I've hated quite a few people since I married poor Mickey," she said. "But I have never enjoyed hating anybody as I enjoy hating Lord Erne's agent. Once, when he was trying to get one of my girls on her back behind a bush, he told her she could do him a lot more good than her stony mistress. She told me. She enjoyed telling me. Then she went to work for him and do him good, no doubt. I have hated him a little more each year. No, a lot more. If I went over tonight to burn him out, would you come and help me?"

"I can think of better things to do with the night."

These cabins were in an indescribable state of disrepair. The thatches were rotten. The smell of want and misery was all about them and the people who lived in them. They received her benefactions more like ill-used dogs than human beings. Their children hid. Their wives peered around the doorposts, half-faced and away again. The men plucked their forelocks and God thank ye, m'lady, God thank ye, m'lady.

Permission to enter? God thank ye, m'lady. "Hold your breath and see everything," she said quietly.

Once was enough. I held my breath. I wanted to hold my nose. I thought of vermin, and my flesh crept and itched. It was squalor of a measure I could not have imagined or invented. Humans lived like this? Did I need to see everything? No table? "We had to burn it, m'lady." What's left to burn? There was no bed: sacking stuffed with straw. The children slept like cattle on straw by a corner of the cold fire. The woman's skirt was sacking.

"They were people once," she said, "long, long ago."

I would not enter the next three cabins. "I want you to," she said.

"I will not." What in the name of God had I breathed in the first one? I stayed out in the wet air, breathing and blowing to clear my lungs of whatever foulness I had inhaled. They were people once, she said. Now they were pigs living the lives of pigs in conditions pigs, clean beasts that they are, would not have accepted.

"One of the things people do not understand about this sort of poverty is that to keep your person and your house clean, you need the means to keep them clean. And without the means to get them, you run out of means. So our sort of Nice People talk about the dirty Irish and live off them. Here he comes," she said. "Now you'll see what I want you to see. Put this in your book."

He was coming at a canter. He dismounted slowly. He was old, or appeared to be old. "Ah, Lady Margaret," he said. He had not expected Lady Margaret.

"Captain," she said with metallic charm, "what a raw day."

He had not come to discuss the day. He was holding down his anger.

"Lady Margaret," he said, "it is being said in the county that Paddy Powers, the Land League agent, has abandoned his bicycle and now rides your horses on his seditious rounds. You, of course, were not aware of this."

"I am aware of everything that goes on in the county, Captain. Past and present. Who sleeps with whose servants and what the randy old goat says to them in bed or in the bushes." She was showing her teeth, but she thought she was smiling.

The captain turned to give me a moment of his time. "Ah, yes," he said, "I had heard in Dublin that . . . I have not had an opportunity to regret Sir Michael's passing and now perhaps you will tell me what this cart and these men are doing here?"

There were provisions for three more cabins in the cart. He knew what she was doing.

"Feeding your hungry," she said without any sort of charm. "Are you going to tell them to stop it?"

"Exactly," he said, and mounted. "You will be good enough, since presumably you brought them here, to tell them to leave."

"No. I am distributing *food*, Captain. *Food*. It is necessary to continuing life. You must have noticed this since you've never missed a meal."

"You will force me to drive them off my land?"

"*Your* land, Captain?" The incredulity in her voice was measured and deliberate. The man was a servant. An important one, mind you, with no restraints upon him—but a servant.

"I'll not debate with you, Lady Margaret. I'll give them cause to leave. You may leave when you please."

He moved his horse toward the cart and took a firm hold on his riding crop. What he intended was obvious. I didn't think about what I was doing. I kicked my horse between his and the cart and its driver and held it there.

"Whoever you are, boy," he said, "you or them makes no difference to me." Only a man conscious of this omnipotence could have said it. We were on his land. He was King. I was Boy. But I had lately become Man and now I felt it.

"You're an old man," I said. "You ought to think twice."

His crop lashed down at my head and caught my left shoulder. I felt the cut through my clothes and grabbed his wrist. Aunt Margaret came across his horse's flanks and struck the beast savagely. It reared and I was slow to let go his wrist. We pulled one another to the ground. Yes, he was old. He was slow to rise. He looked foolish on his hands and knees on the muddy ground. It was humiliation before the men in the cart, the master brought low before the serf. He had no doubt of it. Nobody had any doubt of it. He could not rise quickly. His head was raised to me, his eyes red with rage almost to the point of tears, and his bared teeth were gray. For seconds, only for seconds, I wanted to kick his face, then I was sorry for him and a little ashamed. Somewhere in my spirit, Father was lurking. One of the men from the cart was standing beside me, a club in his hand. I had no wish to prolong the old man's humiliation or to witness more of it. I took the club. "Get your cart out," I said, and mounted. Aunt Margaret rode ahead. I came behind the cart. A rearguard against an aging bully to whom there was nobody empowered to say no.

"*You'll face charges,*" the captain screamed at our backs. "*Rotten scum,*" he screamed again. "*Riffraff.*"

"You didn't introduce us," I said when we were off his land. "It wasn't a social occasion."

"His name's Boycott," she said, "and he'll lay charges. These people have a passion for litigation."

"Nonsense. He couldn't lay charges. He assaulted me."

"We'll lay counter-charges. 'Assault with a deadly weapon while engaged on a work of charity.' That should be good, if we get the right magistrate." But she was not entertained. "You have several witnesses, not including the Cafferty family at the cabin. They don't count. The others don't count without me. But by God I count."

She wanted to fight him. But it was fighting over or about my body, and I found that discouraging. Something else concerned me more than that. When Captain Boycott looked me

over disdainfully, he said, "Ah, yes, I had heard in Dublin
. . ." Heard what? That she was now a young man's darling?
A young man with a name? Riding to Clew House, I was ner-
vous.

We were ready for bed early, piling the fire high. She put out
the lamps and called me to the window. The sky was broken
and the light of the moon fell on the Lough. The wind riffled
the water, and the riffles danced in ranks of broken gold.

She said, "How long does happiness last?"

"As long as you want it to, I suppose." It wasn't the sort of
question I was good at.

"Sometimes other people have a say in that."

I flew a kite. "What do other people know about us?" But
I got an answer I didn't expect.

"What would you do if I told you I didn't want it tonight?"

"I'd put you down and take you."

"You'd rape me?"

"Call it anything you like. I'd put you down."

"Well," she said, "I don't want it tonight."

For a while it was a fairly equal struggle. She made small
whimpering and moaning sounds as we struggled, and they
were to me not different from her ecstasies. Then she weakened quickly. "You're too strong, you're too strong," she
whimpered, and though she gave me no help, I had no difficulty. Nor had I any control. The struggle drove me mad
for her, and I was brutal.

It may have been a long time before the hammering on the
landing door of her apartment eventually reached me.

"They'll go away," she whispered. "Don't stop."

They did not go away. Her maid was calling now, and
pounding.

"You go," Aunt Margaret said, "and think of something.
Damn her."

Think of what? I want out in my dressing gown. "What's
the trouble, Bridie?"

"There's a man for m'lady, and she doesn't hear me."

"Somebody at this time of the night?"

"It's Paddy Powers, sor, she always sees Paddy no matter
what time it is."

"Well, I'll see if I can wake her. Tell Mr. Powers she'll be
down presently—if I can wake her." I closed the door.

"If it's Paddy Powers I have to see him," Aunt Margaret

said. "Let me get down there, and come after me soon. I want you to know Paddy. He's Land League, and this is his county."

In a while I followed her downstairs. Bridie was waiting in the hall. "Her ladyship says in there, sor," she said, and pointed to what had once been Sir Michael's study. It was a small room overlooking an enclosed vegetable garden. "Michael loved looking at vegetables," Aunt Margaret told me without smiling. I never knew if her comments on Sir Michael were the outward and audible signs of inward and bitterly ironic laughter at her fate. The room was book-lined, there was a large desk and some comfortable chairs and a small fireplace. "The books are all mine," she said when she showed me the house. "I don't think Michael ever read a book—unless it was an account book." It would be a very thick account book.

Paddy Powers was a messenger from Michael Davitt. Davitt was in jail in Sligo, where he had been taken that day from a platform for urging his peasant audience to seize food for their families rather than let them starve to death. Her ladyship had been generous in the past months, but now they needed money to allow Parnell to go on a rampage across the country, scaring Dublin Castle because they were thinking of revoking Davitt's ticket of leave and sending him back to jail to finish an earlier fourteen-year sentence. All this, but reluctantly, Paddy Powers went over for me on her instructions. And they needed Lady Margaret's good offices at Dublin Castle, he said; maybe a word that a trial for Davitt in Sligo would cause less trouble in the country than would the revocation of his ticket of leave, for that would send him back to jail in England. (He had been sentenced to fourteen years for gunrunning when he was young.) The League could handle a trial if it was held in Sligo, but what could they do to prevent near-insurrection if Davitt went back to jail for the seven years still hanging over his head? Ireland would burn. Paddy's eloquence was almost orchestral.

He was a big woolly-looking elementally eloquent young man, and persuasive. But he didn't need to persuade. I had never seen her face so full of calculation. She offered him a bed for the night. He couldn't wait. She gave him the money he needed and roused her groom and sent Powers home in her coach, his bicycle lashed behind it.

She sat at the desk for an hour and a half and showed me

what she wrote. It was addressed to Jennie Churchill, to be read by her and passed by her to the Irish Secretary with a copy for Randolph, who was in London fumbling his way through another parliamentary session. It said in part:

Please ask them to consider that the immediate imprisonment of a one-armed Irish peasant like Davitt for another seven years for urging poor men not to let their children starve will cause a more destructive uproar than a trial in Sligo for incitement will do. Out here I am close to the situation, and the mood is explosive. Must we cause ourselves deeper trouble? Is it not better to try the man for his latest offense than to rouse the 500,000 members of the Land League to destructive rage? I am thinking of the Queen's Peace.

I gave it back to her. "A one-armed Irish peasant?" I said, not too pleased. I admired Michael Davitt. So did Father. "A better man than Parnell," he told me.

"My dear," she said like the chaplain at the Royal School, "what is the purpose of the letter? That is all that matters. Its purpose is to succeed. That, and maintaining one's access to the people who exercise power. And, of course, one's usefulness to them. Yes?"

"Usefulness to them? Whose side are you on tonight?"

"Mine, darling," she said. "Come back to bed."

But it was some time before we went back to bed. We lay on the rug in the warmth of the fire, and she talked. Her talk was confused and full of anger; it spoke fiercely for the serf without warmth for his humanity and was full of personal malice for her own kind, as though the serf was a weapon through which she might effect a personal revenge. Then, "What have I been saying?" she asked me.

"Don't you know?"

"I wasn't listening." She was smiling at the fire.

We lay there for half an hour more, touching one another with peculiar indifference. I could not fathom her state of mind.

"You must know Paddy Powers better," she said. "I'll arrange it," and there was another long silence. She kissed me, teased my equipment, and lay back again, tired of it, it seemed.

"Do you want to sleep?" I asked her.

She turned on her side and lay staring at me and did not answer. She was silent for so long that I thought she had forgotten my question.

"I have nowhere to go," she said at last.

"What does that mean?"

"I don't belong to the serfs and I don't belong to their lords," she said, "that is what I mean," and lay on her back again. And, as though things without relation to one another drifted through her mind, "They say Lord Kilroot's bastard young brother is really his son."

"I've heard that story."

"His father died when he was eighteen. They say he wept for a week, and to console himself got into his mother's bed like a baby. She was my own age then. They say she kept him there. I often think about them."

I could think of nothing to say. What was there to say?

"Paddy Powers can show you things. I'll arrange it."

I wanted to sleep.

"Do you think of me with any respect, Alasdar?"

"How can you ask such a question? Of course I do. Respect and very deep affection."

"Very deep affection." She said it over slowly, thoughtfully, as if to examine it from every angle. "They say maids always know how many slept in a bed. Did you know that?"

"You told me once."

"Doesn't that amuse you?"

"I haven't thought about it since."

"Think about it now."

"What should I think?"

"Well, it was one of Kilroot's maids who first said he was mounting his mother. Their whole staff said it was a passionate love affair. It's supposed to have gone on till she was past sixty. She's eighty now, and he never married. The baby was born more than a year after her husband died. They never tried to explain it."

"I've only heard the vague talk, never the details."

"Very deep affection. Is that a kind of love? I mean, could a man be loyal to a woman, stay with her till she ran dry, because he loved to mount her?"

"I'm sure he could. Yes, I'm certain of it."

"I think about the Kilroots. It was so safe that way. I mean, family. Not strangers. We're like that. Not strangers."

"No."

"Alasdar?"

"Yes?"

"I have nowhere to go. Nowhere but you." She was crying.

"Don't cry." Stupid ineffectual counsel. I took her in my arms.

"Alasdar."

"Yes."

"There is nothing I wouldn't do to please you. Tell me what you want, and I'll do it now."

And she was a fine arranger. Paddy Powers was riding around the countryside on her horses on Land League business but she said a word and he had time for me and I don't think he liked me that much. Powers treated me with a kind of Irish cordiality that is cold at the center. The coldness isn't visible. One doesn't see it, one feels it without being able to isolate and identify it. Father had an unerring instinct for it, or antennae that feel it out. At the height of his fame he would say to Isabella or Robert Garrett of some greeter, Orange or Home Rule, who received him with fulsomeness: "I mustn't turn my back on that one." He was invariably right.

I had this feeling about Powers. He tolerated me, I was sure, because Aunt Margaret paid up and they needed her money and her good offices. I traveled the county with Powers, and Aunt Margaret was growing bolder—we traveled the county in her carriage. Powers didn't show me everything, he let me see what he saw, hear what he heard, what he said, and my book stirred in me again and with it a smoldering anger. I wrote, Aunt Margaret read and discussed, and Powers explained with cold patience, and a story began to emerge. She sent sections to Murray, the publisher, who sent back praise and suggestions and wanted to see it all as it progressed. I had a purpose of my own again, though I had almost forgotten Trinity. And Aunt Margaret was cold and astute and critical when what I wrote was under examination. She even decreed an adjustment in our sexual activities— what she called "quick daytime bashes," all unscheduled, took the place of long and now tiring marathon nights, with a sweet, gentle slow session when we went quite late to bed. It was more a domestic mood, and she obviously liked it, for apart from travel with Powers, we did everything together and there was real companionship it it. I found my "very deep affection" deepening.

It was in this state of mind and spirit that I learned from Paddy Powers of the miseries of the life of a process server. The papers were full of them, for Parnell—who was president of the Land League—cried out to the peasants, "Hold on to your homesteads," and Davitt organized them to take that literally. They took it to mean increasing and often brutal violence, which Davitt deplored, and though Parnell also deplored it, his speeches encouraged it.

An eviction order had to be served within three days of its issue. That meant putting the order into the hands of the tenant to be evicted, or nailing it to his door, within the three days. Getting near the tenant or his door had become quite risky for process servers. They had almost given up trying to reach the condemned man or his door in daylight, even with police escorts. I listened to Powers's tales of the tactics of the peasants. There was wild comedy in them: the majesty of the law brought to naught by people who couldn't read the notices meant to expel them from their homes. There was cruelty, too, and savagery as wild as the comedy. The livestock of landlords was killed in the fields at night. Worse, much more of it was mutilated than killed. It was Irish excess, the inflamed anger that feeds on itself and knows no bounds, an epidemic hysteria, and for what? In this case not Home Rule, not nationalism, not a chauvinistic hatred of England or the Queen, but for land reforms, tenants' rights, and a new bill to control rents and compensate evicted tenants for improvements they might have made on the landlords' property. Davitt pleaded with the peasants to stop the killings and the mutilation of dumb beasts. Parnell joined him in his appeals, yet his words encouraged it. Captain Moonlight, they called these operations. Comedy or savagery, it was Irish drama, raw material, and at first that was all it was to me. Aunt Margaret at this time did not encourage me to see it in any other light. It was some time before I saw the cunning progress through which she led my mind, and when I saw it, I was grateful for it.

But it was Powers who served as her tool. He said one day as we rode in style on the serfs' business, "Lady Margaret says you're a writer, writin a book."

It was nice of her to magnify and advertise my standing. Perhaps the euphoria created by hard work on the book—in the end it was as much her book as mine, though till now I have not had the grace to acknowledge this—and frequent short and vigorous intermissions on the floor, on the edge of the bed or on the bed, helped her to believe it. What is important is that she did believe it.

But Powers left me with the impression that he was not impressed. "I suppose you'll only be usin the funny bits?" he said. He didn't smile but granted me this dignity with a too-deep sobriety. There was a suggestion of hidden disdain on his sober face. The Irish peasant, I had to learn, is often a solemn laugher.

But unknown to me and at Aunt Margaret's insistence, he took part of my manuscript to Davitt, now awaiting trial in his Sligo jail. "He read it," he told me later. "So did I."

"What did he say?"

"He said there's somethin missin."

"Did he say what?"

"He did." The Irish have this sometimes infuriating, sometimes entertaining gift for answering the question asked. It's pigheadedness I told Aunt Margaret; anyone else will anticipate the final question in the initial question and answer both. It's a dance, Aunt Margaret said; they like to dance, with their tongues and their feet.

"What is missing?"

"Anger," Powers said.

It was after that that I saw the change come in Powers's attitude to me and in Aunt Margaret's attitude to what I had already written. The book was now my passion. Father wrote: I have been to Dublin twice lately. Why are you not at Trinity? I replied: I am deeply involved in my work, I assure you. I shall return to Trinity quite soon. What Aunt Margaret said was much more important. The more I reread the manuscript, she said, the more I think we're being too objective. I feel—and she puzzled carefully for the right words—that we are only observers. We are not—what do I mean?—we are not inside our people yet. Do you think I'm right? She was always careful, always cunning, and I was always grateful, learning from her, and under her guidance, from the library in the house. See now how he did this, she said of a passage from Mr. Dickens, or from Mr. Stevenson's new book, or from Mrs. Beecher Stowe or Mr. Twain, whose work was reaching us now. "That is the way to do this bit." I was at school again. And Powers was suddenly willing to show me what I had not yet seen.

"Did her ladyship mention that Boycott's got eviction orders for the three families she fed?"

"She did."

"He wants their arrears, and they haven't a penny."

"So he'll throw them out?"

"He won't, y'know."

"I don't follow you."

"We won't let him. They'll hang on to their hovels, the way Parnell told them to. You should see that for your book."

I still had a vague distrust of the man, perhaps because I had felt his distrust for me. "I'll talk to Lady Margaret about it. When will it happen?"

"The morrow night they'll try to serve the orders."

"I'll speak to her about it."

"Aye. Ask her if she'll let you." He was looking the other way. He offered help, but not yet without disdain. The only mind I had was Lady Margaret's mind?

Perhaps it was. She was very thoughtful, but she was smiling. "Yes. Yes, I think you should see it. But don't let them catch you. I'll have to say a word to Powers about that. He'll see to it."

"Don't. I'll see to it."

"Yes, certainly you will. I'm overanxious for you, darling."

"We don't guess the way they come at the cabins," Powers explained to me. "We decide that for them. The roads are all closed."

We were riding bicycles in the pouring rain. It had stopped for no more than a few hours in the time we had been in Mayo. My machine was a model for women and too small for me. I did not look like Captain Moonlight with my knees up to my chest. Powers had ridden a bicycle up hill down dale, day in, day out. "Come on, come on," he kept saying, waiting for me with ill grace and the suggestion in his bearing that I would be a liability. My legs were sore. Only my pride kept me from turning back. I could hear him telling Aunt Margaret, "Thon's the soft one."

A large body of men was gathered at the crossroads. Rocks and tree trunks blocked the road in four directions. Other men, I learned, were in the waterlogged fields, closing the gaps between rain-filled peat holes. There was nothing to see but a blackness beyond the roadblock. Process servers, their police escort, and the defenders of these three homesteads must all work blind except at the closest quarters. A man rode a bicycle up the road from the south.

"They're on sidecars," he called across the rocks and tree trunks. "Three servers and thirty peelers." He passed the bicycle over the barricades and climbed over himself. "There'll be sore heads this night, I'm thinkin," he said.

"Maybe worse," Powers said. "How far?"

"A mile by now and no lamps lit on the cars."

"They're not comin this far then. They're in the fields by now. You, you, an you—go along the ditches till you find the horses and cars. Cut the harness, put the wheels in the bogs, drive the horses to hell and farther. The rest of you go on out an wait for them. They'll try to go roun us—far right an far left. Don't try runnin to meet them, now. Don't wear yourselves out in them fields. Wait for them behind the stone walls. Let them through, then come in behind them. They can't hear your feet for the suckin of their own, an remember—they don't go far when a club gets them on the back of the thigh. Away on, now." They had all done this more than once.

They were part of the darkness. We could hear their boots sucking and soughing in the sog now that they were off the roads. All of them carried clubs. In a little while there was no sucking and soughing, only the sound of the pouring rain.

"What do we do?" I asked Powers.

"We stan here in the rain." He pushed a club into my hand. "An meet anybody that gets through."

"The two of us?"

"Aye. They fight the peelers out there. The servers sneak away. If any peelers get away to help them, there's more of us on the other side of the road. Then we fight more peelers, an the servers think this time they're well away. If they get near the three houses, there's men up there. But over my left shoulder, three hundred yards up the slope, there's one of the houses. Cafferty's house, where you were when the captain clipped you one. We're waitin for the server that thinks he can come this way, roun the hill and then down behind the house."

"Will he be armed?"

"No."

"Then why do we need clubs?"

"They're awful hard on the legs."

Then nothing but the sound of the rain. I was a spectator.

He had done all the explaining he needed to do. Now I could watch or go home.

The yelling began on our right, to the south of us. It sounded at first like anger, like Zulus trying to strike terror into the minds of their enemies. I could imagine what a fight with clubs might be like in fields so wet that quick movement was impossible, in dark so thick that friend might be foe until it was too late.

"Somebody will get killed," I said.

"Sometime. No evictions, nobody gets hurt. Shut up."

We heard the crack of wood on wood, and now cries of pain.

"Somebody's getting hurt."

"It's not the little children up the hill." I tried his patience.

But the children up the hill could very likely hear the fighting. Their fathers were behind the doors, waiting, with clubs, to hear a sneaking approach, to throw open the door and strike down the server's hammer, to leap out to protect their hovels. They were their own last line of defense.

The new commotion came from our left, to the south. In the thick blackness far beyond the new yelling, horses screamed.

"Jesus Christ," Powers said. "I'll kill the shits myself." He spun and paced and swung his club at a tree trunk. "Jesus Christ, they ruin their own cause!" he yelled at the rocks.

"What is it?"

"Nothin." He had his club up. For me, I thought, and shifted my own.

But I knew horses and their sounds. I knew a great deal more about them than Powers would ever know. "They're multilating the animals," I said.

He took control of himself. "It's ruin for us."

"Is that all. You don't think it's bad for the horses?"

"Fuck off," he said, and walked away. He didn't care about the horses. The man had neither thought nor feeling for the meaning of excess. He cared only about the damage the mutilators of dumb beasts were doing to the tenants' cause. To Davitt's denunciations of this mindless savagery, some in the cities in their safely detached anger yelled: Do you care more about beasts than homeless children? They're only the landlord's beasts, some in the countryside yelled. How does a mutilated beast help homeless children? Davitt asked at his meetings. To the sane ones he appealed for an end to it, "before you sicken the world." It was not the sane who did it.

"By Christ they'll pay for this," Powers shouted, and swung his club at absent bodies.

There was fighting behind us now, on the north side of the road. Some policemen had fought their way through. Somewhere in the black wet dark, three process servers with eviction notices, hammers, and nails were loose, looking for holes they could sneak through. The dark was their friend, the rain was their friend, the fighting in which they were not involved was their friend. Powers seemed unconcerned.

"He has to come this way," he said. "He can't get roun the other side of the hill."

"Who?"

"A big fellow by the name of Milford. He has the notice for the Cafferty house up the hill. He has to come this way to go round the hill and down to the back of the house. Don't let that wet club slip out of your hand when you swing it."

I had not thought of swinging it against some clerk without a club of his own. I had come to see. So far I had only heard the rain that soaked me, the clash of clubs, the shouts of anger, the cries of pain, and the screaming of dumb beasts.

"Quiet now," Powers said. "He has the cover he needs with that fightin. He'll come by here on his own, waggin his big smart arse. Out of a hundred they've tried to serve in Mayo, only three got through in the last two months—and this bastard Milford had the three of them."

I heard a sound close by, like the sound of rain washing gravel.

"Down, out of sight," Powers whispered. But he stood as clearly visible as a man could be in this pit of blackness. He must think of himself as Cuchullain at the Gap.

I tried to dry the handle of my own club on my wet clothes. Powers backed away from the barricades and stood in the middle of the road swinging his club like a pendulum, and the sound of rain washing gravel came closer and stopped. For a while there was nothing but rain on the road, rain on the grass, rain on our heads. My ears were tired from straining.

I couldn't tell where the voice came from.

"Bejasus if that great bloody lump standin there in the middle of the road isn't Paddy Powers himself. God, you're the great one, Paddy."

Paddy was searching the dark. He was not finding.

"Come on over, Milford," he said, pretending knowledge.

"Over what, Paddy? Where d'ye think I am, boyo?"

"I know where you are. I want you here, you dirty black bastard."

"Bejasus ye soun fond, Paddy. This is no kissin matter, unless you're thinkin to kiss me arse."

"Come on over, Milford."

"I won't come empty-handed, Paddy."

"Come anyway you fancy. You'll go home naked."

"That's what you have in mind, is it?"

"Come on over."

He did not come over. Something came from somewhere. I cannot be certain that I saw it. I think now I saw it bounce off the side of Paddy's head, but how can I be certain in that black darkness? Paddy went down like a pig at the slaughter-house. Not a sound came out of him, and Milford was up, out of the ditch on our side of the barricade, and away down the road like a harrier and I was crouching behind the barricade as useless as a turtle. I didn't think about Paddy, alive or dead. I didn't think at all when I moved.

Cafferty's was the cabin from which the captain had driven us. That was all I knew. I had in my head only a picture of the pitiful creatures who lived in that squalid place. I made for it. Several times in daylight I had seen it from this crossroad, up there on the slope. I made for it without thought, trying the fields, the shortest route, by instinct, not reflection; clinging to my wet club. There was no thought in my head of what I might use it for.

It is one thing to look at ground in daylight and from a road. It is another to plunge into the same ground in pitch darkness. In twenty strides I was up to my knees in water, and now I knew what that spiky-looking grass covered; a wet bog. I labored through it like a worn-out donkey, my legs dragging water. Above it on a flat place there is a peat bog, but precisely where? I climbed. I could see no more than a few feet ahead of me, and it wasn't far enough.

The feeling of falling in the dark into an invisible hole is very shocking. The solid world disintegrates under you: falling into a hole with four feet of water is terrifying. I went under in the bog hole, my mouth open, gulping air. My mouth filled. My stomach filled with black rancid water and my club was gone from my hands as I clutched nothing to save myself from nothing; choking, flailing, fearing, whimpering. Touching bottom and resurfacing. Merciful Christ it's a bog hole. Up, empty-handed, coughing, spitting, retching, breathing. I had to have my club. The water was too deep for me to bend and search. I had to sweep the hole with my feet, yard by yard, full of dirty water outside me and in me. Coughing, retching, spitting, freezing. When I struck the club, I had to reach it, head underwater. All underwater all over again. Filthy water up the nose. And climb out. The hole was over six feet deep. Throw the club up first, leap at the lip of the hole, get your elbows on top of it. Leap? Out of thick fibrous water? Milford would be headed up the slope now, far to my left, going wide around the hill. He'd have nobody but miserable Cafferty to beat when he came at the cabin from behind. He could eat Cafferty. My boot toes dug the wall of the hole, my forearms and elbows slid off the lip. Again. Again. Try another wall. I found a foothold and was out on my belly and my face. Scrabbling like a dog in the dark on the ground for my bloody club, and when I found it, slap into a stack of turf with my face, bouncing to my back on the ground. Shock on shock, shaking.

I went through the peat bog carefully now. There were men on either side of it and three men somewhere behind it. I began to shout, "Milford's going round the hill," and my legs were pulled from under me.

"Who the fuckin hell are you?" a face said into my face. I shouted with a landlord's accent.

"Milford got Paddy. He's going round the hill."

They didn't wait. They knew the ground, and I followed their shapes upright, scrambling, and on my hands and knees. We crossed the cabin yard and lay behind a dry-stone wall on the slope above it. I got the place to the left of a gap in the wall. "If he comes through it, swing low down," somebody told me. Somebody called at Cafferty's door, "Stay in, Cafferty, Milford's up ahind ye."

We heard him coming. He was running down the slope from the other side of the hill, slipping, sliding, in the clear, and in a tearing hurry. I dare not look in case my white face against the dirty white of the cabin should make me faintly visible. I gripped my wet club, kneeling by the gap in the wall, and he came through it. I was not thinking, but now I was feeling. I would not freeze for nothing.

Swing! I heard the crack. Like a gunshot. He fell like a statue. The weight of the thud surprised me as he hit the ground. They were on him, and he was howling.

"My ankle, you fuckers. You smashed it." He howled. He screamed. He did not fight. He could not fight.

I stood and watched them. They stripped him without thought for his smashed bones and his agony, tore the clothes off him as he screamed. Cafferty brought a lamp. They dragged Milford down the slope, screaming; his leg dragging on the bumpy ground; to the peat bog. They made an armchair of wet turfs and set him naked in it. They piled his clothes out of sight and reach and took his hammer and his nails and the eviction notice from his pockets.

"You can't leave him there," I shouted, the club I hit him with still in my hand.

"Who the fuckin hell are you?" They stood close around me, peering at my stranger's face. One of them said, "He's big Meg's fancyman."

And the dark took them.

"I'll know you, you fancy cunt." Milford shouted at me among his moans and groans and Oh, merciful Jesus it's killin me's. "I know you, you fancy cunt stuffer. I heard them."

I went down the hill full of rage and care for my skin.

Paddy was not at the crossroads. Was there no human anywhere in this desolation? There were no bicycles. I was freezing, chittering like a frightened child. I ran. My thickened, clobber-wet clothes stuck to me like soft ice. My feet swam in my boots. I ran the two miles to Clew House, and my heart and lungs were tearing other great gaps in my chest. Other great gaps because my rage was tearing me asunder.

Aunt Margaret said, "Almighty God. Hot water."

She washed me in the bath, like a mother. I told her what had happened. "One of them called me your fancyman," I said with indignation.

"They do me great honor," she said, and passed on to something else.

But I would not be put off. "How could it enter their minds?" Had she not said they could hear nothing that went on in this apartment?

"Maids, darling, maids," she said. "They always know. And of course, think how they envy me."

She was pleased, for God's sake. She was laughing. "I am very proud," she said, drying me before the fire. "Now, come to bed. And think of it—the girls are lying in their beds thinking, 'Mr. Alasdar is mounting her ladyship, and I wish he was mounting me.'"

She was delighted. She didn't care. In the sound of her laughter, neither did I.

Cleaned by her, warmed by her, and rested, sleep was my contentment. I longed for sleep. When I drifted away, she shook me back to her. She worked, but nothing rose for her. As I left her, hurrying into sleep, I thought I heard her saying, "It will be a boy, darling, a son," but I could not come back. The words were still with me when I woke. It was, of course, a fragment of a dream.

❧ *Eight* ❧

The effects of that fragment of a dream stayed with me all day. How such things work in the mind I do not know, but at breakfast I looked at Aunt Margaret with a new interest and curiosity. I looked at her often—how many times a day?—with lust and through her clothes to her naked body, but always until now only—no, not only, but certainly often—as an instrument to satisfy my surging lusts. This looking was not like that. Instead of the glorious body always available to me and always for whatever use she had taught me to make of it, I saw into it, as it were, to the loneliness ("I have nowhere to go"), to the inexhaustible kindness and the love she declared for me, and the willingness to accept from me—and the gratitude for—the less that I offered in return. And last night she bathed and cleansed me with the care and tenderness of a mother.

"Aunt Margaret."

"Yes, darling?" with marmalade poised over toast, looking at me and smiling, with eyes that—and I thought it was nonsense—also had shining in them a different interest in me.

"There's nobody in the world like you." I brimmed with warmth for her. I could have taken her in my arms, and not with lust, gently.

"Oh. I thought you were about to say something else."

"What did you think I was about to say?"

"I like what you said. Say more."

"You are a most wonderful woman."

"I like that too. Is there more?"

342

"The way I feel, it would tumble out."

"Tumble it out."

"You look very happy." She looked young.

"I am happy. Make me happier."

It was that sort of day. We worked on my—on our—book all morning, writing into what had already been written the anger I saw in the night and did not yet feel. It wouldn't do, of course. I had to feel it, and she said so. But now the skeleton of it was on paper, and the flesh would come. I had Powers's anger to work on also; his anger with the mutilators of dumb beasts, but also his anger at a majority of the members of the Land League, for, he told me on one of our carriage rides, "People like you think every tenant is up an ready to fight, but most of the bastards watch their neighbors bein thrown out on the roads an won't lift a fuckin han to help them. You have to lie and lie like shit to the papers to make them believe we have a half a million men in a fuckin army." And that went in and the story, as it grew, began to look less like a work of devotion and more like the truth.

Aunt Margaret contributed to the germination of useful anger. She said, "If the truth were told about every side in Ireland's disputations, the rest of the world would vomit."

In the afternoon we rode in the rain. "We'll call on the Allans," she said. "Unannounced."

Their house was large and had once been fine, but like the Allans themselves it was now in an advanced state of disrepair. The plaster on their walls was cracked and holed, the roofs of their stables insecure, the large gilt frames on their large family portraits chipped, their furniture very old, its springs broken and its upholstery torn, worn, and shabby. "Mary," said Aunt Margaret, sitting on a broken spring, "what in God's name is pinching my bottom?" The Allans were shabby. They were also righteous and superior. Our hostess spoke of the Irish with bitter contempt. They were savage and undisciplined children, primitive, rather like Africans but without their natural dignity. The intensity of her diatribe suggested a preface to something less general. "Poor Milford," she said at last, "a crushed ankle. He will be a cripple for life."

"Poor Cafferty," Aunt Margaret said, "a pauper's life and a pauper's grave."

"We are disturbed, Margaret," Mrs. Allan said regally, "to hear these stories of Powers using your horses and now your carriage to make his seditious rounds. You do, of course, deny it?" She believed it, knew it to be true; everything about her hostile condescension said so.

"Do I?" Aunt Margaret's smile was brittle. "Of course I don't deny it. Do you ride about the country in the rain on a bicycle?" She looked about the room as though to suggest that, if they had any sense, they would sell their horses and buy bicycles. Then she said it. "Perhaps you should, Mary? If you don't fix this place up, you'll soon be in a worse state than your tenants." The smile was fixed like a bayonet.

Mrs. Allan struck where Irish and Anglo-Irish always strike when the knives are out: at disagreement seen as treachery in their own ranks. "It is so important, Margaret, not to be disloyal to one's own kind."

"But so difficult, dear, when one knows one's own kind so well."

"Do you believe in heaven, Margaret dear?"

"The place with all that harp music, Mary dear? No. It's too much for me."

"From what I hear, that must be a great trial to Michael. Canon Davidson urges us to be circumspect in all our ways, to protect the feelings of loved ones gone before us. He says they know and suffer."

"Poor Mickey," Aunt Margaret said sadly. "Heaven would be such a relief to him now. I don't think he sees much where he is. He went to the other place." And she excused us, smiling her savage smile.

Away from the house she said, "That stupid presumptuous bitch. You've seen them in their decay. But whether they're rich or poor, they are all the same in their own eyes—God's anointed with their feet on the backs of a whole nation."

She didn't speak again till we were alone. I was glad enough of her silence, for my stomach festered with rage, not only because the Allan woman had rebuked Aunt Margaret and thrown me in her face but because arrogance ignorant and unseeing is in itself enraging.

That night she composed a letter to her tenants, and together we made copies of it for delivery in the morning by her houseman, who could read and would read for those who could not. It announced a moratorium on their rents for three years and certain improvements she intended to make on their homes and farms and, when the three years had elapsed, their rents would be half their present level. For a woman so rich it wasn't much of a gesture. She derived very little income from her estates—it came from Sir Michael's shrewd involvement in heavy industry outside Ireland—but it would make things even more difficult for her neighboring landlords, and from that she derived what mattered to her more than income: revenge.

"I'll tell you what will happen three years from now," she said. "They'll see no reason why they should ever pay rents again—and simply won't pay them."

All that day there was no brief and vigorous intermissions. We had too much to do, too many other things to think about, including a visit from a horseback-riding curate who arrived so late that he had to stay the night and another letter from Father. The poor young man, as Aunt Margaret described him, was sent by the rector of their scattered Protestant parish "to look at and report on Margaret Somerville's fancyman." He was a pleasant-enough, harmless-enough creature, suited very well to his calling and no doubt in time would help some desperate Ascendancy daughter to escape from the purgatory of her provincial life. He certainly looked at me and made awkward conversation.

"You are yourself a Catholic, are you, Mr. MacDonnell?"

"Yes."

"I note that you call her ladyship 'Aunt Margaret.' You are her nephew, then?"

"No."

"One of those adopted 'Aunts' then?" with an uncomfortable titter.

"What is it you want to know, Mr. Cranshaw?" Aunt Margaret asked him crisply, and made me sorry for him and amused. She didn't want to be told. He was an unwilling and unskilled inquisitor. Mr. Cranshaw was subjected to a long and detailed account of Aunt Margaret's relationship with our family, and, with, after each segment, including her visit at Christmas, "Is that what the rector wants to know?" And when it was over, "Well, it's past our bedtime. Show Mr. Cranshaw to his room, will you please, dear?"

"A very remarkable woman, her ladyship," Mr. Cranshaw said in his room.

"Very." But by now I found it hard to laugh at him. "And very kind, Mr. Cranshaw. But perhaps the rector already knows that."

"Of course, of course."

"But next time, perhaps he should do his own scavenging? Do you not feel so yourself?"

"I see, I see," nodding and bobbing. "Good night, Mr.

MacDonnell." The poor young man was ashamed. He closed his door, trying to smile.

There are no secrets in Ireland. The thought filled me with defiance. To hell with their tongues and their minds. I knew Aunt Margaret as no one had ever known her, and I was bonded to her in a way and at a depth that neither rectors nor the women of her kind would ever be able to understand. I knew something else about Aunt Margaret. It came to me whole, of a sudden. I knew the meaning of my new interest when I looked at her. I hurried to tell her.

"Open your father's letter," she said.

It diminished my excitement. It was discouraging and it was very brief. "Your retreat to Mayo has gone on quite long enough. Please return to Trinity at once." We had been in Mayo for a month, and Trinity was no longer in my mind.

"Come to bed," she said. "Perhaps it won't rain tomorrow."

That night was different from all the nights that had gone before. She stood naked in the center of the room, smiling her gentle smile, watching me undress. Like a cattle drover I walked around her, looking at her body, and it was glorious in my sight. "You're mine," I said.

"Yes."

"I don't care about anything else."

"Come to bed."

The wildest, most lustful nights we had spent together were not like this. I cried to her what I had burned to tell her. "I love you. I love you. I love you."

In the quiet aftermath, when we laughed, I said, "I had an odd dream last night. All I can remember of it is that you told me you were pregnant."

"I am," she said, "and now I am glorious."

I was not afraid, not even alarmed. I loved a woman, I had made her pregnant, great God Almighty that was glorious. And what a woman, full of greed for me, full of love for me, my friend, my helper, my teacher. I did not say and then I did not think: my mother. We talked most of the night away.

"You'll marry me."

"I'm twice your age, darling. It's impossible."

"Father is twice Isabella's age."

"Your father is a man. Men can do that. Michael did it. You'd be an old woman's darling."

"I hope so."

"Your father would never allow it."

"He couldn't stop it."

"I won't do it. I'm here. I'm yours. That's all we need."

"I shall marry you. I want to marry you. The thing is settled."

"In the meantime, do it that way again."

She was deliriously happy. It was a night of joy and laughter. I have no doubt now that she always intended to marry me. I had no doubt then that it was right, inevitable, but saying that now is nonsense—I didn't analyze it at all, I knew. I wanted the woman for myself. I wanted rights in her, the rights of possession; I knew that without her I was nothing. We loved, and with laughter argued till dawn.

"You'll have it no other way, will you?" she said.

"That is how it will be."

"Then by God that is how I want it to be."

"We'll go home now," I said.

"To Dublin?"

"To Barn House."

"God protect me," she said. "But I'll go."

Now I was afraid. I was caught between two desperations, conflict with the family and the fear of betraying Aunt Margaret by cowardice. I was afraid of Father's magisterial dignity and disapproval. I was afraid of Isabella, and what I feared there I did not know. I was afraid of the laughter or the scorn of my sisters. Tomas I didn't think about.

Father sat in the Captain's chair across the library fire and filled the room. "It is, of course, a very serious step," he said reasonably, and his reasonableness added weight to what must be his concern and disapproval.

"Yes, sir, I know that."

"It is easy to make a dreadful mistake. I made one."

"I know, sir." I felt very young. In Mayo I had not felt young or small.

"Margaret is twice your age."

"You are twice Isabella's age."

"That is not quite the same thing." His tone was chilling. "I have never called Isabella Aunt Isabella. I notice you still call the woman you want to marry Aunt Margaret."

There was no explanation for that. I could hardly tell him it had for both of us an erotic connotation, the tantalizing suggestion of the illicit.

"If you marry her, will you continue to address her in these terms?" I was also afraid of his sense of the ridiculous.

"I suppose not, sir. I've never thought about it."

"Has she?"

"I don't know, sir."

"It is very peculiar. Very, very peculiar. Is there not the suggestion of something unhealthy about it?"

I felt younger than ever. "I don't understand, sir."

"Perhaps you don't," he said. "Perhaps not." He rose slowly, I thought sadly and uneasily. "Well, the others are waiting in the drawing room. Go and get Margaret and bring her there." But he waited. "My boy," he said, "this is going to be very difficult, perhaps unpleasant. But this family cares about you—and about Margaret. We all care, that is why there may be some firm speaking. Margaret spoke frankly to Isabella. She may therefore understand. Do you understand?"

"Yes, sir. Father," but it was not easy to talk, and I came to it haltingly, "you have always been kind and understanding. And I have always been grateful."

"This time, the situation is rather more complex, don't you think?"

"Yes, sir."

"Well . . ." He left me, a little bowed, I thought, and felt guilty.

I had supposed I would have to deal only with Father and Isabella. It shocked me to discover that I must be confronted by the whole family. We are that kind of family. I had always thought this to be an advantage, not to say a blessing. Now I faced it with trembling.

They were not, thank God, ranged in an inquisitorial rank on one side of the fire. They sat, scattered about the large room, but scattered with such casual artistry that I saw Father's hand in it and in my frightened head heard him say to them, "This is not a tribunal. We are a family—remember that and do not sit like judges on the bench." He did not sit with Isabella. That would have been too formidable. Isabella did not sit. She stood, with her back to the room, looking—perhaps—out over the lawns. Kitty and Morag were by another window—reading. At least they had books open in their hands, but their squinting glances as we came into the room were less than casual. Kitty was scowling. Morag was smiling, and her smile said to me, "Bear up, dear brother." Tomas was off in a corner by himself, playing patience. Emily was at the stacks, pulling and pushing books. Father was by the fire, reading the *Belfast News Letter*.

"Come in, come in, Margaret," he said, and with a show of warmth brought her to a chair across the fire. "You rested well, I hope?"

"I slept very soundly, Carrach," she said. Whether it was true or not, I did not know. I did not sleep with her. If she slept soundly, she did better than I had done. She looked refreshed and completely composed, as though this occasion did not differ in any way from any other occasion on which she had been in this room. Indeed, I think her performance on this occasion confirmed me in my need of her.

I stood.

"Won't you sit down, Alasdar?" Not "my boy." It would have been so easy to diminish me to nothing with those two little words. On such an occasion they were the words to use if psychological destruction was to be part of his armory. He did not use them. I sat down.

"Now," he said, refolding his newspaper. He could not endure untidy newspapers. Neither can I. That does not appear to be very important, but as I watched him I began to think of the things we had in common, and different as I supposed myself to be, we looked to me now more and more alike. I knew Father's view: "Sex is unimportant." I also knew the facts of his and Hugh's lives: the little mistress in the little house in Belfast (I learned it from a boy in the Royal School, who learned it from his older brother, who learned it from his father, who said, "The only open thing that papist ever did was live with his niece," for which I thrashed his youngest son and was brutally caned by the headmaster); Cassie Hyndman and her daughter, Agnes, about whom he told me himself ("I was fond of Cassie and, indeed, she loved me. Every young man comes to this experience, and I was fortunate, and I hope you will be fortunate, to come to it through a woman older than yourself and one you can trust." How I cherished that as I waited. He had on that occasion said, and I wondered at the time whether his dry humor was in it, "I understand Frenchmen induce their mistresses to initiate their sons, but that is a practice I could never approve"); I knew my mother had eventually refused him her bed (he told me) and that my missing Uncle Seán was or had been Isabella's husband. And I knew Hugh's record. So, I thought as he folded his paper, to the men of this family sex had been important enough to be an active and varied part of their experience.

"Now." The paper was folded and laid on the floor beside his chair. "Margaret, you know us. You know how we care for one another. You know how much we care about you. That is why we are all here."

Aunt Margaret smiled and nodded.

"Alasdar has told us you plan to marry."

Aunt Margaret smiled and nodded and was marvelously at ease.

To the lawns Isabella said in a husky, rage-filled whisper, "You are twice his age."

Aunt Margaret nodded agreeably.

"Please," Father said gently, and his concern for Isabella could not be hidden. Isabella's temper has become very uncertain, Morag told me when we arrived the night before, and you, my dearest brother, have done nothing to steady it. But Isabella had been warm toward me. We shall put this matter in order, darling, she said, and kissed me as she used to kiss me. Father did not look over his shoulder at her. His hands closed, not in anger but in distress. He knew more of Isabella than he had shared with me, and how could he talk to her to calm her here, as no doubt he could in her room? "I think we must all be very thoughtful of one another," he said now, "and help one another."

Isabella turned. She was staring at Aunt Margaret. Her hands were clasped before her, and her knuckles shone through the skin. "I agree, Carrach," she said in that thundering whisper. "The most thoughtful thing Margaret could do would be to bring the matter to an end."

Aunt Margaret's expression was placid. She returned Isabella's look but did not speak. She had the untouched bearing of an interested spectator, not a partisan.

The books were down now, and the playing cards, and Emily no longer shuffled at the stacks. Everyone else was ready. Emily watched Aunt Margaret from behind her. The rest of them stared at her from every other angle, and apart from Morag and Father and Emily, it was as though venom flew to her from all sides. If she felt it, she gave no sign.

"Margaret," Father said, "this is not an inquisition and it must not become one. It is an unusual dilemma. I don't doubt for a moment that you know it could for both of you become a dangerous, even a disastrous one. Or can I assume that you have not—both of you—thought of all this."

I had not. I didn't want to think about it. There was no need to think about it. The very thought that anyone should consider it necessary was evidence enough that they could not understand and they were ignorant of all things that would give them understanding: our days, our nights, God our nights, and my addiction stirred my stomach and was not to be denied me. Aunt Margaret nodded and did not speak and was very still, and I closed my eyes for I could see her and hear her on that last night in Mayo and my eyes would have told them. I would not tell them anything. How could I tell them anything? And suddenly I was as strong as Aunt Margaret, and nothing, nothing, nothing was going to shake me. And so far, not one word had been addressed to me.

Father put that right. "Alasdar, I'm not going to harp on your years. I admit that this has been done before—I mean a very young man marrying a much older woman. I also know that such marriages have turned out to be very happy ones. I would not think of assuming that the one now proposed could not be happy. We know and love Margaret and we value her deeply. But have you thought enough about the future? Thought hard about it? Talked it over well with Margaret? Have you?"

I gathered myself up. The answer to all his questions was, No, and I was not going to say so. His questions meant nothing to me. I wanted what I wanted.

"Father," I said, "I didn't come to this decision in order to cause you pain . . ."

"I know that," impatiently.

"But I know what I am doing and I am going to do it. If I have to wait till I am of age I shall wait, but I shall live with . . ." Aunt Margaret was too much for me to say after what he had said to me earlier, ". . . her and I shall do it openly. It would be much better for us all if I had your consent."

"I wish you hadn't said that, Alasdar. It sounds very like blackmail." I had had no time to speak to Morag.

Kitty's voice came like a file on a file. "And if you live with her, will you sleep in a cradle while she sleeps in a bed?"

"Kitty!"

She stormed across the room, a little fury. "I don't care, Papa. There's only one word for it. Grotesque." She ran back to a chair and sat down. "No, there is another word for it. Obscene. Love is for the young."

"Papa is not young," Morag said softly. And to me,

"Alasdar, do you love Aunt Margaret or do you want her for her money? I'm not trying to be offensive. I want to know."

"I have my own money."

"Besides hers, that's an allowance. Tell me what I want to know. I want to hear you tell us you love Aunt Margaret. If you can't say it here, among us, what should we think of you?"

"I love her."

"He loves everybody," Kitty shouted. "He's been in love with Isabella . . ."

"*Kitty!* Leave the room."

"I shall *not* leave the room. He has been and he is and you know it, Papa. We all know it. Isabella knows it . . ."

"*Kitty!*"

"*I shall not be quiet.* She was an old man's darling and now she wants to be a young man's darling. She's an old woman. She lived for years with an old man and now she wants a young boy in her bed. *It's obscene.*" She was weeping. Kitty weeps.

Father walked across the room to her. His rage did not force him to hurry. He led her to the door. "Go to your room."

"You are destroying us, Margaret. I shall not forgive you," Isabella said. The whisper had gone. The voice was cold, like a blade.

Father, back in his chair and white, said, "This was not a wise thing for us to do. I agreed to it and I accept the blame for it. I believed we could behave like a family. We shall now put an end to it."

But Isabella was not ready to put an end to it. She came and stood beside Father's chair. "You have not said one word, Margaret," she said. "Why not?"

Aunt Margaret said nothing, but she looked very firmly into Isabella's face.

"I'll tell you why," and the thundering whisper was returning.

Father stood up and put an arm about her. "Isabella," he said, "you must not let yourself be like this. Come, sit down. Or better still, come with me."

"I am not leaving. I shall tell her why she sits there like an earth mother, saying nothing. Because she is determined to marry him. Nothing any of us say will make any difference to her. She has had him, and what she had, she likes. She is determined to keep it for herself, so she will marry him . . ."

"Isabella . . ." My feeble little intervention was scarcely worth making. "Please, Isabella, don't say any more."

"But it is all my doing, Alasdar. I am the one to blame. Didn't I tell you to fly? Didn't I tell you in effect that the way this woman looked at you would tell any other woman who loved you that she was ready to gobble you up?"

"What in God's name are you saying?" Father's face was no longer pale. It was red with embarrassment and incredulity.

"I'm saying that I told him Margaret was his Cassie Hyndman, with jewels, and if . . ."

"You didn't," Emily came slowly in from the stacks. "I told him that. Then I told you I told him. Now I'd like to tell all of you something."

"When I have done with it, Emily. What does it matter who used the words? I told him she had never had a happy day in her life, and if going to bed with him made her happy, why wouldn't he? His father learned on Cassie Hyndman, and why wouldn't he? What woman wants a man who fumbles over her like a schoolboy?"

"That is enough, Isabella. This business must come to an end." Father had her by the arm and was trying to move her toward the door. But I saw then what I had never seen before, that we were alike in another respect: we were the subjects of our women, and neither of us would ever be otherwise. Isabella had no intention of moving. There was more to come, and she was determined to deliver it. I stood now, like an ornament on a shelf, being talked to and about as though I could neither hear nor see, and still Aunt Margaret sat, tranquil and waiting. For what, if for anything?

"Take your hand from my arm, Carrach. I am not a lunatic to be restrained by force." And he took his hand from her arm and looked at me with a despairing: See what you've done to us all? Looked and turned away. If I had gone to him, I think he would have struck me. It was Isabella who mattered most, and I felt for the first time that I was the instrument of damage between us that could not be repaired. I felt sick. It was Isabella who settled my stomach.

"That is it, is it not, Margaret? You got him to bed, and now you will get him to the altar if you can. That is what Wicklow was for, is it not, and those intellectual weekends at Upper Temple Street and Mayo. *Bed, bed, bed, and then baby snatching?*" Aunt Margaret was very still. "And I gave

him to you. He needed a lover, *and I gave him a mother.*"
She shouted it.

She was jealous. I knew it then. It gave me a mean sense
of triumph that I would have waited for her into old age and
now she was in a blind jealous rage that she had handed me
over, like a package, to a woman not a mere eleven years
older than me, but to a woman old enough to have given me
birth. We are a queer complex of loves and hates, of contradictions and needs, of sly self-deceptions and cunning desires.
I think that none of us is free of evil. Evil? That is a strong
word, and it is not what I mean. Corruption? Involuntary
corruption? I cannot go into it with understanding, but it was
when Isabella said "and I gave him a mother" that I knew
she was right. Perhaps we are more to be pitied than blamed
for the ways in which each of us finds some happiness? I understood, too, what Aunt Margaret meant when I plunged in
her and she said, If you were my son it would still be this.
And we two met, and coupled. Can a simple and unconscious
need to have a loving mother, or can the knowledge of having an unlovely and unloving one, give to you a desperate
need to suckle a mother's breast and lie on her belly? In your
manhood? How could I understand these things? I stood
there, detached from them all, scarcely aware of them all,
and thought these things. It was Emily whose voice brought
me back from my thoughts.

"If you have done, Isabella?"

"More than done." Her face was drawn. She was holding
Father's arm.

"Then for God's sake think a little differently and see if it
will bring a little ease. Some men marry women who manage
them, and they want to be managed, and they are happy.
Some women marry men who dominate them, tell them what
to do, what to think, what to know, and they are happy. If a
man wants to marry a mother—for the love of God, let him
be happy."

I saw Father look at me suddenly, and startled.

"And if a woman wants to marry a son, that is where she
will be happy. So why not leave it there?" She looked around
us and at us and smiled and said to Aunt Margaret, "Perhaps
I'm not even close to the truth, Margaret, but I'll always vote
for happiness."

Aunt Margaret said nothing.

Isabella was not quite done. "And you, Emily," she said
bitterly, "what peculiar thing did you want?"

"I wanted to be a virgin. They don't last long in this family. Somebody had to make a stand."

Aunt Margaret said, "Well," and put her hands on her thighs and said, "Well," again. "It has been illuminating and I understand the insults and still regard you as I have always regarded you—with love. I never thought any of you were overwhelmingly orthodox. I never thought any of you gave a tinker's damn. You didn't, Carrach. For that matter, neither did you, Isabella. I understand how you feel, I understand very well. But I shall cherish your son if he marries me, Carrach, and I have a very considerable estate that when I die . . . Now, now, now," and she palmed a retort away, "don't say anything. You've had your say and I've listened very patiently. I am leaving for Dublin. I don't know whether Alasdar will come. I ask him to come. I want him to come. If he turns me away, yes, Isabella, I shall be a very lonely and I shall become a very unhappy old woman. I love him and, yes, yes, Emily, I know why. He loves me and I know why. I'm not a fool and neither is he. People love for their own reasons, and if we make a very odd couple, we'll not have been the first and not the last, and, yes, Emily, happy. But before I go, there's one small thing—very small at the moment—and you have not been told of it because we thought we should be judged on our merits alone. How we've been judged, I'm not quite certain, for this has been a rather confusing confrontation. However . . ."

She stood up. "I'm pregnant."

And she turned and left me with them.

"Perhaps," said young Tomas from his corner, "now that you have your own mother, you will leave mine alone?"

That, for me, was the end of Trinity.

With Father's cool consent, in the presence of all my family, including Hugh and his wife, to the laughter of her peers and in our Catholic church, I was married by Father Mackay to Lady Margaret Somerville, aged thirty-nine, widow of the late Sir Michael Somerville. I was in my nineteenth year.

It was an occasion for uncomfortable compromises. Isabella said to me, "We shall see it through as a family and they'll see us only as one. We shall also be waiting close by, if you should stumble."

Even Kitty found ground on which to move her Catholic

feet. "Well," she said gloomily, "at least now she's a Catholic of a sort."

Emily was herself. "You must have been having a lively time or she wouldn't be carrying one. If intellectual incest is what you need at the moment, enjoy it while it lasts."

Father didn't complete a sentence. "If you need me I'm . . ." and put his arm across my shoulders protectively.

Morag kissed me and put her arms about me and said nothing.

Aunt Margaret was almost cheerful. "I'm quite happy about this Catholic business. I'd be glad to swear that God is oblong and multi-colored if it smooths the way."

Father Mackay was very helpful. He instructed Aunt Margaret during three successive mornings. "If St. Paul could do it in a flash," he said, "I should be able to arrange this in under a week."

Then we retreated for a time to Mayo, away from the laughter of the ladies of Dublin society. Into the silent, smiling derision of the Irish, which so often looks like charm and friendship.

Nine

Work, she said, work, and the way she talked about it, it might have been a cure for something. But we worked. On the book. We worked obsessively, for she was as careful of my pride and dignity as she was of that of her tenants, and only once did she let slip half a remark about how important it was for us that I should have my own achievement. But she took charge of the magistrate who took charge of Captain Boycott's accusations and advised him not to proceed with them.

For a while it seemed that we had turned our minds inward on ourselves. We were happy. Certainly her happiness was to wait on all my needs, and there were times when I was conscious that what I had in my bed was a doting mother; even when she urged me to enjoy her "before my belly makes it dangerous." She was careful of the family also, and while I wrote to them occasionally, she wrote to them often. She wrote affectionate letters to Isabella. They were always about me. For three months Isabella made no reply. "She's jealous," Aunt Margaret said, "she hates the thought of you in my belly. You have to know women, and whether she allowed herself to see it or not, one of her dreams was to have you and Carrach in her own belly." And I liked the thought but did not believe it. Then came a small formal note from Isabella, and the gradual progress toward the birth began.

No horses, she promised me, but that did not cover carriages. The book was always changing. "You must know

357

Connaught," she said, "you must see it in all its squalor."
Since the inns were not fit to stay in, she planned a tour,
wrote to "friends" on the route, inviting us to stay, a night
here, two nights there, according to her estimate of the interest. "Study them," she said, "curiosity will make them eager
to have us, and I shall provide the scandalous or the arid details of their lives," and her laughter was gleeful and malicious. The humor of it appealed to me in a resentful sort of
way. I felt myself to be in an alien and hostile relationship to
her society and it pleased me with slow anger that while they
laughed at us, we laughed at and used them. What I did not
think about and she did not care about was what would happen after the book appeared—if it now appeared, for it was
being written and rewritten in an atmosphere of hilarious ir-
reverence and Mr. Murray was now doubting and impatient.
So we made a progress of carefully selected Ascendancy
houses of the province and saw the quick looks and the smile
as her belly grew and in our room we made notes on our
hosts and their families and on the condition of their tenants.
That is how it came to be a picaresque novel after the Spanish fashion, with something of Laurence Sterne, something of
Swift, something of Cervantes—something of anybody who
was useful to our purpose. It became the journey of two English travelers through Ireland, not this time a contemptuous
account of the lives of the primitive Irish—there had been
many of them—but a comic account of the lives and adventures and the uncouth and domineering gentility of the Anglo-Irish, who were fading, unawares.

Then we went back to Upper Temple Street to write, to
rewrite, and to wait for the child. Father came to stay, then
Emily, then Father and Isabella, then the lot of them. In spite
of the fact that he was fighting an election, he came. A
grandson was more important.

"Margaret, you look like a mountain," Isabella said with
qualified warmth, which we ignored.

"I feel like an empress."

Father said, "Margaret, your first at your age—we must
have the best men in attendance. You're carrying my first
grandchild."

It was Kitty who crept one night to our room and asked,
"Aunt Margaret, what does it feel like to be pregnant?"

"Heavy, my dear, very heavy." Lying there like Mount
Gabriel.

"No, be serious."

"It feels wonderful, and frightening. I shall bear your dear
brother a fine strong son."

"I want to be pregnant."

"Most women do. Get married and get started."

"There are no Catholics I can marry."

"Marry a Protestant or a Nothing."

"And have us all damned?"

"The consolations of religion?"

The telegraph message from Isabella said only, "Father gravely injured, please come at once." There was no explanation,
but it had to have been at an election meeting or a fall from
a horse.

Aunt Margaret was curiously displeased. The book, the
book, she said. Mr. Murray likes what we're doing now, and
he wants it quickly. It was our first near-squabble. Why must
you leave me now? I could have been angry. Instead I responded gently, for she was very large, very heavy, and, as
she said, "becoming a burden" to herself. This was surely to
be the very large child of large parents. I went north with a
mixture of feelings—anxiety about Father and anxiety about
Aunt Margaret. At Barn House both were swallowed up in
murderous rage.

The 1880 election campaign had grown steadily more violent. Rival factions turned meetings into riots, into pitched
battles, into denials of everything all parties professed to
stand for. The people or the peoples of Ireland protest incessantly in the midst of violence that they are a gentle lot, violent only when provoked beyond endurance. If that is the
case, the limits of their endurance are set low, for whether a
dispute is over the corner of a field or the liberty of the land,
the issue quickly comes to violence, personal or collective,
direct or oblique.

When they told me of events at home, everybody talked,
angry and excited and vengeful. Isabella, as Morag who met
me at Carrig station said, was "on the verge." She paced the
library floor, fists clenched, mouth set, muttering now and
then, and as I listened to the others, I strained to hear what
she was saying to herself. The only word I got was "murder."

Three nights ago, they told me, when Father was in full
flight at a meeting—and that meant a level, steady pro-
gression with his fingers turning the buttons of his coat—the
town drunk interrupted him. The family was on the platform
in support. Shorty Shields is a diminutive creature who is

never quite sober. His main—so far as I know his only—occupation is to act as night watchman beside holes dug by town workmen in the streets of Carrig. That these holes needed to be watched was always an entertaining mystery to the town. He staggered up the aisle to ask a question and pointed at Father.

"You's the oul one wi the young fancy wuman. Wheresh the young one wi the oul wife?" He looked around for applause and got it from a group of men standing at the back of the hall. One of them, Morag said, was Willie Ross, the local Orange leader, a man of meager mind and substantial bulk. Thus rewarded, Shields asked his second question. He pointed to Isabella. "Wheresh the wuman from Court House?"

Isabella answered. She jumped down from the platform and stood beside Shields, her inevitable umbrella held like a weapon. "Where is Willie Ross?" she yelled.

"What kin Ah do fer yis, Mrs. McCarthy?" he asked, grinning at his own thrust.

Father stood still. His fingers on his buttons, motionless. But his feet were planted, ready to move. It was Isabella's offensive. Let her act.

"Would you come here, please, Mr. Ross?" she said reasonably.

Ross moved down the aisle slowly, grinning. He was a king in the underworld of religious emotion and religious ignorance. No worse than the Catholic religious underworld, but that was not here. It cared for Father no more than the Orange cared for him.

"Yis, missus?" Ross said, winking to the people close at hand.

Isabella walked around him like a farmer passing judgment on a bull. Ross tried to turn with her, which is what she wanted him to do. Around she went again. Around went Ross. A third time she circled him, and the grin had gone from the big man's face. Near them men tittered, and the tittering spread.

She spoke suddenly, still moving. She spoke to the audience. "Mr. Ross is a big man." She pointed with her umbrella to his rump. "There's meat on those haunches." She pointed with her big umbrella to his head. "There's meat there too, but damned little else. This big strong leader of men is the one who used this poor drunken waste to ask insulting questions. This big brave man hadn't the courage to come up here and do it himself. So why should I punish his drunken creature for doing the gallant Mr. Ross's dirty work?" She had her umbrella by the middle. "Tell me that, Mr. Ross." She was standing before him now. The top of her head didn't reach to the man's shoulder. Her umbrella flashed. It was a savage blow. It caught him across the side of his face, and his hands went up. Two-handed she rammed the sharp point of the umbrella into his fat paunch, and the hands came down. He was backing up the aisle, and she flailed away at his hands, wherever they tried to cover him. She chased him all the way to the back of the hall. It was the day, all over again, when she punished the lout who tripped me in Boney-before. Her fury mounted as she flailed, and the only sound in the hall was the sound of her umbrella on Ross's person. And now it was a flail, for it was broken in two.

She walked down the aisle and stood facing the crowd. Her face was red with rage. Shields had not moved.

"Go and get your money from that fat coward and then go and drink it," she said.

He staggered crablike up the aisle, sideways, the better to watch her.

"Never again," she said, *"never again.* But if some brave man should ever again dare like a squalid coward to raise the name of my poor aunt, I shall not reach him with *this,"* and she threw the broken umbrella among them, making them duck, "I shall reach him with a horse whip. *Understand it and believe it,"* she said, and went back to the platform.

The girls kissed her. Emily kissed her. Tomas embraced her. The children and sister of her "poor aunt" had spoken.

Father's fingers turned his buttons. "Did I," he said, "hear someone say that women are not yet capable of taking an active part in public life?"

As they say of the performers in the music halls, "he brought down the house."

That night the spinning mill burned down. The fire began in the middle of the night. By dawn there was a shell, nothing else. The buildings of the mill formed a square. Fires started in each of the four sides of the square. There was no possibility of accident. Four hundred people were without work. The MacDonnells were without their spinning mill. One did not dare to fight back with Ross of the Orange.

It was only a night later—the police had "no clues, no evidence"—that Father rode around the great rubble and twisted machinery mess of the mill yard, scarcely thinking, he told me. He was deciding not to rebuild. Our flax-spinning days were over. He rode out through the open iron gates of the yard, deep in gloomy thought, and the Orange Lambeg drummers waiting around the corner of the gatehouse as one man—there were six of them—battered their drums. His horse reared and, quite unprepared, he was thrown and dragged for a half a mile. The horse stopped at the gate to the courtyard of Barn House. A leg and an arm were broken, ribs fractured, and his face lacerated.

And still they had not done with him.

The night I arrived, they gathered outside the courtyard gate and beat their drums. They are huge bass drums, fastened to the drummers by a harness and beaten with baked bulrushes. All night long relays of them beat out the mystic rhythms of their lodges to deny sleep to a sick and injured enemy. The police were "powerless." They were in fact afraid. Father lay sleepless and weak and the demonic rhythms of the Lambeg drums imprinted themselves on his brain.

Next day Hugh arrived from Goleen, summoned by Isabella, as I had been summoned. By now she was demonic. "I don't care what the end will be," she said, "but now that you are both here, tonight we'll deal with them. If you don't like my means, go home."

Before the drumming started, we went to the stables, stripped three long-handled yard brushes of their bristles, and padded the heads with sacking. Then we sharpened the ends of the handles and turned them into lances. We bound our horses' hooves in sacking, saddled, and waited.

The drumming began. It may be, as Father insists, that Ulstermen are Hebrideans, not Irish, but if that is the case, these transplanted Hebrideans find in sustained cruelty all the malignant joy the Irish find in it. The sound was maddening, not only because it was meant to prevent a sick and injured man from sleeping. It was primitive, ominous, and threatening. Whatever they choose to call them or however they describe them, these are the war drums of an aggressive breed.

We rode out by the main gates, well below the drummers on the road. They were great iron gates with ornamental oil lamps mounted on them with the old arms of the MacDonnells on the glass. Hugh turned his horse to face them. He dipped his lance. "Remember Rathlin," he said, and three abreast we walked our horses toward the drummers. The high wall of Barn House was on our right, on our left hedge-hidden fields. We had to pass, beyond the fields, a small walled plantation of trees, then turn into a left bend. The house itself abutted on the road, just where the plantation ended and the bend began. Isabella halted us in the heavy darkness made by the tall plantation trees and the trees behind the wall of the house.

"They'll not hear us for the muffled hooves and their own drumming," she said. "First the walk, then the trot, then the canter, then the charge. Let the lances drift on impact, but hold them hard."

First the walk; quickly the trot, more quickly the canter. We were in the bend and they were around it, all unawares in their mindless sound and fury. "Charge!" she yelled, and our lances came down, the brush heads firmly against our shoulders.

They did not see or hear us till we were on them and the lances pierced the drums and went through them. We held hard, and the lances dragged as we passed through their ranks; and the lances spun the drums and the drummers, and pulled back by the force of the spin, sent harnessed men and drums into their spin, crashing to the ground. We wheeled and came back. They were trying to scramble to their feet, encumbered by their great drums, and we prodded them down again with our sharpened spears. Then Hugh was down among them, cutting the harness from Willie Ross. We kept the rest of them on the ground while Hugh threw Ross free from the mass.

"It isn't a woman this time, Willie," Hugh said, "and it isn't an old umbrella."

And he beat him into insensibility.

"Go home," he said to the others, "and don't come back, or as God's my witness, we'll kill you."

"Rathlin!" he screamed at their limping retreat.

We sat by Father's bed, and Hugh told him.

"Remember Rathlin, Carrach," he said.

Once, long ago, very long ago, when Rathlin Island off the north shore of northeast Ulster was our land and in sight of our castle at Dunluce, the MacDonnell men of Rathlin were all ashore on the coast of Antrim when the English landed a force on the island. There was no soul on the island but their wives and the children and the old men and women. All of them were slaughtered, and their men watched from the Antrim shore and from their small boats racing for the island. But when they got there, there were no English and their ship was out to sea; there were only the corpses of their fathers and mothers, their wives and daughters; and their heirs.

"I remember," Father said, "as if it were yesterday."

It was in 1597.

He smiled at Hugh. It was the first time I had seen him smile since I got home. "Why did you stay away so long when we were young, Hughie?" he said, holding his brother's hand.

It happened in 1597, and it was as yesterday? They didn't know it, but they told me something about their strength. They told me, also, something about my weakness. They were MacDonnells. Isabella was a MacDonnell. They made me one.

The election went its course. Hugh won. Parnell won. He led thirty-five Home Rulers back to Westminster.

By a miraculously narrow margin, Father lost. He lost without bitterness. "Next time," he said.

With the exception of Father, they were all there when the baby was born, fussing, worrying, helping, getting in the way of the best men in attendance and an army of nurses; like a Royal Delivery, Isabella said. It was a difficult delivery.

"It must be monstrous big," Morag said, huddling in the drawing room.

But when it was over, I went trembling to Aunt Margaret. She said, "This mountain brought forth a morsel."

The baby weighed only five pounds, three ounces.

"I wanted a son," she said. "What shall we call this?"

"Isabella."

She smiled. "With love or malice?" And went to sleep.

She paid small attention to the child, rarely spoke of her, left her to the nurses or to Isabella when she and Father came (more and more often); then Isabella gave her namesake all her attention. "Well," said Aunt Margaret, "maybe I had it for her?" But she gave fanatic attention to the book. With the birth of little Isabella, something in her was expended. My care and needs were still paramount, but there was no fire in our bed. She was tired, or merely reluctant, and the concern she had never shown before was now her chief concern. "Be careful." She submitted to me passively. She dreaded another pregnancy. Though she was careful never to say it directly,

she made no effort to conceal the fact that the child was a
sour and bitter disappointment. There had been no son in her
loins. I was all she had. It made me tender. Tender? What is
the word? I knew before long that I was sorry for her. Yes,
that made me tender. It also made me tense. Sometimes, at
night, my temper was brittle.

"Last night, the night before, and the night before that,
you were tired. Things have changed."

"I am tired, dear."

"There was a time when you couldn't keep your legs
closed, now you can't get them open."

She cried. A little. Then she hid against her pillow, and I
was ashamed and sorry and tender. Yes, tender. There was
no excitement now. Tolerance? Yes, tolerance.

"Things are well, are they?" Isabella asked, watching me
with eyes that burrowed in my head.

"Things are well." The book was going well. Mr. Murray
wanted all of it at once or sooner. If he recognized Lady
Margaret Somerville and Alasdar MacDonnell as wandering
narrators, he did not say so . . . How he could fail to recognize us and others, I cannot imagine. We were there to be
recognized, amused, mocking; cutting down those who
laughed and raised rents and evicted tenants; we relocated
them, gave them smaller or larger estates, black for red hair,
short legs for long ones.

"Lady Glandore was so marvelously constructed that those
who had been privileged to see her legs—at least a dozen of
her neighbors' husbands—were certain that she wore them
upside down." (Aunt Margaret was very good at deforming
the best features of her victims.) We had worked hard to
solve the problems imposed on us by the old Queen's shadow,
which lay over everything, and Mr. Murray. "I think," he
wrote again and again, "this passage would present us with
unnecessary difficulties. I do not suggest that it should be
eliminated, but in the circumstances given, the implicit will
serve your purpose better than the explicit. It will also delight
your readers, whereas it is in our present climate incumbent
upon them to be outraged by the explicit." And Aunt Margaret would ask: How can we get Lady Dromore into bed
with Lord Larne without mentioning the bed? It was a mirror
of Ascendancy decadence, mindlessness, the cruelty of blind
indifference and incomprehension and farmyard morality
embedded in the background of their tenants' misery. It was
grim and irreverent comedy. Over against their assumptions

of quality and superiority, the book made them merely ridiculous. That was our purpose, for in the eyes of those whom they regarded as their peers in England, they were ridiculous; uncouth, pretentious, and ridiculous—and Irish, which was, to them, the most crushing insult of all and the one we worked on with malicious delight. We called the book *Silk Purse, Sow's Ear*.

Mr. Murray brought it out in the autumn. It is difficult to say one regrets a thundering success with the reading public. That is what I wanted. That is part of what *Silk Purse, Sow's Ear* brought me. If that had been all, there would have been no need for regrets.

Silk Purse, Sow's Ear began in my own excited confusion and ended as satire. In our endless discussions as it was written and rewritten, contructed and reconstructed, we had at last agreed on its purpose—to make a large body of opinion in England laugh at the Irish Acendancy. We had not expected to reach so large a public. It was a public that laughed heartily enough at the for the most part boorish and ignorant Anglo-Irish but did not change its mind about the Irish. One reviewer put it well enough when he wrote, ". . . but would not all of us become a mere onion skin removed from the Irish if we lived long enough among them?" It was the English nose, classic condescension, and not surprising. They did not think differently of us in the North—who were different, we believed—and they had never tried to conceal what they thought. Indeed, they appeared to suppose there was nothing to conceal; what they thought was to them always so obviously true and indisputable.

The early reviewers sold the book. "An Irish Zola . . ." and "Hardy with a light touch and a comic eye," and this sort of thing was too flattering for my belief. Aunt Margaret believed it and was jubilant.

It was Joe Biggar who increased our audience and brought down upon us the wrath of the gods who held most of Ireland and sat in the Commons and the House of Lords. Joe incorporated long passages into his Commons speeches on land reform and rent control, to the cheers of the Irish Home Rulers and the jeers of the Irish Whigs and the English and Scottish members. "Read us more, Joe," the Home Rulers shouted. "Shame, shame," the others cried out, and armed with gossip from Dublin and Mayo, began the slaughter and brought down my house.

It was a Colonel Saunderson, Ulster Unionist and an Orange protégé of Enniskillen, who set the tone and loosed the flood. Protected by the privilege of saying whatever it pleased him to say in the House of Commons, he set the book aside and dealt with me and mine.

"If this young gentleman—and I use the word as a courtesy and not as a fact—wished to expose and satirize the moral and social inadequacies of the Anglo-Irish, he could have done it more completely and more accurately by dwelling in detail on the story of his own premarital relations with the widow of the late and greatly respected Sir Michael Somerville. This lady, twice the reputed author's age and now Mrs. Alasdar MacDonnell, is surely the real author of this squalid and untruthful diatribe. Lady Margaret, as she was when circumstances made marriage with young Mr. MacDonnell advisable if not inevitable, is a fountain of scandalous gossip about Irish society, most of which cannot have been known to her young husband, since he has never been a part of that society. One might say that Mother MacDonnell—as she now is—loaded and may well have had to fire her very young husband's toy cannon—for that is all this venomous, cheap, and untruthful document really is . . ."

There were, of course, cries of "Shame," but most of them were from the Irish members. Hugh remained silent, to protect Father, he said. It was when the later reviewers went to work that sales of the book took a phenomenal leap forward. They had by now been provided with ammunition, and one after the other they worked in "biographical details," the age at which Sr. Michael died and the age at which his widow remarried "young Mr. MacDonnell." And the date of our child's birth. Simple arithmetic did the rest. There was nothing libelous in any of it. To have sued for defamation would have been useless and self-destructive. "The moral degeneracy of the Anglo-Irish," one reviewer said ambiguously, "is dissected by those who know more about it than the Anglo-Irish." It might have been a tribute, but its meaning was not in doubt.

It sold the book and began the swift descent to disaster. Dublin's anger and defensive and derisive laughter showered down upon us; upon our marriage, which had been a minor amusement at its beginning and became a main preoccupation of every poisonous tongue. We had expected anger. I didn't care; I was not part of their society. Aunt Margaret had laughed at the prospect of their anger. In the beginning she was amused enough to frame one review and hang it in the drawing room. It said, *"Silk Purse, Sow's Ear* has done for the Ascendancy in Ireland what ought to have been done for them long ago. It has exposed, with laughter that in the end is like surgery on a limb rotten with gangrene, the preposterous sickness of the Anglo-Irish presence and presumption in Ireland."

Aunt Margaret did not laugh now. In the House of Lords, one ennobled gentleman, Lord Partry, secure in his privilege, and whose estate—which he had not seen for years—we moved from west to east and whose person we had markedly improved in appearance, called her "that pathetic magpie who married an old man for his money and a mere boy for his virility and who lately presented us with the lying evidence that she enjoys both to the full." Shame, shame, a few men with no acres in Ireland cried out. *The Times* declined to elaborate on what it called "Lord Partry's lapse from the standards of the House" and called it "deplorable."

The day she learned of Partry's attack, she sat still and silent for an hour. Then she said quietly, "So that is our marriage? My house is a whorehouse and I am its high-priced whore, and you are the whoremaster. Very well, very well, very well."

She was white. Her face was hard and plain. "Very well, by God," she said, and brushed my comfort aside and went to her room.

It was days before I could reach her, and by then she had brooded herself haggard. In those silent days I tried on her her own treatment of Isabella and she said, "You are hammering different metal." By the time she would talk in more than monosyllables or short sharp statements, her rage had settled deep in her, like ice in winter, and what she would do—whatever it was—was already determined. I knew it, for suddenly she was cheerful, as if a question had been answered, a resolution made, with nothing now to do but carry it out. She was cheerful but it was a sharp and threatening cheerfulness and her smile was like broken glass.

"What is going on in your head?" I asked her.

She sat with her head to one side, smiling that smile, watching me as if to measure what I thought. "My dear," she said, "this is going on in my head: I am your old woman. I love you with the possessive passion of a jealous mother. I am Mother MacDonnell. It was as Mother MacDonnell that I lusted after you. It was as Mother MacDonnell that I conceived your child. It was as Mother MacDonnell that I wanted it. Obscene, is it?" The smile was gone. "But I knew you and I knew myself and there was no difference between us. Was there?"

"None."

"It was ours. What it was, was ours . . ."

"It's still ours . . ." But it was settled in her will.

"And in that place they befouled it in public. They'll say my rage is the rage of a mother fighting for her young . . . it couldn't make any difference now, no matter what they say . . ."

She said no more. She had meant to say more, and I could see it in her face as it changed. She no longer wanted to say more. It was settled in her will, and she was tired of this talk.

That day she went next door to the Parnell house and did not say why. When I asked why, she did not answer. But the fanatic Fanny Parnell, Charles Parnell's sister, became a companion. Fanny's like-minded friends came to the Parnell house and entered ours through the back door. I was not invited to their meetings, and I was not informed of their purpose. I asked. But I caught myself before I could declare my right to know what these fanatic women were "doing in my house." It was not my house. It was the first time I thought of myself as a kept husband. My income was puny beside hers. I had no house.

I think that is why I was able to think about her as I had never done before and had never wanted to do. It was this feeling that something was settled in her will, and something extreme, that sent me roving back over her life. She married an old man—that had been done often enough, and in Ireland more often than enough—but her reaction to the circumstances of her life was to develop an almost barrack-square manner of speaking, to cover the pain she came to feel, or perhaps felt from the beginning of her marriage to Sir Michael. Why did she marry him? For his money? I couldn't believe that. For a child? That was more likely, but from an old man? With that old man it was possible. For a husband? That was most likely. And when plain Big Maggie "killed" the overambitious old man in bed, the fun began. She told me bitterly some of the club stories she heard from "friends" about herself: how John Linane, who was small, said, "I'd like to try her but I want to live." The wounds went deep, and she punished them with her barrack bark and embarrassed them with her sudden and outrageous statements. She rehearsed them, she told me, and went to their occasions armed, waiting for her moments: at Amelia Johnstone's table one night, when Harry Linane's domineering wife had silenced the poor man, Aunt Margaret struck. "Harry, why in God's name didn't you bring that nice little Austrian woman. Then tonight we could all have been allowed to have opinions of our own." That little Austrian woman was Linane's consolation and the scourge with which his wife stripped the skin from his back.

Aunt Margaret was too rich to be ignored or excluded. They made her, in their own defense, a character, a card, an entertainment, and asked her to dine with the people they wanted to see cut down. In her turn she inflicted pain and humiliation for their laughter and grew more extreme. To wound for wounds had settled in her will.

She loved me; I am sure of that. But how did she love me? I don't care much whether in the beginning it was only the lust of a woman who had been denied, to the brink of middle age. It became something else, and if it was mixed up with incestuous fantasies that arose out of the circumstances of her life, well, so did mine. It was the extravagance of her lust I dwelt on now. My own was not modest, but hers was a concentrated and gluttonous insatiability that, when I look back, had the marks of desperation or despair on it. It was extreme from aridity to orgy. To love, to give, had settled in her will. I was to receive all, she to give all.

That, I am sure, is why the book became a passion. I talked of my great scheme for a book while she led me to bed in Wicklow. I must have what I wanted—not spinning mills or tall ships or coal boats, but books to my credit. Even in that she was extreme. And in her response to its reception she was extreme, though now I think all her responses to life's wounds were gathered up in this one thing: the longing to bear a son to a fantasy son, which foundered with a fragile daughter. Even this, in "that place," the House of Lords, was a weapon to wound her with. The passion she gave to my book, the work she did, studying models, learning, teaching me; her happiness in our marriage, her joy in her own malice—all were turned into a public image of squalor when they were, to her, healing ointments for the open wounds she wore.

She was a wounded creature, and I was overwhelmed by pity. I have heard that pity is another form of contempt and do not believe it. It bred in me a new tenderness for her. We were, in a way, two of a kind; our experience was different, our weakness and our need the same. We needed one another.

That is why my bewilderment grew, for now, though she was tender with me and smiled gently and touched me, in bed she was "too tired, my dear" and she was absent from home, sometimes for two days, three days, a week, and would not tell me where. In her second absence I went next door to Parnell's and asked for Fanny. She was "not at home." If I did not know where Aunt Margaret was, at least I knew who was with her, and that made me fear.

It made me fear because Davitt's Land League had been outlawed because of its success and because of the excesses of some of its members, and a more extreme Land League came into being, the Women's Land League. The ferocious women of Ireland took the field in place of their men. The Parnell woman was one of their leading spirits, this woman who feared cats and believed black cats were inhabited by evil spirits.

"Whose money?" I asked my wife.

"Parnell finds the money for them," she said.

"He's cut off their funds. *Whose money?*" I had never shouted at her in anger. "Don't lie to me."

"Most of it is mine," she said, and then, as if in apology, "ours."

"No more," I said. "That Parnell woman is a lunatic."

Very quietly she said, "The money is still mine, Alasdar. While it is mine there will be more for them."

It was a rebuke I could not counter. I was a kept husband. And sex was a concession, passively submitted to when it was not denied. Then it would be given with a wild lustfulness and followed by tears, and again denied. Aunt Margaret died. Something died. I could no longer call her that. It sounded silly. It felt silly in my mouth. Now, it seemed it had always been silly.

Near Christmas I took the baby and the nurse and went north to Barn House. "To think for a while," I told her.

"To think about what?"

"To think about us, Margaret."

"Margaret?"

"Yes."

"You're going to leave me."

"I am not."

"Don't leave me. I need you."

"I am not going to leave you. I am going to have a rest."

"From me."

"From strain."

"You will of course consult Isabella about us."

"I'll not consult anyone about us. I shall think about us."

"About your old woman."

"I did not say that."

"So I am your old woman?" It was sad rather than angry. She was beginning to accept their judgment on her, and believing it to be mine also. So do others destroy us against our wills.

"I do not think that. Would I want to make love to an old woman?"

It was futile. "Come with me," I said. "Please, Margaret."

"Later." And, "If I can."

"You must, I suppose, give your time to Fanny Parnell."

"I'll come. Later. I have things to do first." First. Whatever they were, they came first.

We had not been invited to Barn House for Christmas, at least not yet, and I had not warned them of my coming. I was therefore happily surprised by the warmth of our reception. Morag, Kitty, and Isabella swarmed about the child, but Isabella took possession and sent the nurse, with a girl "to take care of her," to Garden House "to keep her out of the way." Tomas was as pompous as ever, but as cordial, at ten, as his misguided imitation of Father allowed. Emily was kind and gentle, as though I stood in need of her. But at that time it was Father who moved me most. With his arm about my shoulder, a demonstrative gesture for him, he said, "Welcome, welcome, welcome. You come at a wonderful time."

He limped along beside me. "You're limping," I said. "What's the matter?"

"Something didn't set quite right. But I can walk, I can ride, I can work."

They had told me nothing of it. "My God," I said, "my God but they're savages. What have you done to them?"

"Forgiven them, I hope. Ireland has enough anger and not enough forgiveness. They haven't troubled us again."

"To hell with forgiveness. They crippled you."

"We'll not talk about it anymore. You're home."

He would not discuss it further. Nor would Isabella. She took me walking as we used to walk. She took my hand. She kissed me as she used to kiss me. "Home is never complete until you're here," she said, and I forgot my troubles for a little while and my mind was full of other and less complex times.

They had news for me, too. Christmas day was to be a very special day, the wonderful time Father spoke of. Hugh and his wife were coming. The Forsythes were coming. The Garretts were coming, and at dinner a small but important little ceremony was planned. Young Edward Garrett, Robert's son, would put an engagement ring on Morag's finger. Father would not have wanted me to miss that. But why had we not yet been asked? Did we embarrass them too much? Did it have to be endlessly discussed?

"What do you say to that, Kitty?" I asked her.

Morag said, "Kitty has improved. She now thinks it possible that God may have been influenced by the Gospels. 'Little children, love one another' is no longer beyond His understanding."

Kitty said, "But I shall marry a Catholic—if I can find a suitable one."

At dinner, in the middle of urging me to drink more wine, Father asked casually, "When will Margaret get here?"

"Later." There was no further question. Nobody spoke of *Silk Purse, Sow's Ear*. Discretion reigned. I think they would have asked us; I hope they would have asked us, but we were together now and nothing must spoil it. I could see no sign that their welcome was a false front. I feared it, though, and thought I felt it.

The next day's evening paper told: Lord Partry's house near Galway had been burned to the ground.

Such things never passed without comment, without heated, always anxious, often fearful discussion. Not even Tomas mentioned this one, and he read the newspapers with the grave concentration of a lawyer studying a brief. The entire family put on a remarkable performance. They had managed not to mention *Silk Purse, Sow's Ear* or Partry's scurrilous attack on Margaret in the House of Lords, and now when his house burned down they had too many other things to talk about. The fact that they had no knowledge of Margaret's back-door involvement with the Women's Land League wasn't enough to explain their selective silence, and when Hugh and his wife arrived they asked only, Where's Margaret? and extended the silence. I did not intend to break it.

Three days later Margaret arrived unannounced at Barn House. Fortunetly I was out riding and did not have to greet her with troublesome questions in my mind. It surprised me to learn that her first concern on her arrival was for little Isabella—she scarcely knew what the child looked like—and me. I went at once to see her, and after some searching found her in Isabella's room—with the baby in Isabella's arms.

My wife surprised and overwhelmed me with warmth. Isabella told me how happy they all were that Margaret had arrived, and I watched her face for signs of the cost of lying. If they were there, I missed them. They were there. They had to be there. If they were in me, how could they fail to be in them? But Margaret sailed through the rest of the day showering affection, relentlessly gay, and to every appearance indisputably the family aunt she had always been, with the additional advantage that she was also the family sister-in-law, daughter-in-law, niece by marriage, cousin by marriage, jester, clown, and the mother of the first grandchild.

"By God, Margaret," Hugh said at dinner, "you are a formidable woman," and I wondered in just how many respects he meant it.

I went to bed before her. "Please don't fall asleep," she said, and kissed me. "I'll be with you very soon."

It was a promise and a declaration, made before the whole family in the drawing room, made in such a way that it could not be misunderstood. It was as welcome to me as it was amusing to Hugh, and he nodded to me knowingly. I didn't mind. Indeed, I rather liked the idea of them knowing that all was very well.

I waited for her, naked, my splendid equipment in excellent working order. But she delayed her coming longer than I expected, and my mind wandered and a doubt nagged, and the Partry house would not go away. Where had she been before she joined us here?

She came. She heaped coal on the fire. Her smile and her eyes were greedy as they used to be. She undressed slowly, smiling at me as she used to smile. Naked, she cupped her breasts in her hands and kneaded them lustfully. "What do you want to do with me?" she said, standing before the fire.

"Margaret, tell me about the Partry fire."

"Oh, yes," she said, and the smile broke only for a second and shone again. She turned out the light, poked the fire into flame. "I love it by firelight," she said. "Oh, yes, Partry. His house burned down. It was in the papers. I can't think of that now, darling. All I can think of is what you'll do to me." She got in beside me. "Anything you want to do, darling, anything at all." It had the sound of a desperate appeal.

I tried. I tried frantically. I could do nothing.

"I see," she said. "I see." She turned from me and cried.

✑ Ten ✑

Christmas was a delicate time. There were painful memories for all of us, but especially for Isabella. If she gave any sign, it was only in her loving attention to little Isabella. Father and Hugh and his wife watched her, pretending not to. Margaret, gay again in the light of day, said: Enjoy the little darling.

Isabella, with the baby warmly wrapped and in her arms, said to me, "Come and walk with me in the garden." I thought she had something to talk about. She spoke only to the baby and sang small Spanish songs and was happy and said to me, when we came back to the house, "Thank you, darling," and left me.

It was Margaret who dominated the day. While Isabella nursed the baby, ran to see to her needs, carried her on the lawn, Margaret supervised the preparations for dinner, spread mirth about the house, and advised Edward Garrett and Morag on the essential ingredients of a good marriage ("Marriages are not made in heaven, my girl," she said, "they're made in bed and the woman who forgets it has a husband out looking for a mistress," and she looked at me without a trace of spite and said, "wouldn't you agree, my dear?").

The Forsythes, who had met her often before our marriage, came with unconcealed curiosity to see her as my wife and regarded her almost with awe.

"Margaret, you're a very formidable woman," Hugh said again, and whatever harm had been done was manifestly undone.

The girls laughed with her, worked with her. Even Tomas laughed with her. "Margaret," Emily said, "you'll be active when you're ninety."

"At what, Emily?"

"I'd like to talk to you in our room," I said to her in the afternoon, and she hurried there with me like a young girl rushing to new knowledge.

I had no problems this time. Everything was again as it ought to be. So was Margaret.

Dinner was a gala. We drank too much wine. Patton and the servants drank more than their normal Christmas ration, and after the little ceremony of the ring, came by arrangement to drink a toast and offer their congratulations to Edward and Morag. Patton spoke for them, quite boldly and with the voice of good white wine and with some emotion assuring us all that "This first marriage in the family will be a sub . . . subl . . . very, very happy one."

"And do you suppose, Patton, that my husband and I are living in sin?" Margaret asked him.

"Ah, m'lady, I know, we can all see how happy you are."

Father rescued him. "Thank you, Patton. I think two more bottles in the servants' hall will be enough. Don't you?"

"Thank you, sir. Thank you. I think, however, sir, that enough has already been reached."

They may have heard our laughter in the servants' hall. If they did, much of it was not about Patton. Some of it was about mixed marriages. Kitty was happy enough and free enough from piety to make jokes about them. Morag was as quiet and deep as a river and as beautiful as the land, still talking with smiles rather than words. She graded them into tones and degrees of meaning, familiar to those who knew her well, but now she said, "Mixed? Of course it's mixed. Male and female shall cleave one to the other. Isn't that what the Bible says, Edward?"

"What book is that?" Edward said.

Tomas asked her gravely, "What does 'cleave' mean in this context?"

Silence fell like snow. Morag smiled at us all. "The pope," Edward said, "is putting Morag's smile on the Index."

"There'll be children from all that cleaving, Morag," Kitty said. "How will the pope like that?"

"Oh, he won't be personally involved, dear. That's Edward's job."

"Yes," Tomas said, "now I see. My mare . . ." and Isabella swept him to herself, laughing out of control.

Margaret took charge. "I have some news for you," she said, and won silence. I knew of no news she might have for them. "You may have wondered what kept me in Dublin when Alasdar came? I shall tell you, if he hasn't done so already. Have you, dear?"

"No." What would I tell them? Her eyes had the bright light of challenge in them.

"I had business with one of the Viceroy's flunkeys about the girls," she said. "When the court season opens in February, they are to be presented at the Castle, if you will agree, Carrach." The thing had never been talked about, never been thought about; at least not between us. It had never been mentioned to me.

Father did not speak. He managed to look interested.

"Carrach?"

"It's not something we ever thought about, Margaret. Nobody in this family . . . we're not Dublin Castle people . . . we don't really know those people . . ."

"I do." Nothing in it betrayed to them the feeling I knew to be in it.

"Yes." Father poured himself some wine. He drank. He put down his glass with elaborate care. "Of course, the . . . it's very good of you, Margaret, very thoughtful, but of course the girls may not want . . ."

"We do," Kitty said emphatically. "Morag?"

"We do. I've love to go to Popeye's peepshow."

"That," said Margaret, "is the proper attitude."

"But not very respectful," Father said.

"It's not an occasion for respect, Carrach. It's merely an experience. They should have it."

"Well, supposing I was inclined to agree about that, there is the question of a sponsor." Father was groping. He was, unfortunately, groping toward painful ground.

"I shall sponsor them. I have already agreed to do so, if you will agree that they should come."

There was no escape from the question. Father went straight to it. "That surprises me, Margaret. This business of *Silk Purse, Sow's Ear* is still very much alive. I'm astonished that you're still acceptable at Dublin Castle."

"The English," she said, "often sup with the devil. It's a technique of survival. You know that, Carrach."

He knew that. "Isabella?" he said.

"I think we need to discuss it very thoroughly." They knew one another so well. They thought together. They wanted time, without Margaret. Isabella looked steadily at me and said, "We should take a few days. It would have helped us if you'd mentioned it before, Alasdar."

"It's Margaret's idea, not mine. It was her business to raise it, not mine." I did not look at Margaret but I knew she was looking at me, and I wondered whether she thought I had failed her or covered her. I was angry. Isabella knew. Margaret knew. All my recent doubts and questions stormed in my mind. The happy Christmas was over, at least for me.

But the girls were happy. The prospect of presentation to the Viceroy when his mini-court opened in February delighted and amused them. They chattered incessantly about it. The Garretts could see nothing wrong with it, the Forsythes thought it "very proper," Father was reserved, Isabella maintained her cautious "we'll discuss it" posture, and Hugh and Emily refused to take part in any general discussion. Margaret's cheerfulness had a determined quality about it, and I drank enough wine and brandy before going to bed to make my incapacity and disinclination plausible.

But in the morning Isabella asked me to walk with her. She did not raise the question. We walked in the garden and she was unusually affectionate. "You know how we care for you, dear," she said.

"Yes, I know."

"Everything is well with you. Everything looks well."

"Oh, yes." She was probing. It was no accident that in the conservatory, where I did not like to be, we found Father and Hugh.

"Hugh was explaining to me about the reception your book got," Father said.

It wasn't a subject to cheer me, but Hugh went on with his explanation. The Dublin bourgeois loved it. They were Home Rulers, waiting to fall heir to the place and power of the Anglo-Irish. The Anglo-Irish hated it because it presented them as they were and did not know they were—decadent, feckless, and a millstone around the neck of the nation. Yes, they had always laughed at Margaret and valued her only for her money; yes, she had always hated them, but her real reasons were personal, not political, and the Castle people knew this. They had no higher opinion of Ireland's country gentlemen than Margaret had They would probably enjoy the idea of Margaret as a sponsor. It would shock and irritate the country gentlemen, and the Castle laughed at them anyway.

"It's the girls I'm concerned about," Father said. "What effect will it have on them?"

"Carrach," Hugh said, "Morag is marrying an Ulster Protestant and Kitty is looking for a Catholic. What effect can those people have on either of them?"

It was Isabella who put the matter bluntly. "Alasdar, what's she up to?"

It was scarcely a question to ask a husband about his wife. It was the question in my mind, but was I now to confess to my family that my wife traveled and I did not know where? That she conducted a back-door liaison with the Parnell woman and helped finance the Women's Land League in defiance of my wishes—and with her own money? That I had an uneasy fear about the burning of Partry's house? That apart from this very brief period at Barn House we had become careful of one another. That this business and Margaret's attempt to commit me to prior knowledge of it had ended a reconciliation?

"Why should you suppose she's 'up to' anything?"

"Because I know you. You didn't know she had done this, did you?"

"Yes, I did." Could I say otherwise? "It was her surprise."

"Alasdar," Father said, "is all well with you and Margaret?" His voice was kindly, a father's kindliness and concern.

"Well, there are things we'll put right."

"And if I refuse to have the girls sponsored by Margaret, will it make things more difficult to put right?"

"It will take a little longer."

"Do you want us to agree?"

Isabella was the one who always put the knife to the bone. I wanted to say, No, I do not want you to agree. I wanted to say, I don't know what she's up to. I wanted to say, Every day she makes me more uneasy. But I said, "Morag and Kitty are my sisters, not my daughters. Don't ask me to make your decisions for you." It was cowardly. It was also a grievous error.

Back in Dublin, a week later, Father's letter brought his agreement. I knew why he had done it: to make it no more difficult for me to "put things right," and I wanted to write and ask him to change his mind. And did not.

"Good," Margaret said, "good, good, good."

But I saw no more of the Parnell woman in the house; there was no more traveling; some people came to dinner, an Austrian courtier who made Elizabeth of Austria's arrangements when she came to Ireland, two learned men from Trinity College and their wives, Harry Newenham and his little mistress, a clownish country gentleman from Mayo who "loved the book" and roared with delight and did not recognize himself in it, and his wife. But of Dublin society there was no sign.

Anxiety waned. Margaret was happy. Things were normal; she paid no attention to little Isabella, within a fortnight I had done long enough without sex and took my marital rights with mounting pleasure and to a new song, for she said urgently when I at first lacked my old fire, "Give it to me," and night by night with mounting greed I gave it to her and received it from her. Day and night she was full of laughter and I was empty of all my old uneasiness. The swift daytime intermission returned, there was no more fear of another pregnancy, everything was as it used to be.

Father had been wiser than I had been.

Great changes, too. The MacDonnells were going into new things. "The paunch-belly of the North," Hugh called us when he passed through Dublin. Times were not good, and Isabella was always looking, always thinking, always weighing the present against the future. Hugh called her "the general manager."

On a visit to Barn House to discuss what the girls would wear for their presentation we were conducted by Isabella over two factory-building sites in Belfast, one for a biscuit factory ("We hired two master bakers away from Jacob's in Dublin," she said), and the other a factory for the production of tinned fruit and jam ("We're bringing a man from America. James found him for us"). The machinery was also coming from America, where they had, I gathered, made great progress in what they called "canning." It was exciting for a little while. For a very little while. "We don't intend to go down because we couldn't face change," Isabella said. "Carrig Biscuits and MacDonnell's Tinned Fruit and Jam will be selling generations from now."

"Unto Tomas's children and his grandchildren?"

"And yours."

The family was again far more exciting to me than any

factory. It was a world. Sharp Kitty enjoyed her tongue and used it freely on us all. Deep Morag watched us fondly and possessively. She would have three children by Edward, she announced, and they would all be kind and have no interest in politics. Tomas talked soberly with Father, whose patience was inexhaustible. Isabella presided, arbitrated, rendered judgment, and made this world like a pool of sunshine. And Emily: today she was full of sport, tomorrow of melancholy. Dinner was a daily celebration. "A family sacrament," Very Catholic Kitty declared. Very Catholic as she was, His Holiness couldn't compete with the family. We were us. We loved one another. Perhaps it was all or in part relief that Margaret was buoyant and happy and beyond doubt a part of us all.

The great families were moving into Dublin for the Season; with them came the less great, the ambitious, the expectant, and the hopeful of something. Those who did not own town houses borrowed them. The poor came up from their warrens to see the country gentlemen and their ladies, the rich or those who to their country tenants and neighbors appeared to be rich, and were not. Other people came to town: the dispossessed, the evicted, the hungry. They overcrowded the overcrowded slums. Margaret insisted that I needed to see this more than I needed the court clothes Callaghan the tailor was making for me. I was determined to see Popeye's Party. In my knee breeches, silk hose, and buckled shoes, she said, I would look like one of Marlborough's footmen. "I'd prefer you not to be there," she said, "and certainly not as a court fop."

Military bands gave concerts in Phoenix Park and the horsemen and horsewomen galloped on fine beasts. The Shelbourne Hotel was packed with young ladies of quality or young ladies whose families aspired to quality, waiting for the Viceroy's levee to open the Season and to be presented at one of his Ladies' Drawing Rooms and in the slums as many as ninety people were crowded into tenements with one room to a family and two lavatories to a tenement, which were used also as public conveniences by casual passersby. In the great houses of the town, balls of impressive splendor were held, and over one-third of the working people of the city lived six to a room. Rich wine flowed at heavy tables in fine houses in the squares, and the tenements had one outdoor water tap in backyards that were also garbage dumps. Only in Delhi were these scenes of viceregal pomp more impressive than Dublin's. The town reeked of magnificence and tuberculosis, but not in the same districts, and the death rate was the highest in any city in the United Kingdom of Great Britain and Ireland.

I was reading Swift when the Season began, and I found in Gulliver in Lilliput some passages to my taste. Having walked and ridden all over the country around Dublin in the days of our estrangement, it seemed to me that this one had a certain relevance to the Season's setting:

> The country round appeared like a continual garden, and the enclosed fields, which were generally forty feet square, resembled so many beds of flowers. These fields were intermingled with woods of half a stang. I view the town on my left hand which looked like the painted scene of a city in a theater.

When the family arrived and the dinners and dances were in full flood, I thought this one served me well:

> The ladies and courtiers were all most magnificently clad, so that the spot they stood upon, seemed to resemble a petticoat spread on the ground, embroidered with figures of gold and silver.

Many of them went into debt to achieve this embroidery.

Margaret was by far the most magnificently gowned woman I saw in Dublin that Season. Her dinners, which were suddenly being attended, on the news that the Castle accepted her, were elaborate, her humor was outrageous, and her temper poised between rage and derision. Derision of everything and everyone except Father and Isabella and the family. Father humored her, Isabella handled her, the girls roared with her, and Tomas watched her like a young owl.

"You are a forthright person, Aunt Margaret," he said gravely. "Is that helpful?"

"It is to me, Tomas," she said. "And the best is yet to be."

I did not ask myself what that meant. I didn't think about it at all. We were all more than a little infected by the hysteria of the occasion and by a curiosity we had never felt before.

At dinner one night, she told the story of a certain young man who had called at a lady's house to collect and deliver some gifts. When invited to linger "in the interests of the advancement of his education," he ran away without the packages.

Subdued and puzzled laughter. What was she doing? "But my dear Sir George," she said to a knight seated halfway down the table, "when a lady asks a young man to linger, she intends to advance his education."

Sir George was the husband of Lady Mary Colville. Sir William and Lady Elizabeth Burden were there. It was said that Season that Lady Mary and Lady Elizabeth, both in their late twenties, had been the causes of the transfer of two subalterns from their regiments in Ireland to more exacting service in India. Their ladyships laughed with discomfort. Their husbands did not.

"Enjoy this Season, my dears," she said to Kitty and Morag, "see all the fun of the fair. The office of Viceroy may not survive the Churchills—which reminds me, Isabella, that tomorrow you and I will ride in Phoenix Park with Jennie Churchill and Elizabeth of Austria. Marvelous woman that Elizabeth. Did you know that she has in her house here a gymnasium with a trapeze in it and sometimes receives guests hanging from it upside down? By God, that's the way to treat them, and they needn't think any longer that only the Royals and the Fenians can treat them that way." She took a long draft of wine while her guests waited for what to them was the next blow. "By the way, I suppose you all know poor Elizabeth has syphilis? Got it from her emperor. I wonder if Jennie ever got it from little Randolph?"

It was calculated recklessness. It was also too late to withdraw the girls. They were not ill. Too many people now knew they were ready and eager to be presented. And Margaret was, during the week of lavish dinners, burning her boats in a state of cold rage at everything her life had been. Father and Isabella looked ill.

The silences Margaret created were like the hissing of the sea.

And suddenly she was tired beyond reason and that night left her guests, but not before they saw her tears.

Lady Burden said, "Poor Maggie. She's having a breakdown," and took Sir William home. She would dine on it for months.

Father was grim but controlled. Isabella said, "She's ill, dear. We should withdraw the girls and go home."

"It will pass," Father said. "She is tired. All this social business is a strain." But he didn't sound convinced.

"She's gone crazy," Kitty said, "but I want to go to Popeye's Party."

In our room I said, "What in God's name are you trying to do?"

"If you know," she said, "tell me."

But in the morning everything was pleasant. Margaret was herself again, apologetic, full of delight at the girls' pleasure, excited by their anticipation; evidently quite sane. Her "court dressmaker," as she called the sewing woman, put some final touches to the girls' gowns, but even I was not allowed to see what Margaret would wear. "It will be memorable," she said, "a magnificent creation in the most exquisite washed Irish silk poplin." That was all any of us were allowed to know.

It was women's work. Father and Emily and Tomas and myself went to an exhibition of Emily's paintings. Now many of the court set came to see her pictures. A few came and bought. Few of the great families of Ireland's great houses were aware of anything beyond horses and tenants, and of the two, horses were generally preferable. There were a few libraries of some value; a very few of great value. Their owners filled their houses with books and pictures and other works of art. But for the most part such things were exotica and far removed from real life. The Castle was real life. The Ladies' Drawing Rooms were real life, gloriously real life and all too brief, from February until the St. Patrick's Day Ball on March 17, and then to that other real life with the dogs and horses and the problems of social discipline, resistance to evictions, the mutilation of livestock, and now and then to a fine house burned to the ground. Emily's exhibition was left to people of lesser consequence, Dublin's lesser middle classes who were not excluded from the Viceroy's court because it did not occur to anybody that they ought to be included. The better middle classes had a place in the Castle. They too bought pictures and read books and were, Father always thought, quite like the people he and Isabella enjoyed so much in Boston. So many of them, though, Father regretted, were Home Rulers. But they bought pictures. Emily didn't care what their politics were.

It was a cold and blustery day when Kitty and Morag were presented.

Margaret's gown indeed outshone theirs. But it appeared to me that it would be unique among the splendors of the Ladies' Drawing Room which was held in the Throne Room of the Castle. It was a copious garment and its splendor consisted not in its elegant cut but in its decoration, if that is the right word. I have never learned adequately to describe these things; not even inadequately. To be frank, it made me think of a glorious tent, the sort a sultan might rest in from the desert heat. It was, as she had promised, of washed hand-woven Irish silk poplin. She told us in detail of its "construction," as she called it: by weight equal proportions of silk and wool; of wool forty threads to the inch, of silk 280–420 thread to the the inch, "according," as she said, and did not say according to what. Then a dominical utterance on why silk poplin was made only in Ireland: "Because our woolen trade was banned because it competed with England's woolen trade, so our weavers, clever fellows, created silk poplin because it could not be called wool." Her cloth was made, she said, in Elliott's workshop on Weaver's Square.

The cloth itself was beautiful beyond description, certainly to me. It spread out from her shoulders, which were broad, beyond her hips, which were broader, down to the floor, and on the back was embroidered in gold and silver thread a great harp. On the front, a Celtic Cross, and reaching all the way around the hem, "a symbol," she called it but it looked to me very like a hurley stick. I said so. "Perceptive," she said, and smiled a warm smile for me. She was sweetly composed as though whatever conflicts raged in her had all been resolved.

With all this, she carried a bag of the same cloth, fastened at the mouth by a silken rope by which she held it. The gown was buttoned all the way down the front from its high neck to its wide hem. I dwell on it only because it is important.

The poor people of Dublin, having little else to do, were lovers of spectacle. They gave no sign of social envy. Rather they came in their meager coverings to see a parade, the army marching or their betters on display at the Castle. They filled every foot of free space around the Castle gates, and the darling girls from Cork and Clare and Mayo and Meath came in their carriages and shivered in their elegant inadequacy like the chittering poor in their inelegant and involuntary raggedness. Society's daughters and their sponsors were hustled inside where it was warm; the spectators from the slums, perhaps warmed by the sight of so much consequence, stood, sometimes for hours, in the snapping winds.

The anterooms were packed with young ladies, thin, fat, beautiful, ungainly, and all in a state of terror. Their names must be called, and the list and the waiting were endless. Could there be, in such a small country, so many daughters with a title to the subroyal, viceregal nod, all of them in a state of tension dangerous to their dignity? "Make wet before we leave," Margaret bellowed at my stuttering sisters, "at the very, very last minute, make wet. You cannot like Gulliver pee in the Throne Room." Not all that much later, when Agnes in America asked Kitty what she was most afraid of at her presentation, the dear devout girl said, "Wetting myself."

Without such indignities their names were called and an ADC escorted them from the anteroom up the long length of the Throne Room toward the imposing viceregal figures waiting at the other end; the girls and their sponsor moved, the girls at least in a trance. They were aware, they said, but vaguely, of all those who had gone before them crowding the fringes of the room, curious, perhaps envious, for the girls were lovely and no doubt wondering if they in their own progress had looked better or worse. And a little to their left the statuesque tented figure of my wife, bearing symbols on her back and bosom and touching the hem of her garment. She was herself majestic.

On they went, slowly, toward the throne.

His Grace, George Charles, Seventh Duke of Marlborough, was a good man. He had not wanted to be here. He had declined to be here on an earlier occasion. The opportunity to get his son Randolph out of London after his bitter and public quarrel with the Prince of Wales was his chief reason for accepting the appointment. He was heavy-faced, popeyed, and decent. Her Grace, Frances Anne, was a heavy woman, ample, plain, and in repose drooping at the corners of her mouth. Their sons had been less than a joy to them. They had in their own lives deserved better.

The presentation did not take long. A curtsy, a viceregal word, an elbow touch by an ADC, a few paces backward— not to trip on one's train if it had been badly gathered—and over to the wall.

But Margaret did not join the retreat. The ADC nudged.

She paid him no need. The duke and duchess were impassive, watching without understanding. Margaret was unbuttoning her glorious tent, and half-unbuttoned, she dropped it to the floor.

Collective horror roared around the great room and fell into a deep pit of silence. Margaret was dressed in filthy sacking. She emptied her silk-poplin bag on the floor. A wig and a pair of old boots without laces fell at her feet. She kicked off her shoes and stepped into the boots, pulled the wig over her hair, and her voice boomed.

"Six hundred evictions and the year is not yet two months old."

The duke motioned the fussing and frustrated ADC to retreat. He watched and listened with something like interest on his face. Perhaps it was relief. Perhaps it was sympathy.

Margaret turned and progressed in a slow shuffle down the long floor.

"Half the people of this land are starving on charity," she shouted, and a cloud of pale faces watched her progress without belief.

"Men are going to jail for defending their hovels," she bellowed.

"The children of the west sleep on straw," she cried.

"The poor people of this city live in places where you, my friends, would not keep pigs. Where pigs would not live.

"There is no work, there are no crops, there is no food—except on our tables."

Her splendid tent was lying before the throne.

She turned toward the duke and the duchess.

"When will you end this serfdom?" she yelled. "Must it always be done by the sword? When will you listen? Have you no compassion?"

A long time after, Father said to me, "That was not a cry for the serfs. It was a cry for herself."

Kitty and Morag had gone, hustled to their carriage and sent back to Upper Temple Street. A carriage was called for Margaret. Every courtesy was extended to her. "Your gown, m'lady," an ADC said. "Your carriage, m'lady." She paid no attention, to the gown or the carriage, but walked out of the Castle gates in her wig and sacking and her boots.

Futile and ridiculous I pushed and elbowed and ran after her in my footman's clothes.

"Margaret, Margaret, come back to the carriage, for God's sake," I pleaded, plucking her elbow, gripping her arm.

"How much longer will you let them live on your backs?" she screamed at the chittering poor.

They jeered us out of sight, the ludicrous young fop in his buckles and silken hose and knee breeches and the rag woman. She walked back to the house, and I walked with her, gathering attention on the way. A court fop with one of Dublin's carrion poor. But anyone less accustomed to them might have noticed her stride. All I can say for myself is that I did not, could not, leave her.

They were waiting, stunned by what the girls told them. Margaret was utterly composed, even placid.

"Well," she said, "I know you will wish to be far from me now."

Father stood still and dismayed, and Isabella took his hand. The North was on their minds and in their faces. They were counting the cost.

"You used us and the children, Margaret," he said, and his pain was visible. "You used us."

But Kitty kissed Margaret. "Tomorrow there will be thousands of us who will praise you," she said. "Maybe some will even join you."

Emily said, "Thank God all I do is paint Blue Landscapes."

The MacDonnells went home in the morning. A great silence had fallen on the house and on the Season. Followed by chattering and whispering that filled the air like an endless hissing.

I was not angry. I was numb. I had nothing to say to her, to ask her, to rebuke her with or even to demand or plead for an explanation.

I went to another room that night. I never slept with my wife again. She never asked me to again. She never spoke to me again.

I do not pretend to understand. Did all her wounds lead here? I talked to her. She did not reply. What did I fail to understand that might have healed the wounds of her lifetime? I do not know.

She walked the streets of Dublin in the rags and wig and old boots in which she had confronted the Viceroy and cried out for compassion, for herself or the miserable. I followed her about. She wheeled a handcart through the streets of Dublin with on it a small coffin and in the coffin the corpse of an emaciated child.

She was arrested and confined. The child was a work of art or great skill. Where she got it or who made it, I do not know. It was made of papier mâché. I went for her to the prison. She was released and came home, as silent as the child.

She waited, a few days later, on Sackville Street down which the First Secretary was expected to ride in his carriage. He came at a sharp pace and she leaped at the bridle of one of his horses, crying, *"What will you do for the suffering? Have you no compassion?"*

She fell under the horses and was trampled. They bolted and the wheels of the carriage rolled over her.

She died where she lay.

The Duchess of Marlborough, who thought the whole matter "disagreeable," opened a relief fund for the poor.

In her last testament my wife left everything "to my beloved husband, Alasdar Carrach MacDonnell, whose gift to me was the brief and only happiness I have ever known but who, through no fault of his own, came too late to mend what others had already destroyed."

It was dated two days before she died.

I took her to Mayo. Present at the burial in the Protestant graveyard—she was no Catholic—were Father, Isabella, who carried our daughter, Emily, Morag, Kitty, Tomas, Hugh, his wife, myself, two gravediggers, and the curate, who came to spy. The rector was "away."

I did not go north with the family. Isabella took the baby with her. Tomas said, "You will be lonely now, Alasdar."

But it was more than loneliness.

A few days after I returned to Upper Temple Street the postman brought a large envelope with a card in it which said:

VERY RICH YOUNG WIDOWER OF VERY RICH
OLD WIDOW NOW AVAILABLE TO SERVICE
OTHER VERY RICH OLD WIDOWS

On the handle of the front door a maid next morning found a much larger card which said:

VERY RICH OLD WIDOWS THIS
WAY PLEASE
REMOVE FOOTWEAR AND
UNDERGARMENTS BEFORE
ENTERING

The Anglo-Irish were indeed more Irish than the Irish.

❧ *Eleven* ❧

I ran. The pressure of family communication was powerful in
us all. I wrote a brief note to Father saying only that I would
be away for a time, burned it as I might discard a burden I
no longer wanted to carry, wrote a shorter one and sent it,
and began my own long silence.

I am not a wanderer. It did not occur to me to stagger
from place to place, and my earlier notions of the drama of
an Irish life had no place in my mind. I was leaden. Stillness
and separation were what I searched for by instinct more
than thought. I did not "find myself" in Finntown, in Donegal. I went to it with consideration because I knew there was
a roadside inn sitting alone above Lough Finn and the place
was far from anywhere. I had a room. The innkeeper and his
wife attended to all my needs, food, linen, and when I needed
them he bought two horses for me, stabled them, groomed
them, saddled them. But after my first day and night there he
did not talk, for I did not talk. At first I sat. Then I walked.
Then I rode. Presently I thought. In time I felt. I was not the
youth who married Lady Margaret. I was not the young man
who buried her. When I thought, all my thinking was about
the wounded and the wounders. Streams of bitterness ran
through me; and of pity, and in time a measure of reason.
What reason there was centered on the way *Silk Purse, Sow's
Ear* had begun and altered and ended. It was the first stage of
an accumulation of stages in an act of self-destruction. It was
her book, not mine. I could no longer examine all the minu-
tiae of our life together. I didn't want to. What thinking I

did—I call it thought, but my mind leaped from point to point and a settled attitude emerged—ended in a dull cynicism about human life. It made me a silent, watchful man but it gave me also a cold self-critical humor about myself. Humor? It was at any rate self-critical and it presented me to myself as a rather ridiculous creature who to this point in his life had been no more than an aspect of the lives of others. In the mists and rains and winds of Donegal's mountains, I became my own, was as silent as ever, lighter of heart by some degrees, free of the past to some extent, and ready to leave my hiding place, having been six months in it. I went back to Barn House to see my child.

I think perhaps they understood what had happened in me and to me. They accepted my silence. In a little while it grew into something that was not anger but urgency. I was very rich. I wanted rid of the estates I had inherited and the houses in Dublin and London. I sold the houses quickly. The estates were a different matter. I could sell them, but what of the tenants? Sell them also, in effect, to the feckless mockers and evictors?

Or do something with them that would benefit the tenants and hurt, enrage, and perhaps frighten the mockers and evictors?

I created the Lady Margaret Somerville Cooperatives, one in Wicklow, one in Mayo, not out of any philanthropic motive; I did it with quite cynical humor, laughing at the mockers, laughing at myself, and before I was done with it, as cynically doubtful about the tenants as I was about the landlords.

The first cooperative in Europe was founded in the west of Ireland in 1831. I found a priest who had sight far into the future and knew about cooperatives. He found a young lawyer who knew even more about their legal structure. We made Clew House in Mayo our headquarters and traveled between it and the Wicklow house as necessity demanded. It was a gruesome year's work in some senses. The avarice and meanness, jealousy and anger of the tenants at least equaled that of the landlords. During all those troublesome marathon conferences I kept open my option to sell and kept possible buyers in sight of the tenants, to keep their minds on the consequences of failure. Even so, threatened by new owners, their greed for their neighbors' lands was the dominant fact in their minds until at last I said, "I've tried to help you. You don't want to be helped. You can go to hell. I'm selling."

"Who to?"

"Lord Erne." That brought the Mayo lot to heel. Wicklow did not wait to hear who would buy them. The Lady Margaret Somerville Wicklow Cooperative and the Lady Margaret Somerville Mayo Cooperative came into being to a chorus of abuse and predictions of failure from most of the landlords and ludicrous hymns of praise from the Home Role press. I cared nothing about either. I did not look back when I drove away from Clew House. I know why I called them Margaret Somerville and not Margaret MacDonnell: I was flying a flag, shedding a skin, and rubbing salt in wounds.

I went home to see my daughter, who scarcely knew me and did not need me. She had Father and Isabella and the girls and Tomas and Emily. I was loved here, but not needed. That too had its effect on me.

James and Abigail MacDonnell were on one of their progressions through Europe and were staying at Barn House. I listened to James and Father talking about America and Ireland. America, James said, was the Land of Opportunity, the Country of the Future. Father, who was daily less hopeful about Ireland, called it the Country of the Endless Past, the Land of Fantasy, the Dream and Nightmare Country. "We live in fantasies and by fantasies," he said, "and if the Irish ever run the country themselves, things will be worse, not better. It is in the nature of the Celt in isolation to be irresponsible." I thought of the year it took to persuade poor tenants to agree, and could not disagree. I thought also of my own life and supposed he was speaking to me.

I chose to make my announcement at dinner, when all would be there. I had not reached it lightly or quickly. I was here at home, enormously rich and idle. I was here, with my daughter, who was growing and happy without me. And I was here among all the old emotions, and once again, coveting my Father's "wife," but this time with trained and conscious lust.

"James," I said, "I am coming to America." I caused no surprise, no shock, no outcry. Perhaps they expected it and had already talked about it, as they might talk about an invalid's problems and cures.

"Good," James said, and went on eating.

"My only business experience has been in setting up two cooperatives."

"That's considerable."

"Have you by any chance a job that somebody who knows nothing could do?"

"To what end?"

"To learn how to run a business that will make money."

"You have money."

"I didn't make it."

"I have such a job, in your case. Long hours, hard work, token pay till you learn and earn. No privileges, you'd not be my relative, just an employee, learning."

"That would suit me."

"How long would you stay?"

It did not suit me to enlarge on that. "Till I have what I want."

"What about what I might want?"

"If what you wanted suited my ends, that would be fine."

"Suited your ends?"

"That's all."

"We can do business. That sort of thing works both ways."

No member of the family said a word. The conversation flowed again, elsewhere.

In the morning I went for my accustomed solitary ride. I always rode beyond Eden Village and watched the sea. Isabella appeared from behind a small plantation of trees.

"I've been following you," she said.

"I know."

"I came to talk to you."

"I expect you did."

"How long will you stay in America?"

"I have no idea."

"Will you take little Isabella?"

"To take her I would need a woman to care for her. The only woman I want is you. I'm going for many reasons, but one of the main ones is you. I wish you were her mother . . ."

"Stop it, Alasdar."

"I shall not stop it. I wish I had put her seed in you. That is how I think of you. No. I shall not stop it," at her waving hand. "If I stayed here I would . . ." I stopped it "I do not want any more emotional tangles."

"Do you want me to bring her up?"

"Goddamn it, Isabella, haven't I said what I want?"

"I want her."

"Why?"

"She's yours."

"Damn you." I pulled my horse away.

She followed me. "Do something for me."

"I'm doing something for you. I'm leaving."

"When you leave." She handed me a scrap of paper. "That's Agnes Morgan's address. I owe her more than I can ever repay. She knows her own father even less than little Isabella knows you. I write to her sometimes, but she never replies. She refused your father's help when she left. She's a proud girl, and she's your sister. If she needs help of any kind, I want to see that she gets it. Will you see her for me?"

She rode knee to knee with me. "She wouldn't see me."

"You can find a way."

I took the paper. "I'll try."

"Ride home with me."

It was a silent ride. I was recalling other days, old dreams, old fantasies that hopelessly turned to nightmares. Father watched us coming and turned and went into the house. Was he remembering, and was he glad I was going?

"What are you thinking about?" she asked me.

"Father. And you." She left me to my silence.

But before we reached the stables she said, "Alasdar?"

"Yes?"

"Come home to me."

"Do you need both of us to love you? Do you think what I always thought, that maybe he'd die and I'd get you?"

"That is cruel."

"It's also true. But I've no doubt you're right. I'll always come home to you."

A week before I sailed, Kitty told me. "I've been pleading with them for weeks," she said, "and they've agreed at last. I'm coming with you."

I was angry. I was leaving alone. I did not want to take Barn House with me. I was accustomed to being alone. I wanted to be alone.

"We'll live with James and Abigail," she said.

"You will. I shall not."

It was a decision I had not made before. As it turned out, it was a very important decision.

I also made an upsetting error of judgment. I went to see my mother. Why I did it, I do not know. I had no strong impulse to do so. I scarcely knew the woman. I had seen little of her in childhood and nothing of her in recent years. I suppose it was because I was going so far away and the woman bore me; that meant nothing to me. She never acted toward me as though it meant anything to her.

Her woman let me in reluctantly, and I almost turned away. What did it matter whether I saw her or not? Why should I suffer any nonsense?

The house was not well-kept. She was not well-kept. She received me in the drawing room; it had not been dusted for months. She wore black and sat in a large chair that did not allow her feet to touch the floor. I could not bring myself to say "Mother." She stared at me in silence for a time, and as I turned away, angry with her and myself, she said harshly, "What do you want?"

I wanted nothing. I said, "Nothing."

"You came spying," she said.

"I came to say good-bye."

"You said that the day you were born."

It was too much. This time I walked away.

I still heard her screamed abuse of Father and Isabella and Emily, her foul abuse of them, as I got to the front door.

My stomach trembled. She was an ugly sight and an ugly experience. I thought she must be mad. I did not tell them at home that I had gone to see her. I could not think of her as my mother, or as a part of the family. I could not think of her at all.

Part Three

Isabella

For
WILLIAM and HEATHER MORGAN

✑ One ✑

In Carrig the Orange sometimes call me the Spaniard. It came from the servants, who got it from the sparrow hawk when she was at Barn House. But those who are kind still call me the Spanish Lady and those who smile call me the Spanish Umbrella because more than once at a political meeting I have used an umbrella to make a point.

At first the servants called little Isabella Miss Isabella to her face and behind her back Little Spain. She changed all that. "I am Isa," she said before she could say Isabella, and Isa it has been. Little Spain and Little Isa, they said in Carrig after that.

Where did she come from among the distant MacDonnells? Not from Margaret Somerville's blood. She has my color, my temper, my ways. My ways are not surprising in her, for to her I am Mama. My color and my temper are Father's and they came to Isa through whatever strain threw up Father and came again through Alasdar. She is mine. She is Alasdar's. I wish I had borne her. I am Mama. That is how I love her.

"You have gathered them all to you," old Pollard said one day. "You're Mama to all of them."

No. Not to Alasdar. I love them all with a great and boiling love, but I love Alasdar with a special love. Alasdar loved me when he was a boy and a youth. He loved me in that time as a boy and a youth; then, I'm sure because he loved me hopelessly, came the episode with Margaret. I know how this could happen; there was Seán McCarthy, was their not? and the scars remain. But I know, now that Alasdar is a man and far away, that he loves me as a man. I can feel his heartbeat and hear him think over all the miles. That will never change. We are like that. Before God, and if there is a call from heaven to seek forgiveness, I shall not ask for it: I know that will not change. I do not want to understand; I am content simply to know. Why must we always understand? Is it not enough to have?

So I love father and son? In a way for which I could not offer an explanation, yes. And if I had an explanation, I would not offer it. I do not lust for him, but if Carrach were taken from me and I was still young enough to be able, I could bear his son's children. Yes, I would want to. Yes, I would enjoy it. Yet I love Carrach with my whole being; I lust for him and want him to command my body. I want more of his children to move in my belly. I want to pack the family with his children. Now, for fear, he will not let me.

It was a year before I heard from Alasdar. In that year he wrote four times to Carrach and spoke of me. "Give Isabella my love." It was enough. All brief letters, all fond and kind and grateful. "He is stronger," Carrach said. "Tougher." Yes, he would write only "Give Isabella my love." It was like touching and passing in the night in one another's warmth.

Kitty was the letter writer. She wrote incessantly and of everything, like a gusher. Alasdar lived for two months with James and Abigail and then moved, Kitty reported, "to live with some working-class family. The husband is a carpenter at James's mill. I can't understand Alasdar. Where did he come from?" I went and hid and laughed at that, and my heart leaped.

Kitty does not understand Alasdar. But I do. Carrach understands him and was moved in a way Kitty would also not have understood. One day Alasdar will no doubt tell us how he did it, but it was enough for us to know that he had gone to Agnes, she had accepted him—slowly, quickly?—and now he lodged in her house. She knew we were all of one family. Carrach told me early of Cassie Hyndman and in time he told Alasdar. But not Morag and not Kitty. Morag now would understand; Kitty might not. The time was coming when we would have to take the risk. I wrote to Agnes from the time we came back from America. She did not reply. Still I wrote. She never replied. "That child has no relations," Carrach said. "I feel very guilty."

"Go and see her," I said.

"I don't know how. She never liked me."

Now I wrote again to Agnes. At the end of my letter I said only, "Tell Alasdar to write to me." She did not reply. Alasdar did not write to me. The day of the ring was in his mind. I could feel it.

But James and Abigail sent happy reports. "Your young man," James wrote, "has a natural aptitude for business and is making quite outstanding progress. I would bring him—and some of his capital—into our interests, but I suspect that he will fly his own kite when he is ready." Abigail wrote, "I have no doubt Kitty has written fat books on Timothy Buckley, one of James's young men. She is comforted by the fact that he is Catholic!" Yes, Kitty had written "fat books" about Mr. Buckley, who became Timothy and then Tim. God would indeed be pleased that Mr. Buckley was Catholic. For Kitty there could be nothing but God-stamped merchandise. And for the first time I am disturbed by the thought that she might after all marry and live in America, with none of the ties that bind friends and family by marriage into one substance. She could have gone to Scotland for a husband. There are families of substance over there Catholic enough to give the church a pope.

"Alasdar does not go to Mass," Kitty lamented, "and I cannot make him. He says he will go again when you and Father can receive the sacrament in the church in Carrig." Ah, my dear Mother Church that loves the law and cannot see the heart. I thank God for our beloved Father Mackay in his holy disobedience. He has more sense than the Holy Father.

Then Alasdar's first letter came to me one year almost to the day since he went away, with a brief one for Carrach. Mine was very long. It began quite sternly and I laughed and cried with happiness.

"My dear Isabella," he wrote, "you asked me to find out what Agnes needs. What she needs most is her father." And that was all about that. Thump. It was not a message from the old Alasdar but a command or a rebuke from the new.

By the library fire I began reading the letter to Carrach.

"We should discuss that first," he said.

"But there's more, pages more."

"About that?"

"Nothing more about that."

"Then we should discuss it first."

"But darling Carrach, you'll need grounds, easy natural grounds to go near her. They're here, next in his letter."

"Oh? Read them."

I read them:

Willy Morgan is a very remarkable little man. He is timid, lacks every sort of self-assurance except one, and is, as you know, a carpenter. But there has not been a carpenter like him since Chippendale. Give him a picture of some classic piece of furniture and he will copy it. Ask him to design a chair and he will design a thing of beauty. The one thing Willy speaks about and acts on with authority is wood. This little house is overcrowded with beautiful furniture he has made—and he makes it in the kitchen!

It went on like this in detail for four more pages. Then he said:

I have found the business I want to invest in, but my master cabinetmaker withers and retreats from the horrifying thought of being anything more than a weekend master craftsman in the kitchen. I could build a business that would make money and art, and at the same time, but Willy is certain he is not the man I can trust to help me. I need the setting in which to persuade him, and it does not at present exist. Do you think you could give your mind to what that setting might be?

"Is that all?"

"That's all."

"There are," and he peered at the pages, "four more pages there."

"Not about carpentry."

"Do you think," he said, "we might move beyond Scotch whiskey in America?"

"We could think about that. But I don't think Alasdar wants investors. He wants a setting that persuades." I was too happy to hear from him to see the implications of any of this. He wrote me, he wrote me at length, and he was saying, Help me. That was what I needed from him then. I said, "There are more very interesting things."

"Read them."

I read them. "Tell Father that Isa is not his first grandchild. Agnes has two sons." Thump. That was all. It was cunning.

"Two grandsons?" Carrach said. "There's more about them?"

"No. The rest is about Isa and her education and unbringing."

"Indeed?" With a very happy smile. The post was full of rewards.

"Indeed yes."

"So fatherhood is stirring in him?" A delighted little chuckle.

"He wants to see her."

"We must ask him to come home." But without conviction; he had not grown accustomed to Alasdar's distant absence. And there was another reason.

"I think we shall not. Carrach, two of your children are calling to you."

"And you are determined to revisit America. I take it we both have our reasons. You don't offer me much choice, do you?" Suddenly there were clouds in his eyes where there had been laughter.

"None at all."

I am sorry they killed Seán McCarthy. I'm deeply sorry and haunted by it. That sparrow hawk put Pinkertons to work, and they are very famous and very clever. They must know a great deal of what took place. The woman, in spite of her long silence, hangs over our lives like the blade of a guillotine. But they did not kill Seán McCarthy because of me, and I shall not kneel to her because of him.

Carrach is haunted by what happened. That is why I gave him no choice. The way to lay a ghost is to walk through the haunted house in the dark and come out with cobwebs on your face and fingers. No ghost brushed you and chilled your spine—only cobwebs. We must go and sweep the cobwebs in the haunted house.

I know that when I was young, in my hysteria I created the situation that led the Fenians to McCarthy. It meant heartbreak for Carrach and death for McCarthy, and my father's hand was there, but hidden, They did not kill him because of me. He was a thief and an informer. He was a vile and squalid creature in whom I was deceived, but I will not excuse myself. I was stupid and willful and led myself into a condition in which I wanted to kill him. I threatened to kill him. If I had not escaped from him, he would have forced me to kill him. I do not plead my innocence of the thought. In Andalusia, someone, my father, my cousins, my mother's brothers, would have killed him in the light of day. My father's motives I will not question. I led them to McCarthy. Father sent them to McCarthy. Whether he meant them to kill him, I do not know; I only know, and he knew, that when the Fenians found him they would kill him for what he had done to them, not to me. That was his way of dealing with McCarthy? Let it be.

We tried to save McCarthy in spite of what he was. That has not comforted Carrach. That garden in the house in Cambridge still comes to him. I have the excuse; Alasdar is calling him, Agnes is calling him, he must take the occasion and go and lay the ghosts and tear down the cobwebs from the dark places. He must exorcize McCarthy.

"We are coming," I wrote to Alasdar.

His reply was long and austerely businesslike and made us laugh. He wrote like the official organizer of a tour. But he added a postscript that said more to me than all the rest.

"You have made me very happy."

It was not addressed specifically to one of us, but it went straight to where he sent it.

He came to us alone, at the Palmer House in Boston, and did not wait for shy Carrach to decide how he would greet his son. Alasdar clasped his father to him, held out one hand to me and pulled me to him and put his arm about me and I was in both their arms and my head swarmed and my heart leaped and pounded and the world was whole.

Then, "Now," he said and untangled us all and led us to our chairs and looked so official and produced a folder. "Let's get to it." It was an American way of speaking. I suppose it was an American way of doing? I don't know. It was too abrupt to be our way. But it set me laughing; he set me laughing. It was half hysteria, half joy . . .

"*Oh where, oh where has my little boy gone?*" I sang, and laughed and went to him where he sat, and cradled his head in my arms. Yes, against my breasts. Carrach was laughing. I think it was genuine laughter.

"Now," Alasdar said again, and pressed his face hard to my breasts and unfolded my arms and said, "*Isabella!* We have work to get through."

Carrach said, and there was no question this time that his

laughter was real, "I'm afraid he has gone—your little boy. And mine." We sat down together primly, trying to match Alasdar's sober bearing. But we could not. Laughter commanded us.

"I'm sorry darling," I said. "It's such a joy to see you, Alasdar."

"For me, too," he said, as though someone else had asked for another lump of sugar. "The first thing to be done is to tell Kitty about Agnes. That's your responsibility, Father."

That was a cooling experience. We were in the hands of the young man whom Carrach often spoke of as "our son," and I longed to overwhelm him with my love and was suddenly called to order by a voice that was, God help me, the voice of Margaret Somerville in her drill-sergeant days. "Please pay attention, Isabella. I think you had better deal with James and Abigail. It may seem natural that Father should do it, but if it comes from you, that will take the sting out of it."

"What sting?" I could smile him out of this manner. "You mean that because Carrach and I are not married it should be easier for me to tell James about Cassie?" If necessary, laugh him out of it.

He smiled. "All right," he said, "I am a bit pompous. But neither situation is going to be easy."

"Delicate," I said, "you call all these situations 'delicate' in your letters."

"Well, they are delicate."

"Alasdar, this is our family. We're not dealing with outsiders."

"Agnes," he said, "has to be dealt with . . ."

"Darling, we don't *deal* with people, we're not *dealing* with Agnes. We've come to *visit* her."

"Isabella, you amaze me. You deal with Father, you deal with us, you have been dealing with us as though we were a pack of cards. So now, deal with Agnes. The only place you can meet her is in her own home, and the only terms are her terms. That'll be quite a change for you, dear."

Carrach said very crisply, "You sound very like me when I was your age, Alasdar."

He looked astonished. "Do I?" Then he looked slyly pleased and tried to hide his pleasure.

"When do we see Kitty? I take it that is thoroughly organized?"

"Here, tomorrow. I told her you arrive tomorrow. Tomorrow evening, Abigail and James at their house. Next day, Agnes and Willy at their house . . ." They were very much alike, in some ways. They were amusing one another.

"Alasdar," I said.

"Yes."

"Come next door with me." He knew what I meant. He had not mentioned her, asked for her, and it seemed even thought of her. But he knew.

"Is she asleep?" he said. He had been thinking of her all this time. The new Alasdar had a new discipline that cost him something. I began to wonder what it might cost me.

"Asleep and very tired. Come." I took his hand.

She was sound asleep. "She's not like me at all," he whispered.

"She's like me."

"I hope so," he said, "I hope so," and kissed my hand and dropped it as though it burned him and walked quickly back to his father. "I have taken a house for you for three months, on Whiskey Hill, near James's," he said. "Tell me about Morag and Emily and Tomas." Like a drill sergeant, full of discipline.

Kitty astonished us. Alasdar refused to be present while Carrach talked. Carrach refused to talk unless I was present. Kitty sat with her knees together and her hands in her lap, like a mother superior bearing up bravely under news of an affair between a sister and her confessor, the expression on her face was of very young austerity; I dreaded the moment when she must say something.

Carrach talked. He took his time. "Cassie was my mother's personal servant and her friend . . . older than I was by a good many years . . . childless . . . Hyndman at sea . . ." The bones in my fingers shone. Still that small face was full of mother superiority. Her gaze was set on her father's face, but the eyes said nothing.

He had finished. She did not speak to Carrach. She turned to me. "Isabella," she said, "I have written you a great deal about Tim Buckley."

"Yes, dear." What was her little head about to say to her father but at me?

"Knowing Tim and loving him as I do has taught me to understand a great deal about you and Papa."

"Yes, dear?" It was safer to say only, Yes, dear. I wished

she wouldn't bring Buckley into it in this context. It sounded much too final.

"Isabella, I have heard amazing stories about Uncle Hugh when he was young."

"Yes, dear?"

"And I know, of course, about Alasdar's adventures."

"I see."

"And now, Papa."

"Yes, Kitty?"

"Tell me, Isabella, knowing what I feel about Tim, and knowing what I do about the family—I mean, Morag can scarcely wait for the wedding night, I mean, for various reasons, mostly to do with the bad publicity about Aunt Margaret's adventures, she's been kept waiting and she is certainly feeling it. Her letters. Well!"

"You had a question, Kitty?" A little pressure in the tone.

"Yes. Tell me, Isabella. Do you think the MacDonnells might be the horniest family in Ulster?"

"*Kitty!*" I don't think Carrach knew he was going to shout.

"Don't 'Kitty' me, Papa. Agnes Morgan isn't mine, she's yours, so don't 'Kitty' me. Just tell me when I can meet her and where I can meet her. I might even like her."

"Alasdar lives with her."

She went crimson. "Is that where he's been? Why, that treacherous, rotten . . ."

"That what, dear?"

I dealt with James and Abigail.

Abigail sat like Queen Victoria on her throne. James sometimes planted his elbows on his knees and covered his face with his hands. Through his fingers, I thought I saw his teeth, snarling or smiling, I couldn't tell which, and to tell the truth, I didn't care which. There was a story about James and a Mrs. Hildegarde Ritt, an attractive young widow who used to leave Lowell "for a little break" every time James took an "important trip." And there was Abigail's comment on their childless state, "We have had no crop but a lot of fun sowing the seed." She made a good MacDonnell.

When I had finished, James stood up, struggling against a smile. "And now you need a drink, Isabella?"

"So do I," Abigail said.

"Well, well, well," James said, chuckling like the ringing of the stopper in his crystal decanter, "you might, without stretching a point, describe Carrach as the Father of the Province."

"James! That's scarcely appropriate." Abigail hid behind her glass, enjoying the inappropriate. News of this sort was supposed to be received soberly.

"Do you think not, dear?" James said very soberly. "I now know so much about Carrach that the only surprising thing about him is his dignity."

"It wasn't at all inappropriate, Abigail," I said. "Our son Tomas is also what is called a bastard. But of course there is a difference. He was born at home."

I hoped my face was straight enough.

Abigail's head went up like the head of a startled horse. "Yes," she said uncertainly. There was a confused expression on her face. "Yes, of course. Yes, I see."

And so we came to Agnes.

I do not like the thought, but there have been times in recent years when I believed Carrach was putting his past in order, "amending," as he said one night, "the thin trail of guilt that follows me about." That made me fear I was part of it, but that was not so. This "trail of guilt" was for things not done that ought to have been done. At first, when he talked about it, my fear was that he was preparing for death. While he recovered from the Orange drummers' affair, he spoke often, in depression, of "the need to balance the account," as though he expected soon to come to judgment.

One night I lost patience with him and berated him for morbid fancies. I had known about Cassie and Agnes for many years, but when he told me, I saw no reason to discuss it or probe into its details. In any case, Father and Mother were busy creating me about the time Carrach and Cassie were engaged on Agnes. It was scarcely reasonable for me to be concerned about what had been done before I was born. Young men have experiences, older men have mistresses. The wise woman leaves it there, and we were too close and far, far too active in bed for Carrach to have or to need a mistress now. But there were things about this business that plagued him increasingly, and in time it all came out. There was nothing between us that we could not talk about, and honestly. That was possible because we came to one another always, in need and for support. What is love but an excitement of the genitals, if it does not take all, forgive all, understand all, and sustain the loved one? We sustained one another. The night of my hasty impatience, he told me of things promised and not done; promised to his mother and not done for Cassie and Agnes.

I have never felt contempt for myself. Anger at myself for stupidity, selfishness, or bad judgment, but never contempt. Perhaps this is because I have never been a good Christian and only an indifferent Catholic and have not therefore felt the need to grovel before any throne in heaven or on earth. Carrach—no matter what the Church might say—is a good Christian and a humble man. What are the words? He is of a humble and contrite heart. He has loved me with a great love; he has never felt sinful about it. He made promises to Grandmama about Cassie and Agnes and meant them deeply and was too easily put off by Cassie's refusal to depend on him for anything. We grow more sensitive with the years; as our troubles grow, so does our awareness of the meaning and cost of the troubles of others.

It was a great blow to Carrach to find his own child working as a spinner in his own mill. Ah, yes, *his own child*, there are those to say. He did not feel any great blow when other men's daughters worked as spinners in his mill. How can we love all mankind? Is it not what we feel for our own that makes us aware of what other people feel for theirs? He felt that. Is that not what the family is about—to love our own and care what becomes of them? Each family, loving? I do not make excuses; this is what I believe. It is what Carrach believes. Agnes is his own. He did nothing. The trail of guilt follows him and plagues him more and more, and he did nothing. One of the things that plagued him most was that apart from the MacDonnells and Willy Morgan's family, Agnes had no relations, or none that Cassie knew of. Now his fear was that, with justice on her side, the rejected would reject him and his.

I am his. I think with him. This family is ours. We have defended and protected it and sought to keep its elements together, however far they travel. Even my father returned to us. Wherever we go, we always return. And Agnes was one of us, and there are old debts to be paid. Not just to Agnes, but to the family. Debts of love.

"It is time, Carrach," I said.

"It is long past time," he said.

And so we came to Agnes.

But I went first to the little house. Prepare the way for me, he said. He was afraid. She was afraid. They were both afraid of the same things: that the differences in their lives might mean differences in their ways that could block the road to an affection that ought to grow.

She was heavier than when I last saw her. She was a Forsythe, with all the features of Carrach's mother. When she is old she will be a perfect reproduction of his mother, including her heavy hips and breasts. That would help to put him at his ease with her: she looked like one of the family. She was trying, also: little oddities of speech had disappeared. "The boys have to learn to speak properly," she said. "I wish Willy would."

"Does it matter? You love Willy."

"Oh yes, I love him. That's enough, isn't it?" Then she said, "You put a lot of store on love, don't you?"

"I've loved your father since I was sixteen."

"I don't just mean that. I didn't let you come to see me in Boneybefore. I didn't answer your letters. Why did you keep writing?"

"Because you're his—like Kitty or Morag. Do you want to hear about your father?" We were drinking tea at the kitchen table. Willy and Alasdar were at the mill, the boys at school. There was time.

"About my father and mother? My mother told me a lot about both of them. She was a lot older than he was, and he was very young. She was always happy about it and never ashamed. She liked talking to me about it. She said she asked him for me. Did you ever hear that?"

"I know it's true."

"I look very like old Mrs. MacDonnell."

"You look very like your grandmother MacDonnell."

She smiled. "Yes, my grandmother. Hyndman saw it. He tackled my mother about it. He went on about it. 'Why is there only one?' he said. 'Why is she like the oul lady? I tried hard enough to start one. Why did it happen once and never again?' Do you mind me talking about it? Doesn't it make you jealous and angry?"

"Why should it? You and I were born a few months apart."

"I'd be jealous if it was Willy. Hyndman was jealous. He beat her. But only once. Then for the rest of her life he never said one word to her again. Can you imagine that? In that little cottage all those years, and never a word out of him." She poured more tea. There was something on her mind, and she hesitated to say it. "Can I ask you an honest question and get an honest answer?"

"Don't you know that? Why would I be anything but honest with you? Don't you know what I owe you?"

"Well, then. What does he want?"

"He wants you."

"Me? You mean he would stand up and say, 'Aggie Morgan's my own daughter'?"

"Isn't that what he's doing?"

"Yes, but he's doing it in America. That's a long way from Carrig and Boneybefore. Would he do it there?"

"Morag's getting married when we go back. He wants you and Willy and the boys to be at her wedding."

"Is that the truth?"

"You're going to find out."

"Tell me more about my father," she said, smiling.

I knew she had talked for months with Alasdar about her father. Her need to talk about him was endless. It was time for her father to talk to her. The ground was well-nourished.

❧ *Two* ❧

They were both well-briefed. She desperately needs to know you, I told Carrach. There's a need in her that says she has to have her father. He desperately needs to know you, Alasdar told Agnes, he wants his lost daughter; and with supporting evidence to both of them. The grandsons will take you more than halfway, I told Carrach. He'll be proud of the boys, Alasdar told Agnes, so bring them in early. Be lavish in your praise of Willy's furniture, I told Carrach. She's very proud of his craftsmanship and is grieved that he hasn't the drive to take Alasdar up on his business. Father knows furniture, Alasdar told Agnes, talk about Willy and his craft and we'll get Willy off the ground before long. If Willy can be moved, Alasdar said, the boys will have the chance to be anything they want and Willy will have given it to them, nobody else.

He came to her in her little parlor in three long limps, shy but warm, and took her hands. He kissed her cheek. And then he had nothing to say. He had rehearsed what he would say. This? No, not this. Then this? Not this. Everything sounded staged and silly to him. It will come when I need it, he said. But it did not come. Tears came instead.

"You're welcome in my house," Agnes said.

"I wish you were in mine, Agnes," he said.

"Oh, well, someday, maybe?"

"Soon, I hope." Words are hard to come by when the moment comes.

It was not a big moment in the life of America. They were not big days in the life of the world when Carrach married

416

Elizabeth McCarthy, when Alasdar and Morag and Kitty were born, when I came to Barn House, when Tomas was born.

If Carrach had not given Agnes to Cassie Hyndman, other things would have happened and the world would never have known that these things had not; and the people who walked past Agnes's little house would have seen no difference in their world. But these things did happen, and the people passed down the street and still were not affected. Yet it was a very big day in the little house.

"This is Willy, my husband," Agnes said with steady pride, "and these are your grandsons."

"Did you bring us anything?" William said at once, and held his hand to be shaken.

"Why do you walk lopsided?" John asked.

"Oh, God," Agnes said.

The strain was diminished by them and the day enlarged.

He had brought them something. He told them why he walked lopsided ("I fell off a horse"), and he said, "Tomorrow we'll all go over to our house and you'll meet your Aunt Kitty and your Cousin Isa."

And after the nervous strain and the laced-up emotion, the problem of talk. What is it safe to talk about? What turn of phrase will open an old wound or inflict a new one? What casual reference that is part of one social setting will make an alien and discordant sound in another? What small habit—at table—is good, or bad and the creator of pain or embarrassment?

Alasdar's presence in the house had made small changes in their ways. Agnes had watched him and made the changes, imposed them on Willy and the children. Agnes learned. She was fiercely ambitious for her sons. They were carpenter's sons, but if she could arrange it, work for it, drive Willy to it, they were not to be carpenters. Harvard College, Alasdar told us, is where she wants to see them, "and she will not accept that from Father. She wants to see it earned. She's very much an Ulster Protestant. Nothing is real or her own if it has not been earned."

That night we ate at her table and the wine Alasdar bought expanded our growing lightness of heart. "I niver tasted wine till Alasdar come," Willy said, marvelously bold, "but Jasus it's great stuff, great, great, great," and he giggled with wine and pleasure.

"Willy," Agnes said with delighted disapproval, and smiled on him possessively.

"Another glass, Willy," Carrach said, and was himself in a state of high levity.

"Och, aye," Willy said, "I can feel sorry the morrow mornin." He raised his glass to Carrach. "Y'know, Mr. MacDonnell, they always called you Oul Stuffy down in Boneybefore, and I'm tellin you the God's honest truth—damn the bit of it. Y're bloody great company."

But after that, it was caution and doubt.

The next day, at our house on Whiskey Hill, while the boys happily entertained Isa, unaware of the fitness of things in an adult world, Agnes said, "Last night it was lovely. I was very happy. But maybe it was only the excitement and the wine."

"What in God's name does that mean?"

"We don't fit."

From then on, I heard that often. They didn't "fit." As if an Ulster childhood prepared you for a place in the world into which you "fitted" and no other place would do, or was available—or was natural. And it was true—in Ulster. But she wasn't in Ulster. She was in the land where poor Ulstermen had become presidents, and one of them from her own village; where Ulstermen had been the core of the revolutionary army, asserting control over their own destinies, their right to rise as high as their ability could take them; where Ulstermen who came with nothing were leaders in every profession and business and trade.

When Carrach made it clear that he wanted all of them home to Barn House for Morag's wedding, Willy said lamely, "That's very nice of you," but Agnes said, "No. We wouldn't fit." And, "Anyway, that's part of the trouble—we haven't the money."

"But, Agnes," he said in dismay, "I'm asking you. You're coming as my guests."

"You mean you're paying the fares and everything?"

"Of course." He knew it was dangerous ground. The word "charity" was in her mind, and he could hear it.

"We couldn't even afford a present. We'd look right poor relations."

"Coming would be your wedding present. You couldn't offer a richer one."

"Aye," she said, "I couldn't offer any, and when they were saying so-and-so gave them this and that and the other, they'd say, but the bastard daughter brought her precious self. No thanks."

"Agnes," he said, pleading, with desperation.

"We don't fit. You're too late," she said. "We don't fit."

It was Willy. Yet it was more than Willy, much more. Perhaps we were too late. It was pride. It was pain. It was fear. But it was also Willy. "This thing about Willy and the furniture business with Alasdar," she said days later. "I'll tell you what he said. He said, 'They come to give us a lift up. But I don't want to take charity, love.' That's what he said."

I asked her, "Do you call Willy's talent and Alasdar's money charity, Agnes? It's an equal trade. Alasdar can't do it without Willy's talent. Willy couldn't do it without Alasdar's money. That's equality, not charity."

"I know that. He can't see it. It makes no difference anyway."

I reached for her at the real center of her hopes. "It would make a lot of difference to the boys. Wasn't it Harvard College you talked about? Earned by Willy's skill?"

"Aye."

But we left it there. It was too delicate to hammer. We left in gloom, and Carrach and I went for a night to the Palmer House in Boston, to lay ghosts in Cambridge. It was not the state of mind in which to embark on such an enterprise.

Late at night we took a hired carriage to the house we had lived in. It looked unoccupied. There were no lights; nothing to suggest the house was alive. We knew every foot of the place in daylight and darkness and walked around the house to the garden that ran down to the Charles River.

"It was here they seized him," Carrach said, and stood on the spot. "I tried to save him, Isabella," he said, justifying himself.

"I know you did, darling. You've come. There was nothing you could do, there's nothing you can do. You are not to blame."

"She hired those Pinkerton people."

"We've lived through everything. We'll live through whatever she does with it."

"Yes. Oh, yes." Perhaps he was reassuring himself. Perhaps he was reassuring me. He did not sound reassured or reassuring.

We heard the footsteps rustling in the grass, and my very soul chilled. They came from three sides and stopped.

"What precisely are you doing here?" a man said from the darkness.

"I can't see you, sir. Where are you?" Carrach said, always calm in danger.

"It's quite enough that I can see you. What are you doing here?"

"I lived in this house a good many years ago," he said, always reasonable. "One night something quite dreadful happened where I'm standing. I haven't been able to rid myself of the memory. I came to stand here and try to lay a ghost, sir."

"Lay it somewhere else," a younger voice said angrily, "and get the hell out of here."

"Thank you, sir. I apologize for being here. I thought the house was empty."

He took my hand and slowly, very slowly, for he would not let me rush away, we walked around the house and out to the carriage. Ejected trespassers.

A third voice, also young, said, "The big one limps."

We did not see them. We drove away.

"Like two schoolboys," Carrach said miserably. "Just like two trespassing schoolboys, and the big one limps. Is that what the whole thing adds up to? Farce?"

Perhaps it was the perspective he needed? In the morning he was in good spirits and we took the train to Lowell. "What we need," he said, "is a few days by ourselves. Why don't we go to Gloucester?"

Next day we went to Gloucester. He seemed to have forgotten everything but me. "When I want too much of you," he said, "tell me you don't want any more."

He could not want too much of me. I asked for more. His passion for me was my assurance of life, of place, of purpose. I had always wanted to bear his children, many children. Tomas was not an act of carelessness but of choice. But Carrach was strong and cool and careful. Another one, I said. Let us wait and think, he said, you have time. Time? He took time. He was careful. When the next one came, again my hastiness was my undoing. Now I pleaded with him: Give me another child, darling. I thought the violence of his passion for me here in Gloucester would make him forget all carefulness. But whether it was night or day, from somewhere down in those quiet depths caution came in time, and lying in my arms he said, "You still have many years, my dear. When we get them all settled and have everything in order, we'll do it again." I was over thirty now.

Everything in order? He frightened me when he said things like that. They made me think of him as a man who walked with his own shadow even when he was not in the light. "We have Kitty and this Buckley fellow to cope with yet. Talk to me about Agnes," he said again and again. "Explain a woman to me."

"A daughter," I said.

We dealt gently with Agnes. There were no more attempts to persuade her about anything, and there were fewer invitations to our large house. "Agnes," Carrach told her, "this is where we live. It is therefore home to you in any way you want to mean that, night or day." He left it there, and we spent more time at her little house.

"Why?" Agnes asked me. "There's no room in my house."

"Because this is your house, Aggie." No argument, no elaborations.

Instead, Carrach talked to Cousin James. "I want Willy off work for a bit, James. Can this be arranged?"

"Can he afford to be off work, Carrach? What will his wife do without his pay?" It was to James a perfectly natural and a quite simple question. Willy was one of his hands. Willy worked for pay. Somebody else would have to do his work, for pay. James would have to pay. James was no charity.

"If you'll pay him in the usual way so that he doesn't know, I'll reimburse you."

"How will he collect his pay if he's not at the mill?"

"He might," Carrach said patiently, "suffer an attack of acute intelligence and go down for it."

For a week, we went to different places every day. Carrach hired a carriage. We rode on the first morning of Willy's surprising holiday-with-pay through the Acre where the still-flowing Irish immigrants lived. It was the custom for the carriage trade who lived on Whiskey Hill to take their guests on Sunday mornings for carriage drives through the Acre "to look at the Irish." The Morgans had never seen the Acre. It was Irish, it was Catholic, it was miserably poor—some of the newest arrivals were still in sod houses—and it frightened Agnes. Life was precarious enough with her husband in steady work and valued by his employer. "It's the dread of Willy getting sick," she said. "You can never get sick."

Willy looked at the Acre and the people in it and said with an unhappiness that went home to his own little house, "What chance have their wains?"

"As you say, Willy, what chance have their wains?" Carrach did not elaborate. He did not apply the message. Willy was doing that himself.

We drove from the Acre to the places where the lace-curtain Irish lived, the older immigrants who were seizing the day, who had worked harder than they or their fathers had ever worked in Ireland, who were becoming, indeed had become, a political force in the state and were determined on their place in the American sun. They or their fathers came here from the Acre, rising. For the most part they were not much interested in Ireland or Ireland's affairs. They were interested in a local magnate, a General Butler of Civil War ill-fame who lived on and was bitterly hated by his equals on Whiskey Hill. We spent hours talking of him and listening to James's denunciations of him. General Butler had political ambitions, the Irish had social goals. The two came together. The general failed to persuade the mill owners that ten hours was a more reasonable working day than fourteen. So the general bought a mill of his own and the votes of the Irish by reducing the working day to ten hours. The other mills conceded eleven. It was not enough. The lace-curtain Irish could count. They were by now a majority in the town.

"The children of these people," Carrach said, "are going up."

Willy said nothing. Agnes said nothing, but her eyes were hard and bright and her mouth set. I watched her hands as she looked from house to house. They were fists.

Next morning we took the train to Boston. This was my day. While Carrach and Willy walked about the town, Agnes came with me to the shops. We bought nothing. We looked at things of high quality for growing boys and bought nothing and kept our appointed time with Carrach and Willy, who had, we discovered, been in furniture stores where Willy explained to Carrach the defects in the manufacture of the goods on display.

Lunch, and without explanation, a carriage to Harvard College. We walked in the Yard, saying little. Carrach stood beside Willy under the gateway. "This is the gateway," he said with apparent foolishness.

"They're nice gates," Willy said.

But Agnes knew. Through teeth tightly shut and to herself she said, "They'll pass them," and looked back into the Yard. Then she looked at Willy and nodded. She was nodding to herself. I think she was unaware of us; only of her children and her husband. She looked at Willy as though about to lift him out of a deep pit and plant him on higher ground. Our women have always been like that.

We spent the week that way. It was a tiring week. At the end of it, as a last reminder to Willy we rode again through the Acre and among the lace-curtain Irish and came back to dinner on Whiskey Hill.

We talked a lot that evening about work. "Work isn't enough," Carrach said. "Hard work isn't enough. This family has always been a working family. But hard work will not it-self get you anywhere. It's work and opportunity together that make sense and progress."

"You can work till you're old and crippled," Agnes said, "and at the end you're just old and crippled."

"Yes, Agnes, yes. That's the truth," Carrach said. Neither of them looked at Willy. He looked disconsolate. I think he despaired of himself.

Late that evening, when the Morgans had gone home, Alasdar and Kitty and her young Mr. Buckley came to the house. They had been together to dinner at the home of Buckley's parents in Boston. I was less puzzled—but dis-pleased—by Kitty's passion for this plain young man than I was by the discovery of a close friendship between Buckley and Alasdar. They spent a great deal of time together, talk-ing. They sat about, with papers and pencils, "doing sums," as Kitty put it, and did not explain. They did this at our house and, I learned, at the Buckley family home in Boston, but never when they met at Agnes's house and never at James's house. It was difficult to ask questions, and they offered no explanations.

Kitty took a great fancy to Agnes. They had the same hard will, the same sharp tongue, and Kitty—who once barred her friends from riding at Barn House because one of them asked if a tenant's farmhouse into which they had been invited was clean enough to drink tea in—found Agnes very much to her taste. She also found in herself a great fondness for Willy, who talked to her more freely than to any of us except Alasdar. She made Willy laugh. "She does the dishes with Willy, for God's sake," Agnes said, "I had to show her how." And Kitty took Buckley there. His father came as a child of the famines to Boston. He grew up there, through hard times. When I was small my father talked a lot about the hard times, Buckley told us. I think the father's talk must have left its mark on the son. He was at home with Agnes and her family. He too "did the dishes" with Willy.

I liked him well enough. He had, I learned from James and Alasdar, a genius for selling. He was in charge of that operation at the mill, and in spite of the fact that times were not good, James's piece goods and his made-up goods were selling. Buckley had devised a system of what he called "market discovery," which told him what women wanted, and from it he worked out, with James's designers, what they would get that more or less resembled what they wanted. "If we go on like this," Buckley said, "every country and small-town woman in America will look like every other one." He was one of the instruments of this sameness of look, but he didn't like it. James had big plans for him and his talents. I was to discover that Mr. Buckley had big plans for himself. They included Kitty.

That meant America, and it worried me. But if in the end she married him—and Carrach was reserved about the prospect—we could use him at home. If he could sell look-alike dresses in America, he could sell jam and biscuits and tinned goods and coal at home. If that could not be brought about, Mr. Buckley was a threat to my family, helping to scatter it far and wide, weakening my strong fortress. I saw him in that light. Alasdar said he would always come home to me. He would come home to me and he would come home to Isa. These were strong chains to bind us. Kitty made no such promises.

They came that night brimful of wine and talkative, but I think they came intending to talk to a purpose.

"Well, all we need now is Willy," Alasdar said, and settled himself with more wine.

"You intend, of course, to enlarge on that," Carrach said. "For example: 'We.' Who are 'we'? And what about Willy?"

"'We' means Tim and myself. Willy means a master craftsman. Without him, we can't do it."

Then all their "doing sums" was explained. They had been very busy: machinery had been costed, everything had been costed. Buckley, on his travels, had done most of the work and together they had searched for what Alasdar called factory space and Buckley called plant. They had found what they wanted at Watertown, west of Boston, and Alasdar had taken an option on the place and on a house standing in four acres of ground, "for Agnes and Willy." What Alasdar would lose if Willy continued to tremble was not great. He could afford it. "But we must have Willy," he said.

"I'll sell," Buckley said. "Alasdar will manage. Willy will design, pick his craftsmen, and astonish America with his product."

Kitty was nervous and silent. All she said was, "Help us, Papa, Isabella."

"Us?" I said.

"Yes. Us." No more, but the little mouth was firm. Kitty was going to marry this man, over our heads if she had to. And stay in America.

"And has Isa any place in your plans?" I asked Alasdar, groping my way, but to where, I wasn't sure. Toward some way of keeping us from being scattered on the the wind; what way I was now too nervous and puzzled to see. But if Alasdar and Buckley and Kitty and Willy were to be in this thing together, Alasdar would stay in America. That filled me with a vague dread.

"A very large place, Isabella," he said, "but one thing at a time." He closed a door on me. I couldn't doggedly pursue the question. In any case I was trapped by my own pursuit of the family. I had pursued Agnes. I had tried to pursue Willy. I had thought of a business for Alasdar to put money in, a business with expert managers, and of a rising place for Willy, of the future of his boys. And of Alasdar leaving it to them and coming home. I had not thought enough. "You're the family persuader," Alasdar said, "will you help us with Willy?"

"We've tried," I said, feeling hopeless for more than one reason. I saw no way around Willy's deeply ingrained diffidence, and they were making their own lives, their own futures, and there was no place in them for me.

"I think," Carrach said, "Anges will do it for us," and there was nothing left for me to say. His eyes told me to say no more.

Buckley and Kitty left us. They seemed well content with whatever they thought they had accomplished.

Alasdar lingered. Several times he began to say something and left it unsaid. At last he said to Carrach, "Thank you, sir. I'm grateful." All of them appeared to know that some understanding had been arrived at.

"I'll walk you to the corner," I said when Alasdar rose to go. But we walked to the corner of Mansur Street in uncomfortable silence. Standing across the street from James's house

I said, "So you will not come home to me?" And I added, as I might have used a knife, "Or Isa."

"You are trying to be cruel, Isabella. It doesn't suit you." He was cold.

"At this moment it suits the situation very well. You are leaving me to bring up your daughter . . ." But I had no real spirit to be cruel.

He had. "Isabella," he said, "Margaret is dead. She is dead in me and I am back where I started, with you. I love you. You know damned well how I love you. And what am I to do? Cuckold my father? Would you let me?"

"You know damned well I would not. You know damned well I don't want it, haven't thought it . . ." I was tripping over my tongue.

"I wouldn't let myself. I wouldn't let myself think of it. So what is there for me? I love you and you have Isa. I love her, I love you. I can think of nothing better, unless it was to have you both. And I can't. What else is there to do or say?"

"You could of course find another Margaret Somerville and she would bring up Isa." I wanted to hurt. I wanted to yell at him. I wanted to touch him.

"Damn you," he said, "damn you." But he didn't leave me. "You love my father. What more do you want, in the name of God?"

I left him. I ran back to the house and did not go in. I stayed in the garden for a long time, till Carrach came to look for me.

"She will marry that Buckley," I said to cover myself, "and be lost to us. And Alasdar wants her to marry him."

He put his arm about me. "Come in," he said. "There's a chill in the air." He led me to the door. "The young have lives to live," he said. "We still have Tomas and Morag."

"And Morag is going." I could cry now, and he would think it was for that.

"And Isa," he said. "We still have Isa."

Sometimes, I think he reads my heart.

✑ Three ✑

I had no choice. The reins were out of my hands and I had to ride with the family. It was my family. Kitty arranged it all. We were to have dinner at Agnes's house, and Buckley was coming. Agnes was party to it. She was torn by panic; panic about her food and panic about her husband. "Oh, my poor Willy," she said. It was to be the night of the assault on poor diffident Willy. Alasdar bought great quantities of wine.

We ate and drank heartily. Agnes was nervous, and tender with Willy. Her love for him was mother love, protective and hopeful; hopeful for Willy, hopeful for her sons, but in her face the fear that something would hurt Willy before the night was done with.

There was an artificial gaiety about us all. At least in my case it was artificial, for I felt that by this night's work I was helping to dig my own grave. I had used Alasdar's determination to have a business of his own and Willy's skill as a craftsman to help bring Carrach to Agnes, to draw his other bastard child into the family, and now my schemes threatened to rob me of two of his children. I did not want them in America. I wanted them near me, making their lives close to mine. But I was committed to furthering a cause I now wanted to fail. But as the night wore on and the wine did its appointed work, their gaiety grew more spontaneous, mine more melancholy. Willy was not a drinking man. The genuine pleasantness of his nature was released by the wine, and the dependent tenderness of his love for Agnes was uninhibited. "I wish we had the wherewithal to do this every

427

week, love," he said to her. "It's lovely. It's just lovely," and he came around the table to kiss her.

"Willy!" she said. "For goodness, sake," and was happy.

We washed the dishes, put them in their places in the cupboards Willy built, and gathered again around the table. I felt a warm fondness for this kind and good little man, and my mind raced over all the ways in which we might use him at home. Surely we could make his furniture in Ireland and sell it in Ireland and England and, why not, in Europe?

It surprised me to learn that Willy had been involved in the preparations already made by Alasdar and Tim Buckley. It was Willy who told Tim what machinery to look for and where to look for it.

Alasdar produced his papers and spread them on the table. "Well, Willy," he said, "we're ready."

"Ready for anythin," Willy said happily.

"We know exactly what our costs will be, Willy. We have an option on a building in Watertown and on a house standing in four acres of meadow. That'll be the house of the most important man in the business." He waited.

Willy said, "That's lovely," and smiled at somebody's good fortune.

"Tim has done a lot of work on the market. It's enormous, Willy. People are getting richer. They want good things, beautiful things, in their homes. We'll put on the market furniture called Watertown Design and it will be selling a hundred years from now. How does all that strike you?"

Willy grinned merrily. "That's bloody great, Alasdar."

Agnes watched him with loving anxiety.

"There's only one thing missing, and without it we can't launch the business, we can't fill the house in those four acres, and we can't fill people's houses with beautiful things. We need the master craftsman."

"Oh?" There was no cheerfulness in Willy now. He knew now what was coming. He looked around the table at us all, and to me at least there was a pitiful accusation in his eyes. In his own house, at his own table, we were ganging up on him. He looked down at the table and his head sank lower. The wine was turning near to tears. "Ah can't," he said. "Y'know Ah can't. Ah'm ony a joiner, a workin man. Don't go on at me."

"Willy," Agnes said pathetically.

There are many Ulster voices but there is one that is common. It is the startled voice, the tones of a child in a grown man. It has its own music but it is the voice of inherited modesty, of inbred humility, of accepted and ingrained inferiority. I forgot my own fears enough to want to weep for Willy. This voice comes from a deep sense of class that survived slavery and serfdom and a fixed loyalty to Big House dominance in a society where places are firmly fixed. The very lilt of the voice is tentative, apologetic, with a startled wonder in it. It is Willy's voice.

"Ah couldn't, love," he said. "Ah couldn't fit. I'm a workin man, love."

"You can do it, Willy. You're great."

"No, love, no. Don't go on at me, love."

Kitty bought the wineglasses we used in the little house. Wineglasses are not needed in houses like Agnes's. I watched Kitty's hand, tight around her glass. I knew what was going to happen. The glass cracked in her grip. Her blood flowed.

Willy was the first to move. Cold water, salve, bandages. He was gentler than a woman. "Am I hurtin you, Kitty?" Willy was all kindliness, all care, all goodness; humble and selfless. Kitty was silent. "Yer a brave wee girl," Willy said.

When it was done, Tim said, "You handled that like an expert, Willy."

"Och, y'have to, at the shop." That was all. It was something you had to do quickly in a carpenter's shop. Willy didn't know he was kind and good and selfless.

Carrach had been still at the table, as still as a statue. "Willy," he said, "I've been watching you for weeks. You know exactly what you're doing at your job, you know exactly what has to be done. When we talked about lathes, wood, lamination, anything to do with your skills, you *knew*. When you talked about that furniture in the Boston shops, you *knew*. About your job, you have no doubts about yourself. Away from it, you're one big doubt. Why?"

"I'm sorry," Willy said, still watching Kitty. "Are y'all right now, love?"

I left the table. They didn't see me go. They were fixed on Willy. I went to the boys' room and woke them and brought them down, sleep-drugged, to the kitchen. "Sit there and be quiet," I whispered, and pushed them to the floor. Willy's children were the tools that would help me pry my own children from my side.

Perhaps Kitty had been talking. Now she was almost shouting, "Dammit, Willy. You are that class of man. You're making me angry with you. Will you listen to them? *Will you for God's sake think well of yourself?* Will you stop making me angry?"

"I'm sorry, Kitty." He had done something wrong. He didn't know what. He was sorry for it.

I motioned Kitty out of her chair and sat beside him. "Willy," I said, "take a good look at them. You came here for them, didn't you?" I was stern. Maybe I sounded rough. I took his hand. "This is the country where they can climb. You told me that."

"Aye."

"They haven't many more years in school, have they?"

"No."

"Then what?"

"Work. They'll have t'get jobs."

"What jobs?"

"I don't know what jobs."

"Agnes knows. She doesn't want them in those jobs. She wants them in Harvard College. She wants them to be doctors, lawyers, university professors, anything but mill workers."

"Aye. Ah know."

"There's a house in Watertown, a good big airy house with four acres of meadow around it. There's big pay. There's education for the boys, futures for them, money for you and Aggie, a future for both of you, and a decent comfortable old age. You are exactly the man they need. Willy, you hurt us all when you undervalue yourself. We know your value. Agnes knows your value. You do not. Will you wake up and see what good things you've got in your hands and your eyes and your brain? Will you?"

"Is that what you think?" Willy said in a voice of humble amazement.

"*Yes!* Dammit, Willy, haven't they been telling you?"

Agnes said, "Willy, will you listen, love?"

It took the entire evening. I talked. Only myself and Willy talked. The evening lengthened, and we talked. We sat still and stiff. The boys' marbles rolled on the floor with their whispers. Slowly Willy grew and talked.

"Agnes," I said, and Agnes knelt by Willy's chair.

"Willy, love," she said. "Why do we support General Butler?"

"Oh, he's for us, love. That's why."

"Willy, there's men die in the mills at thirty-five. There's men get hurted every day." She was Ulster again and her speech was his. "What're ya gonta do if ya git a chisel through yer han? If ya lose a han? Don't we live in the fear of it, for God's sake? Don't we, Willy?"

"Aye."

"Willy, there's not a workin man that has wains that doesn't think of the big hole he walks over—an it's only covered wi paper. All our lives, love, we walk over a papered-over pit. Look at them, Willy—walkin over paper. An if anythin happens to ya, down we go through it into the hole. Isn't that the God's truth?"

"Aye."

"Do it, Willy."

"Aye." He took her head between his hands and laid his brow on hers. "Wud ya help me, love?"

"I'll always help ya, Willy."

"Aye. Ah know ya will."

It was midnight. He said, "Aye, well, as long as Alasdar doesn't leave me on my own—I could try, couldn't I? Ya think I'd be good at it, do ya now? Honest to God, Aggie?"

"Honest to God. I know ya'd be great at it."

"Maybe Ah could try, love?"

"Ya could try, Willy."

Agnes took the boys back to bed. We all heard her say on the stairs as she meant Willy to hear her say, "You're both going to Harvard College. Daddy'll get you there. Oh, he'll get you there, all right."

"When? Will he take us tomorrow, Mammy?"

Willy was rubbing his palms together, staring at nothing, nodding his head, flexing his resolve. "Aye," he said aloud, deep in his thoughts, "aye. Bejasus, aye, right enough."

As long as Alasdar doesn't leave me on my own, he said. I had helped to win Willy for them. I had lost Alasdar for myself. Now he would not come home to me.

❧ *Four* ❧

The thing was done and I had faithfully played my part in seeing it done.

Alasdar would not come home to me. A man does not establish a business in America, a business which he intends to make into something very special, and leave it in the hands of others while he trots home to Ireland. To think otherwise was one of my self-serving stupidities. What I had contributed to the success of our family assault on Willy produced in me a nervous bitterness, a disturbing uneasiness in my stomach that stayed with me for days. My strong fortress was falling, and because I had been its principal architect, I was committed with the others to dismantling its walls. The Watertown decision and the conscripting of Willy were family enterprises.

I was afraid also of myself. I think I'm honest with myself, and for the first time I asked myself why I was and always had been so desperate to have Alasdar come home to me. The Margaret episode was dreadful, it was my fault; I knew then more clearly than at any time since I agreed to his being sent to the Royal School that I was too close to him, too fond of him in the wrong way, and when I got over my rage with Margaret for having agreed to marry him, it became almost a relief to have him married. And safe from me? Can a woman love a father and his son? I know that Anna Davidson loved Charles Davidson with a deep and abiding love. She was his second wife and a great deal younger, and we all admired the way she had taken on the task of being mother to his growing son. But one night Charles came home from London unexpectedly and found them having sexual intercourse on the floor before the library fire. He divorced her—they were Protestants—and disinherited his son. Charles was broken by it, his son drank himself to death, and poor Anna went out of her mind and had to be locked up. All she ever said was, "I loved them both so dearly. They were both mine." I frightened myself. I love them both so dearly. They are both mine.

But I have never allowed myself to think of intercourse with Alasdar. I know even by saying "I have never allowed myself" that I condemn myself out of my own mouth, that something was there to be suppressed. Suppressed, but not because I had consciously thought of it; I would have supposed it a very wicked thing; suppressed only because it was a dangerous thing, disruptive, destructive, and a source of anguish.

Well, something was over. The wind took us and we were being scattered, thousands of miles apart. We had won Agnes but she also was far from our family fortress, and what I had helped to accomplish bound her to this place so far from home. That seemed to matter less than Alasdar's defection, and that too filled me with a fear that love for a father and his son was my real motive in working with all my strength to bind the family to me and keep it near me.

My thoughts distresed me; I had chained them down within me when the matter of Buckley and Kitty came to a head. That young man did not ask Carrach's permission to marry Kitty. They came one night soon after the evening at Agnes's house. Buckley had asked to see Carrach "on a matter of great importance." It was Kitty who insisted that instead he ask again, to see us both on this greatly important matter. We had no doubt what it was all about. I had no doubt that Kitty expected my support.

He did not ask permission. He said to Carrach, and took me in as an obvious concession with an inclusive turn of his eyes—my inclusion, I had no doubt, was at Kitty's insistence, but it was reluctant on Buckley's part—"We came to ask your blessing on our marriage."

He enraged me. "Not our permission?" I said.

He looked me right in the eye. "No, Ma'am," he said.

"You do not wish to modify that?" I asked him.

"How do you modify an absolute negative?" he asked me.

Carrach removed the matter from immediate and what he later called "fruitless contention" by saying, "The subject isn't altogether surprising, but you will, I'm sure, understand that we have to think about it?"

"Of course, sir," Buckley said, and read quite correctly that there was a division from which he might profit. They withdrew from us quickly, for the atmosphere was unpleasantly electric and my anger was written very large on my face.

"A blessing, but not our permission," I raged, pacing and hugging myself with fury. "That's an insolent brat. And he wanted to exclude me."

Carrach is always placid when I am furious. "Have you been happy with me, Isabella?" he asked me gently.

"Of course I have."

"Did I ask your father's permission?"

"He's your brother. You didn't need it."

"Did I ask my brother's permission to take you without marriage to give you a child . . ."

"We didn't need it."

"Are there rules to free us and different rules to bind them?"

We loved one another so greatly and we had loved so faithfully and so long. It always seems, does it not, that when we break the rules it is for good and sufficient reason? Who could reasonably doubt us? But when others breach even good manners, there is little excuse for them? My Carrach knew me very well.

"No, my love, no," I said, and knelt by him. "But he will keep her here, thousands of miles from us."

"That's the reason?"

"That's part of the reason."

"At sixteen, you sneaked off to me. Your own rules?" He was smiling. He could have said, You also ran away with McCarthy, but he said, "He's a fine young man. He's going into a family business."

"Not a family business. Alasdar's money alone. Are you going to say yes to Buckley?"

"They'll marry no matter what I say."

"Then bind them to us."

"And how would that be done?"

"Put money in their company. Make it a family business."

"Alasdar has decided to take his own road. He doesn't want our money."

"*Bind them to us.* If it has to be done with money, use money."

"We'll talk about it. If it can be done, I'll do it."

But I went to see Alasdar. I wanted to see him. We had not exchanged a word since the night at Agnes's house. I could endure his absence from Barn House when I knew I could not see or hear him better than I could endure his silence when he was near. He saw me in James's drawing room; he received me as he might receive a stranger. My head was a little wild. He sat at a distance from me. "Yes?" he said. It was so distant.

"If you love me, why do you ignore me?"

"Because I love you. Is there anything else?"

"If you ignore me, why do you tell me you love me?"

"Because you want to hear it. You love to hear it. I love to say it. You are avaricious for love, Father's love, my love. You have both. Now, why don't you be content with that?"

"I love Kitty too. I don't want her to marry without Carrach's permission. Buckley intends to marry her with or without it. So does Kitty. That will make enmity in the family. I don't want that. Do you?"

"Won't he get Father's permission?"

"He refused to ask for it. He wants only our blessing."

"Will he get yours?"

"No. Not yet anyway."

"Will he get Father's?"

I would not lie to him. Nor would I tell him what Carrach said. "He would find it a lot easier to give if Buckley was bound to the family."

"Kitty is surely quite a bond?" His little smile was mocking.

"Three thousand miles from him? Threads break, Alasdar."

"You, Isabella, are not a thread, you are a ship's rope and you have a long reach. Who should know that better than I do?"

"But Kitty can't know it as you and I do. Can she, Alasdar? Kitty doesn't want to be my lover, does she, Alasdar?"

"I don't want to be your lover. I want to be your husband, and that can't be. So now, what are you up to?"

"Would you prefer to discuss it at that level?"

"Much."

"Very well, then. I want you to do something for me."

"What?"

"This business of yours. I want us to invest in it, a very large investment."

"And what you want, you try to get. So tell me why you want it."

"Because I have loved and given my life to the family. I brought Carrach here to reclaim Agnes. All I have done is help to separate us all. We are being scattered. Two of you are in America now—thousands of miles from us. I do not 'want you to go your way alone, separate from us. I want bonds of the heart . . ."

"And of the pocket?"

"And of the pocket. Do you think for a minute that is of no consequence? It is your business. You will run your business without interference. You know your father. But I, I, Alasdar, want it to be a MacDonnell business. I want Buckley, if this marriage is to take place, bonded by self-interest to this family. I'm sure he loves Kitty. I don't question it. But I want his self-interest to cement him to us. Not to you, not to Kitty alone. To this family. What money is he putting up?"

"None."

"So."

"What does that mean?"

"Do you want Kitty to marry him?"

"I do if she wants to."

"Do you want your father to agree?"

"Naturally, if Kitty does."

"Do you want me to help him to agree?"

"If Kitty wants it, I want you to. I know you can."

"I know I can. Kitty knows I can. I would do it—if Buckley were to be bonded not to a furniture factory but to a family. When he works for your factory, I want him to be working in this family."

"And the same applies to Agnes and Willy?"

"The same."

"You really are a ruthless bitch, aren't you, Isabella?"

"Yes, Alasdar, I am. But that's not news to you."

"No, that's not news to me. You flung me into Margaret Somerville's bed to get me off your conscience, then you screamed when she said she'd marry me. And now, a bit of blackmail. That's what it is, isn't it?"

"Of course. Yes."

"I'll think about it. But you knew I would."

I rose to go. That was what I wanted to hear. "On the other hand, you might do it because I want you to."

"Oh, yes, I might do it because you want me to. But you have another gun at my head, haven't you? I might do it because you have Isa? Isn't that something you haven't mentioned?"

"That too. And you do think that's very important, don't you? You may want to take your own road far away from the family, Alasdar. Or is it far away from me? Why are you able to be so free of us?"

"I'm afraid I'm not free of you."

"But you are able to be a father far from your child because we are the family. Because home is still us. To Isa in particular, Alasdar. What about your own conscience? You can invest her in us, because we are the family, home is with us. We are not so dispensable, are we? Surely we can invest mere money in you?"

"What a crude way to put it."

"Yes, isn't it? I'm going now."

He came and stood before me, close to me. I wasn't sure whether he wanted to slap me or take me in his arms. I would have welcomed even a slap to show me that I created some turmoil in him. "Much as I love you," I said, "I would at this moment like to slap you." The turmoil was mine. What I knew suddenly and without question was that in very different, very intimate circumstances, my turmoil would be no less wild but far from angry.

He turned away, and as he turned he said, "Get away from me." I was alone in the room. I was very much alone.

Our house was only a short distance from James's. I covered the distance almost without knowing I had walked at all. Carrach was crossing the hall as I came through the front door. "Isabella," he said, and was alarmed, and for a moment I was too upset to realize that my distress was visible, "what on earth's the trouble?"

"I've been down to see Alasdar at James's house." Our house was higher on the hill.

"Should that upset you?"

What was I to say? I'm another Anna Davidson? I want your son to take me on the library floor? "We were talking about Isa." I said it sharply. It was true. We had talked about Isa. I had blackmailed him with Isa.

"Well, should that upset you?"

I was in my own trap, and my impotence threw me into a fury, with Carrach, with Alasdar, with Buckley, with Kitty, but most of all with me. "Yes, by God, it should. Your bloody son doesn't know his arse from his elbow." It covered anything and everything and nothing.

His eyes and mouth were wide open. I thought: He's going to tell me not to be vulgar.

His laughter boomed in the hall. It drained away my fury. He often drained away my furies. My energy drained away with my anger.

"Let's go to bed and get to sleep," I said, and he put his arm about me.

I needed more than a night's sleep. Anyway, I didn't sleep, or I slept badly and woke tired and irritable. It was not the proper state of mind for the day I had to face. When I'm in this state, my stomach is nervous. I lose my temper quickly and know I'm unreasonable. I regret the things I say and do. Carrach, when I'm like this, says, "I think you were born in the caves of Granada," by which he means that I'm behaving like one of the half-civilized gypsies who live in the caves. He leaves me alone. That pacifies me because I want to be near him and my stomach calms down and I seek him out. "I'm sorry" is all I need to say.

This time I had no chance to tell him I was sorry. Alasdar and Buckley came early in the morning and asked him to go with them to Watertown, "to see the plant," they said. That pacified me a little. I jumped to the conclusion that this was a ploy of Alasdar's to invite Carrach to invest in their company. But Alasdar came and went from the house with no more than "good morning" and "good-bye" to me, and took Carrach away. "We'll be a little late getting back," Buckley said, but there was nothing about him that suggested he was privy to any special knowledge. If he was, he concealed it. They left the house before nine.

It was some time before I put the pieces of the day together.

Kitty came before ten. She was brimful of sweet charm, and when Kitty is like that I raise the drawbridge and wait. Her chatter was idle, and sweet charm and idle chatter from Kitty are like the trot before the canter before the charge.

Her theme was Barn House. What happy lives we all had there, what delights, what closeness we enjoyed; how we Christians (she said MacDonnells) loved one another there.

"Yes, Kitty?"

She knew I was waiting. The horses. Had any woman in the world ever ridden as I rode? No mother ever loved and cared for her children as I had loved and cared for them. (She made me feel like a mare, hopping from horses to good mothers.) And Papa, what happiness I had given him. I had been positively noble about Alasdar and Aunt Margaret, and what happiness they had known together was largely my doing. I was that sort of person. I opened the road to happiness for other people.

Ah! "Tea, Kitty?"

Tea came. Kitty went on. No matter where we were in the world, we would always be together. Think of Uncle Hugh and Aunt Isabella. Aunt Isabella was an Andalusian and Uncle Hugh had met her and loved her and married her in Spain when he was "quite young." But before that he had adventured in the world, and "none of us knew where he made his fortune."

"I do, Kitty." Interruption surprised her. "I also know my own family history. But tell me more about it." And I smiled. I hope like a hunting polecat.

"Aunt Isabella's family was never poor, of course."

"Horses and fighting bulls," I said with my smile.

"Yes. Tim's family—his grandfather and on and on far back—were tenant-at-will farmers in Ireland. They were always very, very poor. His grandfather brought Tim's father here in a coffin ship."

"He has told us several times. Are there new details?"

"They are such fine people. Tim's father climbed. By sheer will and talent, Isabella. They're quite rich. Tim takes after him."

She was watching the street. I turned to see why. Agnes was coming across the lawn. "Tim is so fine, Isabella. I love him so much. Please love him, Isabella."

"Was it not possible to begin there, Kitty? Was that hour-long rigmarole really necessary?"

"I was afraid."

"Of *me*? Whatever happened to that loving-mother theme? You were afraid of me?"

"Help me, Isabella."

Agnes was at the door of the room. "You wanted me in the family," she said, "are there secrets, or can I come in?"

Kitty played instant hostess. "No secrets, Agnes. Come in. The tea's still hot. I'll ring for another cup."

Two pieces fell into place. Alasdar and Buckley came to take Carrach away. Kitty came to soften my heart and came to the point only when Agnes arrived at the door. They were all in it. Agnes was in it. We ganged up on Willy. They were ganging up on me.

Apart from Alasdar, they were always my children. Now they were young adults. In a way, I was amused by it. Only in a way. It was counterattack. There had been many counterattacks since I came first to Barn House to mother them in my sixteenth year, but they were children then, and their ploys were children's ploys, conspiracies of the very young and very loving. This was not the same.

"Willy kept them," Agnes said. "They'll be home very late."

"Willy? They came for your father. Did they take Willy?"

"What could they do without him? They're going to plan the layout of the place at Watertown."

"May I ask," I said, "about their jobs? They do have jobs to go to."

"No, they don't have jobs," Agnes said cheerfully. "They all resigned a week ago. They're on the Watertown payroll now. Didn't Alasdar tell you?"

No, he didn't tell me. "Has James known nothing about all this?"

"No. Alasdar says he's angry."

"Do you blame him?"

"No. I don't blame him but I'm sorry for him. They're looking after themselves. That's what James does, isn't it? They were all his hired hands. He wasn't giving them anything. They all worked hard for their money."

Well, we MacDonnells had always looked after ourselves. I had helped to bring this MacDonnell back to the family. That too was amusing in a way. Kitty was less pleasing, much less amusing.

"Isabella, I'm not going home for the wedding."

"Morag's?"

"Mine."

"Do you expect an announcement like that to make your father happy?"

"When he had to understand something, you always showed him how."

"And you expect me to do it now? To make him understand that you don't want to be married at Carrig?"

"I'm asking you to."

"When no marriage has been arranged."

"And by God this one isn't going to be." Her little face was red. "I'm marrying Tim. I'm marrying him by choice. I'm marrying him here and as soon as I can. I'm marrying him while you and Papa are still here."

She was on her feet. She was a formidable little creature. For a moment my heart stirred for her. It would have been my own attitude—if there had been any need for it. I didn't see the need. If this marriage took place, there was no reason why it should not take place at home.

"Kitty, you seem determined to make your father needlessly unhappy," I said sharply.

"Why, in God's name? I can't understand you. Look, I want to get married. I am here. Tim is here. Agnes and Willy and Alasdar are here. James and Abigail are here. You and Papa are here. What else is there to say?"

"Why the hurry? It's not the way we do things."

"It's not the way you and Papa did things. Was there a storm about that? How can you and Papa talk about the way things are done . . . ?"

"When we're not even married? Is that where we've come to, Kitty?"

"No, no. I don't mean that. Isabella, I love you too much to mean that. You know that."

"Then what do you mean?"

"I mean that there is no way we do things. It's all in your mind. It's family, family all the time with you, and this is family. Tim will be family."

"And you can guarantee that?"

"Isabella, what are you up to?"

It was Alasdar's question. Did they all think always that I was up to something?"

"Must we be your children all our lives?" she shouted. "You'll have our children. You have Isa. You have Tomas. You have William and John. You'll have Morag's children. You can have more children of your own . . ."

"Kitty!" It was a low blow. I knew it was not meant meanly, that it was her tongue unleashed against odds.

She was on her knees beside me. "Isabella, I'm sorry. I didn't mean to hurt. Forgive me, please, forgive me."

I said nothing. I could not have spoken then. I had pleaded with Carrach for another child . . .

"Isabella, I don't want to defy Papa. I want to have a happy wedding, a quiet wedding, here where I'll live. It's very, very simple." She was in tears now. Tears have not always worked for Kitty. "Agnes will be my matron of honor . . ."

I looked at Agnes. She was quite composed. "Have you already agreed, Agnes?"

"You wanted me in the family, Isabella. My sister asked me. I said yes. Should I have asked you first?" She was smiling. It was Grandmama MacDonnell's smile. It was gentle. It was also like iron.

And I felt foolish. I had no arguments. I had known that for half an hour. Perhaps I knew it sooner. Perhaps I knew it when I talked to Alasdar. I had no children now, except Tomas and Isa. I could not treat any of them as children, except Tomas and Isa, and Tomas was growing out of my reach.

"Isabella?"

I must have been brooding. "Yes?"

"You remember the fight Morag and I had, when Emily gave us all hell?"

"No. I was not well at the time. I only know what Emily told me months after it."

"Morag said some pretty strong things, Isabella. She said I would be the first of us to get to bed with a man."

"That was delicate of her."

"She was right, I want to be pregnant before her." She was grinning. "Do you understand that?"

I walked to the window. Sometimes Kitty reminds me of myself when I was young. Now she reminded me of those days at Barn House when the most urgent, the most immediate necessity was to get to bed with Carrach. I was a MacDonnell. Kitty was a MacDonnell. "Yes," I said, "I understand that."

"Talk to Papa, Isabella."

She was always a knowing child with knowing ways. She was a knowing woman now. "We'll talk about it." But I did not promise what I would say.

It was very late when Carrach came home. He was tired and I didn't want to trouble him. But I asked him just the same, "Did Alasdar ask you to put money in his company?"

"No. Did you expect him to?"

"I hoped he would."

"Did you ask him to?"

"Yes."

"That's a pity."

I had grown so accustomed to having my way.

❧ *Five* ❧

Kitty's wedding was as she wanted it. There was no invitation from Alasdar to join his company.

There were problems with an Irish priest. When he discovered that Agnes was a Protestant, he raised difficulties. Kitty disposed of him quickly. "My sister is not a problem to me," she said, "I'll find another priest. You, sir, lack both grace and charity."

It was her idea to be married in Watertown and to hold her small reception in Agnes's new house. The only people present were MacDonnells and Buckleys, and a gnomish little priest named Corcoran, who protested, "I'm not Irish, I'm American," and won the Buckleys' approval. Mr. and Mrs. Buckley were tolerable. Mr. Buckley struck me as being a shrewd ambitious man who had worked hard at becoming an American. He had no interest in Ireland and no sympathy for Fenians. "If they're so fond of Ireland," he said, "why don't they go back there? But they don't, do they? No, by God, they don't. They live the good life here and want to see blood run on Irish streets . . ." But he was pleased that his son was marrying into "the Irish aristocracy."

"Hebridean," Carrach said, and since that sounded like a mystery, Mr. Buckley dropped the subject.

James and Abigail were courtly. Willy was delightful and full of his favorite German white wine. Carrach, for the most part, was silent. Alasdar also; he, as Willy put it, "stood for Tim," and the thing was accomplished.

When it was time for the bride and groom to leave, Abigail

443

asked Kitty in the hearing of our small company, "And where are you going, my dear?"

"To get pregnant," she said, and left in the silence.

"May I come home with you?" Alasdar asked us.

That night, just before we went to bed, he said casually, "I'd feel happier if you came into this business with me."

Carrach was no less casual. "Oh," he said, "we've always tried to do what made you happy, Alasdar."

"And you, Isabella?" He was smiling one of Morag's ironic little smiles.

"Your father makes those decisions," was all I could muster. I would have preferred to break something over his head. He was mocking me. Had he removed himself so far from me that now he could mock me?

"Well," Carrach said, climbing into bed. He stretched himself and tucked his hands under his head. "Well, well," he said.

"Well, well, what?"

"I don't know how you engineered it," he said, "but you did it very well."

Let him think so. I turned my back to him and went to sleep.

It was time to go home.

A sharp letter from Morag, without the softness of her nature in any part of it, said:

> You and Papa will, of course, come home eventually? My wedding was shelved in the public commotion and embarrassment of the Margaret Somerville debacle. It is now being delayed by what I might call the Anguish over Agnes and the Capers of Kitty. Do not pretend surprise if you should one day come home and find me the married or unmarried mother of several children. Do not let my plans interfere with your plans. On the other hand, I am finding it difficult to see why your plans, whatever they are, should interfere with mine....

It was very strong stuff for Morag, who usually dealt with what she saw as difficulties with a push and a little gentle irony. Tomas was no more helpful to the spirit. Kitty had been writing him with great frequency—would Buckley ever come to the point where he told her to shut up?—but about what, I had no notion. Now I learned of it.

Harvard. Old Dr. Houston's son took over his father's practice. While Tomas lay ill from that dreadful fall, young Houston became his friend. He went often to the doctor's house, they talked medicine endlessly (like his father, young Houston was a healer of spirits as well as bodies and saw the two as one), and we knew that sooner or later the announcement would come: I want to be a doctor. That was why, when Morag and Edward Garret spoke to us about marriage, we spoke to one another about succession in the family's businesses and Edward was there. Tomas, if he pursued his course, would not be there. With the kind of passion young Houston had bred in him, he would one day be a distinguished doctor and a teacher of young doctors. And now he wrote of medical schools and "Jack Houston says," and "Kitty says," and "When, later on, I complete my M.B., I ought to go to Harvard for further study." Whether he would ever return to Ireland was a question in his mind, "for if I see no civilized future for the Irish, how could there be one for me?" But, "Kitty thinks I should come to Harvard when I have reached that stage, and stay in America."

It blurred my mind. I saw this family like a little army in the night, moving the balance of its strength from Ireland to America while we at home grew older and weaker. What it said about us I did not want to hear. It was time to go home. To, as I saw it, a depleted home. Even Isa was not as she had been when we came here. She knew her father now. He had—very cunningly I now thought—showered attention and affection on her, and she grieved to leave him. That ought to have pleased me and did not. Only part of her was returning with us to Barn House. Carrach was no longer Papa but Grandpapa. Alasdar was Papa, and he made the most of it. And I was going home, depleted, to a depleted home that was on the brink of further depletion. In a way I did not understand—for the feeling was like a vague discontent—it seemed to me that those who came to the station to see us off (Alasdar, Agnes, Willy and the boys, and James and Abigail) were looking into the future while we were returning to the past. And the thing that troubled me the most and was not well-defined in my mind was that the future was bright, like American sunshine, while the past, which I championed, extolled, and idealized, was as murky and uneasy as a wet day in Donegal.

Even so, past and future pulled both ways in more than

one of the young ones. (I say young ones, and perhaps it says something about my state of mind that day, for Agnes and I are in age only months apart. I felt old.)

Carrach dealt with each of them in his orderly way. We stood together, they formed a line. Perhaps people in the station thought they were a reception committee welcoming what the Americans amusingly call "visiting firemen."

As the least of these, so to say, James and Abigail and mutual expressions of pleasure and gratitude. Then the boys, and Carrach held them in his arms and had trouble maintaining his composure. He whispered things none of us heard. The boys cried. Then we heard Carrach in an overflowing voice, "Come and see me, come and see me." And Willy, "It's been very nice," he said and made room for Agnes. She was in her father's arms; "Willy can't come to Morag's wedding," she said, "and I won't leave him." He said, "I know, I know, we'll come back."

Then Alasdar. He took my hand in his left hand and embraced his father with his right. He did not let my hand go free but pressed it hard till it hurt and the pain was pleasure. It said: I still love you.

"You're my senior partner now, my boy," Carrach said. "Make the thing flourish."

"Oh, yes, we'll succeed."

Underneath the composure, old love and old mutual dependence stirred in both of them.

"Morag's wedding," Carrach said.

"We'll be there." Then Alasdar kissed me. On the cheek. "Be Isa's mother," he said, and meanings darted in my mind and she hung from his neck and wept.

We went through the gate, walking without looking back. It was Agnes who sent through me a shock I shall never forget.

"Father!" It was almost a scream, and there was anguish in it. We turned, full of alarm.

"Come back!" she cried.

We hurried back to her. "I wanted to say it," she said, "I never called you that." She was crying.

"Och, love," Willy said gently.

Sometimes I think life begins to wind down and sends us small signals that that is what is happening. There is a period, as this begins, when the signals are not seen. I did not see them in myself at first. Past thirty, strong and healthy and supple, it did not occur to me that there were things I once did with ease on the back of a horse and now might not do with the same ease. One of them was to fling a flat Spanish riding hat ahead as I rode at full gallop and snatch it without slackening stride as it touched the ground. I could do it with ease when I was seven and seventeen and twenty-seven. And now? Thirty-four is not old. I am young. I do it now once out of three attempts, and dragging myself back into the saddle is a labor—well, it is a lot harder than it was even two or three years ago.

It was Carrach who said, when Tomas beat me at it five times out of five, "I think time is telling you something, dear." I had not noticed till then that time had anything to say to me. So, I said, I am older. It was nothing.

Carrach's signs were different. Mine said merely that I was less supple. His were ominous to me, for he read them. We were standing one day in the orchard some way to the east of the lawns before Barn House. The ground there slopes down to a small cliff above the sea—it is a drop of no more than a hundred feet—and among the old apple trees we had built a small summer house where we often sat, talking, or silent, looking at the sea. It was standing before this summer house one evening that Carrach first disturbed me with life's little signs. He had needed reading glasses for quite some time—several years indeed—and had lately had them exchanged for stronger ones. He was looking with such intensity at the scene before us that I asked him what he saw.

"Everything," he said. "If I lose my sight, I want to be able to recall every detail of this scene."

"Why are you talking like that?"

"My eyes are so often so very tired now. I hate to read."

"Then we must rest them, but don't talk of losing your sight."

He paid no attention to that. "Isabella," he said, "look. There's the table where we picnic. There are the benches where we sit. We've kept this place this way for years. We've spent hours with the children here, and every tree is in place. If you go blind, do you think your imagination alters what you remember? Or do you simply not remember properly?"

"You're not going blind."

"Of course I'm not, but it's interesting to wonder."

There were other things, but it was only after the blindness talk that I paid them much attention. He rode less and less frequently, and when he did, he was stately and slow and very careful. After riding, he limped from the stables through the courtyard to the house, looking very, very weary.

Going to bed had been with us from the beginning a kind of ritual. We had always gone to bed at the same time. It never occurred to me to go to bed without him, nor he without me. Mind you, from the beginning and for many years there was a most urgent reason for that. It continued each night for many years, before sleeping and on waking. Now that he was in his middle fifties it was not the fiery compulsion it used to be—at least not in him—but it was still an occasion we cherished at least four nights of every week, and not indifferently. It was when we came back from America after Kitty's wedding that sometimes he went to bed without me, before me, and was asleep when I came to our room.

Then he said, in the firm way he had when it was time to stop talking about something and act, "I think we'd better get Edward Garrett into the company." First I thought his reasoning about Edward was my reasoning about Buckley. "No," he said, "it's simply that I'm tired and you're going to need a head man to manage your managers, and he's practically running Robert's mill. He has brothers to replace him there."

I learned not to comment on comments like these. But more and more I took these sayings to my heart and was deeply troubled by them. It was as though he were cooperating with the years in winding down his life and preparing me for it. Yet there was nothing wrong with him. It was a state of mind; not constant, but occasional enough to be a pattern in the mind.

Yet there was a joy about him when we were all together for Morag's wedding. Alasdar came, Kitty and Buckley came, Kitty, I think, padding her swelling little belly a bit; the senior Buckleys came, and Mr. Buckley was impressed by Barn House where he slept and by Garden House where the Garretts slept, and Mrs. Buckley thought the whole place "quite a spread" and "worth a million," and Patton worth another million in spite of his years, but nobody mentioned Court House to them. Father and Mother came, and the Forsythes, of course.

Kitty was right. There was no MacDonnell way with

weddings. "Only our families," Morag said, and was married by special license in a little chapel great-great-great-grandfather MacDonnell had built, when he built Barn House. It was in a locked-up attic. It had not been used since Catholic Emancipation and had to be redone for the occasion and the altar given legal ecclesiastical standing—whatever that is—by the bishop. Even Patton did not know it was there, and he had served the family all his life. Emily called herself Michelangelo and supervised its redecoration. The day after the bishop completed his consecrating exercises, Father Mackay brought the Garretts' Protestant minister, the Reverend Raymond Davey, a Presbyterian reconciler among the clergy, to "say a wee prayer over the place," and Patton sat in the chapel and, he told me, "said a wee prayer myself, ma'am." When all was done that it was apparently thought necessary to be done so that God might be present in His own House, they were married, by Father Mackay and the Reverend Mr. Davey, and to this day whether they are Catholic or Protestant I do not know. It was Carrach's joy in the presence of his children that was my joy then.

Agnes and Willy did not come. There was an exchange of letters that grieved Carrach. First, they could not come because, with Alasdar and Buckley away, Willy could not leave the plant. In the end, though, Agnes wrote a letter that filled her father with pain and admiration. She said:

I am content to be your daughter, but I think you must be sensible about this, for your own sake, but also for Hyndman's sake. I once worked as a spinner in your mill. There are girls in Carrig who remember me well, but as "Cassie's girl," not your daughter. It's enough for me that you came to me. I do not need these people to know who I am. I know and you know who I am. There is no need for Hyndman, who has endured his humiliation in silence, to have it made public in the village he lives in and you own. I could come with the boys and leave Willy to his work. He wants me to. But for these reasons, I will not come. What is most important is that I know you will understand.

He was grieved, but he understood. He was also sentimental, and without explanation to Patton, had four chairs reserved in the chapel with place cards on them that said only Agnes, Willy, William, John. Nobody asked questions about the cards on the chairs. Something much more horrifying happened that shattered his joy and came like a foretaste of the winding-down I saw in so many of his attitudes.

The service had begun. There was no guard on the house, for no one thought it necessary. All the servants, Catholic and Protestant, were in the back chairs of the chapel, all in their Sunday best and all sharing in the happiness of the two families, Catholic and Protestant.

The Reverend Mr. Davey, looking in his Geneva gown and white banns like a figure from a Dutch painting, had stepped forward beside Father Mackay to ask his question: "Who giveth this woman to be married to this man?"

"I do," Carrach said, and stepped back.

The rustling and murmuring began among the servants. Carrach glanced over his shoulder, and the pleasure on his face died. He looked suddenly old and haggard. Father Mackay looked down the aisle, and anger spread on his benign face. We all looked around.

That woman was walking slowly up the little aisle. The sparrow hawk had come to her daughter's wedding.

The ceremony went on. Carrach turned back to face the priest and minister. Our darling children knew nothing but that at last they were being married. All eyes were front again, except Alasdar's and mine.

The woman walked slowly up the aisle, her eyes searching. She was dressed in black, with a black veil on her head and a black band on her throat.

"What in Christ's name . . ." Alasdar said.

I took his hand. "Be quiet."

She was searching for a place to sit. She sat in the chair marked Agnes. She picked up the place card and read it. She held it in her hand and sat in silence through the service. Now and then she glanced at the card, but almost always her eyes bored like drills into the back of Carrach's head.

The murmuring among the servants died, but the nervous unease in the place was tangible; it rippled through the little chapel like an infection. It burned in me like a fever. I took Alasdar's hand to restrain him. I held it through the service to restrain myself.

Father Mackay pronounced the benediction. He made the sign of the cross on their foreheads. His face had on it the stillness of fear. "Go in the love and sight of God," he said gently. *"Go in peace,"* he said with great firmness, and stared at the woman.

She stood up as Morag turned. She darted into the aisle, clutching the Agnes card. Morag stood as if paralyzed. The woman rushed to the door of the chapel and barred the way.

"I hope," she said in a shrill voice, "she has more peace and love than I ever had."

Then she turned and ran. We heard her clumping on the attic stairs. Patton hurried after her.

I heard Carrach say to Morag, "Go now, dear, Patton will see to it." Dear, faithful Patton.

In the drawing room, the strain was like wire. Emily said to me, "Is Court House well-covered?"

"Yes. Why?"

"I think I'll burn her and it tonight."

Mr. Buckley felt no strain, only curiosity. "Who in God's name was that?" he asked me.

"That, Mr. Buckley," Emily said quickly, "was my sister."

"Oh," he said, not quite clear about things. "I never saw her before. Does she live here too? Nobody ever mentioned her."

"No, she does not live here. She lives in a special house, some distance away. We speak of her only at night." Emily's anger was running away with her tongue. Her face betrayed it.

"Oh," Mr. Buckley said, "oh." He wasn't sure what to say next. I think he was not sure what to think. "Oh," he said. "A special house? That's it, is it?"

Tomas was standing behind Emily's shoulder, watching Mr. Buckley's confusion with some sympathy. "The woman you ask about," he said helpfully, "is my father's wife." He lived with it. There was nothing strange about it to him. His father had a wife who was a stranger and not too well in the head and was kept at Court House in considerable comfort. But his family, his father and mother and sisters and aunt—they were here, in this house; at home.

Mr. Buckley looked hard at Tomas, searching, it seemed, for some sign that no one was, as he sometimes put it, "joshing" him. There was no such sign in Tomas's face. Mr. Buckley looked at Emily. He looked at me. He glanced about the room. Maybe he was searching for something to say or somewhere to go.

"I see," he said, "I see." He looked unhappy. He looked again at Emily, then at me. Then he looked across the room at Kitty and his son, who were talking intently with Edward and Morag. He looked at them thoughtfully for a long time, and we waited, for it was not a moment to walk away.

In a sick voice he said, "I see," and seemed to shrink.

Six

The days that followed were black. Our guests hurried away.
Kitty and Buckley lingered a few days and went home. "I'm
so afraid of her," Kitty said. "What will she do?" Only
Alasdar remained. Carrach limped about the lawns, and
Alasdar and Tomas walked with him. Often they walked arm
in arm. Often all four of us walked together, Alasdar's hand
in his father's, Tomas's in Alasdar's, mine in my son's. We
talked very little, but we were together. The days passed
quickly, the nights slowly. And as slowly, Carrach recovered.

"But it's a foretaste," he said, and having said it, seemed
to gather his spirit. "I will not cower in a hole in the
ground," he said. "I will not walk away from what I have
waited so long to do."

Alasdar and Tomas spent more and more time together,
talking about America, about Harvard, about doctors. At first
I thought little of it. They had always had a peculiar frank
closeness that made them sharp with one another, but without
intent to hurt. Now their friendship was warmer. It seemed to
me that Alasdar was cultivating it and Tomas responded like
a boy who at last was finding something he had always hoped
for.

There were conferences with Robert Garrett. Would they
fight the election for which the writs had now been issued?
Father and Mother came again, up from Goleen now that
parliament had been prorogued.

"No," Father said, "it will be vicious. Foul. With Pinkertons hanging over your head, you can't fight. She will find a way to cover you in dirt."

"I did not kill him, Hugh," Carrach said. "Your Fenians did."

"We're not talking about facts, only about the use they'll make of dirt."

"No," Alasdar said, "you can't subject Isabella to this sort of thing."

"Yes," said Robert Garrett. "He should fight. We have to beat them, dirt and all."

"Yes," Carrach said, and as I listened to them, all my rage grew till I felt it in me like a demon.

"We will not live that way," I said rationally. "We shall not run from anything," I shouted irrationally. "Do not use me to make your father less than he is."

Carrach said quietly, "I shall fight it and I shall win it, Alasdar."

"And if you win it, what will you have won?"

"Mostly, I think, myself," Carrach said sadly. I did not know at what cost that might be done.

The day Alasdar left, Carrach said to him, "When I win, will you come home again and celebrate with us?"

"Win or lose, we'll all come home to you."

I shall always come home to you, he had said to me once. I hid from him in my room, and he came to me.

"I shall always come home to you," he said, and closed the door.

The day after Morag's wedding, that woman began her horse-riding antics again. She rode at twilight, like an apparition. She shut herself up in Court House after young Mac-Neice, who called on her at all hours and was the talk of the town and a gnawing worry to us, went off and married. "She's out again. Something is going to happen."

"I shall drive her off our land with a horse whip," I said in my fury. "The articles of separation are supposed to protect you from molestation."

"Do nothing," Carrach said. "People see. They judge. It's a kind of persecution, and persecution turns stomachs." And, he said, with a sardonic grin, "My limp is an election asset. I shall use it."

"The woman isn't in her right mind. Only a crazy woman would start this again."

"I think probably she is out of her mind, but it's best to do nothing."

"Why? You have plenty of evidence. Houston would sign her away. You could have her committed."

"I'm afraid life doesn't work that way. You know that. Has she something from Pinkertons? She told Hugh so, but we don't know. Do we want it claimed that that's why we want her committed? To get her out of the way? When MacNeice was visiting her at Court House, what did he get from her? If we commit her, and he got something from her, think of the effect if they claimed that as the reason why we put her away."

"But this is not why you won't do it, is it, Carrach?"

"No, this isn't why. Isabella, I married her. She bore the children. She would have to be raving mad and a danger to our lives before I could face doing it. She's done crazy things, I know, childish things. She's a childish creature. Maybe she's mad, but she's not mad enough. Not yet."

So, it wasn't fear of her that restrained him. It was his own decency. "We'll be sorry," I said, but there was nothing I could do to change his mind. I tried. He would not be moved.

"Leave her," he said. "In the end it will all come back on her."

But I rode out and followed her. When she rode east across our land, where did she go? She turned north and west, and as the darkness grew deeper, climbed the back tracks around the base of Knockagh Hill, which rose like a halved pap on the edge of the estate, the north side sloping down to green fields, the south side of a cliff eight hundred feet high and sheer to its base, where a sally garden flourished. I sat back from her and thought of her with murder in my mind. It would be easy to ride her off the edge. Horse and rider would fall into the sally garden and lie hidden by the trees. They might not be found for months. But horses' hoof prints tell their story. If I had to do it, that was not the way.

She sat on her horse a little way back from the edge of the cliff and looked down on us. What was she thinking? Oh, certainly of us. Of the destruction she hoped to bring on us? No doubt. She sat there, looking down on us, and I think she imagined herself to be some angel of destruction gloating on the landscape she intended to lay waste. I turned my horse away and came home, but my fury raged and my mind was dark.

"You missed dinner," Carrach said. "Where were you riding in the dark?"

"I followed her. She sits on the edge of Knockagh, looking down on us."

"Never," he said, "never, never, never do that again."

Yes, it was a vicious election. The very viciousness of it brought out all the quiet power in Carrach. We sat on his platforms, Tomas, Edward, Morag, Robert Garrett, Emily, and myself. It was too dangerous and too frightening to bring Isa with us as we had once brought Tomas. "Ireland," Tomas said reasonably, "is not a very reasonable place, is it? I wish Alasdar was here. He's not afraid of them."

No, it was not a very reasonable place. Carrach limped to the front of his platforms. "This is my Catholic daughter," he said, "and this is my Protestant son-in-law, her husband. We could all live like this in Ulster. And this," and he limped across the front of the platforms, "is a bigot's gift from the wilder Orangemen of this constituency." It always brought a cheer.

But soon it brought less encouraging things. "Will youse interjuse us t'yer Spanish hoore?" a voice began it.

Carrach stood silent for a long time. The audience fell silent, stilled by his long stillness.

Then he said, "I knew this election would be fought by foul means." He spoke very quietly. "I decided to fight it in spite of that. What I am fighting for is worth fighting for. Now," he said, "if the gentleman who asked that question is small, let him skulk in the crowd, hiding. But if he is not, I wonder, since his size must make him feel quite safe, if he would show his courage and come down here?"

A big man pushed his way out of the crowd and strutted three-quarters of the length of the aisle. He stopped. "Am I big enough for yis?" he asked.

"Oh, quite, quite," Carrach said amiably. "Now, gentlemen, you will note as I walk to the steps here, that I am a cripple. A man, very like this man, organized an accident that crippled me for life." He was in the aisle, limping slowly, talking slowly. "He did so because he did not share my opinions. For that, he crippled me. He did it from hiding, as this large man asked his question from hiding." He was looking out over his audience, left and right, and they watched him, puzzled and fascinated by this strange electioneering. "This large man is no braver than the man who crippled me." He was standing broadside to the man, speaking now to the people on the right side of the hall. The fingers of his right hand were pointing to the man's grinning face. Suddenly they shot into the idiotic face, into the eyes, and Carrach, as the man clutched his eyes, lashed at his stomach, and as he bent, at his face, again and again. The man went down. He lay without movement or sound on the floor. Carrach limped back to the platform.

"I said I would fight this election," he said calmly, "and by the Lord God, I shall."

They heard him out.

He won, that night. It was a brief victory. Within a week an anonymous pamphlet appeared. It was scrupulously accurate in detail. It bore the name of no author, no printer, no political party. It was merely a statement, credited to "the American private detective agency, Pinkertons," of what had taken place, in Providence, in Cambridge. It made no accusations, offered no opinions. It was the sensation of the entire campaign. It appeared in people's hands at meetings, on the streets, even in churches. Where it came from was a mystery to everyone who handled it.

"Where did you get it?"

"A fella give me one."

"What fellow?"

"Ah niver seen him before in me life."

The papers discussed it, condemned it and those "who resorted to these gutter tactics," then attacked Carrach for his views. He made no attempt to refute it. He blazed like a furnace, no longer fingered his button, no longer spoke in measured terms but pounded the table before him, thundered, did not talk politics but "civilization" and "the way we want to live and are not allowed to live." He denounced hatred, bigotry, prejudice. He sang the eloquent praises of fellowship, of mutual respect, of "hope for Ulster." It was not a political campaign. He had become an evangelist. At no time in the weeks that followed did he mention the name of the sitting member, MacNeice. He behaved as though there was no election, but a mission, a revival.

Filth poured down on our heads. Men brought in from far places stood in his audiences with placards held high:

WHO MURDERED MCCARTHY?
WHERE DO YOU KEEP YOUR WIFE, MACDONNELL?
SHOW US THE SPANISH HOORE
HOW MANY BASTARDS HAS MACDONNELL?
HOW MUCH DID YOU PAY FOR BELLA?

and tributes of that quality.

Throughout the whole campaign, not one of them mentioned that woman's name.

Emily said to me once, "I wonder what else MacNeice got from her?" and when I said nothing, "When we were young, she had a dirty mind. She thought about nothing but getting Hugh to bed."

I do not know. I do not want to know. What I know is enough. Harold MacNeice got from her what his family wanted, and knowing what he might have paid for it was no comfort to us. But the visits that were the talk and laughter of the town were all explained and our anxieties about them justified: whatever else that pair did at Court House, they plotted together against us. MacNeice, the member hoping to return to Westminster, disassociated himself from the pamphlet. Carrach, with a bitter smile, read the terms of the ambiguous disclaimer in the papers: "I refuse to be associated with this unfair and ungentlemanly revelation of the domestic affairs of my opponent."

The papers also reported that, "Mrs. Elizabeth MacDonnell of Court House, Carrig, has refused to meet reporters to discuss the contents of the pamphlet or to confirm its alleged facts."

No. She had already given it all to Harold MacNeice for just such a time as this.

From that first week, almost every meeting ended in a spreading fight. The crowds grew larger, the fighting fiercer, the police more impotent. MacNeice's meetings smaller. The sport was at the MacDonnell meetings.

We sat on the platforms, on farm carts in fields, always there, always silent, and always grim and frightened. But Carrach, to us and to most of the people in his audiences, and certainly to the newspapers, seemed to grow larger, his passion more passionate, his courage greater. We were driven from platforms and farm carts by showers of—empty—whiskey bottles, beer bottles and—full—jars of MacDonnell's jams. Emily sat, or stood firm behind a wooden placard of her own, which she used as a shield. It said:

I AM MCCARTHY'S SISTER
I VOTE FOR MACDONNELL

Carrach was struck on the forehead by one of our jars of jam and fell unconscious. That was the worst fighting of the whole campaign. It spread to the country roads and left us alone to attend to our wounded. After that, the police, frightened by the nearness of Carrach's escape from serious injury and perhaps death, suddenly shed their impotence and formed a barrier between the platform and those who came to fight and inflict injury on us and on others.

There was a fury in the air I had never known before. It had many faces, grinning, laughing, snarling, howling, sneering ugly faces that boiled and merged before us like an ocean of hate. It continued even to the doors of the polling stations, and sometimes inside them.

It stopped.

A great calm settled on the countryside.

Even the stillness was frightening as we waited for the counting of the votes. It was a silence hard to assess. Carrach assessed it.

"They're struck dumb," he said.

The new member of parliament for Carrig was Carrach Tomas MacDonnell—by a huge majority.

The *Belfast News Letter* said:

> The people of Carrig constituency did not vote for Carrach MacDonnell's politics. He did not offer them any. They voted for his quality and courage as a man and the quality and courage of his household against a hooligan campaign of foulness that brought only shame to the Unionist cause. The people voted for Carrach MacDonnell's decency.

"Perhaps," Carrach said, unconvinced, "perhaps," and after all the clangor and struggle and strain, seemed suddenly to have no interest in the affair. Struck by inertia as though by a debilitating disease, he said, "Will you cable the children, dear, and bring them all home?"

"For a celebration?" I knew there was no celebration in him.

"No, no." He was staring sightlessly into the flames of the

library fire. "No. Just to see them. I think I need to see them. Don't you?"

While we waited for them, one thing was accomplished.

Carrach did not go to Westminster. He showed no interest in going, spoke not one word on politics, declined to go to London, or Dublin, or Belfast to meet Parnell, who had gone back to parliament with at his back seventy-five members of the Home Rule faction. Carrach was tired. It was weariness of the body and weariness of the mind and spirit. Now that the campaign was over and won, it filled him with disgust.

"They soiled you," he said. "I soiled you by running. I disgust myself."

Point by point he tore himself down. "Everything flows from my actions," he said. "If I didn't love that woman, why did I marry her? I don't think I even liked her. I took her to breed her. That was all. Alasdar was the only object of that marriage. There had to be an heir. Why?"

He was digging up the roots of my family obsession. I had given myself to the family with such a passion since the day I walked into Barn House; he was asking, Why?

"I ought to have refused to marry," he said. "I ought to have waited. You came in the end, didn't you?"

His tenderness and care for me had never been greater. It was in practicing that care for me that one thing was accomplished. "You must have good sound help always at your elbow," he said, and negotiated with Robert and Edward Garrett for Edward's transfer from Robert's company to ours. But I noticed that in the definition of responsibilities on which Edward sensibly insisted, some of Carrach's most important functions passed to Edward.

He was a much more than competent young man, and I didn't mind this new arrangement. What worried me was what I believed to be Carrach's assumption behind it—that life for him was rapidly winding itself down. His limp grew worse, he was losing weight, he spoke wearily, he could not sustain himself for long when he made love to me—scarcely once a week—and his ironic eye was turned again on himself. "I feel nauseated all day," he said once. "I think it begins in the morning when I look in my shaving mirror."

He paid little attention to business and spent hours every day with Isa and Tomas. His talk with them was most often of Alasdar and of me. "Papa will be home soon and Mama is always here," he told Isa. "Remember," he told Tomas again and again, "you can always turn to Alasdar if you need to."

He is waiting to die. He does not say so, but he believes he is dying. He must not die.

I shall not let him die.

He has placed Edward in position to assume the headship of the companies. Carrach has no more interest in politics, no interest in Ulster, no interest in his theories about Ulstermen as Hebrideans. "I am sorry for them," he says. "Generation after generation they will be the same." He has washed his mind of them.

I must find ways to restore in him his belief in life, even his own life. We ride the boundaries of the estate. He rides with difficulty now. He will not ride in the late afternoon. She will be there, defiling our land, goading us, taunting us with her presence, noting his decline, defying him in his weakness.

He says, "I would like to build a high wall all around our boundaries, with only a great door in it and the door barred and locked."

I cry to Robert Garrett, to my father and mother, to the Forsythes, "Come and be with him. Talk with him of everything." They come, they talk; he talks softly, listlessly, and always of the past. "Ireland is the past that never ends," he says. "It disgusts me, for they prefer the past and its miseries to the future and its efforts. They prefer past wrongs they can hate to a future they don't know and have to build." He muttered about it, to himself, to them, to me. "What about you, Tomas?" he said. "Have you written another letter to Alasdar about America?" As though he had a purpose. Sometimes his eyes were wet.

"He is dying by his own will," they say.

I shall not let him die.

"Carrach, live for me."

"I have lived for you since you were a child, why should I change that?"

But it is an evasion. He did not say, Yes, I want to live, I shall live. He is thin, bent, gaunt. He won his victory. There are victories that destroy. They cost too much.

My own guilt burdens me. What have I done to help bring to his mind and spirit this weight of hopelessness? Was not I the meaning and joy of his life, and am I this no longer? I do not know what or how much I have contributed to his state of mind. I go over it again and again till my head aches. Is it Alasdar? What did I do in America to sow some seed that is growing now? What did I say? Why is he pushing Tomas toward Alasdar, as if to hand him over? But I showed no sign in America, said not one word that could be understood or misunderstood. What is it, love? I ask him. What have I done to you? Done to me? he says, you have brought to me everything that is good in my life. I cannot argue that with him. I have to be so discreet, so careful of his thoughts. Don't leave me, I say. Not willingly, he says, but we do not choose the place or the time, do we, my love? Is it exhaustion from that fearful election? Despair that Ulster will always be the same? The dispersal of the family? If it is that, what am I? Not enough, now. That strikes at my heart like a bill hook. It strikes, too, at my conscience, for if I am struck down by the thought that I may no longer be the very core of his existence, what must he think and feel that I have fought to keep the children bound to us, have wanted Alasdar to be always near me—am I maybe, in his mind, an Anna Davidson without her courage to act? What more would he need, after all these troubles, than to have this in his mind?

Then the children came.

Kitty was swollen with pride and her child. Morag was pregnant. New life was everywhere.

"I took right away," Kitty said.

"Edward was very efficient," Morag said with one of her smiles.

Alasdar was silent and watchful. "He's very ill," he said.

"He's improved a lot," I told him. "He has waited for you with great longing."

"And you?"

"That is enough, Alasdar," I said, angry and guilty at my own joy in seeing him. "Do not destroy your father. *Help* him."

They spent hours together every day, talking, and always Tomas was there, and often Isa. Carrach was happy. He touched us all, lovingly, and said we had brought nothing but joy into his life. He held me in his arms in the presence of the children and said, "Isabella has been our strong anchor. She has loved us all with her whole heart. Never forget that."

The next day, without announcement, and having once again declined to come, Agnes and the boys drove from the station. Carrach was not to be contained. His joy was like wine in excess. "Patton," he said, I think without giving it any consideration, "this is my daughter Agnes. You remember her mother, Cassie. These are my grandsons." And Patton looked stunned and did not know what to say and hurried to the servants' hall to share his news and his astonishment. "The slate is clean," Carrach said, "and, God, what a relief that is." But whatever we do, we touch the lives of others. The slate was clean for Carrach. It was dirtied in public for Hyndman. The word spread like fire in a field of wheat.

"Your house is bigger than our house," William said, and took John to get lost in the servants' quarters.

The house was filled with laughter. Each day he looked better. There was color in his gaunt face. His limp had life in it. When Father and Mother and the Forsythes came, they marveled at the change in him, at his laughter, at his talk. It was always family talk. "Do you remember when—" But Father said to me, "Keep Alasdar here as long as you can. That will help." Carrach was turning a corner.

The night of our great family banquet he was closer to gaiety than he had been for months. "Next year," he said, "we are going to America again. We must go now to see them every year. We have grandchildren all over the place."

We danced that night to the music of local fiddlers. Kitty stood off from Buckley and looked endearingly ridiculous. Morag and Edward were like young lovers, which was what they were. Carrach danced with Agnes, with Kitty, with Morag, with Emily—and with me. It was awkward. His thick-soled boot made it ridiculous. He laughed at his efforts and tried to do a little jig. The fiddlers laughed with him and applauded him.

Alasdar danced with me. "I was riding," he said. "I saw that woman riding to the north of us. What is she doing on our land?" He was angry.

"Say nothing," I said. "Leave it alone. He's happy."

"Why was she there?" he persisted.

"Leave it alone. You will do nothing or say nothing to bring him sadness. If you persist, then go back to America."

It had rained very heavily that day. I had things to see to at Garden House and had not seen to them. Presently I said I would ride over and get them done.

"I'll come for you," Carrach said. "I'll give you an hour and ride over."

Ride over? He no longer enjoyed riding. Why would he ride at night?

"It's pouring," Alasdar said. "You stay out of the wet and I'll ride over for her."

"No, no. I shall go for her. I have something to talk to her about."

"Your father will come for me." I wanted none of that. Carrach felt well. He was happy. Nothing else mattered. I rode alone to Garden House. What did he have to talk to me about that could not be talked of in bed?

Perhaps it was an hour later. I was still busy. The rain had stopped. I heard the shot. Poachers, I thought, and thought no more of it. This was not a night to bother about poachers. Then my work was finished. I waited. He did not come. Poachers? I wondered. But poachers work with snares, not with guns. We have only rabbits and birds, and you do not shoot birds at night. Yet someone fired a shot. The sound had come from the little wood. How long ago? I could not now be sure. Some time ago. Carrach was very late. He was never late.

I asked one of the girls who was looking after the guests at Garden House, "Did you hear a shot?"

"Yes, ma'am," she said, "maybe from the trees."

I went outside.

"Don't go looking by yerself," the girl said.

But now I was afraid. I walked to the bridle path through the little wood and stared into it, afraid to move under the trees. Then I heard his horse, and panic whipped me. I ran up the bridle path, my face struck by the low branches. His horse was standing, restless, by the entrance from the meadow beyond.

He was lying on the sodden ground.

It was raining again.

He was dead.

♔ Seven ♔

I do not remember much.

I remember horror, terror, and desolation. I must ride for Alasdar. I ran down the bridle path.

But I cannot leave my darling lying on the wet ground. I ran back to him to shelter him from the pouring rain. The rain must not pour down on him. It ran down his face into his open mouth. I was like a rabbit trapped by dogs, go, stay, go, stay, turn, turn, turn, and he was dead, in the rain. I do not know what I did. They did not tell me. I do not ask.

They say I did not speak again to any of them for a month. I know myself. I know I must keep control. They say I wandered the house day in, night out, searching for Carrach, opening doors, looking into rooms, saying only *No?* as if to say, Is he not here? But I do not know, I do not remember.

I know it was at Goleen that I came again to my right mind. Alasdar and Tomas took me there. They say I wandered the land, riding, searching for my beloved Carrach in all the places we knew together. They say they followed me wherever I went, watching over me. Then one day, on Mount Gabriel, where we had never been together, I said, "Carrach is dead. Take me home." That is what they told me.

But I do not remember. I do not want to know. What did he want to talk to me about that dreadful night? Was it some pain I caused him? Some wrong I did him? The wild anguish runs deep in me, for I shall never know.

The police say he was murdered by someone he knew; that

he sat on his horse at the mouth of the bridle path, talking to someone he knew. The hoof prints tell them this, they say. The murderer was on the fringe of the trees among the deadfall and last autumn's leaves, leaving no trace. The murderer shot him through the heart and he fell to the wet ground. I saw him on the sodden ground. I do not know these other things; only the police know these other things.

But I know that my darling lay on the wet ground, dead, in the rain, and the rain ran down his face into his open mouth.

The day we came back to Barn House a storm was blowing across the Lough. I walked down to the shore. The rain drove in clouds. The trees behind me bent and whipped in the gale. The rain soaked me, the wind tore at me. Sometimes, far out, the clouds opened and the sun came through, shining on the gray and black water like molten silver. Then it was shut off like a light, or it died by inches, gray and desolate. Alasdar and Tomas and Emily stood back in the trees and watched over me. Alasdar and Tomas—were they always together now? What did they think I would do to myself? The sea was slate gray now, and raging, the heavy sky was low and rain and cloud lay on the water only a little way from the shore. The little boats strained at their moorings as if they were pleading for mercy to the maker of storms.

Somebody would plead for mercy. I closed my eyes and turned my face up to the rain and opened my mouth. The rain ran down my face and into my open mouth. I could see him, lying there on the wet ground, dead, in the rain, and the rain ran down his face into his open mouth. Somebody would plead for mercy.

Who?

The storm that grew in me grew slowly, but it grew daily.

Alasdar watched over me and Tomas seemed almost always to be with him, like a dependant. Alasdar declared no love. He stayed and the months passed and he was tender and kind and I was grateful. But it seemed that now I had no feeling for him beyond fondness and gratitude. Wherever we went, whatever we did, if it was possible he brought Tomas and Isa with us. When she asked questions he could not answer, he said, "You'll have to ask Mama that one, dear." There was a closeness that was a source of strength to me. We were a little family. Alasdar, like Carrach, was all patience. Was there nothing that could exhaust his patience? He was patient too with Tomas, who went often to Carrach's grave and rushed home from it into my arms and into Alasdar's arms. "Help me," he cried to Alasdar.

"I'll always be near," Alasdar said, and held him.

"Alasdar," Tomas said one day, "I do not love Ireland."

"I love Ireland," Alasdar said, "I love the land, the skies, the seas around her. But I will never live here again."

"That is what I mean," Tomas said. "Tell me more about America."

That filled me with dread. Alasdar would leave again. Tomas would one day leave. He dreamed of America. I would go with Emily to Garden House, but I would be alone in the world, without Carrach, without Alasdar, without Tomas.

"Do not talk about America," I said.

And one day I asked, "What will you do about Isa?"

"When I go back I shall take her with me," Alasdar said, and did not explain, but he looked at me as if to see what was in my face, in my head, in my heart.

I was afraid to ask what was to become of me, for I had been gone from him in my silence and had been distant when I returned from it and he did not speak to me of love. A great desolation settled in me, like a solid piece of my own body. Once I loved Garden House. Once I told Carrach we would live there. But I could not live there without him or near the wood where he was slaughtered, and the storm grew in me. Someone robbed me of my love.

Carrach left Garden House to me, knowing I loved it. He was a far richer man than I had known, and left me generously provided for. Garden House and its environs were the least part of his provision for me. There was a clause in his will making provision for Isa, but it had a condition attached: that Alasdar would henceforward attend to all my needs, "protect and care for Isabella, who has been Isa's mother almost since her birth." And there was a further condition respecting Isa's inheritance: that Alasdar should be a father to Tomas "so long as he has need of one." He left me also the key to an iron box that sat in Pollard's office. I was to ask for the contents of the box when it pleased me to do so. In all the anguish of his going, I forgot about it and did not ask.

He left Court House to Hugh, my father. Alasdar commented on that. "There's his irony in it," he said. "He got that woman from Hugh and he left Hugh to deal with her." He confirmed the settlement he made with her and added to it a little "for her material comfort," on condition that, if my father required it of her, she would move from Court House at his request and find for herself another place to live.

We were all provided for, including Emily and Agnes. He left Barn House and its lands to Morag.

"He understood everything," Alasdar said, and I did not ask what he meant. My Carrach was not here. I did not care what Alasdar meant. I had no mind for his riddles.

But there were other riddles. The police did not solve them. What would they discover if they solved them? Who killed Carrach MacDonnell? The Orange? Some MacNeice lackey? What gales would blow if the answer to their riddle was an answer nobody wanted to hear?

But I wanted to hear it.

Now it was known far and wide that Agnes was not Hyndman's but Carrach's daughter. She had come to celebrate the election victory. She had come as one of us, with her sons. She had not gone near Hyndman. Oh, that Carrach, they said in the town, he knew how to handle women. And Cassie! Who would have thought fine upright Cassie, old Mrs. MacDonnell's servant-friend, was opening her thighs to young Carrach? Morag got the talk from her friends. They're saying it was Hyndman, she said. Was it Hyndman?

I rode to Boneybefore. Hyndman did not answer my knocking.

"He niver answers the knocker now, mistress," the woman next door said. "Ye jist have ta walk in." And she stood, watching. Carrach's Spanish hoore had come to see Hyndman, who killed Carrach.

What did I care now what they thought or said? I would live out my days among them and never know them or need them. They liked me once. Carrach and Alasdar and Emily said they loved me. They voted for Carrach because he was brave and good and honorable, and I was "ma'am" and "Mistress Isabella" and there was no blame. But back in their minds there was the knowledge: She's not his wife; he's her uncle and she's his fancy woman. The months had passed since the election and their emotions had time to settle and their votes to be reconsidered, for he was dead now and the shelter of his own time and his mother's time was no longer over me. Mistress, she called me, but I knew in the face that looked across the little fence at me that without him I was only his leftover woman, the mother of the bastard I conceived with him on my belly in America. Niece, yes; but his Spanish hoore.

I opened Hyndman's door and went in. He was sitting by the little open grate, crouching, his shoulders bent, his legs together and pulled back at the side of the very low chair he sat on, and his hands were clasped together in his lap. He did not look up. His face was yellow and shadowed by the flames of the fire. He looked satanic with his black hair and his pie-bald face and eyes that had the light of the fire in them.

I said, "Hyndman."

He paid me no heed.

"Hyndman."

Nothing about him said he was aware of me. Nothing about him moved. "Was it you, Hyndman?" I said, and perhaps he heard me; perhaps the wall heard me. He was as still and stony and silent as the wall.

"If it was you, Hyndman, and I can prove it, I won't go to the police with anything I know. I'll come here and I'll kill you myself. Do you hear me?"

There was no sound, no movement. *"I will kill you myself,"* I said. But when I turned to the door, my rage drained from me. This poor creature could not kill anyone. He was not here at all.

Then I heard his voice, clear and strong. "Hoore," he said.

I turned on him with my riding crop ready. He was still; still staring into the fire; still as a stone; crouching.

A hundred yards out of the villiage, Alasdar was waiting. "Where have you been?" he said.

"Go to hell."

"For you, I've been there."

He had been here at Barn House with me for five months now. He had said nothing; nothing like that, nothing of love; only kind things, helpful things, things that help to rebuild the mind and the spirit. And I had been in his company most of every day and had scarcely looked in his face.

"You went to Hyndman, didn't you?"

"Yes."

"You accused him, didn't you?"

"I said 'if.' "

"If *what*?"

"If I found he did it, I would kill him myself."

"Don't do it again. Don't go near him again. Have you heard that?"

"Yes."

"Come home." He said it sharply, as though he had every right, as though he had taken me over. As though it was his place and would not be questioned.

I felt contented, riding beside him. In these months I had felt no contentment. That night we sat with Tomas by the library fire. They talked of the future, Tomas's future, medical schools and their merits. They talked as though Alasdar had rights; a father's rights, willed to him in Carrach's testament. Tomas talked and listened as though he knew he was Alasdar's inheritance. As a son.

"Tomas," Alasdar said, "leave us, please. I want to talk with your mother."

But he did not talk with me. He said nothing. I think he had something to say to me and decided not to say it. He stretched his legs toward the fire and closed his eyes. Sometimes he opened them long enough to put a coal on the fire. Then he rang for Patton.

"Patton," he said, "I think we'll have a glass of warm milk before we go to bed."

"Yes, sir."

"With a little whiskey in it."

"Yes, sir."

"And, Patton, I think we'll make it a habit. Every night. As you always did."

"Yes, sir."

He did not speak while we sipped our warm milk. When we had finished it he said, "It's bedtime. Let's look at Isa and then we'd better get to sleep."

She was sound asleep. He was smiling. He took my hand and bent over her. "I love you," he whispered, and kissed her forehead and rose and said, "and you too. Now, get to bed." That was all.

The sparrow hawk was still riding. I had to stop that woman. She was riding over his grave. And Father came to settle some things about Court House. This was the time to do it.

"I'll deal with her," he said, "I want you to keep well away from her." He had served her notice to quit and she would not.

He rode out to meet her and said almost nothing to me of what passed. Perhaps very little passed. "She was not quite sober. She called me Black Hughie and laughed at me," he said, "and she said Morag could get an injunction to stop her, but how much more bad publicity could the MacDonnells stand? 'Taking their mother to court' was how she put it. In the meanwhile, leave it. There are other means to deal with her."

One of them was to sell Court House, unless I wanted it. If I wanted it, he would give it to me and I could evict her. I hated the house and all its associations. "Then I shall have electricity put in and increase the price and get rid of the place," Father said, and made all the arrangements to have the work done. "If she doesn't move out, she'll be extremely uncomfortable."

She did not move out. Father and Mother came from London now and then to observe the progress made by the contractors. It was slow progress. It was persecution, the woman wrote to Pollard, to Father, to Alasdar. She wrote to Alasdar every day. She rode over our land every day. She was confident, arrogant, and abusive. "Take me to court," she wrote Alasdar, "let the whole world see what the MacDonnells are prepared to do to their own mother."

She was drinking. We learned this from the workmen. But she rode every day. "It's very hard on the workmen," Clugston, the contractor, complained. "She's half drunk half the time. The place is dangerous." Pollard appealed to her, threatened her, but she would not move. "Take me to court and let the reporters hear your case," she wrote to him.

Then Clugston came one day to Barn House carrying a long paper parcel. Alasdar had taken Tomas and Isa to Belfast for the day. The man would see no one but Mister Hugh. "Not you, ma'am," he said. "Only your father." Father was riding. The man waited. He had two hours to wait. He would leave no message. "If I have to wait all day, I'll wait," he said stubbornly.

For such a long wait, whatever Clugston came about took little time. They were in the library together for no more than ten minutes. When he left, Father sent for me. He was pale with anger and distress. The long parcel was lying on Carrach's desk. It had been opened and the paper was loosely wrapped about the object it covered.

"I think," Father said, "you'd better hear this sitting down." And he added, "And you'd better get a firm grip on yourself, for you have a shock coming."

It was about Court House. It had to be about Court House; Clugston had no other business with us, and Father owned the place, was the only one the fellow would talk to. I watched Father as he took one layer of paper off the long object. Already, I felt sick.

"This thing," he said, "was found under the floorboards of a cupboard at Court House." He went on unrolling sheets of brown paper. "From its condition I would say it had been there a long time. It is rusted, but it has been used since it was first put under the floor, and not very long ago." The paper was off. My father held a gun in his hands.

At first I had no feelings except nausea. I could not think. I could not look at the gun. It had been missing from our gun rack for a long, long time; since before Carrach brought me back from America.

"Look at it," Father said. "Is it Carrach's?"

"I have looked at it. Yes, it's his."

Feeling came slowly as my mind came back to me. It came with the pain that comes to a sleeping leg when the circulation begins again. It came to my stomach, to my heart, to my head, and a long cry like an animal's cry came out of my mouth.

He took me by the hair on the crown of my head and shook me. "You will keep control of yourself," he said. "I want no bloody nonsense."

"No."

"I shall cope with this," he said. "Do you understand that?"

"Yes."

"Clugston says he has to tell the police. He says if he does not and the workman who found it talks, he will be in very serious trouble. You understand this?"

"Yes." But my mind was working.

"He will tell them in a day or two. He will explain the delay by saying he thought nothing of it at first and then he thought, It was found in a Catholic house and what Catholic keeps concealed arms for any good purpose? Do you hear me?"

"Yes." He was talking to me as though I were a foreigner who did not understand anything.

"You will do nothing," he said, "*nothing*. I will deal with this."

"Yes." But, oh, how fast you will have to be, to be faster than I shall be, I said in my head.

My heart was roaring. Great cries of anguish and of rage were tearing through me, and I strangled them in my throat. The sound of them dying came out of me like the gagging of a mongol. You will have to be quick to be quicker than I shall be, my head said to him, and he could not hear me.

"Do you hear me, Isabella?"

"Yes."

"I loved him too," he said, and I thought he too would cry out.

I rose and put my arms about him and kissed him and said, "Dear Black Hughie. My dear and darling father." And I walked toward the door, holding hard on my heart.

"*Isabella,*" he roared, and came after me. "You will leave it to me," he said, and took me in his arms. "It will be all right, my little one," he said.

"Yes, yes, yes." But my tears would not wait till I reached my room. "I love you. I love Mama. And, oh, how I loved my Carrach," I said and the gates broke and he lifted me and sat down in Carrach's chair and cradled me on his lap in his arms, as he had done when I was a child.

I found the sacking and the cord in the apple loft and tied the sacking to my back under my cloak. Then I rode north-west up toward Knockagh to wait for her. The police would come to see my father about the gun. They would want to see Alasdar. They would want to see me. All we could tell them was that years ago the gun was in our gun rack. Then while we were in America it was not. Now, as we understand it, it was found in Court House, concealed under a cupboard floor. We knew nothing more and could tell them nothing more. I went over it in my head.

"And where can we find Mrs. MacDonnell? Her servant says she went out riding yesterday" (or would it be the day before? It would be according to the day the contractor told them of the gun) "and has not returned."

"And have you searched at the foot of Knockagh's face? In the sally garden? This is where she sat on her horse, planning his murder?"

She would be somewhere behind me now on her weird nightly pilgrimage to look down on us. Part of her destruction had been accomplished. What did she plan for us next? Was it Father? Was I the one? Or the children? Her own, mine, Alasdar's? There was nothing I could not, nothing I did not believe of her. On the back slope of Knockagh I rode into a copse and wrapped my horse's hooves in sacking. There would be no hoof prints to tell that more than one horse came to the cliff tonight. In any case, I would walk to her very silently. She would not know I was there. If she survived for a little while in the sally garden—and that was not likely—she would not know who made her animal bolt in the dark and fail to stop at the cliff's edge.

I was very calm; nervous, but calm. My stomach was nervous, my head was calm. All my thoughts were ordered. Each step in her progress was known to me. Each step in mine was already determined. She would pass this copse. I would watch her pass. In time I would follow her. By the rock outcroppings below the summit, I would leave my horse and walk. I would walk to her very, very stealthily. She would not know I was there. She would not know I was there. She would not know I was there. She would not . . . When they found her and her animal, there would be gashes in his hindquarters but they had nothing to tell. Piercing rocks and branches would make wounds very like the raking gashes of a cattle prod with nails driven through it. Poor beast. It was a pity to have to hurt or kill the beast. Poor dumb inoffensive beast. It was an old animal. It had not wronged us. It had not entered my mind that she might be drunk. We knew. Father had seen it. The contractor said it. I did not think of it. Now I thought of it with a sort of horror and disgust.

She came, *singing*. She was drunk. It is a strange thing: I felt a strong revulsion at the thought of killing a drunken woman. She was Carrach's murderer. Why should I care that she was drunk or sober?

She passed up the slope, always in my sight, and I pulled my horse to the fringe of the copse. As soon as she disappeared on the broad summit, I would ride to the outcroppings. I would watch her. I could not harm her.

But I pulled my horse back in a small panic. There was a rider behind her now. The horse's hooves were not muffled. I heard now and then the clink of iron on stone. And I saw the figure on a rise against the sky. How could I not know him? He taught me to ride when I could barely walk; I knew his seat. He had a glorious arrogance on a horse, and I could not let him soil himself by taking our revenge on this drunken creature.

I kept far behind him till he reached the summit. I could not hurry. My own horse did not like the sacking muffles on his feet. He lifted them high and splayed them wide, like a child walking in his father's boots. He snorted his annoyance. But there was wind in this high place. It came from the south. It blew his snorting over my shoulder. I left him at the outcroppings, tied to a gorse bush.

I did not want my father to kill her. That was for me. Carrach was mine. I bore his son. I raised his children. I loved him as no brother could. My mind had been prepared. I had been able. But the stomach heaved at the thought of killing her when she was drunk. The police could have her. The gun was there if they could use it to hang her. She would be sober then.

He was dismounted, his horse tethered far back on hard ground. They were talking. They must have done much talking while I scrambled forward up the slope over rough ground. He held her reins close to the bit and faced her on the horse's right side. If I came too close and he looked to his left, he could see me against the sky. Her horse was standing broadside to the cliff's edge. I came forward very slowly, stepping high in the heather. But it crackled under my feet. He did not look. She did not look. Yet he at least must hear me.

I stood not more than twenty feet from them. I could run and cry out to stop him. The wind blew their words to me in snatches. Snatches of sentences, odd words, drunken and derisive and bitter tones. Hers were derisive and drunken. How she got this far I could not understand. When I was a child in Andalusia, revenge was normal, but to be acceptable and not to dishonor the avenger, it must be equal. This jeering creature was helpless. My father was Irish, not Andalusian. His voice did not suggest that he cared about such distinctions. She was mounted, he was on foot. Perhaps he thought that made them equal? So far as I could see, he had no weapon but a riding crop. She would ride him down. But she was very drunk. It was a wonder she got this far; it would be a miracle if, unmolested, she got back without falling from her horse. The recklessness and relaxation of drink almost certainly got her here, but exhaustion and nausea were reaching her now.

Suddenly she was sick.

She held the horn of her saddle with both hands and bent in the awful misery of vomiting and was sick on the beast's neck and left shoulder. Again and again she vomited, then retched helplessly, then sat still and voiceless and bent with the awful stillness that follows.

Father was standing back from the horse's head out of the wind and the spew's way, and she sat, slumped, helpless, and motionless. I heard her drunken and sick misery with peculiar clarity. It was like a little cry of despair.

"Why don't you help me, Hughie?"

He stood there. He said nothing. She had done and said all she could. She sat still on the patient old beast, bent like a question mark, her head hanging, and against the sky she looked like death, riding. They stood there, doing nothing, saying nothing, the wind blowing as if to unsettle the fearful tranquillity of their silence.

I know him. He could with ease have driven horse and rider off the cliff. This drunken, vomiting, and spent demon he could not touch, any more than I could. But there were things I could say to her, wanted to say to her, was determined to say to her. Then the police could have her.

I walked to them.

"You couldn't do it," I said to him.

"Not with you watching."

"You knew I was there?"

"There was a horse missing from its stall. I watched you follow me up the hill from the trees."

"I want to talk to her."

"I think she's beyond hearing."

"Elizabeth," I said.

Perhaps she was beyond hearing. She said nothing, did nothing. Her eyes were closed.

"Elizabeth," I said again, and moved closer. "You are an ugly and an evil woman. You killed him. We have the gun you stole and used. Tomorrow the police will have it. Get yourself and your possessions out of Court House. I hate you with all my strength. If I meet you sober I shall kill you where I find you. Get away from us and never come near us again. If you do not go now, then whether you're drunk or sober, whether the police want you or not, I shall kill you. No matter what happens to me. I shall kill you." I was cold, I was cold in my body, in my heart, in my head. Now that I was speaking to her, I felt no pity. I could have killed her now. But not with my father watching. Now that I had spoken, I felt only contempt for her. I could have killed this creature without feeling. "Get home," I said. "Get off our land. And take yourself away where we cannot see you. If you do not, I swear to God I shall kill you."

She did not move. I waited for her to move. "Move, woman," I shouted.

She moved very slowly. She opened her eyes and raised her

head and looked at me. "The pair of you?" she said. "Up here alone with me?" She looked at my father. "What did you bring this hoore to help you do, Hughie?"

"*Move*," I screamed. "You heard what I said to you. Before God I shall do it. *Move*."

"Oh, yes, I'll move," she said. Her voice was weak, with the hollow sound that follows sickness. She pulled her horse around and backed it a pace or two. It faced me. She straightened in her saddle as if to gather herself for the ordeal of a long ride down Knockagh, drunk and sick, sick and drunk; hanging with weakened hands to the saddle horn.

Then, with a lunatic scream, she kicked her horse at me.

I knew that old beast. It had been mine. It was as tired as she was herself. It did not jump at me. It reared in fear and it hooves pawed. I did nothing calculated. My action was instinctive. As the horse came down I lashed at it with my crop, to defend myself, to turn it away from me. Father leaped to protect me and lashed at its neck. It reared again and did not turn away from me. She came off, too sick, too drunk, too spent to loose her foot from its stirrup, and the horse backed, trampling and dragging her. I jumped for its head and it backed and its hind legs missed their footing on the edge. I had the reins and the beast was clawing the rim of the cliff with its hind feet, struggling for a footing where there was none, and I was being dragged to the edge. I fell and slid along the ground toward the edge. Father threw himself and struck my arm savagely, and my hand went limp and the reins fell free and the horse fell free, screaming.

But the woman went with it, in silence.

"Merciful Christ," my father said.

"You missed dinner," Alasdar said. "Where in God's name have you been in the dark?"

"We were sitting by the shore at Kilroot," Father lied. "She's sick. She's going to bed."

Alasdar came with me. I lay on the bed. He pulled my boots off. I wanted to be sick and could not be sick. I was incompetent with exhaustion and fear.

"Isabella," he said, "I'm here."

I heard him but I was beyond speech.

"I told you I would always come home to you," he said.

I heard him but I was slipping away. I know he brought blankets and covered me. I know he kissed me.

"Isabella," he said, "I came home for you."

I think he said "for you," but I was very far away and his voice was far, far away. Perhaps he said only "to you." I know he took my hand in his.

❧ *Eight* ❧

I know where I am in my silence. It is a lonely place; there is no one else there. All the time, when I am there, I am searching. My search is always for someone I love. I cannot think of life without loving. I did not go all the way to this lonely place when Alasdar covered me and I went to sleep. He sat there all night and I dreamed. It was such a vivid dream and stays with me because it is real.

I was running to the doorway to this lonely place—I always run, never walk or ride, and I am always off the ground. It is like one of those dreams in which you float just beyond the grasp of those who reach to seize you; you strain to stay out of reach, and there is terror in it. That is how it has always been, and always I have wanted to escape and reach the place where I shall find my love. But running toward this lonely place my terror was not this time of being seized but of running out of reach, and my arm was stretched back and I cried out to be caught.

Alasdar caught me by the hand. He drew me back from the lonely place. When I woke in the morning I knew what had been done. He was holding my hand. He held it all night and did not let me run to the place where I am always alone. I felt warm and safe as he drew me back. When I awoke, he was there.

"You have a visitor," he said, and Isa came under my blanket.

"Mama has all her clothes on," Isa said. "Why, Mama?"

Alasdar said, "Last night Mama was very, very tired and

lay down and fell asleep. She will now take off her clothes and sleep some more."

"Why don't we get in beside her, Papa?"

"Why don't we, indeed?" he said.

It was three days before the police came. Clugston, the contractor, ought to have brought the gun to them, they said. They wanted to see it. You're certain it belongs to this house? they said. We were quite certain. It disappeared from the gun rack years ago.

Can you tell us, now, where Mrs. MacDonnell might be? they asked.

"Sergeant," Alasdar said, "there isn't a soul in this town who doesn't know we have no dealings with my mother. You know where she lives."

"Aye. She isn't there. She went out on her horse the other day and hasn't been seen since. Neither her nor the horse."

"Didn't her servant come to you to report her missing?"

"Aye. The next day."

"You've been searching?"

"Where would we search? You can *see* a horse."

"She's very odd. But Court House at the moment is not a comfortable place to live in. She'll have gone somewhere."

"On a horse?"

Three days later they were back. Someone cutting stakes in the sally garden came on horse and rider.

"She'd been drinking a lot, we're told," the sergeant said. "Was she?"

"Clugston says so. We don't know." Alasdar spoke for all of us. Father and I said nothing. They asked us nothing.

The sergenat seemed tired of the MacDonnells. He had lost interest in the gun. "Aye, well," he said wearily, "I suppose you'll bury your mother?" It was heavy with accusation—of heartlessness, indifference, neglect, cruelty, and all unnaturalness.

Alasdar said, "Naturally," very curtly, very coldly.

And that was done. That door was closed. "I shall attend to it alone," Alasdar said.

Morag looked at me and said, "I never knew her. She was not my mother. You are."

Emily said, "I don't want to, but I'd better go with Alasdar and the priest."

And so, that is how it was done. Father Mackay said,

"Poor creature. She was one of that strange breed that never loves anybody."

"She once loved Hugh, God help her," Emily said, and left the room.

Morag and Edward moved into Barn House. The rest of us stayed a little while, then moved to Garden House. Morag resisted the move, but she was mistress of Barn House and Edward its master. The bed was theirs. I had no one to share it with me and no right to lie alone in it.

Worse, the little wood behind Garden House was haunted. He lay beyond it, in the rain. How could I live near that place?

"I think," Alasdar said, "we should take Tomas and Isa and travel for a while."

We were rootless now, that was our problem. Father and Mother no longer came to Carrig. "We shall not come again," he wrote.

For a little while we stayed with them in London. For a little while we stayed with my relatives in Andalusia.

"When are we going home?" Isa said.

Alasdar put his arm about me. "Where we are is home," he said.

"Then why do you not sleep in the same room?" she asked him.

For a little while we stayed in Rome. For a little while we stayed in Vienna, in Athens. We rented a villa for six months near Geneva and stayed in it a month. Kitty's child had been born, a girl named Isabella Cathleen, and we had not been there. Morag's child had been born, a boy named Alasdar Robert, and we had not been there.

"I feel homeless," Tomas said. "Why can we not have a real home?"

We were always together yet not quite together. Events and emotion and pain had aged us both. Aged? We were young but we were both much, much older. The passions of which I was capable such a little while ago seemed to be spent. Alasdar was grave now, grave and gentle and kind, always kind. Of his patience there was no end. He spent a great deal of time with Tomas, and I was certain that my son's lovingness toward me was Alasdar's influence. Tomas had always had Carrach's reticence; now he had Alasdar's warmth. I think they had talked together about my need for love. And

Tomas returned again and again to his theme. "Mother, I want a home."

After all the years, we had no home. It was right to say to Isa, Where we are is home, but home is also a habitation and a place, and we had no place. Emily needed a place. I made over Garden House to her. She would be close to Morag, who was her favorite; she could grandmother Morag's children.

Habits of mind formed: Where we are is home. We. It was "we" in the beginning of our futile wanderings because— what other word could we use? "We might go to Athens." And, "We'll have to sit down and talk about Isa." And there was an inescapable domesticity about it; always in hotel suites, or rented flats or in rented villas, we wandered into and out of one another's bedrooms because they and we were there. Papa and Mama, Isa said. I was the only mother she had ever known. What else would she say? A kind of domesticity grew. It grew of itself, without intent. Edward wrote to Alasdar about affairs. We discussed them. You should deal with that, he said. Tim wrote to him about affairs. We discussed them. He dealt with them. Agnes wrote about her new pregnancy. It was being difficult. We worried about her and could do nothing helpful. And she said, "I had a father for such a little while."

And then without knowing it, we were quite together. We knew it consciously one day when I was a bit unwell. A German maid had taken Isa for a walk, and Alasdar and Tomas came to my room to keep me company. Two weeks earlier I had sent for the contents of the iron box left in Pollard's office.

Very early that morning, I lay in bed and read what Pollard sent me from the big iron box. It was a series of small black-bound books, each sealed with a clasp and a tiny lock. Pollard sent the little key, and I wondered whether he had read the books and felt unworthy. He was an honorable old man.

Long ago, at Goleen, Carrach began to set down his thoughts and the movement of his heart. Down the years, though only at intervals, he had recorded our story. Its love, its passion and its pain were here and all of it addressed to Alasdar and myself and at times my mind swam and my heart swelled, for through the years he had watched us and loved us and understood. I wept, for he understood not only my faithfulness to him but my love for his son and Alasdar's love for me.

He made his last entry during that time when he was, I believed, winding down his life. Then he took the books to Pollard and locked them in the iron box. This is what he wrote:

"I have no fear of death, no matter how it comes. What I fear is separation from you, Isabella and you, Alasdar, for that is the worst death can do to me—rob me of your presence. But I have this great comfort, that you love one another and as time passes and wounds heal, you will care for one another. I shall not put it more plainly. I say only this: I do not know whether there is a Heaven or a Hell. I know only that there are lives, now. I cannot believe that with one life to live any of us should wait for death to discover whether we should or should not have given rein to the joy and the peace our hearts need. And I say to you with a full heart and without blasphemy: Love one another as I have loved you. I cannot bequeath one to the other in my last Testament. I cannot, even in the privacy of this little book, presume to dispose of your lives. I can say only Love one another and do, then, what your love tells you to do."

I wept. I dressed. I took the books downstairs and roused the concierge and put them in his furnace. Alasdar need never read them. I had read them; that was enough. Then I went back to bed and in time they came to keep me company. I knew what Carrach wanted us to do. The only questions to be answered were: How? And, When?

Alasdar stood by the window, his hands in his pockets, his back to me, and said, "Isabella, we want to talk something over with you." There was something not quite usual about his voice. Standing there, he looked very like Carrach, sounded like him. I thought this, and it was not painful. There was pleasure in it.

"I hope it's about why we should not spend any more time in this pointless place among these pointless people?" The Prince of Wales was in Baden and all the poor man's followers were there, cluttering the place with themselves and their silliness.

"I suppose it is, in a remote sort of way. It's about us," he said, "and, of course, about Isa." He was somewhat less masterful, somewhat more uncertain, than he had been for months. Women feel the changing of the wind just before it happens.

"About us?" I said, "and about Isa?" to avoid anything else.

Tomas was lying across the foot of my bed. Alasdar came

and pulled a chair to my bedside and sat down. "Isa has got to be settled in her own place," he said. He looked very firm now. He had said this several times lately, then left it.

"Yes," I said. "Please, dear, pour me some mineral water."

He poured my water, gave it to me, and sat down again and said nothing. Then he said, "It's a year now." He did not say, Since Father died.

He was studying my face, searching, I knew, for signs. Tomas was watching me with marked intentness.

"Yes." I sipped my water. Alasdar was so like Carrach. I had seen it before, of course, but now it blazed at me from beside my bed. I loved him. The weeks that were past had peeled away the layers of my reluctance to say it, but I had not said it. I did not love him as I loved his father. I knew, in spite of the warmth that moved in me as I sat in bed and watched him, that the wild joy I had known in bed with Carrach would not be in any bed I shared with Alasdar. This warmth was gentle, companionable. But that I wanted to share it with him and to share it now, there was no doubt in me. Now I could be truthful with myself. I had always wanted to share it with him. I was another Anna Davidson. I had merely been more afraid of the storms that raged in me and the destruction they could wreak. I loved them both so dearly. They were both mine. The way to keep both was to have only one of them. Now there was only one of them, and my body was making demands that felt sweet.

"Alasdar," I said, "we're both much older now."

"What does that mean?"

"Isa must have a home. That was what you wanted to talk about?"

"I said so." He was cautious, and nervous again, and it made him irritable, with himself, with me.

Tomas said, "Mother, I want a home of our own."

"Well, suppose we try to be practical about it?"

"That's what I'm being," Alasdar said impatiently, and was very nervous.

He had been the one always to come to me to tell me his love. I would have to be the one to help him come again to me, now that he was free to do it. Now he was afraid to do it. "You are her father," I said, "and I am the mother she knows. You said, 'Where we are is home.' Is that what you think now? That's how I see it."

"That's how I see it," Tomas said.

"And you, Alasdar? Do you still . . . ?"

"Mother," Tomas said soberly, "he wants to get married."

"Oh? Does he have somebody in mind? Or can he speak for himself?"

"I have you in mind," Alasdar said.

"And do you intend to ask me?"

"He's asking you," Tomas said sharply.

"You two have talked it over and you both think it would be wise? Is that so?"

"Isabella," Alasdar said, "for God's sake"

"Is that so, Tomas?"

"Yes."

"Have you got Isa's approval?"

Tomas said, "She already thinks you're married."

"So all you need is my agreement?"

"Isabella, will you marry me?"

"Of course," I said.

"We have the license and the priest," Tomas said.

"We have, have we?"

Alasdar was smiling. Tomas was laughing. "It's really quite odd," he said, "my brother is going to marry my mother. Does that happen often?"

"Not very," I said.

He came to me nervously on our wedding night. He was afraid of coldness, of restraint, perhaps even of reluctance on my part. We had talked about it. I shall be happy, Alasdar, I told him, but I can only love once the way I loved Carrach. I know, he said, and came to me nervously. But I had waited several nights for this night. I wanted this night. He was tender and gentle and kind. He was like Carrach. Was I, after all, another Anna Davidson? There was no restraint. We were both MacDonnells.

In the morning he said, "You have time for at least two more children."

Yes, that was about right. To be quite safe.

"The first one should start at once. I think we should leave nothing to chance."

"I thought you'd left nothing to chance in the night."

"We'd better be sure."

And when he had once again assured himself and me that he had done everything in his power to make me pregnant in one night, he said, "Kitty and Tim and Agnes and Willy and all their children, and Abigail and James are all in America."

"Yes."

"There are enough MacDonnells over there to keep you busy manipulating them till we are old."

I didn't speak.

"Then there's Thomas and me and Isa and the one we started in the night."

I smiled at the ceiling. Maybe he thought I thought there still ought to be more?

"And the two more after that."

"Two more," I said.

He leaped out of bed as full of energy as a man who had slept well and rested all night.

"I have passages booked," he said. "Get out of bed and let's go home."

I watched him dressing and thought of Carrach. He was so like Carrach. And yet there was a difference, and I liked the difference too. Carrach will be pleased now, I thought, and knew what Alasdar meant after the reading of the will when he said, "He understands everything." He had left me to Alasdar's care. Carrach was the MacDonnell. He left me to his heir, the MacDonnell. To build another family fortress?

I got up. In my mind was a thought that had been there often since we were first in America, Carrach and I: Ireland is the past, like a wet, dark day in Donegal. America is the future, like spring sunshine.

"What are you thinking?" Alasdar asked me. "You're smiling."

"About sunshine," I said. "And I have a lot to do. Let's go home."

About the Author

Shaun Herron, Irish by birth, has lived in the United States, Europe, and Canada and has now returned to make his home in County Cork, Ireland. His two previous books published in Signet editions are *The Bird in Last Year's Nest* and *The Whore Mother,* both of which have been met with critical acclaim.

Big Bestsellers from SIGNET

- [ ] **TORCH SONG by Anne Roiphe.** (#J7901—$1.95)
- [ ] **OPERATION URANIUM SHIP by Dennis Eisenberg, Eli Landau, and Menahem Portugali.** (#E8001—$1.75)
- [ ] **NIXON VS. NIXON by David Abrahamsen.** (#E7902—$2.25)
- [ ] **ISLAND OF THE WINDS by Athena Dallas-Damis.** (#J7905—$1.95)
- [ ] **THE SHINING by Stephen King.** (#E7872—$2.50)
- [ ] **CARRIE by Stephen King.** (#J7280—$1.95)
- [ ] **'SALEM'S LOT by Stephen King.** (#E8000—$2.25)
- [ ] **OAKHURST by Walter Reed Johnson.** (#J7874—$1.95)
- [ ] **FRENCH KISS by Mark Logan.** (#J7876—$1.95)
- [ ] **COMA by Robin Cook.** (#E8202—$2.50)
- [ ] **THE YEAR OF THE INTERN by Robin Cook.** (#E7674—$1.75)
- [ ] **MISTRESS OF DARKNESS by Christopher Nicole.** (#J7782—$1.95)
- [ ] **SOHO SQUARE by Clara Rayner.** (#J7783—$1.95)
- [ ] **CALDO LARGO by Earl Thompson.** (#E7737—$2.25)
- [ ] **A GARDEN OF SAND by Earl Thompson.** (#E8039—$2.50)

THE NEW AMERICAN LIBRARY, INC.,
P.O. Box 999, Bergenfield, New Jersey 07621

Please send me the books I have checked above. I am enclosing
$_____(check or money order—no currency or C.O.D.'s).
Prices and numbers are subject to change without notice. Please
include the list price plus the following amounts for postage and
handling: 35¢ for Signets, Signet Classics, and Mentors; 50¢ for
Plumes, Meridians, and Abrams.

Name_____

Address_____

City_____State_____Zip Code_____

Allow at least 4 weeks for delivery